Praise for *Ivory Apples*

"*Ivory Apples* is a legendary fantasy novel of the great-nieces of their Great-Aunt Adela, almost as celebrated and mysterious as the book itself, and the charming superfan Kate Burden—a sort of wicked Mary Poppins on the dogged hunt for hidden magic But magic has always its own desires, far beyond any fan's dream."
—Peter S. Beagle, author of *The Last Unicorn* and *Summerlong*

"*Ivory Apples* is like a set of Russian Matryoshka dolls: stories within stories within stories within stories that keep you reading all the way to the bottom. I finished in eight hours and now want to read it again."
—Jane Yolen, author of *The Emerald Circus*

"Neil Gaiman hasn't written anything half as good as *Ivory Apples* . . . If you enjoyed books such as *The Poppy War* by R. F. Kuang, *Deathless* by Catherynne M. Valente, or *War for the Oaks* by Emma Bull, you'll love *Ivory Apples*."
—*Little Red Reviewer*

"An absorbing fantasy about the power of art, family secrets—and obsession . . . Goldstein has crafted a dark, suspenseful tale in which the power of the faery world is appealingly disruptive and dangerous."
—*Kirkus*

"A contemporary fantasy that is wholly original. I want to read it again and again."
—Ellen Klages, World Fantasy Award-winning author of *Passing Strange*

"Lisa Goldstein is writing some of the most exciting fantasy out there. *Ivory Apples* is terrific."
—Jo Walton, author of *Among Others* and *Lent*

"So many contemporary fantasists have learned from Lisa Goldstein's weird, wise, humane and graceful example; her books comprise the best sort of magic school. Now, in *Ivory Apples*, she leads us deep into a wondrous grove that only she could scry. Goldstein is a true enchanter."
—Andy Duncan, author of *An Agent of Utopia*

"A powerful fairy tale set without compromise in the modern world—the characters are convincingly real, and the magic is genuinely enchanting and perilous."
—Tim Powers, author of *Alternate Routes*

"Lisa Goldstein's work invariably surprises and inspires me. *Ivory Apples* is no exception. A vivid tale of magic and its consequences, filled with beauty and terror."
—Pat Murphy, author of *The Wild Girls*

"A fine, swift, effervescent fantasy."
—John Crowley, author of *Ka* and *Little, Big*

"It's great, I loved it, you will also love it."
—Tor.com

Praise for Lisa Goldstein

"She has given us the kind of magic and adventure that once upon a time made us look for secret panels in the halls of wardrobes or brush our teeth with a book held in front of our eyes, because we couldn't bear to put it down."
—*The New Yorker*

"Lisa Goldstein is the perfect, born storyteller. Her story pulls you in and wraps you round, and it is hard to think of anything else until it is over."
—Diana Wynne Jones, author of *Howl's Moving Castle*

"Lisa Goldstein's work deserves to be celebrated along with that of Alice Walker and Shirley Jackson."
—Lucius Shepard, author of *Life During Wartime* and *The Jaguar Hunter*

"Lisa Goldstein . . . never writes the same type of story twice, and she never disappoints."
—Mark Graham, *Denver Rocky Mountain News*

"Goldstein's style remains unerringly unaltered. There's a subtle beauty to all her work; a charm which draws the reader in and keeps them there, not wanting to put the book down until it's finished. And this is another thing I like about Goldstein—no sequels. Her books are solid and complete in one volume and never seem to leave you with that 'unfinished' feeling."
—*SF Site*

"Goldstein fearlessly rubs the dreamlike logic of fairy tales up against stark realism, and each one makes the other more real."
—*BoingBoing*

Praise for *The Uncertain Places*

"Goldstein's complex and ingenious plot transplants the forest realm of European folktale, where witches grant wishes with strings attached and you'd better be careful which frog you kiss, into the sun-drenched hills of Northern California in the 1970s—and beyond."
—Ursula K. Le Guin

"An exquisitely beautiful, eerily compelling modern fairy tale."
—*Library Journal*, starred review

Other books by Lisa Goldstein

Novels

The Red Magician (1982)

The Dream Years (1985)

A Mask for the General (1987)

Tourists (1989)

Strange Devices of the Sun and Moon (1993)

Summer King, Winter Fool (1994)

Walking the Labyrinth (1996)

Dark Cities Underground (1999)

The Alchemist's Door (2002)

The Uncertain Places (2011)

Weighing Shadows (2015)

Collections

Daily Voices (1989)

Travellers in Magic (1994)

IVORY APPLES
LISA GOLDSTEIN

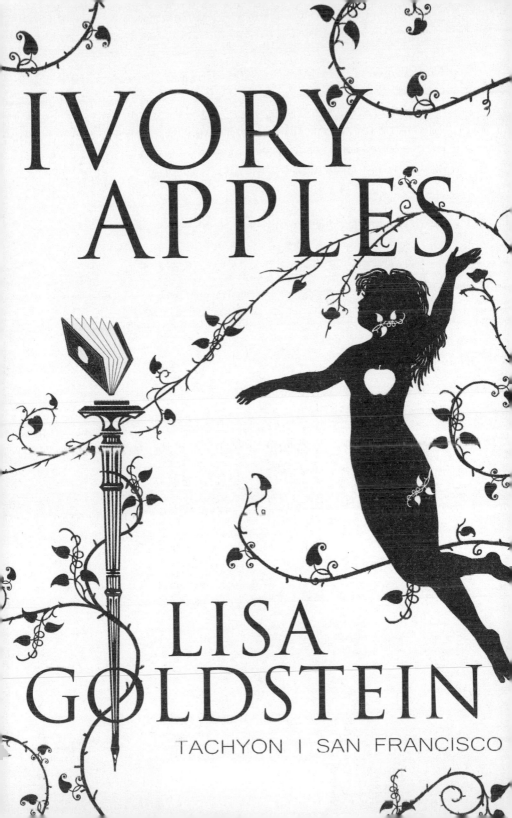

IVORY APPLES

LISA GOLDSTEIN

TACHYON I SAN FRANCISCO

Ivory Apples
Copyright © 2019 by Lisa Goldstein

Interior and cover design by Elizabeth Story

Tachyon Publications LLC
1459 18th Street #139
San Francisco, CA 94107
415.285.5615
www.tachyonpublications.com
tachyon@tachyonpublications.com

Series Editor: Jacob Weisman
Project Editor: Jill Roberts

Print ISBN: 978-1-61696-298-2
Digital ISBN: 978-1-61696-299-9

First Edition: 2019
10 9 8 7 6 5 4 3 2 1

To Lucius Shepard:

Thanks for all the crazy phone
calls. I still miss them, and you.
The best joke in here is yours.

CHAPTER 1

THERE WERE A LOT OF THINGS I didn't understand about Great-aunt Maeve when I was growing up. For one thing, although she and my father insisted that we call her Maeve Reynolds, that wasn't her real name. We'd seen that name, Adela Madden, on the book she'd written, *Ivory Apples*, which had been published a long time before I was born.

My sisters and I asked my father Philip about this, of course, but all he told us was that she valued her privacy, and that we weren't supposed to give away her real name to anyone. For a while I thought Maeve was some kind of secret agent, hiding out from people who wanted to kill her, and whenever we went to visit her I'd look for proof of this theory. I never found anything, though.

We usually saw her about once a month. My three sisters and I would pile in to our ancient VW station wagon, and after the usual fights over who got the front seat we would drive to the post office, where Philip picked up Maeve's mail. The letters and packages were all addressed to Adela Madden, and I wondered why other people got to use her real name when her own family had to call her something else. This was one mystery Philip could clear up, though: the letters were from fans of her novel, and they knew her only by the name on her book.

Then we'd take the twisting highway out of Eugene, Oregon,

which was where we lived. The houses grew farther and farther apart, and trees crowded up to the road as if to watch us go by. Sometimes Philip would swing out into the oncoming lane to pass the car in front of him, and I'd hold my breath until we returned to our lane.

After a long drive we'd take the exit at a small town. The town flashed by as we passed: a restaurant, a gas station, a single stoplight. And then another branching off and another road, this one smaller and filled with potholes. We were driving through trees now, the only car within miles, and we would tell stories about how the world had ended and we were the only people left, until the stories scared us too much to keep going.

It took an hour or two to reach Maeve's house. I know this sounds imprecise, and I have to admit that back then I never really noticed my surroundings much—except for those times when Philip tempted death in the other lane, of course. Instead my sisters and I talked or argued, pinched each other surreptitiously, sang or played games.

This time I'm talking about, the visit that changed everything for me, it was 1999, and I was eleven years old. After me came my younger sisters in steps of two years, Beatriz, Amaranth, and Semiramis. (My mother had disliked her own name, Jane, and had chosen increasingly florid names for us. She had even started to regret naming me Ivy, which she said was becoming too popular.) Semiramis's birth had been difficult, and Jane had died a few months later.

Philip did his best with us. He taught engineering at the U of Oregon and spent a lot of time with his students and colleagues or writing for journals, so we had a housekeeper, Esperanza, come in to cook our meals and clean up. On the weekends when he wasn't too busy he'd try to do things with us, or take us to interesting places. Still, we grew up fairly wild, and with little idea of how girls, much less women, were supposed to behave.

As we pulled into Maeve's dirt driveway we could see her outside, working in the garden. We spilled out of the car, delighted with our freedom after being caged up together.

We didn't run toward her, or hug her. We never did. There was a formality to her, a distance, that seemed to forbid it. "Hi, Aunt Maeve," we called out.

She stood up and brushed her hands on her skirt. She was tall and heavy, with most of the weight around her middle and thighs. Her hair was thick, a wiry gray, and she wore it brushed back from her forehead. Her face reminded me of a stone, rough and open. She wasn't as ugly as this makes her sound, though; something about her gave her the presence of a queen, or a goddess. I saw a Greek statue once that looked like her.

She headed toward us. She went with a bobbing clumsiness, like I imagined the Little Mermaid would when she first tried to walk on land. "I moved this stone over here, but it doesn't seem very happy in its new spot," she said to Philip. "They're very conservative, don't you find, stones."

She made a lot of comments like that, said a lot of things I don't think Philip understood. His way of dealing with it was to change the subject. Maeve was really my mother Jane's aunt, someone Philip had inherited after Jane had died, and though he tried to treat her politely, his frustration would sometimes show.

"Well, we made it," he said. "I brought your letters."

"Oh," she said. "Letters."

People from all over the world wrote her letters but for some reason she disliked reading them, and Jane had taken over her correspondence. The job had grown until most of the fans got an answer, if only just a form letter, and then when Jane died Philip had taken over.

I'd watched them go through the mail once, and it had been so boring I'd never done it again. She got checks from publishers around the world, what seemed to me like a lot of money, and she would sign them for Philip to deposit later. A producer had written, wanting to make a movie of her book, but she tossed his letter in the trash, much to my disappointment.

Most of it, as I said, was fan mail. Some of the letter-writers told her how much they liked her book; some sent her presents; some asked questions. She and Philip decided which ones needed replies, and then Philip would make some notes and answer them when he got home. Some had theories about the world she had created, and these she would set firmly in the pile that got a form letter.

A few times Philip asked about something the letter-writer raised, but she would just shake her head and smile with her lips closed, as if opening them would let all her secrets come flying out. "I like to keep things mysterious," she'd say.

The day that I'd watched them, Philip had tried to get her to use email, and to take a look at a website someone had created for her. She refused to get a computer, though; she said she was too old to learn how to use it. Philip had sighed quietly. I don't think she realized how much work she made for him.

"You kids want to wander around a bit?" he asked us now. "Just stay together and don't go too far, okay? And keep away from the river."

I left them opening letters and packages in the dining room. It was only in the last year that Philip had allowed us to go outside; before that we'd had to do all our exploring indoors. The house was made out of wood and glass—really more glass than wood, with enormous windows surrounded by walls weathered like driftwood. It was crowded with all manner of things, most of them presents from her fans, candles and vases and plants, stones and shells and masks and figurines. Paintings of scenes from her book lined some of the walls, and the rest were filled with bookshelves, and with stacks of different kinds of boxes, carved wood, painted tin, old orange crates from California with pictures of bright yellow suns.

Despite all this we had grown tired of staying in the house, and the woods outside seemed to beckon us. They started at the back yard and stretched out for miles; a creek ran through them, and there were open meadows where you could sometimes see deer.

I was the oldest, and my sisters were used to following wherever I led them. As I moved into adolescence, though, I wanted more and more to strike out on my own, away from my sisters. Now I imagined Beatriz piercing the silence of the wood with her chatter, and Amaranth hurrying ahead, impatient for a destination. Semiramis just looked at me, smiling, but even that seemed an invasion of my privacy.

I told them firmly to go away, but Amaranth still followed me a ways into the wood. "I told you, Rantha, I don't want to look after a bunch of babies," I said, and she finally left me.

I did feel a glimmer of guilt as I went on. I knew that at nine years old, Beatriz was too young to look after the other two, and that although Philip was pretty relaxed with us he would be angry at what I had done. But the feeling of freedom was so intoxicating that I shrugged off my guilt and went farther in.

The trees here seemed sized for me, not too tall or too close. It was late summer, and some of the leaves had already changed color or dropped to the forest floor. A pale, watery sun sieved through the branches, lighting some places and leaving others in shadow. I passed familiar landmarks, a mossy stump, a fallen tree with other trees sprouting from it. Birds sang in the distance.

I was thinking about my mother, something I'd been doing a lot lately. Jane had died five years ago, and Amaranth and Semiramis, who were seven and five now, didn't remember her. Even Beatriz had forgotten some things—and, most terrible of all, my own memories were starting to fade. I felt as if, once the last remembrance of her was gone, her time on earth would be erased, wiped out as if she had never existed.

I missed her dreadfully, and her absence seemed to take on more weight as I got older. This year I had gotten my first period, and Philip had tried to help me but had gone mute with embarrassment. And I knew there was more waiting for me, other things outside of his experience: makeup, high heels, boys. And sex, a word that seemed tinged in red whenever I thought of it.

I had started thinking about words that year, and I wondered if there were words or phrases to capture this feeling of loss. I turned over words like coins—"sorrow," "desolate"—but none of them seemed to fit. Well, maybe I'd find something later, in one of the books I was always reading.

I stopped. The woods around me had grown dim and the trees seemed different, crowds of thick, tall pines, their branches blocking the sun. It looked like another forest entirely, older, shaggier, wilder. And it had grown silent, all the birds hushed now.

I felt a spark of terror and began to hurry, trying to find my way out. Trees crowded around me, looming like giants, closing off the paths I tried. Branches caught at my clothes. The air turned cold and sharp and tasted like iron. Things moved at the edge of my vision, as if herding me somewhere. The woods grew darker.

Finally I saw a stream running across my path, so narrow that one step would take me across it. I left the path and followed it deeper into the wood, thinking that it would lead to the creek. The woods still looked strange, though, and the stream never joined up with anything, just ran silently through its bed of mud and moss and stones.

It disappeared several times in the gloomy light, and I had to stop to look for it. The air grew colder, shivery. I heard splashing up ahead, and I ran toward it.

The woods opened out, and in the sudden light I saw a lake. Giant mossy rocks stood on the opposite bank, one piled atop the other, and a waterfall cascaded down them. A great forest stretched out in the distance, a forest I'd never seen or heard of before, and a mist lay over the tops of the trees, turning the leaves gray and the trunks the color of bone. More trees lined the shore, nodding to their reflections in the water; they had leaves of red and gold, the fiery colors of autumn, though it was still summer, as I said, and the leaves near Aunt Maeve's house were mostly green.

And there were people, laughing and sliding down the rocks or scattering through the gusts of leaves. They had pointed ears, and fingers and toes as long and gnarled as twigs, and their hair, brown with a greenish tinge, was tangled with leaves and flowers and berries. Their eyes were longer than other people's, green or black or gray, and seemed lit from within by gleeful mischief. They were tall and short, though none larger than a child, pale and dark, some of them beautiful and some with strangely exaggerated features—a wide mouth, a nose like a potato. They dressed in rags of rust and red and green, or gossamer shawls that trailed them like wings. Someone was playing a set of pipes, and someone else tossed circlets of flowers, which the others caught and set in their hair.

And lying in the lake, naked and completely at ease in the water, was my great-aunt.

"What—?" I said.

She looked up. "Ivy, no! Get back to the house! Go!"

"What is this place?"

"Please, just go back. I'll explain later."

The children stopped what they were doing and came toward me, their wide mouths open in laughter. The music turned jagged, discordant. "Now! Hurry!" Maeve said.

I became aware of her urgency, finally, and turned to go. Someone slammed against my back. Then he pushed his way farther, *through* me, into me. I felt him turn and insinuate himself inside me, his sharp fingers pressing up against my breastbone.

Maeve said something, but I couldn't hear her. A high, crazed hilarity had taken hold of me, like champagne bubbles rising through my body. All my senses seemed heightened, as if I had never truly experienced the world before. The red leaves blazed, the air tasted like fresh apples, the music was intricate and full of subtle changes. I wanted to laugh, to grab a flute and play it, to slide down the rocks into the lake.

"Oh, Ivy," Maeve said. Her voice was low and beautiful, the words like the beginning of a song. I turned to her, dazzled.

I struggled to ask questions, to hear myself over what sounded like everything in the woods singing at once. "What—what's happening?"

The creature turned and nestled more comfortably within me. How did he fit there? Most of the others I'd seen had come up to my chin.

He was urging me back to Aunt Maeve's house. Without thinking, I went toward the path.

I made an effort to stop, to look back at Maeve. She must have seen my anxious confusion, because she called out to me. "Try to keep him at bay, especially at first. But also pay attention, and choose wisely."

"But—what is he?" I asked. And was he male, as I'd been thinking of him? But I felt certain he was.

The creature's pull grew stronger. Finally I stopped fighting and headed along the path. Maeve called something behind me, but I couldn't hear her.

Well, why not do what he wanted, after all? For one thing, he knew the way back and I didn't. But for another, the excitement he'd brought was still fizzing through me. I knew Maeve was right, that I should fight him, but just then it seemed too difficult. Everything around me was opening up, calling to me, overwhelming me with new sights, sounds, sensations.

I stopped often as we walked through the woods, looking at a flower or up at the sky. A beetle crawled up a tree trunk, and I lost myself for a long time in thinking about its life, its purpose, all its varied and intricate connections within the forest.

We emerged from the woods at dusk. A light shone at the back window of Maeve's house, but the rest was in darkness. Fear broke through my enchantment finally, and I remembered forcing my sisters away. Had Beatriz gotten lost? Was Philip waiting in terror, wondering what had happened to us?

I hurried inside. They were all there except Maeve, talking together in the kitchen. "—give her more time before we call the police," Philip was saying.

"Give who more time?" I asked. I wanted to laugh at the absurdity, the idea of calling the police while I was right there in front of him. At the same time, though, I knew I had to clamp down on my giddiness, the sense that I was held to earth by the lightest of tethers.

"Where the hell have you been?" Philip asked.

"Just in the woods," I said.

"Didn't I tell you to stay close to the house?"

"I did stay close." The lie took me by surprise, as if it had come from outside me.

"Then why the hell are you back so late?"

"I lost track of time." Then, belatedly, I thought to say, "I'm sorry."

"Beatriz says you left them." Next to him, Beatriz smiled smugly. "Didn't I tell you to stay together? Who knows what could have happened?"

I couldn't help but feel sorry for Philip. He still thought that his logic worked, that he could list my misdeeds and I would understand what I had done wrong. He didn't realize that he was up against something irrational, something that made a mockery of all his rules.

"Nothing happened, though," I said. Then, urged on by my newfound sense of mischief, I said, "I saw Aunt Maeve in the woods."

"Never mind that," he said. "You know Beatriz isn't old enough to look after the others."

"She was swimming in a lake. And she was naked."

"What?" Beatriz said. "Aunt Maeve? What did she look like?"

"Like Aunt Maeve, but without her clothes on."

"That's it," Philip said. He rarely got mad at us, but when he did he made up for months of even temper. "You're grounded for a week. No, two weeks. You think you can leave your sisters behind, and come in here late and—and with your clothes all torn, and make up ridiculous stories about your aunt—"

This seemed terribly unfair. After all, he hadn't gotten angry at the things I really had made up. "I did see her."

"I don't want to hear about it. We're leaving. Now."

"Aren't we going to wait for her? What about dinner?"

"Now. Let's go."

We went out to the car and drove off. I planned to sulk conspicuously all the way home, but to my surprise my resentment was fading. Instead I felt astonished all over again by the world, by the stars lighting up the sky, the hook of the crescent moon, the hiss of the wheels on the road.

For the first time I wondered what would happen if this feeling never went away. The creature had already gotten me in trouble, and that was over something fairly minor. I could feel his sharp-edged knees pushing against my ribcage, sense him chafing against his boundaries, urging me to let his chaos loose into the world.

I hadn't been good enough to merit the front seat; instead I was sitting directly behind Philip. Suddenly I saw myself taking the wheel and wrenching it around, hurtling the car out into the oncoming lane.

I felt a shiver of excitement, imagining the carnage. The next instant my excitement changed to horror. How could I even think such a thing? But this wasn't me; it was the promptings of the thing inside me. Wasn't it?

Aunt Maeve was right—I had to keep him at bay. I tried holding my breath or breathing deeply, tensing and loosening my muscles, but he continued to blaze up though my awareness, laughing silently.

Finally I found a way to block him. I had to ignore him—or not ignore him so much as think around him, understand that he was there but not feed him with attention. It was easy, in a way, but hard too, because I longed for that intoxication again, the way he'd changed everything, remade the world into something bright and fresh and new. I kept wanting to reach for him, to feel that wild excitement coursing through me.

"You're very quiet back there, Ivy," Philip said. "I hope you're thinking about what you did, how dangerous it was."

"Yeah," I said.

Beatriz giggled, thinking I was being sarcastic. I meant it, though. It was dangerous as hell. I understood that now.

CHAPTER 2

I knew I needed Maeve's help, needed to know what had happened to me, who those creatures were. But being grounded meant I couldn't use the phone, at least not until Philip went back to work. It was Monday afternoon by the time I could finally look up Maeve's number and call her.

The line sounded scratchy, filled with static, as though I was calling another country, or another era. She didn't answer, though I tried every few hours, willing her to pick up the phone. And if I couldn't reach her, I'd have to wait another month before I saw her again.

Even without her I was learning what the creature's presence meant in my life. For the most part, I was able to keep him reined in, but every so often I'd forget myself and reach out for him again. School started a week later, and I found myself laughing inappropriately in class, or raising my hand when I didn't have the slightest idea what the answer was. Once I watched my hand move out to slap the person in front of me, and I had to grab it and hold on tightly to stop it.

I got some strange looks, and I heard murmurs and laughter several times when I passed groups of students. I was an adolescent, that time when nothing is more important than what other people think of you, and with each question, each puzzled look, I'd vow to keep the creature under tighter control.

Philip came home early one day and found me on the phone, trying to call Maeve again. He took the receiver away from me and hung up. "I said grounded, and I meant it. Go outside and play with your sisters."

I wasn't supposed to go anywhere if I was grounded. I didn't remind him, though, just ran outside before he could change his mind.

We lived a few blocks from Amazon Park. Philip used to take us there because it was so close, but also because it had a good playground for kids, with swings and slides and a dinosaur you could climb on. Lately we'd been going over by ourselves, to play at the creek or walk through the trees or watch the dogs in the off-leash park. Sometimes people asked us where our parents were; apparently they thought we were too young to be out on our own. Philip told us that when he was a kid he could wander the neighborhood and no one thought anything about it. He didn't know what had changed, why adults nowadays felt they could interfere the way they did, but he warned us that we had to be polite.

Now I saw one of those adults, sitting on a bench between the playground and the pool. The sun lit her face like someone in an old painting, and my first thought was that she was too beautiful for these ordinary surroundings. Her hair was tied carelessly and spilled down her back, the light burnishing it from brown to old gold. She wore a gray pullover and black pants tied at the waist, and she was so thin and sat so straight that her clothes seemed to drape her without touching her body.

It took me a while to notice that my sisters were there too. Semiramis was on the bench next to the woman, and Beatriz and Amaranth sat on the grass at her feet. Amaranth was looking at her eagerly, waiting for a chance to jump into the conversation, and Semiramis seemed delighted. Only Beatriz sat a little apart, her expression impassive, as if waiting for more facts before she made up her mind.

"You must be Ivy," the woman said as I came up to them. Her eyes were light brown like her hair, the color of Philip's scotch. "Your sisters have been telling me all about you. I'd know you anywhere, though—you're all so similar. Come and sit with us."

I was at the age where I hated being compared to my sisters, to anyone really. I wanted to be admired for myself, to be thought exceptional in some way. I couldn't deny that we looked alike, though. Our hair was reddish-brown, and so curly that Philip couldn't manage all the knots and tangles when it grew out and had to shepherd us to the hairdresser every few months to crop it short. Our eyes were a mixture of gray and green, different for each of us. I'd once heard a friend of Philip's praise our high cheekbones, which we'd gotten from Jane. It had never occurred to me before to pay attention to cheekbones, and I felt annoyed—yet another body part for people to notice and make a judgment on, another thing to worry about.

It might have been the comment on my looks that made me

wary of this new woman, or maybe the fact that Amaranth and Semiramis seemed to have formed a bond with her, and I felt like an outsider. I sat on the ground near Beatriz, as far away from the woman as I could.

"She's telling us what we're going to be when we grow up," Beatriz said.

"I'm sorry, I haven't introduced myself," the woman said. "My name is Kate Burden. I was just telling Beatriz here that I thought she would"—she paused, and Beatriz looked at her expectantly— "that she'll be a pearl diver. Yes, that's it. You'll dive off those great tall cliffs and go deep into the water, and you'll come back with those rare black pearls that are only found in one or two places in the world. Then you'll have to smuggle them out, to walk past the customs people and pretend you're just another tourist, and all the while you'll have a fortune hidden in your suitcase."

Usually when people asked Beatriz what she wanted to be she came up with phrases like "metallurgical engineer" or "biological re searcher." I couldn't imagine her smuggling anything. But she was smiling now, as if she'd totaled up all her calculations about Ms. Burden and they'd come out positive.

"Me, do me!" Amaranth said.

"And Ivy here," Ms. Burden said. She turned to study me. "You'll be a famous artist. No, a writer, or a dancer."

I was startled, though I tried not to show it. I'd been thinking a lot about writing lately. Meanwhile Amaranth scowled at her, and I remembered that she'd once told me she wanted to be a dancer.

Ms. Burden laughed. "No, I guess I was wrong. It's Amaranth who'll be the artist, obviously."

Without thinking I said, "Well, that was an easy one." The creature wanted to say more, something cutting, and I struggled to control him.

Ms. Burden looked at me again. Her light-colored eyes seemed infinitely deep. I wondered how far she could see, if her gaze went all the way within me. "Well, sometimes what's obvious is the same as what's true. You shouldn't be so quick to discount the obvious."

It seemed profound, a truth spoken by a wise woman. But was it? I was too young to know, I realized that much.

Philip had urged us to be polite, though. "I'm sorry, Ms. Burden," I said.

"There's nothing to be sorry for. And please don't call me Ms. Burden—it makes me sound ancient. My name's Kate."

She *was* old, though, thirty or even forty. She had a few delicate wrinkles on her forehead, like lines raked through a Japanese sand garden.

"And who's left?" she said, looking around at us. "Semiramis? Oh, I love your names—they're all so fanciful. I think Semiramis will be a lion tamer."

Semiramis growled. "A lion tamer, not a lion, Ramis!" Beatriz said, and we laughed. Semiramis beamed, thrilled with the attention.

"And what do you do, Ms.—Kate?" I asked.

"Me? Oh, I've done a great many things. I traveled all over the world, teaching English, and I worked for a rare-book dealer, looking for treasures in old bookstores, and I was a bartender for a while, and I worked in Hollywood as a makeup artist . . . Oh, that reminds me!"

She dipped her hand into her purse, and when she brought it out she was holding several bottles, blue and red and green and one that glittered. "Do you know how to put on nail polish?" she asked.

We shook our heads. It certainly wasn't anything Philip had ever taught us. She and Semiramis sat with us on the ground, and we spent the rest of that afternoon brushing our nails with colors and covering them with sparkles.

"Why did you have so many jobs?" Beatriz asked. I noticed that she was sitting up straight, trying to imitate Ms. Burden's posture. It annoyed me, though I didn't know why.

"Well. The truth is that an old woman cursed me, a long time ago. She said I'd never be able to rest, never have a family, that I'd wander the world for a long time. That's why I did all those things, why so many things happened to me. But she also said that I'd find a family one day, in the last place I thought to look for it."

The sun was setting by the time we finished our nails. Beatriz's polish had gotten mixed in with dirt—she was never very clean, though she walked and moved with the elegance of a duchess—and Amaranth had painted her fingers as well as her nails. I hadn't managed to keep within the lines myself, and I felt unhappy as studied my hands. The only one of us who looked good was Semiramis; Ms. Burden had done her nails.

We said goodbye and headed home, waving our fingers in the air to dry them.

"Do you believe her?" Beatriz asked me, as we left the park and crossed the street. "About the curse?"

It was strange hearing someone so logical talk about curses, and I thought it was a sign of how much Ms. Burden had won her over. "I don't know," I said. "No."

"Why not?"

"Well, I think she . . . I think she said all that so we'd wonder if *we* were her family."

"Well, maybe we are."

My stomach cramped. Or was it the creature, moving inside me? Beatriz and I bickered a lot, but we rarely disagreed over anything important. "We don't need anyone else," I said. "And we especially don't need a replacement for Jane. Nobody can do that."

"She didn't say anything about replacing Jane. And anyway, she can't possibly know that—that we don't have a mother."

"Why not?" I think this was when all my suspicions coalesced, when I started to question everything she'd said and done. Who shows up at a park with four bottles of nail polish in their purse?

"Well, how could she?" Beatriz asked.

"And another thing," I said. "All that about a curse—it's hokey. It's like a bad movie." I remembered the word I wanted and brought it out proudly. "Clichéd."

"No it isn't."

"You just haven't seen a lot of movies, that's all."

"Oh, you just think you're so superior—"

It was an old argument. Of course I was superior, I was two years older, after all. We continued along those familiar lines until we got back to the house.

If I couldn't reach Aunt Maeve, I thought, at least I could read her book. I'd read it before, of course, but Philip had said then I was too young for it, and I think he was right. I hadn't understood all that much, anyway.

It took place in a small village called Pommerie Town, in what might have been the United States a hundred or maybe two hundred years ago. Strange things went on there, though few people spoke about them. One morning, for example, the people who visited the library found a river flowing down the center of the room, with a Japanese half-moon bridge connecting one side with the other. And yet no one said anything about the changes; instead they went about their business as usual, crossing the bridge when they needed a book on the other side.

All the clocks in town ran backward one day, and another time a great dancing mania seized the people, who stopped what they were doing, found a partner, and danced until their feet bled. Things went missing and turned up in odd places: under the blankets in someone's bed, inside a fish caught in the river. The chief alderman took his hand out of his pocket while making a speech and a bracelet glittery with emeralds dropped to the floor, a bracelet no one in town had ever seen. As everyone argued about where it had come from, the alderman, who had been as surprised as all the rest, suddenly admitted that he'd been embezzling from public funds.

Whenever something unusual happened an apparition would appear soon afterward, a small skinny man driving a coach no more than four feet high. The man, according to the few people who would talk about what they'd seen, had dark spiky hair that shot out around his top hat, and the coach looked more like a house or a castle, with sharp turrets and chimneys and a roof fenced in by iron spears. The horses neighed, the whip cracked, the bridles jingled, but the man himself never spoke. Instead he would doff his hat and open his mouth wide in soundless laughter.

Almost no one in Pommerie Town mentioned the changes, or the spiky little man. Some seemed truly not to see them; others had to force themselves to say nothing. But a few people, braver souls than the rest, would talk about them in whispers, and only among themselves.

I was pretty sure I recognized the coachman. My creature laughed a lot as well, his mouth as wide as a trumpet bell.

I wondered if Aunt Maeve had one of the creatures within her too, and if its presence was why she had written her book. It gave another meaning to Ms. Burden's prophecy that I would become a writer, an uncomfortable one.

It began to rain for days on end, and there were times when we couldn't meet Ms. Burden in the park, when we had to come home straight after school. Still, we saw her as often as we could. Even I started looking forward to those meetings. Whatever else I thought about her, those games were fun.

One day she took a pack of cards out of her purse and dealt a card to each of us. "Now look at your card," she said. Then, as Semiramis opened her mouth, she said, "Don't tell anyone what it is. One of you has the Joker, and you're the Murderer, out to kill us all. The way you kill someone is by looking at them and winking, and they have to drop dead. The rest of us can guess who the Murderer is, but if you're wrong you have to drop dead too."

Amaranth gave herself away by winking at Ms. Burden the minute the card was in her hand. Semiramis got the Joker next and could barely contain her giggles; that and the fact that she couldn't wink and had to contort her face instead ended her turn immediately. Still, they seemed to enjoy themselves, and Beatriz and I had long runs where we murdered nearly everyone.

A squall of rain fell, and I saw darker storm clouds massing in the distance. I felt disappointed; I could have sat there and played cards all day.

The others wanted to keep going too, but I got them up and made them hand their cards back to Ms. Burden. "Goodbye," I said, hoping to hurry them along.

"Goodbye," Ms. Burden said. She was still sitting on the ground, looking bereft, the rain pattering around her. I wondered what she was going to do for the rest of the day.

"Come to dinner with us," Beatriz said.

I stared at her. None of us had ever invited an adult home for dinner; it had never even occurred to me.

"Oh, no, I couldn't possibly," Ms. Burden said.

"Why not?"

"Well, there won't be enough."

"Sure there will. Esperanza makes enough for an army."

"Yeah, come with us!" Semiramis said.

All my suspicions of Ms. Burden came flooding back. What did she want from us? Was this what she'd been aiming for all this time? Who carries a pack of cards in their purse?

"All right, then," she said.

We ran down the streets through the rain, Ms. Burden holding her enormous purse over her head to keep herself dry. Amaranth burst through the door shouting, "We brought someone for dinner!"

Philip came downstairs. Ms. Burden waited for someone to introduce her, and then, seeing that we didn't know even the most basic rules of politeness, she moved forward. "Hello, I'm Kate Burden," she said, brushing her hand against her pants and holding it out. "I met your children in the park—they're enchanting company."

Philip shook her hand, glancing briefly at all the colors on her fingernails. Then he looked at her, his gaze lingering on her face, and suddenly I understood. I felt sick, a slow dragging pain in my stomach. She didn't just want to take Jane's role as our mother; she wanted to marry Philip, to insinuate herself completely into our lives.

My sisters didn't seem to notice anything. They looked eager, excited, probably hoping he would like her as much as they did.

"I hope I'm not intruding," she said.

"No, not at all," Philip said. "Esperanza always makes too much anyway."

"Is Esperanza your wife?"

"No, she's the housekeeper." Was I imagining it, or did she look relieved? "Come on, let's eat."

We went into the dining room and sat around the table. Esperanza came out from the kitchen with a salad, then returned with a platter of roast beef. We ate in silence for a while, and then Philip asked, "And what do you do, Ms. Burden?"

I looked up, interested in what she would say. I'd asked her the same thing, and she had never answered.

She took a bite of roast beef. "Kate, please. My, this is good. What do I do? Well, right now I'm unemployed, unfortunately. My last job was working at a bank, but they let me go."

"She was a makeup artist in Hollywood once," I said. I was starting to wonder if she'd made up that story, and most of the other stories she told us, and I wanted to see if she'd lie to an adult. And maybe the creature had given me a nudge here, had wanted to add his own pinch of mischief.

"Really?" Philip said.

"It was a long time ago," Ms. Burden said. "But yes, I'd love to do something like that again."

"Why did you stop?" I asked.

"Oh, it's a long story. My mother fell ill, and I had to nurse her, and then when all of that was over the job was gone."

"That wasn't very long."

"Ivy!" Philip said. "Ms. Burden—Kate—is our guest here."

The creature stirred, became more alert. "Well, why say something is a long story when it takes you five seconds to tell it?"

"Ivy!" Philip said again.

"Oh, that's all right," Ms. Burden said. "I know what she means. It felt like a long time to me, that's all. She was ill for years, and I spent most of my time taking care of her, and then she died."

I had another rude comment all ready, but now it seemed stupid and ill-considered and I said nothing. We had all stopped at once, in fact, stopped everything, eating and talking and breathing, and I knew that we were all thinking of Jane.

"Our mother died too," Amaranth said finally.

"Did she?" Ms. Burden said. "It's a terrible thing, to lose a mother so young."

Amaranth nodded, though I was pretty sure she didn't understand yet what Jane's death meant. Ms. Burden looked at Philip, clearly wanting to know more but not sure she could ask. We hadn't told her about our mother's death; we rarely talked about it with outsiders.

"Jane died five years ago," Philip said. He shook his head. "Well, let's talk about something more cheerful. And Beatriz, finish your dinner."

"I am finished," she said. She'd left about half the roast on her plate, though she'd eaten the salad. This was more of her wanting to imitate Ms. Burden, I knew, trying to starve herself into thinness.

"What do you do, Philip?" Ms. Burden asked.

He told her about working at the university, about engineering, about each new crop of students arriving seemingly more ignorant than the last. This was one of his pet subjects, and it took us through dinner and into dessert. To her credit, Ms. Burden seemed interested, asking questions and nodding in all the right places.

She made to leave soon after that. "Well, thank you for looking after the children," Philip said at the front door. "You really don't have to do so much with them."

"Oh, it's no problem—they're very well-behaved."

Philip looked at us, startled. She waved her multi-colored fingers at us one last time, and then she was gone.

CHAPTER 3

The creature and his enchantment was always with me. Sometimes I found myself wanting it like an addiction—and sometimes, usually when I was very tired or unhappy, I would loosen his bonds and let myself be carried along by his whims.

Once after I did this in school I noticed a group of students staring at me. One of them started to vocalize the theme to *The X-Files*, and I realized that I had just said or done something with no memory of what it was.

Another time I—or he—let out an enormous fart while we were crowding up to go into class. Luckily no one believed I'd ever do such a thing; instead the kids blamed one of the school outcasts, a boy who smelled like sour milk.

I felt bad when they made fun of him, but the creature didn't seem to care. He didn't appear to think about fairness, just did what he wanted, whatever made him laugh. Later, though, he had me pick a flower and leave it on the boy's desk, and the boy floated in a daze of happiness all that day.

And once, at lunchtime in the cafeteria, I picked up a flute belonging to someone in the school orchestra. I had never even held a flute before, but somehow I found myself playing the song that had captivated me in the grove. I left the cafeteria and went out into the hall, still playing, and other students followed me, dancing and laughing. More and more kids joined in, until dozens of them were lined up behind me, spinning down the corridor.

I found myself in front of a padlocked door and started to turn away. The creature seemed to know how to work the combination, though, and opened it in a matter of seconds. I went through the door and saw a set of stairs. I knew it was dangerous, that I had to stop, but I was still in the grip of the creature's madness, transported by my high mad glee.

A woman came running out of a classroom. "What are you kids doing?" she said. "Get away from there, right now!"

Most of the students melted away. "You there!" she said. "What are you thinking? That door goes up to the roof."

I wanted more than anything to go outside, to smell the fresh air around me. I made a great effort to rein the creature in. "I—I don't know," I said.

"You don't know! That's it—you're spending a week in detention, starting today."

The flute's owner hurried up, panting from her run. "That's my—my—" she said.

"And give her that flute," the teacher said.

I began to get a reputation around school. Some people thought of me as strange, unpredictable, and started to avoid me. Others seemed admiring, but these were scary, edgy kids, not people I wanted to be friends with. My friend River took me aside and told me she was worried about me.

At different times I felt resentment or anger, or a sense of loss for my old life. And sometimes I even felt hatred, hatred for this creature who had upended everything, who was turning me into an outcast.

Another change was happening to me, something I only understood later. I'd always liked words, the sounds of them, the way they flowed and chimed and merged with other words to bring something new into the world. Now words seemed to cascade through my mind, lovely words like "simoom" or "cardamom," jagged, arresting words like "quotidian" or "physiognomy," and I'd have to stop what I was doing and look them up.

After a while I was able to grab hold of this chaos, to see a way through it. I made lists of words and scraps of sentences, then used Philip's computer to arrange and rearrange them, patching them together in different ways. And the more I did this the more I reached for, the more I went beyond the rules I'd learned from books and in school. I got so deep into words that it felt as if I'd pushed myself into them, through them, that the letters on the page had been sentinels keeping me out, and I had found a path between them.

One day our English teacher gave us an assignment to write anything we wanted. I started on a boring description of a trip my family had taken, too self-conscious to let anyone see the pieces of writing that were so important to me. But something, the creature maybe, or my own pride in these scraps, made me print out one of them and turn it in.

A few days later the teacher asked me to stay after class. Somehow I knew that he wanted to talk about his homework assignment, so while I waited impatiently for the class to end my mind flickered through dozens of things he might say: what I'd turned in was terrible, it was great, he didn't understand any of it.

What he wanted, though, was nothing I'd thought of. "Where did you get this, Ivy?" he asked.

"What?"

"This poem. Who's the real author?"

"It's not—" I wanted to say that it wasn't a poem, but for the first time I realized that that was exactly what it was. "It's mine. I wrote it."

"Oh, don't give me that. Eleven-year-olds don't sound like this."

"I did—"

"You know, they keep saying that kids your age know all about computers, much more than old people like me. But don't worry— even I can look things up on the internet. And you better believe we're serious about plagiarism here. When I find out where you got this, I'll be talking to your parents, to the principal."

"I didn't copy it! Go ahead, look it up—you won't find it."

I tried protesting some more, but he dismissed me. I wondered why he thought I'd plagiarized it. Did he really think it was by someone famous? I wasn't that good, I knew that much. Still, I was glad to find out what it was I'd been writing all this time.

I don't know if he ever talked to the principal, but Philip got a phone call that evening, just as he was heading to his room to work.

"Wait, what did you say?" he said into the phone. There was a pause, and then, "No. Never." . . . "No, I'm telling you she wouldn't do that. She works hard on her assignments—she'd never copy some-one else." . . . "Maybe you should trust your students more, then." . . . "All right, this conversation is over. You keep looking for some great poet who wrote my daughter's poem, and if you find one you get back to me. But I'm telling you now, that's not going to happen." He hung up without saying goodbye.

I waited for him to ask me if I'd copied the poem. Instead he stood by the phone awhile, scowling to himself, and then turned to me. "Well, he seems to think you're one of the greats of literature, Ivy. I guess I should see this poem."

I felt embarrassed showing it to him, since it still wasn't where I wanted it to be. I waited nervously while he read it.

"This is good, Ivy," he said finally. "Very good."

I was at the age where I had a hard time accepting compliments. At the same time, though, I felt a rush of love for him. He had be-lieved me over someone in authority, he'd taken time out of his busy schedule to defend me, and he'd even liked the poem.

"Yeah, well, what do you know?" I asked. "You're an engineering professor."

"I know enough to answer your Aunt Maeve's letters. And some of them come from critics and English professors, and no one's ever guessed what my background is."

I never heard anything more about the poem, and I got my usual good grade in English that year.

Finally, after what seemed like forever, it was time to visit Aunt Maeve again. We crowded into the car and set off, first for the post office and then onto the highway.

The trees had started to change, matching the fiery leaves I'd seen in Maeve's grove. The sky was gray, overcast. I sat without saying anything, holding my excitement inside. The creature seemed eager as well, moving within me, alert to his surroundings.

Every so often Philip would remind us of the importance of keeping Adela Madden's name a secret, that we had to call her Aunt Maeve if we mentioned her at all. He had come up with a kind of chant during our earliest visits, and he started it again now. "Who are we visiting?" he said.

"Aunt Maeve!" we shouted. I came in a little behind my sisters, still thinking about all the questions I had for her.

"What do we call her?"

"Aunt Maeve!"

"What name do we never use?"

We kept quiet after this question, because, of course, we weren't supposed to say her name. I used to giggle at this part when I was younger, and Amaranth and Semiramis giggled at it now.

Maeve wasn't working in the garden when we pulled up. We ran outside and swung the rope of bells hanging from her door.

"Well, hello," she said, opening the door and looking out at us. "How good of you to stop by." She seemed surprised, as if she hadn't expected us, as if we didn't come visit her every month.

We filed into the house. I waited until everyone had greeted her and then said, "Aunt Maeve, I need to talk to you."

"Of course, dear," she said. "What about?"

"About—something important. You know what."

Her puzzled expression was back. "I'm afraid I don't."

"Well, you can do all that later," Philip said. He looked unhappy, probably thinking I wanted to discuss women's stuff, that he had failed me again. "Let's get to the letters."

It was raining outside now. My sisters and I left Philip and Maeve to their work and wandered through the house. It was cold inside, with all the windows letting out warmth, even though Maeve had turned the heating up.

Amaranth found a deck of cards and tried to get me to play Murder, but I felt cooped up, jittery, unable to settle to anything. Finally

I went into the study, took down a copy of *Ivory Apples,* and picked up where I'd left off.

There were more strange things happening in Pommerie Town now, too many for the people living there to ignore. Some left their homes and workplaces and did shocking, uncharacteristic things: an opera singer spent an entire evening on stage just laughing, and another man gave all his money to someone he'd feuded with for years. Marriages frayed, secrets were revealed, and the constabulary were called out to break up fights or stop thefts, though fewer and fewer of the police were showing up to work.

The first time I'd read it I was on the side of the merry-makers and against the stodgy burghers, but this time I noticed that my sympathies were shifting. I'd liked Quentin Foxtree, for example, who'd left Pommerie Town to travel in foreign parts, but now I felt sorry for his wife Tabitha and their four young children, whom he'd abandoned without a single thought. I admired how Maeve had managed to manipulate the reader, without fully understanding how she did it.

A few hours later Philip came back to look for us. "Come on, we're having dinner," he said. Maeve usually called the Italian restaurant in the nearest town and had them deliver take-out for all of us.

"I want to talk to Aunt Maeve," I said.

"Oh, right. Just be quick."

I hurried into the dining room. Dinner hadn't come yet, and Maeve sat at the table, surrounded by piles of letters and empty envelopes.

All at once I couldn't think what to say. She'd said she had no idea what I wanted to talk about, but how could she have forgotten, when it had happened only last month? It was as clear as an illustration in my mind—the trees, the lake, the music and dancing . . .

"Listen, I wanted to ask you—" I started.

She looked up. "What is it, dear? Is it the bees?"

"The—the bees?"

"There are so few left, I know. But I planted all that spiderwort in the garden, and some lavender, and I think they're coming back."

"No, nothing about bees," I said. I hurried on. "Last month, well, I was walking through the wood, and I saw you in the lake."

She stayed silent, and I forced myself to continue. "And I saw these other people too, these—these small people, like children. And then one of them, he got inside me somehow . . ."

"Ah." She nodded, finally, and I let out a breath of relief. "The sprites, yes. Well, it's unfortunate, what happened to you. But fortunate, too, maybe. Your life will never be the same, anyway."

I liked "sprite"; it described them much better than the ugly word "creature." "But what are they?" I asked.

"Well, I can tell you a few things. Show you some things, anyway. The best answers are always in books, don't you find?"

She went to the living room and looked through the shelves. "Mmm," she said, going down the rows. "Mmm. Yes, that one, and this one's good too . . ."

She came back with an armful of books. "Here you go. Read these and we'll talk about them next time."

I looked at the titles. My frustration returned, soared to new heights. She had brought me *Ivory Apples*, I saw, and something about American Indian folktales, and a book on tricksters, and *The Wind in the Willows*. "How are these supposed to help me? And I already have your book." I didn't mention that I was reading it, or say anything to encourage her. "And *Wind in the Willows*? I mean, come on—it's babyish, it's a book for Beatriz, or even Rantha."

"Have you read it, child?"

I hadn't. I didn't say anything, though.

"Just take them, see what you think." She pulled out *Ivory Apples* and handed me the rest of the stack.

The doorbell rang, the food she had ordered. Philip opened the door and carried everything into the dining room, and Maeve stayed behind to pay the delivery-person. Philip had once complained after he saw her give one of them a fifty-percent tip, and she had pointed out that the nearest town was thirty miles away, and that she had to give them some reason to drive so far, after all.

We went in to eat. I couldn't talk to Aunt Maeve with everyone else there, of course, so I said very little during the meal. Then we left, and as I said goodbye Maeve put the stack of books into my arms.

I felt the sprite caper within me as we headed toward the car.

Ms. Burden took some photographs of us one day in late October. Beatriz invited her over for dinner again, and I saw to my disgust that she was on her way to becoming a regular fixture.

It rained heavily over the next few weeks, and we didn't see her until early November. When we met her again she'd brought us some presents, Photoshopped portraits she'd made of us. Semiramis was riding a lion, Beatriz was poised to dive from a tall cliff, Amaranth was dancing, and I was working at a computer.

She'd knocked some manners into my head by then, and I knew what would be the polite thing to say—that my twelfth birthday had been yesterday, and that this was the perfect birthday present. I didn't say it, though. Although my sisters clearly loved theirs, I wasn't sure how I felt about mine.

It wasn't just that I had the most boring of the four, a picture of me sitting and staring off into space. It was that she'd put so much time and energy into them. The technology wasn't very good back then, so she'd mostly pasted our heads on other people's bodies, and the sizes and proportions were off. But the parts she could do, the shading and the backgrounds, had to have taken hours.

Why had she done it? Why did she spend so much time with us? She was beautiful, as I said, and could probably date anyone she wanted, so why didn't she? I wondered again if she was trying to get close to Philip. She didn't flirt with him, though, or I didn't think she did, but a lot about adults still seemed mysterious to me.

It's amazing how much kids have to learn in a short period of time. Not just what words mean, but recent history and pop culture and manners and how to do some things and when not to do other things . . . Earlier this year there was a big deal about Bill Clinton being impeached, and when I watched the news with Philip they kept talking about Watergate, as though of course everyone knew what Watergate was.

I don't know if other people do this, but whenever I came across something I didn't understand I'd save it up until I heard about it again. A few weeks after the news anchor had mentioned Watergate I saw an article about it in a newspaper Philip had left lying around. Which answered that question, but where was I supposed to go for more pressing problems?

All I had were the books Maeve had lent me. Most of them looked dry, scholarly. I'd finished my copy of *Ivory Apples* and so, despite what I'd told her, I started on *The Wind in the Willows*.

At first I didn't understand why she'd given it to me. The stories of Toad and Mole and Rat seemed old-fashioned, and yes, a little babyish. Then I came to the chapter called "Piper at the Gates of Dawn," and I knew.

The Piper was the sprite inside me, or an idealized version of him. Like my sprite, he played music, and like my sprite, he played music, and he made his surroundings dazzle with beauty.

He stirred within me at that thought, and I had the idea that he liked this view of himself. He liked the name Piper, too, and I thought that it might be what his fellows called him. But he and the Piper in the book had some differences as well, and I reminded him of the mean tricks he had played on me, the things he had tried to make me do. He seemed so drawn to the name, though, that finally I gave in.

He danced like a leaf on a twig. It was as close to a conversation as we'd had, and I felt myself softening toward him. In response I heard music, the song that had played in the grove.

Maeve was more responsive the next time we visited, even answering a few of my questions.

"Did you read those books I lent you?" she asked.

"Some of them," I said.

"What did you think?"

"I don't know. Well, they were about tricksters mostly, weren't they?"

"That's right." She tilted her head to the side like a bird, waiting for more.

I didn't know what she wanted. I wanted to keep her talking, though, and so I went on, saying whatever came into my mind, hoping I would hit on the right answer. "And there are stories about tricksters all over the world, right, Legba and Eshu and Loki and Susa-no-o, and all those American Indian stories about Raven and Coyote. And you put a trickster in your book, didn't you—that coachman? But what does that have to do with—with what happened at the lake? Are those—those sprites I saw, are they tricksters?"

"You can't hold on to Trickster. If you think you have him, he'll change shape, he'll get you looking in one direction and escape in another."

"I don't know what that means."

"Trickster doesn't mean anything. Trickster just is."

"Look," I said, feeling frustrated again. "I'm twelve years old, okay? It's hard enough being this age—that's what Philip says, and he's right about that. And along with everything else I have this— this thing, this trickster, making me do things I don't want to do, things I would never even think of by myself. I feel like some kind of freak. I *am* some kind of freak. And I can't talk to anyone about it, no one except you. God knows what Philip would say. You have to help me. You have to tell me what to do."

"Do? Why do you have to do anything? You just have to be. Like Trickster."

"So I should—I should try to learn from him?"

She laughed. "Oh, no. No, I shouldn't think so." She seemed to take pity on me then, because she went on, "He isn't there for you. Nothing he does is for you, to help you. But he's given you a gift nonetheless. Hermes, you know—did you read about Hermes?"

I nodded.

"What did he do, do you remember?"

There had been an essay about him in one of the books Maeve had given me, but all I remembered from it was the intriguing word "psychopomp." I decided to guess. "He was a trickster too, wasn't he?"

"That's right. He stole the sun god's cattle. They're connected to fire, most of them. They steal it, or they bring it down to our world, like Loki, or like the Great Hare in some Indian stories."

I waited for her to go on, but she seemed to have finished. Philip chose that moment to come into the dining room. "There you are, Ivy," he said. "Are you ready for dinner, Maeve?"

"Yes, I think so," she said. "I'll go call the restaurant."

She started to leave. I wasn't finished talking to her, though—I needed a lot more answers. "I don't want any cattle!" I called out to her retreating back.

She turned to face me. "How is your writing coming?"

I looked at Philip, enraged. "Did you tell her?"

He shook his head, his expression puzzled. "No, dear, no one told me," Maeve said.

But how could she have known? I hadn't shown my writing to anyone except Philip, not even Beatriz.

CHAPTER 4

On December 31 we all stayed up to welcome 2000. Philip had explained that this was wasn't the turn of the millennium, that the count would start next year, but we didn't care about that; we were just excited that we didn't have to go to bed, and that Philip let us have some champagne.

Beatriz had been worried about the Y2K bug, the theory that computers couldn't handle the new date and would flip back to 1900, causing problems all over the world. She'd taken Philip's computer downstairs, and after midnight she booted it up and then sat back in relief; everything seemed to be working fine.

A few days into the new year Beatriz talked Philip into framing the portraits Ms. Burden had given us, then hung them up in the front hallway, making them the first thing Ms. Burden would see when she stepped inside. The next time she came over for dinner, my sisters could barely contain their excitement.

Ms. Burden did not disappoint. "Look at that!" she said. "They look wonderful up there. But where's yours, Ivy?"

"I lost it," I said.

"Oh, what a shame. I'll print you out another copy."

"No, that's all right."

"It's no problem."

"I don't—I don't really want it."

Philip turned toward me, his expression clearly telling me to stop being such a misery. For some reason, it made me want to behave even worse.

"I wonder if I could use your bathroom," Ms. Burden said.

We only had one bathroom, ridiculous for the five of us, and we all tried to get up as early as possible to be the first one to use it. Philip gave her directions and she headed upstairs.

We drifted to the table. My sisters seemed listless, uncertain, as if they needed her presence to inspire them. Even I felt it at times, that spark of excitement she carried with her, the way she seemed to promise marvels.

Esperanza came out from the kitchen with a platter of goulash, and we realized that Ms. Burden had been gone for a while.

"She should be back by now," Amaranth said.

"Maybe she got lost," Philip said.

"Oh, come on—it isn't that hard to find," I said. The meat and spices from the goulash smelled wonderful, but we wouldn't be able to start until Ms. Burden came back. "I'll go find her."

"No, don't—it wasn't that long," Beatriz said, no doubt worrying that I'd antagonize her somehow.

I stood up. "I'm hungry now," I said.

I went up the stairs before she could stop me. I walked as quietly as I could, though I don't know what I was expecting. That she'd steal something, and I'd catch her red-handed, and we'd never have to see her again.

Even so, I was startled to see her in the room I shared with Beatriz, looking at my desk. "What the hell—" I said.

She turned around. She seemed as unruffled as ever, with no trace of guilt. "Oh, dear. I'm afraid I got lost."

I went over to my desk and straightened out some of the piles, though she hadn't touched anything. "For ten minutes?" I asked. "And what the hell are you doing in my room? Did you think this was the bathroom?"

"It's such a big house."

"Not that big."

She spoke over me. "What interesting books you read." She looked back at my desk, where I'd put the stack of books Maeve had given me. "Folklore and history and novels—oh, and *Ivory Apples*! Have you read it? It's my favorite book in the world."

I nodded.

"You're so lucky, reading it for the first time. It changed my life. And these other books—you must be very intelligent. Where did you get all of them?"

I didn't want to tell her about Maeve, even though the name would mean nothing to her. "A teacher gave them to me," I said. "And you still haven't answered my question. What are you doing in my room?"

"I want to get to know you better, that's all. Is that so terrible?"

"Is that why you're going through my stuff?"

"Look, Ivy—I think we got off on the wrong foot here. This is what people do when they like each other—they want to know more about the other person, to share things. You know what I think? I think you don't believe anyone could like you. That's why you're so suspicious of me, why you think I have an ulterior motive."

Was that true? I didn't think it was. My friends liked me, or they had, before Piper had come and turned my life upside down.

My sisters did too. Still, maybe she was right. Maybe, at her age, she knew things I didn't.

"We should go to dinner," I said.

"I still need to use the bathroom. I'll be as quick as I can, I promise."

"It's down that way. At the end of the hall."

She headed for the door. As I watched, my foot swept Beatriz's thumb-piano into her path. She stumbled over it and swore, then looked at me sheepishly.

"Sorry. I'm terribly sorry. I hope I didn't break it. No, it looks all right. What on earth is it?"

She picked it up and plinked a few keys. I stared at her, reminding her of her promise to hurry, and she left quickly.

Had Piper moved the thumb-piano or had I? Maybe it was both of us. We had both wanted to do it, anyway.

I waited in my room until she came back, just in case she wandered off somewhere else, and then we went downstairs to the dinner table.

"Sorry, I got lost there for a bit," Ms. Burden said to Philip, as she sat down. "You must be very proud of Ivy—she's reading at a level far beyond her age."

"Well, sure," Philip said, trying not to look too proud of me in front of my sisters.

"And *Ivory Apples*," she went on. "I love that book. Do you know there are rumors that Adela Madden is still alive?"

The name acted on me like a shock. I heard Philip's voice in my head: *What name do we never use?*, and I stared at Amaranth and Semiramis, trying to warn them not to say anything. They were busy squabbling with each other, though, and I don't think they'd even heard her.

I wondered again why we couldn't talk about Adela Madden. Philip's instructions had been so entwined with my earliest memories that at first I hadn't thought about it; I'd just gone along with what he and Jane had wanted. Maeve liked her privacy, Philip had said, but it seemed like it was more than that. And did people really think she was dead?

I decided to ask Philip later. "It's all so puzzling," Ms. Burden said. "There's even a website about Adela Madden, with all kinds of theories. And people do research—do you know no one's heard from her for forty years, since about 1960? No newspaper articles or television appearances, and nothing official like a marriage certificate. So she's probably dead, but no one's ever found a death certificate either."

Philip nodded, no expression on his face. I could see he felt uncomfortable, that he wanted to change the subject, but of course she didn't know him as well as I did.

"And, you know, why would someone write such a great book, a masterpiece, and then just disappear?" she went on. "So she has to be dead, right? But then there are people on the website who swear they've seen her, even talked to her."

I looked at my sisters again to make sure they said nothing, but Amaranth and Semiramis were still arguing, and I don't think even Beatriz was paying attention. Philip was still saying nothing, probably hoping that the conversation would fizzle out on its own.

"I'm sorry," Ms. Burden said. "It's one of my passions, that book. I know I go on about it, I bore people to death sometimes. Just ignore me, please."

"No, it's all right," Philip said. "It's a good book."

Piper laughed soundlessly. And it *was* funny, seeing the person who knew *Ivory Apples* better than anyone except Aunt Maeve, who had answered countless questions about it, acting like just another reader. I felt something rise within me, a hot-air balloon lifting free of its moorings, and I had to quash the urge to laugh out loud.

I missed some of the conversation, and when I started listening again they'd changed the subject. "Do you ever go into their bedrooms?" Ms. Burden asked. "My mother would have skinned me alive if I'd left my room in that state."

"Really?" Semiramis asked, her eyes wide. "Skinned you?"

Ms. Burden laughed. "No, that's just an expression. But she did hit me a lot—in my memory I'm always running away from her, and she's always catching up and slapping me."

"What?" Amaranth said. "Why did she do that?"

Ms. Burden looked flustered. "Because I did something wrong." She turned to Philip. "Don't tell me you never punish your children."

"Well, sure I do," Philip said. "I don't hit them, though."

"Oh. Well, she could be pretty harsh sometimes, my mother. She liked things neat—she hated it when something was out of order. Once I put a book in the wrong place on the shelf—they were alphabetized, and I didn't know that names that started with 'Mc' went in with names starting with 'Mac'—so she took the book out and started hitting me with it. And then later, whenever I looked at that part of the shelf, she'd come up behind me, very quietly, and hit me on the back of the head with another book. And then she'd say, 'I hope you learned your lesson. 'Mc' and 'Mac'—they're the same thing.'"

"That's—that's horrible," Beatriz said.

"Well, I did learn my lesson. I learned to watch out for her before I went to that part of the bookshelves."

She laughed a little, but another expression looked out from behind that one, like a lost child peeking out from behind a curtain. For the first time she seemed vulnerable, exposed.

My sisters looked shocked—and I did too, probably. Ms. Burden must have noticed our reactions because she said, "Well, we should probably talk about something else."

"But it must have been horrible," Beatriz said again. None of us had ever realized that parents could be cruel; we'd thought, because of our own parents, that they had to love their children. Sometimes they could be absent-minded, like Philip, or gone, like Jane, but that love was non-negotiable, instinctive, built into the contract from the beginning.

"Well, I turned out all right," Ms. Burden said. "I was able to move out, finally, and I didn't see her for years. I didn't even come to her funeral."

Hadn't she said she'd been with her mother when she died? I was excited to have caught her out in a lie, but at the same time her story had been so terrible that it seemed unfair to press my advantage.

She was so careful when she spoke, though, that I didn't think I'd get another chance. "Wait a minute," I said. "You said—didn't you say you nursed her until she died?"

She turned to me. "No, that's not what I said, Ivy. I did nurse her for a while, but she died much later."

"Yes, you did. You said—"

"I should think I'd know when my own mother died."

She had said it—I was sure of it. I opened my mouth to argue, but the rest of them had moved on. I learned something then that I was able to put to good use in later life, that most people don't want to believe someone is lying to them, that they will make excuses for the most blatant untruths.

"Anyway," she said, talking to Philip now. "I still can't believe you let them keep their bedrooms in that state. I mean, the floor's just covered with their things, Ivy's and Beatriz's. I could barely make it through the room."

She was smiling as she spoke; she'd probably say she was just teasing if we became offended. Still, I was furious. I wanted to ask her why she'd gone snooping if it was so crowded in there. What right did she have to criticize us?

Philip spoke first, though. "You know, I don't think it matters," he said mildly. "I just want them to be healthy, and to find what they want to do in life, and be happy doing it. And no matter how messy it gets, they always seem to know where everything is."

"Ivy couldn't find her homework this morning," Beatriz said.

"Shut up, Beatriz," I said. Why did she always have to take Ms. Burden's part? "I did so."

"Yeah, after about ten minutes. You almost missed the bus."

Dinner ended soon after that, thankfully. Ms. Burden left, and Philip went to put Amaranth and Semiramis to bed. I sat at the table, waiting for him.

Finally he came downstairs. "Can I talk to you?" I asked.

Just for a moment he looked impatient. Then he nodded, and I could tell he was trying to put out of his mind all the things he needed to do, the countless tasks adults busied themselves with, and focus on what I wanted. "Here, let's go sit down," he said.

We went into the living room and sat on the couch. To my annoyance, Beatriz came in and took the chair across from us.

"I didn't know Maeve was supposed to be dead," I said.

"Well, she isn't *supposed* to be." He paused, as if trying to decide the best way to explain it. "But she—Adela Madden—she doesn't want anyone to know anything about her. It's fine with her if people think she's dead."

"Why, though?"

"She—well, she doesn't like being bothered. You know that. If her fans knew where she lived they'd eat her alive. They'd come to her house, or follow her around, or call her up—there'd be no end to it. A lot of them want to know why she's never written another book, and she got tired of answering that question."

"Why hasn't she?"

He didn't seem to have heard me. "And some people can be obsessive—do you know what that means?"

I nodded.

"They might threaten her, or—or hurt her in some way. Someone sent a dead rat to her publisher once."

"Uck," Beatriz said.

"I still don't get it, though," I said. "Other people have fans, and nothing ever happens to them. People want fans, I thought."

He shook his head. "Well, part of it is that she's become more of a hermit. She used to go out sometimes, go into Woodbine instead of paying people for deliveries, but she stopped doing that a while back. She even sold off her car, though I told her she should keep it for emergencies."

"Okay," I said. "But there's another thing, too. Ms. Burden, when she went to the bathroom—I found her in my room, looking through my stuff."

"You did?"

"Yeah, remember? She said something about all the books I read."

He sat up, looking worried. Finally, I thought. Finally he understands, he sees it too. There's something wrong with her.

Everything I wanted to say seemed to burst out at once, like opening an overstuffed closet. "She's—she's obsessed, like you said. She keeps talking to us, trying to get to know us, and then it turns out that *Ivory Apples* is her favorite book, and she wanted to know, she asked me about Aunt Maeve—"

"Really? What did she say?"

"She wanted to know where I got my books. The ones Aunt Maeve gave me."

"What did you tell her?"

"That I got them from a teacher."

Philip nodded, looking relieved. "Good. I don't like you to lie, you know that, but I suppose in this case you didn't have a choice."

"What if she already knows about Aunt Maeve, though? And that's why she's interested in us?"

"How could she? Maeve's been very careful when it comes to her privacy, very smart. The book came out in 1957 and pretty much disappeared, and then in the mid-sixties or late sixties, somewhere around there, people started reading it and it got rediscovered, it became very popular. They did a paperback edition and Maeve—well, she was still Adela then—she started getting a lot of money, and fan letters, and people around the world were reprinting it. And then one day her sister Lydia—that was your grandmother, Jane's mother—she came to visit and found all these unopened envelopes with checks in them, and she started taking care of Adela's finances. They got a bank account together and Lydia deposited all the checks. And she answered the mail too—there wasn't that much of it then, and she thought the fans would like it, that it would help sales of the book. Then she died, and your mother took over. So the last time anyone dealt with Maeve, the last time they saw her in person, was around 1960, like Kate said."

I'd thought it had been Jane who'd started answering the fan

letters, but it had been going on longer than that, for two genera-
tions. It seemed ages ago. No computers, black and white television,
diseases with ancient names, like polio . . .

"Well, she still could have found out," I said. "Ms. Burden. Someone could have told someone else. The thing is, I just don't trust her.
There's something, well, off about her. Something wrong."

He got that look, the one where he knew he had to say something
but felt embarrassed about it. "Did she—has she ever done anything
inappropriate?"

I wasn't sure what he meant. "Like what?" I asked.

"We talked about this, remember? If someone tries to touch you
where you don't want to be touched, or says something that makes
you uncomfortable, or—or grabs you—"

"She does touch us a lot."

"She pats us on the arm!" Beatriz said, her voice scornful. "That's
not what he means."

"Does it bother you when she does that?" Philip asked.

"No!" Beatriz said.

"Okay, look. Probably she's just trying to be friendly. Could you,
I don't know, give her a chance? She's doing her best."

"What if she asks us about Aunt Maeve again?"

"Well, then, you come talk to me."

He studied me, his eyes clear and steady. And that was the way
I'd remember him later, that sincere, slightly puzzled expression. That
look of his that said he was trying, that he really did want to understand.

CHAPTER 5

A few days later it seemed I got my wish, and Ms. Burden disappeared. We didn't know she had gone at first; we just noticed that

she hadn't come to the park for several days, and we thought that she must be busy with other things.

The days turned into weeks, then months, and I began to hope she would stay away forever. It seemed that I had never taken a full breath around her, that I was always worrying about what she wanted, whether I might give away something by accident. Now I felt myself stretching out luxuriously, filling all the spaces she had occupied.

The others wanted her back, of course, and they looked for her at our usual spot every day after school. After a few weeks they started going through the rest of the park and even beyond, to the surrounding neighborhood.

"What if—well, what if something happened to her?" Beatriz asked once, after another unsuccessful day in the park. "Do you think we should check the hospitals, or the police?"

I shook my head. "I'm sure she's fine."

"I wish she'd given us her phone number."

"Yeah—it's weird she didn't."

"It's not that weird."

"Really? She keeps telling us how much she likes us, what great friends we are, but we don't even know how to get in touch with her? She never even told us where she lived."

Beatriz couldn't say anything to that. But I saw I'd made her unhappy, and from then on I tried not to criticize. After all I'd won— she was gone.

My sisters started going to the park every few days, then every week, then only a few times a month. But after about six months they seemed resigned to her absence, saying "if she comes back" and not "when."

I was in middle school then, in a school near the park in fact, so I walked the few blocks there and back. Beatriz and Amaranth and Semiramis still went to grade school on the school bus. Whoever came home first was supposed to get the mail, so I was the one who ended up finding the postcard.

It had a picture of a fountain the size of a building, with statues of horses and men cavorting through the water. A caption underneath said, "Trevi Fountain, Rome." I was turning it over idly, wondering who we knew in Rome, when I saw her name.

A few months ago I would have been shocked to hear from her, and alarmed that she might come back. Now I felt only curiosity, a desire to know where she'd been. "My dear Ivy, Beatriz, Amaranth, and Semiramis," the postcard said. "I am so sorry I haven't been in touch with you. I had an opportunity to travel through Europe, and I couldn't possibly turn it down. I've been to England, Spain, Italy of course, Greece, and Turkey. Today is the first day I've been able to finally sit down and write you. I wish you could be here with me and see all the wonderful places I've seen. Much love, Kate."

I was still standing by the mailbox when the school bus pulled in at the curb, and my sisters came clattering down the stairs. "We got a postcard," I said.

"Yeah?" Beatriz said. "Who from?"

"Ms. Burden."

"What? Really?"

Her face opened up, like an empty house filling with life and light and conversation. She grabbed the card from me and read it aloud to Amaranth and Semiramis.

I couldn't help but think, my second time through it, that Ms. Burden wasn't a very good writer. "Wish you were here" was the worst kind of cliché, and if you traveled to all those places you should at least describe some of them.

For just an instant Beatriz looked disappointed, as if she'd expected more as well. Then Amaranth said, "Let me see, let me see," and Beatriz passed her the card.

"When is she coming back?" Semiramis asked.

"She doesn't say," Beatriz said.

"She might not be," I said.

"Of course she is—she says—" Beatriz took the postcard and read it again, then looked up at me, doubtful. "What, do you think she's going to stay in"—she turned the card over—"in Rome?"

"I don't know."

"I think she misses us. Look—it says 'Much love' here."

I didn't think that proved anything, but I kept my opinion to myself. We got a second postcard about a week later, this one with a castle in Germany on the front and another vague message on the back. And then a third one, the Arc de Triomphe in Paris, where Ms. Burden had written, "I miss all of you very much. I think it might be time to come home."

"See?" Beatriz said, as triumphant as whoever had built that arch. "She's coming back."

She'd said she *might* come back, I thought. But even I was starting to think Beatriz was right. And my worry, that nagging feeling that Ms. Burden had something wrong with her, began to slither back.

Still, so much time had passed that I wondered if I had exaggerated the menace I'd sensed from her. I even felt a small excitement, thinking about those meetings in the park. What would she come up with next? Would she bring us something from Europe?

Piper jumped up and down in extravagant disgust, though, saying as clear as words that he wanted her to stay away for good. Could he have been the one who'd distrusted her all this time, and not me? After all, he'd been there when I'd met her—could he have influenced me somehow?

But what if he was trying to warn me about her? Well then, I thought, he should come right out and say it. I was tired of being crabby and cynical, the one who let the air out of everyone's balloons. I wanted to set down the load of my suspicions, to walk on lightly without them.

We saw her sitting in the park the next day, as if she'd never left.

"Is that—?" Beatriz said, but before she could finish the sentence Amaranth and Semiramis were racing across the grass.

"Kate!" one of them shouted, and the other one said, "We missed you!"

She lifted Semiramis into the air. "Look at you, Ramis, you've grown so much," she said, putting her down. Semiramis beamed, and Amaranth scowled when Ms. Burden didn't pick her up as well. And I was scowling too—when had she started using our nicknames?

Beatriz and I had come up by then, and she drew us all into a hug. When we pulled apart I saw that she looked tired, and the lines on her face had deepened; she could have been gone years instead of months. She was still thin, though, still wearing all those loose light-colored clothes. Her scarf was pale green and something I thought might be called charcoal, and I wondered if she'd picked it up on her travels.

We sat down around her and she told us about the places she'd visited, the adventures she'd had. She was still talking by dinnertime, and of course my sisters invited her back to the house.

"Kate!" Philip said when he saw her. "Where have you been? Everyone's missed you."

"Didn't you get my postcards?" she asked.

"Oh, yes, of course. Europe somewhere, wasn't it?"

I looked at him in amazement. Hadn't he seen how closely my sisters had studied the postcards?

"We each got one of them, to put up in our room," Amaranth said. "I took the Paris one."

"The Arc de Triomphe, of course," Ms. Burden said. "You know, it's right in the middle of a traffic circle, with all these cars driving around it. And there are these people standing under it, looking at it up close, and I just couldn't figure how they'd gotten there. It looked like they'd all run out into traffic, but I didn't think so many people would risk death just for a tourist attraction. I must have stood there for, oh, five, ten minutes, watching them. And I was just about to throw myself in front of all the cars when I saw some people go into a tunnel."

We laughed. "Which one did you get, Beatriz?" she asked.

"The fountain in Rome," she said, and Semiramis said, "I have the castle!"

"And you, Ivy?" she said, turning to me.

I blinked. "You only sent us three of them."

"Really? Honestly, I meant to send you more. I certainly would have, if I'd known you'd each take one."

Didn't she know how many she'd sent? She hadn't seemed to have put a lot of thought into them, just picked up a generic postcard from every city she passed through.

We went to dinner and ate in silence for a while. Finally Amaranth said what we were all thinking: "Why didn't you say goodbye to us?"

"And why didn't you write us sooner?" Beatriz said. She was looking at Ms. Burden intently now, adding this new fault to her scorecard. Ms. Burden seemed to have lost a few points, I was pleased to see. "We were worried—we didn't even know where you were."

"Well, but I did write to you," Ms. Burden said.

"Not for a long time," Amaranth said. "A year."

"Not that long, surely. I left at the end of January, and it's September now, so"—she counted on her fingers—"only eight months. And I sent you those postcards a few months ago."

Esperanza came out of the kitchen with two bowls of noodle soup and set them down in front of Philip and Ms. Burden. Ms. Burden blew on hers to cool it and then spooned out a sip. "Mmmm, this is wonderful," she said.

"Last month," Beatriz said, her jaw tight. "I can show you the dates on them."

"The dates on what, dear?" Ms. Burden said, taking another sip.

"On the postcards."

"Oh, dear." Ms. Burden put her spoon down. She frowned. "Well, the truth is that I was swept away. By a—a man, someone who seemed wonderful, maybe the love of my life. Well, I thought so at the time, anyway. He told me he wanted to take me to Europe, but he was leaving the next day and I had to give him my answer right then. So of course I said yes."

"And then what?" Semiramis asked. She seemed already won over.

"Well, we got along famously for the first few months or so. But he was always hurrying me along, never staying in one place for more than a day or two. I didn't have time to write, or do much of anything else. And then, well, he left me. Right in the middle of Spain, and of course I didn't speak the language, or have a lot of money—he'd always taken care of our finances. And he'd carried my passport in his backpack, too, though I don't think he meant to take it with him. It took me a while to sort all of that out."

"Oh," Beatriz said. We were silent for a while, thinking about being dropped in a foreign country without money, without knowing anyone.

"Why did he leave you?" Semiramis said.

"Ramis!" Beatriz said. "You can't ask someone that."

"Oh," Semiramis said. "Well, I wouldn't have left."

Ms. Burden smiled sadly.

"How did you get back?" Beatriz asked.

"Through the American embassy. And thank God for them—I'd probably still be in Spain if it wasn't for their help."

"What was your favorite place?"

Ms. Burden seized the change of subject gratefully. "You know, I think it was England. Well, except for the food. There was this one pizza place in London—my God, it was horrible. I don't think you're supposed to put warmed-up peas and carrots on pizzas, but maybe that's how they do it there."

She talked about her travels all through dinner. Then she excused herself, saying that she'd learned a little Spanish and wanted to thank Esperanza for the meal. Philip went to put Amaranth and Semiramis to bed, and only Beatriz and I were left at the table.

After a while I realized that Ms. Burden hadn't come back. I remembered her looking through my things, and a small cloud of suspicion formed in my mind. I went into the kitchen and saw that she was helping Esperanza with the dishes. She dried a fork and then opened a drawer in front of her.

"No, they go over there," Esperanza said.

"Oh, *lo siento*," Ms. Burden said. She looked up and saw me. "Did you want anything, Ivy?"

Just making sure you don't steal the silverware, I thought. "No, it's okay," I said.

CHAPTER 6

I came back to the house one afternoon to see my sisters standing on the doorstep. "I lost my key," Beatriz said.

"Again?" I asked.

"Hey. I only did it once before."

"Twice," I said. "At least."

I let them in, and Beatriz and I went to the junk drawer in the kitchen to look for the spare key. We piled things around us on the kitchen floor—twine and a box of matches and playing cards and an old ashtray from back when Philip smoked—until we reached the bottom.

Beatriz sat back. "I don't see it here," she said.

Suddenly I had a horrible thought. "What if Ms. Burden took it?" I asked. "She was here, remember, helping Esperanza do the dishes."

"Oh, God, Ivy," Beatriz said. "First you think she's snooping around in our room, and now she's stealing things . . . Why would she take our key, anyway?"

"To get inside the house. Duh. To snoop some more."

"And why would she do that?"

"Because—because she's looking for something."

"For what?"

"I don't know. Something about Maeve, maybe."

"Oh, come on. She said once that she likes *Ivory Apples*, and you just made up this whole story about her . . ."

I stopped listening. I felt cold suddenly, my skin prickling with static. She might have been here, might have looked through our things. Might have found out who Maeve was, and gone over to her house to do something terrible. To put a dead rat in her mailbox, or worse.

I stood up. "I'm calling Philip," I said.

"You can't. Only if it's an emergency, he said."

I went to the phone and dialed his office number. But Philip, too, thought there was nothing to worry about, and told me we could talk about it when he got home.

How could I not worry, though? There was plenty of evidence around the house—the letters Philip answered, for one thing, and the listing in our phone book. I paged through the phone book and saw that Philip had just written Maeve's first name and phone number, not her address. Well, all right, but no doubt there were other clues scattered around, things I hadn't thought of.

I paced through the house, jittery and anxious. A key sounded in the lock at the front door but it was only Esperanza, come to clean and make dinner.

Beatriz and the others had gone, probably to the park to talk to Ms. Burden. I could head over and confront her, but I was sure she'd deny everything. Then she'd put on that hurt expression I'd seen before, heartbroken that I could even think such a thing. For now I could do nothing to do but wait.

Philip came home a few hours later. He took one look at me and ushered me into the living room. "What about our phone book?" I said, even before I sat down. "Her name's in there, and her phone number."

"Only her first name, Maeve," he said. "And Kate would think of her as Adela Madden, wouldn't she?"

That much was true. I relaxed slightly. "Well, but—"

"Let me explain a few things, and then you can ask me whatever you want," he said. "I have an office where I take care of Maeve's business. Well, she rents it for me, really—I told you she's paranoid. Everything connected to her and her book is over there, nothing's at our house. Except that one listing in our phone book, but I'm sure that's okay."

I hadn't known any of this—though, to be fair, I wasn't all that interested. I hadn't even realized that Philip didn't write the letters at home. "Seems like a lot of work," I said.

He laughed, a tired laugh that sounded like he'd thought the same thing, many times. "Well, I've streamlined it—I use form letters a lot. But I promised your mother I'd do it. She was worried Maeve would starve to death up there on her own."

"So there's nothing to connect you to *Ivory Apples?*"

"Nothing." He smiled. "Your mother signed the letters with my middle name, David, and said she was Adela Madden's secretary. I use the same name, but I dropped the secretary part—it made me feel like an imposter. If I gave some of these people my real name they'd track me down at the U and I'd never get rid of them. Do you feel better now?"

"Yeah. Yeah, I do. Could you call her, just to make sure she's okay?"

"She won't answer the phone. I'll try, though."

Philip did call Maeve once or twice, but, as he suspected, she didn't answer. I couldn't shake the idea that something had happened to her, and when it came time to visit her I ran for the car.

It was October, cold and clear, and leaves skittered along the highway. I fidgeted with impatience as we drove, unable to settle until we got to Maeve's house.

She was out working in her garden again. I was so relieved that I let go of my hold on Piper, and I felt him leap sharply at the thought of freedom. I tugged him back and got out of the car.

"Something very disagreeable has happened," Maeve said when we reached her. She wiped her hands on an old shirt. "A woman keeps calling me."

I glanced at Philip. "What woman?" he said, though I was sure he knew as well as I did.

"I don't know what woman, do I? She called me Adela, my first name, if you please, and said she wanted to visit me. And when I demanded to know why, she said that she had something to tell me, something I'd like to hear. But I already know I won't like anything she says, that I don't even like *her*. Have you told anyone about me, let anything slip?"

I looked at Philip again. "Yes, Ivy?" Maeve said. "Is there something you want to tell me?"

"Ivy—well—has a theory," Philip said, and he told Maeve about the missing key.

"Well, for God's sake, change the locks!" Maeve said.

"We already did. Ivy wanted to."

"Good for her," Maeve said. "Tell me about this woman, this Kate."

"She didn't do it!" Beatriz said loudly.

We rehearsed all the old arguments again. Maeve said nothing, just studied us, expressionless.

"Well," she said finally. "I changed my phone number. And this time, Philip, you memorize it. Don't write it down anywhere."

"All right," he said. "Why did you answer the phone in the first place?"

"Well, she kept calling. Finally I thought it might be you, that there might be an emergency. How did she know who I was, though?"

"We don't even know if it was her. It could be someone just dialing randomly."

"Someone who knew my name? My old name?"

"I don't know."

"All right. Well, let's go in and start on the mail. You did bring the mail, didn't you?"

That seemed to end it. Philip would deal with Maeve, and I could stop worrying about her. So I thought, anyway.

We usually ate out on Tuesdays, Esperanza's day off. A few weeks after our visit to Maeve we were sitting in a restaurant when I noticed Amaranth and Semiramis whispering together and pointing.

I don't remember what restaurant it was, only that, since Philip wasn't great on fine cuisine, we'd probably gone to some kind of diner. It was dim and a little dingy, so I had a hard time making out what they were looking at. "What's so funny?" I asked.

"Nothing," Amaranth said, trying not to laugh. Semiramis giggled.

"Well, it has to be something. You wouldn't be laughing so hard if it wasn't."

"Oh my God," Beatriz said. "It's Kate."

"What?" I said. "Where?"

Finally I saw her too, at a table against the wall. She looked very strange, out of place, as if a gazelle had wandered in out of the jungle to order a hamburger.

"Oh, my *God*," Beatriz said again.

"What?"

"She has a boyfriend."

I looked closer and saw a man at her table. The first thing I thought was that he was nowhere near good-looking enough for her. He had curly, mouse-colored hair, already receding from his forehead, thin lips, a boxy chin.

Amaranth stood up, eager to join them. "Wait a minute, Rantha," I said. "I want to watch them for a while."

"Why?"

"I don't know. See what she does when she isn't with us."

"She isn't doing anything."

"Maybe she wants to be alone," Philip said. "Have a vacation from you kids, for a change."

Semiramis squealed in laughter at something Beatriz said, and Ms. Burden turned toward us. It was hard to tell in the murky light, but I thought I saw her frown.

Then, very quickly, she smiled. "Well, hello!" she said.

She got up as though to come toward us. I darted over to her and caught her at her table before she could move.

"Hello, Ivy," she said. Papers were scattered all across the table. She swept them into a briefcase, then closed it with a click like a knuckle cracking, a sound of finality. "Does your family come here a lot?"

My sisters had followed me over. "Sometimes," Beatriz said. "What about you?"

"This is my first time, actually. I've already eaten, or I'd ask you what's good here. Oh, where are my manners?" She turned to the man with her and said, "These are my friends, Ivy, Beatriz, Amaranth, and Semiramis."

"And what's your name?" Beatriz asked him, sounding very much like Ms. Burden.

The man cleared his throat and said, "I'm Ned."

"Are you the man she went to Europe with?"

Ms. Burden laughed. "No—we're just discussing some business."

"What kind of business?" I asked. "What do you do, Ted?"

"Ned," he said. The mistake had been Piper's, I realized, but I thought it was pretty funny anyway. "I'm a legal aide, I guess you'd say. I fill out forms, things like that. Dot the t's and cross the i's."

"No, it's the i's that are—" Amaranth started.

"It has to be done, unfortunately," Ms. Burden said. "And there's a lot to do, so we need to get back to it."

"Forge ahead." Ned chuckled.

I knew enough to realize that she wanted us to leave, but my sisters were still staring at Ned. We weren't used to seeing her with anyone else, or being told to go away, and I think they felt jealous—especially after she'd been gone for so long.

"I'll come talk to you when I'm done here," she said.

"Okay," Beatriz said.

We went back to our table. "He isn't her boyfriend," Beatriz said to Philip, sounding disappointed.

"No? Who is he?"

"He's helping her with business."

"What kind of business?"

"She didn't say."

"She never told us anything about a business," I said.

"Well, she doesn't have to tell us everything, does she?" Beatriz said. "What are you thinking —that her business is breaking in to people's houses and stealing their keys?"

I laughed. I imagined a chain of keys around her neck, chiming softly, taken from houses all over town. "Yeah, maybe," I said.

We left before she did, so we never got a chance to ask about her business, or Ned. And somehow, when we sat together in the park and talked, it never seemed the right time to bring it up.

CHAPTER 7

This next part is hard to write, hard to live through again. For a while we continued as we always had. We visited Maeve, and I tried to figure out the answers to her riddles; we saw Ms. Burden in the park; I tried to keep Piper under control. I turned thirteen in November, and in December we all stayed up for the new year again.

Then it was January 15, a date I've never forgotten. Ms. Burden had joined us at dinner again. She had been doing that more since she'd returned, to the point where she no longer needed an invitation, just asked if she could come back with us when we walked home. She didn't impose overmuch, though, maybe once or twice a week.

This time she told us about some noises she'd been hearing from her basement. "It sounds like there's something down there, or someone," she said. "Sometimes I hear crying, or—or howling. And then things start to bang around, or make a loud crashing noise, like they're falling down.

"It only happens at night," she went on. "I looked down in the basement a few times during the day, but nothing seemed out of place or fallen over. So I knew I had to check it out at night, but the thought of going down there in the dark just terrified me. Finally I couldn't stand it anymore—I wasn't sleeping, just waiting for something to happen. So I bought the biggest flashlight I could find, and then when I heard the noises again I went down the stairs, and I turned on the light . . ."

She paused for a long time. I was just about to ask what had happened when she went on.

"And then I saw . . ." she said, ". . . I saw absolutely nothing. I'd cleared out a lot of the basement, all the heavy stuff, so if anything fell over it wouldn't make much of a noise, but everything was exactly where I'd left it."

"And then what?" Amaranth asked.

"That's it. That was last night, and I haven't been down there since."

I'd noticed before that she wasn't a very good storyteller. A long pause like that should be followed by something dramatic, at the very least.

"Could it be a cat?" Philip asked. "That would explain the crying noises, and maybe it knocked something over."

"Well, I thought that too. I even looked for paw prints, but I couldn't find anything. But honestly, I think you're right, that's what it is. I hope that's what it is, anyway. Everything else I can think of is, well, it's sort of terrifying."

"Like what?" Amaranth asked.

"I don't know." She laughed shakily. "Maybe I'm being haunted."

Philip looked at her, a stern gaze that I had seen from him before. He was telling her not to frighten the children, to keep the conversation light. And she seemed to get his point, because she put her hands to her mouth briefly, as if to take back her last words.

"Well, what I mean to say is that I just can't figure it out," she went on. "I'm at my wits' end here. I haven't slept at all for—it's been three nights now."

"Why don't I come back with you, take a look at your basement?" Philip said. "Maybe it's your house settling, something like that."

She looked at him gratefully. "That's very kind of you."

All my old suspicions surfaced again. What did she want from him? Was she trying to get him alone, away from us kids, and then seduce him?

"I left my notebook at River's," I said quickly. "Maybe I could go with you, stop by her house and pick it up."

She scowled at me. She really did, I wasn't making it up. There was something she wanted to do with Philip, and I would get in the way.

He turned to Ms. Burden. "Where do you live?"

She gave him her address, but he didn't know the street. "You'll have to show me. And where does River live?"

He'd only dropped me off there about a hundred times. "McMillan Street."

"All right, then. Come on."

"I want to go too!" Beatriz said.

"Someone has to stay here, make sure Amaranth and Semiramis get to bed," Philip said.

"Esperanza can do it," Beatriz said. She ran to the kitchen to ask her.

"That's not fair!" Amaranth said. "Why can't I go with you?"

"Because it's your bedtime," Philip said. "You and Semiramis are going to bed, right this minute."

"Esperanza says she can stay," Beatriz said as she came back, sounding gleeful. "What's your house like? Is it big?"

"Well, you'll see it when we get there," Ms. Burden said. She stood, as if to urge the rest of us to start moving, and we got our coats and left.

Nobody said much on the drive over. It was dark, and rain hit the car with the sound of fingernails tapping. Every so often we plowed through pools of water, and fountains shot up around the car. Philip turned on the heater but I still felt cold, and my coat did little to warm me.

I didn't pay much attention to our surroundings, though. I was puzzling over the fact that Ms. Burden had never told us she had a house, had never once invited us over. And I didn't know a lot about finances, but I wondered how someone without a job could afford to buy a house.

We parked at River's house and I got out of the car. Of course I hadn't left my notebook there—that was just an excuse so I could go with them. But they were watching me, so I knocked at the door and talked to River's mother when she looked out.

"It isn't there," I said when I came back to the car.

Then it was Ms. Burden's turn to give directions. We drove for a while and came to a neighborhood I'd never seen before, with an auto painting shop and a mini-storage and other businesses, all of them closed and dark. We were near the Rose Garden, I knew, where we'd gone several times with Philip. I wondered why Ms. Burden spent so much time at our park when this one was much closer.

Finally we turned down a street of small, rundown houses. Ms. Burden pointed out the window, and Philip pulled over to the curb.

Weeds had taken over the front lawn, urged on by all the rain that winter, and our feet squished through mud as we went up to the door. The paint on the walls—once white, now a sort of gray—had started to peel.

We went inside. The living room had almost no furniture, just two folding chairs, a television on a small table, and some bookcases stuffed with books. The place was freezing, the cold gusting in through cracks somewhere, and it smelled of books and stale grease.

I felt a profound disappointment. I had been expecting something dark and glittery, a pirate's cave filled with treasure. Even if that had been an impossibly romantic vision, she should have had more than this bare room: wonderful old toys and Photoshopped artwork, maybe; shelves of leather-bound books with gold-stamped titles shining in the firelight; colorful hangings and patterned rugs and rare plants.

The bookcase seemed to be the only interesting thing there. I scanned the shelves and saw a few editions of *Ivory Apples* before Ms. Burden called to us to follow her. I turned and caught a glimpse of a book called *Games and Pastimes for Young Children.*

I looked around for Beatriz, wanting to show her what I'd found, but Ms. Burden was hurrying everyone into the kitchen. It was as stark as the living room, just a stove and refrigerator and sink, and a Mac set up on a small table. There was nothing on the Formica counters, no toaster or microwave or coffee maker, and no dishes in the sink or any traces that she had ever eaten a meal here. I had the sudden thought that if I looked in the cupboards they would be empty.

She went over to a small door closed by a padlock and used a key to open it. "Down here," she said.

I peered inside and saw a narrow wooden staircase. One side stood against the wall, but the other opened out into space, with no railing or handhold. Halfway down, the light ended and the stairs disappeared into shadow, a darkness that seemed to move, to billow, like a pool of black water or a vast sea creature.

"Get away from there, Ivy—it isn't safe," Ms. Burden said. I moved back and Philip went to stand at the head of the stairs. "The cord for the lightbulb is down there at the bottom, unfortunately. I don't know why they couldn't have put a switch up here—it would have made it so much easier."

She was chattering, talking quickly but not saying anything. I had never seen her like that, and I wondered if she felt nervous about letting us into her house.

She handed Philip a flashlight and he started down, moving carefully. I watched him go, watched as he passed from light into shadow. The sound of his footsteps faded, as though the darkness had soaked them up.

Something howled. The howl wavered up and down the scale, eerie and infinitely sad. I felt hairs rising up on the back of my neck, as if I had hackles.

There was a long, loud, dull noise, and then a shout: "No!" or "Oh!" Then a thud, and a trailing arc of light.

"Philip!" I yelled. "Dad!"

Beatriz came over and stood behind me. I didn't see Ms. Burden anywhere. Where had she gone?

Beatriz and I shouted Philip's name again. "What on earth has happened?" Ms. Burden asked, coming in from the living room.

"He—I think he fell," Beatriz said. "He isn't answering."

Ms. Burden looked around the kitchen. "Oh, dear," she said. "I don't—I'm not sure what to do here. I gave him the only flashlight."

I started down the stairs. "No!" Ms. Burden said, sounding more confident now. She grabbed the back of my shirt to stop me.

"Let go of me!" I said. I tried to turn around, to face her. "Right now, or I'll—"

I didn't know what I would do. She could tell that I meant it, though, because she let go. "You're not going into the basement, not after what happened," she said. "I'm calling 911."

"No, he's down there, he needs our help . . ."

"You can't do anything for him. We have to call an ambulance, the EMTs. You can't carry him out by yourself."

She was right, unfortunately. She left the kitchen, and I climbed back up the stairs and stood next to Beatriz, saying nothing. Beatriz reached out and took my hand.

What was I thinking, in the long minutes before the ambulance came? I think now that the answer is nothing, that my mind had become a complete blank. I couldn't wonder what had happened to him, because the answer might be too terrible, and I couldn't concentrate on anything else.

The EMTs came inside, and the small kitchen was suddenly full of people. What sounded like dozens of voices bounced and boomed off the flat sterile surfaces, EMTs calling to each other and talking into their radios. A man went down the stairs and turned on the light at the bottom.

"What is it?" someone called into the stairwell.

"We're gonna need the stretcher."

"What happened?" I asked.

No one answered. Some of the EMTs went outside and came back with the stretcher. They maneuvered it into the small space and headed down.

"Could you move your kids into another room, ma'am?" a woman called up.

"Sure," Ms. Burden said. "Come on, Ivy, Beatriz."

I stood where I was, still holding Beatriz's hand. Ms. Burden broke us apart—she was surprisingly strong—and pulled us after her into the living room.

"What's going on?" I asked.

"We have to stay out of the way, let them do their jobs," Ms. Burden said.

"We weren't in the way," Beatriz said.

We looked at each other. I watched as she turned pale as paper, as the same thought occurred to each of us. Why wouldn't they let us see him?

I couldn't think about that just now. "We aren't your kids," I said to Ms. Burden.

"What?" she said.

"That woman called us 'your kids.' You should have told her we aren't related."

"Oh, Ivy. They're busy doing their jobs—I can't bother them with something so trivial."

It didn't seem trivial to me. I was going to say so, but just then the EMTs came through the living room with the stretcher. I tried to get a glimpse of Philip but they blocked my view—on purpose, I think now.

They fit the stretcher through the door. Then I heard them slide it into the ambulance, heard the doors close and the ambulance drive off. There was something strange about all of this, something missing, and after a while I realized that they hadn't put the siren on.

One of the EMTs came back into the house. "Hi, I'm Marla," she said. "Why don't we sit down?"

"Come on, Beatriz, Ivy," Ms. Burden said.

Beatriz and I sat on the flimsy chairs, leaving Marla and Ms.

Burden standing. "Well," Marla said. "It's bad news, I'm afraid. Your husband—"

"He isn't her husband!" I said.

She looked confused for a moment. "Well, I'm sorry to tell you that he died. He—"

"No!" Beatriz said. "No, that isn't true!"

"I'm afraid it is. We'll have a better picture later, but for now we think he fell down the stairs."

My face felt wet. I put my hand up to my cheek and realized that I was crying.

"What's your name?" Marla asked me.

"Ivy."

"And your father—was he your father?" I nodded. "What was his name?"

"Philip Quinn."

"Do you have any tissues?" she asked Ms. Burden.

"Sure. Just a moment."

She got up and came back with some paper towels. Beatriz had started to cry now too, and I handed her a few.

"And are you—his girlfriend?" Marla asked Ms. Burden.

"No, she's—"

Ms. Burden interrupted me. "No, I'm just a friend of the family."

"Do they—can we call their mother?"

"Their mother is dead, unfortunately."

Marla's expression, already sad, deepened into pity. And immediately I understood that we would see this for the rest of our lives, that everyone we met from now on would feel sorry for the poor orphan children. That they would all think they knew us, based on that one thing, and they would know nothing about us at all.

"Well, who can we call?" She turned to me. "Did your father ever talk about, well, what would happen if he died?"

I remembered a talk we'd had, a long time ago. "Yeah," I said, shredding a paper towel. "He said we'd go to his brother's family, in Indiana."

"Okay, good. Do you know the brother's phone number?"

I shook my head. I'd met him a long time ago, but I didn't remember him very well. Leonard, his name was, a duller, drabber version of Philip. Would we have to move out to Indiana, live with a bunch of strangers?

Marla suggested that we should go to our house, see if we could find some information somewhere. We went outside and headed for Philip's car. Ms. Burden went toward the driver's seat, but Marla reached it first. She opened the door with Philip's keys and we drove off.

When we got home, Ms. Burden went into the kitchen and talked to Esperanza in a low voice. I followed her, in time to hear Esperanza say something, sounding shocked.

"Shhh," Ms. Burden said to her. "We can't wake Rantha and Ramis. They'll have a hard enough time of it tomorrow."

They still hadn't heard, I realized. He was still alive for them. At that moment I envied them more than anyone in the world.

Ms. Burden headed to the shelf of cookbooks, which was where we kept the phone book. How did she know that, though? Even worse, I suddenly remembered that Maeve's phone number had been in there. She'd told Philip to take it out, but had he?

"Let me look," I said, grabbing the book before she could look through it.

"What are you doing, Ivy?" she said. She pulled it toward her and turned away from me.

"I'm the one who should go through it. It isn't yours, it's ours."

"Let her look, Ivy," Marla said. "She'll know better what to look for."

"Why?" I asked.

No one answered. A long time passed, with just the sound of flipping pages. "Here's something, someone's name and then the word 'Lawyer,'" Ms. Burden said "Do you know this name, Ivy? Nate McLaren?"

I shook my head.

"Well, let's call him." She looked at the clock over the stove. "Good Lord, it's after midnight. Look, I'll tell you what. Why don't you and Esperanza go home"—this was to Marla—"and I'll stay here with the family? I can call the lawyer in the morning."

I didn't want her to stay over; she'd already intruded enough into our life. "Good idea," Marla said. She looked exhausted.

She headed for the door. "Call me if you have any questions," she said as she left. "Or even if you just want to talk. Bye now."

Esperanza came in from the dining room. She put her arms around us, and I started to cry again.

"*Pobrecitas*," she said. She stepped away to look at us, and I saw she'd been crying as well. "If you need me, you call me, okay? And I come here tomorrow, see how you are."

I nodded, and she followed Marla out the door.

"Where should I sleep?" Ms. Burden asked, yawning.

"Not in Philip's room," I said.

I expected Beatriz to object, but she'd caught the yawn from Ms. Burden and couldn't say anything. "No, of course not," Ms. Burden said.

We didn't have any more rooms, though. Beatriz and I shared one, and Amaranth and Semiramis another, and Philip used the third as his bedroom and office. "On the couch?" I asked.

"All right," she said. "Do you have a linen closet?"

A linen closet? A moment later I worked out that she meant a place for sheets and pillowcases, and I showed her where it was.

Then we went to bed. I couldn't sleep, though. Instead, I tossed and turned and thought about everything that had happened, over and over again.

CHAPTER 8

"Ivy, get up," someone said. "We have to get going."

Who was that? I was home, in my own bed, but the person speaking wasn't anyone who lived here.

I opened my eyes. Ms. Burden stood over me. And then, like a great gust of wind sweeping through me, I remembered that my father was dead.

I wanted to curl up and go to sleep, to burrow back into that warm cocoon of unknowing. "Get up, Ivy, please. We don't want to be late."

"Late for what?"

"I called the lawyer. He wants to meet us at his office. He says he has Philip's will."

"Oh." I looked over at Beatriz's bed, but it was empty. "Don't come into my room."

She laughed. "Really? Beatriz doesn't mind."

"Well, stay on her side, then."

"Come on, Ivy, we shouldn't fight, especially now. We have to stick together, help each other out."

Why? I thought. But I threw the covers off and sat up.

"Oh, and I told Rantha and Ramis about your father," she said.

"What?"

"I said—"

"I should have been the one to tell them. They're my sisters, after all. How are they doing?"

"I don't know. I think they might be too young to understand."

I wasn't sure about that. Amaranth, especially, was starting to figure out what had happened to Jane.

I got ready and headed downstairs. My sisters were already at the table, eating breakfast.

Ms. Burden paced back and forth across the dining room, stopping every so often to look at her watch. "We have to get there by ten o'clock," she said. "Beatriz, wipe your face—you have jam on it. And Ivy—oh, dear. Is that what you're going to wear?"

I'd grabbed the first things I saw, some jeans and a Ducks sweatshirt. "Yeah, why not?"

"Well, you know, a lawyer is a very—a dignified kind of person. We have to show him some respect."

"Why? We'll never see him after today."

"There are conventions, rules. Ways of doing things that people have agreed to."

"So? I never agreed to them."

She sighed. "Could you please just put on a skirt? For me?"

"I didn't shave my legs."

That sounded like Piper, not me; he was the one who made personal, vaguely embarrassing comments. I realized I hadn't felt Piper since . . . since Philip had died. That made sense, though—Piper didn't like sadness, didn't seem to understand it.

Well, that would be a way of keeping him away. Of course I'd have to feel this unhappy, this empty, for the rest of my life. Still, right now I couldn't imagine anything else. How were you supposed to keep going when your life had broken in two?

I went upstairs and changed my clothes.

When we got to the car Ms. Burden took the driver's seat, Philip's seat. It seemed wrong to me, a usurper on the king's throne, but I told myself not to be so melodramatic.

Ms. Burden drove downtown and then parked and led us into a four-story office building. We took the elevator to the lawyer's office, and a woman at a desk waved us into the next room.

"Hello," a man there said. "You're the Quinns, is that right? I'm very sorry for your loss. My name is Nate McLaren—I'm Mr. Quinn's lawyer."

He had a round face, with rimmed half-glasses down near the tip of his nose, and a mustache so bristly you could shine shoes with it. He took us all in, his expression half sad and half kindly, as if he'd practiced the right way to greet people in mourning. Then I told myself not to be so harsh; he might be a decent person, someone who genuinely wanted to help us.

"I'm afraid I hadn't expected so many of you," he said.

He dragged some more chairs to a table in the corner and we sat down and introduced ourselves. I thought he looked up when Ms.

Burden gave her name, but maybe I imagined it. There was no reason why he should have, anyway.

He picked up some papers on the table, pushed his glasses up,
pulled them off. "So," he said, looking up at us. "The first thing I
have to tell you is good news. Your father had a life insurance policy,
a big one, because he knew you'd need it if he wasn't around. So you
don't have to worry about finances for many years yet. You'll get the
entire sum when you come of age, and there's enough there for you
to go to college."

He beamed through his mustache, as if he'd said something
remarkable. I hadn't really heard anything past his first few words,
though, which had caught me and suggested an entire story in the
space of a few seconds. The good news was that it had all been a mistake: the EMTs had been wrong and Philip was still alive. It took me
a while to drag myself back to reality, to force myself to pay attention.

My sisters were all nodding, so I nodded too. "So maybe I should
read the will itself," Mr. McLaren said. "Being of sound mind, so
forth, so on . . . In the event of my death I would like my good friend
Katherine Burden to be my children's guardian—"

"What!" I said.

"What?" Ms. Burden asked, an instant later.

Mr. McLaren looked at her. "Is there a problem? That's you, isn't
it? Katherine Burden?"

"Yes, it is," she said.

"Okay, very good. And you'll be able to be the children's guardian? There's a sum set aside for their maintenance, a good-sized
amount, so you won't have any trouble on that score—"

"*I* have a problem with this," I said, finally getting my voice back.
"We were supposed to go to our uncle in Indiana."

"Yes," Mr. McLaren said. He took his glasses off. "So this is a re-
vised version of Mr. Quinn's will, dated, let's see, October 22, 2000.
He's signed it, right here, and had it witnessed by two people, and
then he couriered it over on the twenty-third. All legal and above-
board." He looked at Ms. Burden. "Did he tell you what he'd done,
that he'd made you the children's guardian?"

She shook her head. "No. Honestly, I'm surprised as they are. And delighted, of course. I'd love to take the children—I already feel we're very close."

"Let me see it," I said. I slid the will closer. I had the crazy idea that she'd forged it, but Philip's signature looked just as same as all the other times I'd seen it. I pointed to the two signatures below his. "Who are these people?" I asked.

"His witnesses," Mr. McLaren said. "I don't know who they are, colleagues maybe. One minute."

He went to his desk and used the intercom to talk to his secretary, then came back to the table. His finger hovered in the air, pointing toward him, and he walked into it, pushing his glasses up. It would have been funny at any other time.

He sat down and looked over the will again. "There's a bequest of ten thousand dollars to someone named Esperanza Suarez," he said. "Do you know who that is?"

I didn't feel like talking, or cooperating in any way. "She's our housekeeper," Beatriz said.

"Oh, very good," Mr. McLaren said.

The woman we'd seen in the other room came over to him and handed him some papers. He flipped to the last page and turned it to face me. "So this is the will your father made in 1994. That's when his wife died, your mother, is that right?" Beatriz nodded. "He told me he knew he had to make some provision for you children if anything happened to him."

I looked at both signatures, the earlier and the later one, as if the answers I wanted would be written there. They were very similar, with only slight variations. So the newer signature probably wasn't forged, I thought; a forger would have copied it exactly.

"The witnesses are different," I said.

"Well, that's not surprising," Mr. McLaren said. "The wills were six years apart, after all. He probably couldn't find the same people, or didn't know them anymore."

I was furious at everyone. At Philip, who had done this without asking me, when he knew what I thought of Ms. Burden. At

Ms. Burden, for agreeing to it. Even at Uncle Len, who I blamed for not being enthusiastic enough about taking us in, for making Philip change his plans.

"Well, that's the general outline, anyway," Mr. McLaren said. I added him to the list of people I hated. "I'll have to talk to Ms. Burden here, work out the details, but you kids can be assured that you're provided for."

"And this way you won't even have to move," Ms. Burden said. "You can stay in Eugene, go to the same schools, keep all your old friends. That's good, isn't it?"

I turned to her. I felt Piper rising up triumphantly within me, felt his blasphemous joy, and for the first time I welcomed him completely.

"Listen, you malicious, mendacious, overweening smudge," I said. "You hanger-on of other people's families. You envious giraffe. My father's dead, and there's nothing remotely good about any of this."

I hadn't even known Piper could talk. He wasn't finished, though, or I wasn't; I wasn't sure which of us was saying these things. "You thief, you cut-rate Bonnie and Clyde. You—"

Everyone was looking at me, stunned. "I had no idea you could express yourself so well, Ivy," Ms. Burden said drily.

Mr. McLaren cleared his throat. "I'm sorry you feel that way, Ivy. Unfortunately, your father's will is clear on this point."

The jubilation I'd felt from Piper was ebbing now. I sat back in my chair, saying nothing. We didn't seem to have any choice; we were going to go home with the person I was starting to dislike more than anyone in the world.

"It won't be as terrible as you think," Mr. McLaren said. "You'll see."

CHAPTER 9

He was wrong, though. Things *were* that terrible, or worse. It was a Möbius strip of terrible—awful events coming back around over and over again.

There was the funeral, for one thing. The day after we saw the lawyer, Ms. Burden sat Beatriz and me down and looked us over, her eyes bright. "Is there anyone you think we should invite to Philip's funeral?" she asked.

Beatriz shrugged. "We didn't really know his friends and stuff," she said.

"I was thinking more of relatives—aunts or uncles or cousins, like that."

Aunt Maeve! How could we have forgotten her? But Philip had told us often enough not to mention her to anyone outside the family. And my suspicions of Ms. Burden had returned stronger than ever, especially after she'd become our guardian.

I made some kind of face at Beatriz, hoping that she'd guess my meaning. "Well, we have an Uncle Len," she said. "He lives in Indiana somewhere."

"Uncle Len, good," Ms. Burden said. "Here, I have an idea." She sounded cheerful, too cheerful for what we were talking about. "Let's look at your phone book."

We paged through it slowly, looking at names, some familiar or nearly so, some we'd never heard of. I grew more and more anxious the closer we came to the "M"s. Philip hadn't written down Maeve's new phone number, I knew, but I didn't want Ms. Burden even to see a crossed-out name, to know that Maeve existed.

Our phone book was a ring binder, with hole-punched pages that could be added or taken out. When we got to "M" I saw that Philip had done exactly what I'd hoped: he'd taken out the old page and rewritten all the names except Maeve's on a new one. Ms. Burden held the page between her fingers and flipped it back and forth for a while, saying nothing.

I let out my breath softly. Beatriz seemed relieved as well. We became tense again when we reached the "R"s, in case he'd put her under "Reynolds," but she wasn't there either.

"I guess that's all, then," Ms. Burden said when we came to the end. She'd written down a few names, including Uncle Len's. "Unless you can think of anyone else?"

"No," Beatriz said, and I shook my head.

Beatriz and I discussed Ms. Burden a lot, mostly after we'd gone to bed and turned the lights out. How often had we talked like this, two distant satellites, beaming our signals out through the darkness? Those conversations always seemed different from everything else in our lives, nothing to do with the daily world of school and homework and the rest of our family.

"We have to find her," Beatriz said. "Aunt Maeve."

"We don't have her phone number, though. She changed it after someone kept calling her, remember? And you saw the phone book—Philip never wrote it down."

"Well, could you find her house?"

I sketched the route against the darkness, trying to follow it through the trees and the highway. "I don't think so," I said. "Anyway, how would we even get there? I don't think a bus goes anywhere near it."

"Take a taxi. Tell them to drive around a while and look for it."

"Do you know how much that would cost? There's no way we could afford it." I thought of something else. "Philip used to deposit those checks for her. What if she runs out of money? Or food?"

"God," Beatriz said.

We said nothing after that. We were both thinking about Aunt Maeve, I knew, imagining her alone in her house in the middle of the woods.

The day of the funeral I put on my favorite dress, one with a print of bright red and yellow flowers. I thought that at least now Ms. Burden couldn't complain about my clothes. But when I came down to breakfast she had that reproachful expression I was starting to find so familiar.

"You can't wear something that colorful to a funeral, Ivy," she said.

"He liked this dress," I said. That wasn't true, actually. He'd never said much about our clothes, just asked if they fit.

"Well, you don't look very sad about your father's death."

"Why should I care if people think I'm sad or not?"

"It's a convention, like—"

Beatriz came down then, and Ms. Burden found some fault with what she was wearing as well. But Beatriz didn't argue, just went back to our room and put on another dress. By that time Amaranth and Semiramis had shown up, and in the confusion I never did change my clothes.

A light rain was falling when we got to the chapel. Hundreds of people seemed to have come out for the funeral, and somehow that finally made it real to me. I could no longer imagine that Philip was just at work, that he would come through the front door at any moment.

My sisters and I didn't know anything about funerals, so Ms. Burden made all the decisions for us, including finding a minister. But when the minister started to talk we soon realized that he'd never met Philip; the man he talked about could have been almost anyone. Even worse were all the references to God, when Philip had been an atheist.

My attention started to wander. I thought about the real Philip, the man who had tried to be both a father and mother to us. He'd failed sometimes, but he'd succeeded a lot more, and even when he came up short we knew he loved us.

When the service ended I spotted Uncle Len, who stood alone, without his wife and children. We moved from the chapel to the cemetery, and I made my way toward him. "Why didn't you want to be our guardian?" I asked, too unhappy to try to be polite.

"I never said I didn't, Ivy," he said, opening an umbrella and holding it over both of us. He had the same air of grave bewilderment as Philip. "I can't imagine why my brother changed his mind."

"Can you talk to the lawyer? Tell him we're going to live with you after all?"

"I can't go against what Philip wanted. And he had his reasons, I'm sure—he always did."

School was awful as well. People had already started avoiding me, and the fact that not one but both of my parents had died seemed only to make me stranger in their eyes. There were whispered rumors: that I'd killed both of them, that my family had done something horrible and been cursed for it.

Beatriz had started middle school the previous semester and she talked to me sometimes, but she had her own friends to hang out with. I ate lunch by myself, mostly, and tried to act as if that was my own choice. Piper helped here; being around him had shown me how to deal with embarrassment.

I still missed my father terribly. Losing someone close is like losing a part of yourself, an arm, maybe. You keep trying to do all the things you used to do, reaching for a book, opening a door, passing the salt. And then suddenly it hits you: a part of you is gone, and it's forever.

It hurts like an amputation as well, a pain that never seems to go away. Once while Beatriz and I were walking to school I stopped and sobbed for ten minutes straight. There was no reason for it; nothing had happened to make that day worse than any other. But I had to sit down on the curb and give in to my sorrow until it ended. Beatriz sat next to me, saying nothing, waiting until I finished.

If it hadn't been for Beatriz I don't know what I would have done. Philip's death had brought us closer, and we were fighting less and talking more. She even seemed, ever so slowly, to be coming around to my point of view, that there was something wrong with Ms. Burden.

She'd noticed, for example, that Ms. Burden did very little around the house. After the funeral she'd visited the lawyer to do some lawyerly stuff, get instructions or sign things or something, but since then she was usually on the phone or studying her computer.

"Did you notice how quickly she made herself at home?" I said one day, as we were walking home. "She even took over Philip's bedroom, even after I told her not to."

"Oh—you told her," Beatriz said, laughing her snotty laugh.

"What's so funny?"

"Well, she isn't going to listen to you, is she? Or me, or any of us. She does what she wants." She hesitated. "Here's the weirdest thing, though. She used to hang out with us all the time, remember? Playing games, or telling us stories, or just talking for hours. When was the last time she did any of that?" A wistful tone had come into her voice.

"It's like—like she got what she wanted, and she doesn't have to do that stuff anymore."

"What does she want, though?"

"I told you. Our family."

"Why? And she didn't plan what happened, you know that. She wasn't the one to—to do that to Philip."

"Maybe she did. Do something."

"Oh, come on. She wasn't even there, remember? She came into the kitchen later."

"She still could have done it. I mean, strange things happen." It was the closest I'd come to telling her about Piper.

"Is that how you explain it?" Beatriz said. "Strange things happen?"

"Okay, maybe she—she loosened the stair somehow. Made it so he'd fall if he stepped on it."

For just the briefest moment she considered it. "No—I don't think she'd do that," she said finally.

We started running to answer the phone when it rang, hoping it would be Aunt Maeve. Sometimes it was one of Beatriz's friends, or a parent calling to arrange a play-date with Amaranth or Semiramis. Usually, though, it wasn't anybody, just someone trying to sell us something. Ted-or-Ned called once and asked me to leave a message for Ms. Burden, but I never did.

Of course it was Ms. Burden who answered the phone when Maeve called. It rang after we'd gone to bed, and even though we ran down the stairs in our pajamas she had gotten there first.

"Yes, this is Philip Quinn's house," we heard her say. Then, "No, I'm sorry to have to tell you that he died."

Exclamations of shock came from the phone, loud enough that we could hear Aunt Maeve's voice. "Let me talk to her," I said.

Ms. Burden waved me away. "Yes, I understand," she said into the phone. "What did you say your name was? . . . But I've never heard the children mention a great-aunt—how do I know that's who you are?"

"It's Great-aunt Maeve!" I said. "Let me talk to her!"

"Hush—I'm on the phone, Ivy," Ms. Burden said. "Ivy here says your name is Maeve, is that right? . . . Well, I suppose we could come visit you. Where do you live?"

I grabbed the phone away from her. "Hi, Aunt Maeve!" I shouted into it. "It's Ivy!"

"Hello, child," Maeve said. "I'm so sorry to hear about your father. How did it happen?"

Ms. Burden reached for the phone, and I darted away. "He fell down some stairs. Listen, I don't have a lot of time. Could you come over? There's things I need to tell you."

"Oh, dear. I don't leave my house very often, you know. Can you come here instead?"

"I can't drive. I'm only thirteen."

"Well, can you get someone to take you? And maybe they can bring my checks, too."

"Give me the phone, Ivy," Ms. Burden said behind me. "Right now."

"Is that the woman I was talking to?" Maeve asked. "Be careful—I don't trust her."

"I don't either," I said. "Quick—how do we find your house? What's your address?"

Ms. Burden snatched the phone away from me. "No, wait—" I said.

Ms. Burden listened intently, then scowled. "Hello!" she said. "Hello, are you there?"

She put the receiver down. "She hung up," she said. "Never do that again, Ivy. Never interrupt me while I'm on the phone."

"She wanted to talk to me, not you."

"But who was she? What did she want?"

"Our aunt Maeve. Great-aunt." I realized I'd let her name slip in my excitement. Still, the name by itself didn't mean anything. And if Ms. Burden had been the one calling her before, she had to have known it already.

"But why didn't you mention her earlier?" she said. "When I asked you about your relatives?"

"I don't know. I forgot about her."

"We could have invited her to the funeral, if you'd just considered other people for a change. If you hadn't been so selfish. Instead she had to hear about your father's death from a stranger, over the phone. How do you think that made her feel? How old is she?"

"I don't know. Seventy, maybe."

"What's her last name?"

I knew enough not to tell her that. Hell, Semiramis would have known. I gave her the first name I could think of. "Quinn. Like us."

"And where does Maeve Quinn live?"

"I don't know."

"How can you not know?"

"We—we didn't see her a lot. And it was a long drive. Bend, somewhere like that."

I knew a lot of people in Eugene went to Bend for vacation, knew that it was over a hundred miles away. If she wanted to waste her time going there and asking questions, I wasn't going to stop her.

"Which one was it? Bend, or somewhere like that?"

"Bend. I think."

"And you're sure you didn't see her more often? I heard her say something about her checks—what was that all about?"

"We—Philip found a bunch of checks lying around one time when we visited her. So he took her to the bank and made sure she deposited them."

Beatriz risked a glance at me, looking impressed. I felt pretty impressed myself, with how quickly I answered her questions. I wondered if Piper was helping me. He was a terrific liar, I knew that.

"What kind of checks?" Ms. Burden asked.

"I don't know! How would I know?"

"So here's this old woman, living alone—she does live alone, right?" I nodded. "Living alone, forgetting to deposit her checks. Running out of money, maybe, not paying her rent, unable to buy food. Starving, maybe. And you only saw her once in a while? You weren't worried that something could happen to her, that she might die if you didn't keep an eye on her?"

That did it. It wasn't the questions, though they were getting harder to answer. It wasn't that she was making me feel terrible, as if I had set out to torture my aunt on purpose. It was the fact that she kept after me and after me, that she just wouldn't let it go.

"I don't know!" I said again. "I was only a kid, and Philip didn't tell me everything. Why are you asking me all these questions?"

"Well, don't you think we should visit her, try to help her out? She didn't seem all there on the phone, poor dear. Did she give you her address?"

"No. You took the phone away before she could say anything."

I thought she'd get mad at this. Instead she said, "You don't seem to know very much about your own family."

"I guess not."

"Well, sleep on it. Maybe you'll remember something in the morning."

But the next day, fortunately, she seemed preoccupied, and I managed to leave the house without any more questions.

Beatriz and I were walking home from school one afternoon when she said, suddenly, "Okay, you win. There's something really weird going on."

I tried not to grin. Beatriz hated admitting she was wrong. "She wants to find Aunt Maeve for some reason," I said.

"Yeah, but why?"

"I told you. Because she likes *Ivory Apples*. Because she's an obsessed fan."

Beatriz shook her head. "I don't know about that. But I think you might be right that she might have—might have done something to Philip. So she could get closer to us, though I don't know why she'd want to. Remember how she asked him over to her house? Like she really wanted him there for some reason."

I nodded.

"We could go over there, take a look at those stairs. Figure out what happened."

"What good would that do?"

"If she did do something, if she messed with the stairs, then it's a crime. It's murder. And we could go to the police, or that lawyer."

Piper stirred at this. And suddenly I had a strong feeling of anticipation, as if someone had opened all the windows in a stuffy room, letting in strong, sharp, bracing air. Or as if spring had started at that moment, every tree and flower in the world stirring in excitement.

We talked about it for the rest of the way home, working out the details. I felt hopeful, for the first time in a long time. If she was a murderer she'd go to prison, wouldn't she? And we'd get another guardian, Uncle Len maybe.

CHAPTER 10

Beatriz unfolded a map as big as a bedsheet. We were sitting next to each other on the bus, tracing the route to Ms. Burden's house.

It had been amazingly easy to put our plan in motion. Ms. Burden usually hung her purse by the door, out of sight of where she was lying on the couch; I had only to dip my hand into it and pull out a batch of keys, and separate hers from Philip's. Then I found some mail that had been forwarded from her old house and memorized the address. The map showing bus routes had come from a drawer in the kitchen.

It had all gone so well that I couldn't help worrying about what lay ahead. "What if she already sold her house?" I said. "If there are people living in it?"

"Then we just say we're looking for her and go away," Beatriz said.

There was something else bothering me, though. I hadn't completely realized, yesterday, what it would mean if she'd killed Philip. It meant that she was a killer, someone who got rid of people and seemed to feel no remorse for it. That she had killed my father as easily as swatting a fly. I felt a helpless, choking anger, that feeling you get when you've been treated unfairly but are powerless to do anything about it.

The bus came to our stop and we got off, then walked the three blocks we'd seen on the map. The neighborhood looked even shabbier in daylight, and so did the house: the roof was missing a few shingles and two of the windows were cracked.

We looked at each other for courage and walked through the unkempt garden. I rang the bell. We didn't hear it ringing inside the house, so I knocked loudly. No one answered.

I pulled out the two keys. One was much larger than the other, and it opened the door on my first try.

There was more dust on the furniture, but otherwise everything seemed unchanged, cold and still and unwelcoming. We went on into the kitchen.

The door to the basement was closed again, and locked with the padlock. Why had she locked it? Was it to keep something inside, the thing that made noises maybe?

We looked at each other again. Beatriz made no move toward the door, and I remembered she hadn't looked into the basement the last time we'd been here either. I put that together with other things I'd noticed, and finally I realized that she was terrified, and trying hard not to show it.

I didn't want to unlock the door either. I felt for Piper, hoping he would inspire me, would goad me into a wild flight down the stairs. But Piper had shrunk himself into the smallest space possible, trembling and chattering his teeth in an exaggerated show of fear. He would never do anything he didn't want to, I knew that much about him. But if even he was frightened, what did that say about what lay behind the door?

I used the smaller key on the padlock and opened the door quickly, then peered down into the darkness.

"Crap," Beatriz said. "We forgot to bring a flashlight."

I remembered that for some reason the light switch was at the bottom of the stairs. With Beatriz so frightened I would have to go first and turn it on. I stepped through the door, my mind as blank as I could make it, and started down. "Don't come after me until I turn on the light," I called, pretending to both of us that she wasn't afraid.

I moved slowly, feeling for each step before I put my foot on it. And I kept to the right, my hand brushing against the wall to guide me.

I came to the shadowed part, where the light from the kitchen didn't reach. It seemed to be rising and falling in places, as if it was breathing. I took a deep breath of my own and continued down. The darkness slid over my mouth, my nose, my eyes.

The air seemed heavier now, like wading through tar. I had an immediate desire to go back, as strong as if I had heard a sharp voice commanding me to turn around. It was getting hard to breathe.

A howl came from the basement, starting deep and climbing higher and higher, finally breaking on a note it couldn't reach. It sounded like the grief of some huge animal, a rhino or a whale.

We both screamed. "What was that?" Beatriz yelled from the kitchen.

"I don't know!" One of my feet was hovering over the step below, and I jerked it back and stood still, listening.

Suddenly I couldn't stand it anymore. I took the last few steps at a run, forgetting that one of the stairs might be loose. I reached the bottom before I expected it and stumbled.

"I made it," I called to Beatriz when I'd righted myself. "I'm going to turn on the light."

I felt along the wall. Something crept across the floor with a slithery sound. "I can't find the switch," I said. A whimper had come into my voice.

"There isn't a switch, remember?" Beatriz said. "It's a cord, hanging from the ceiling."

Oh, thank God. I reached up and felt the cord brush my hand. Or was it a spider web? I jerked away, then forced myself to go back to it, to grab it and pull. Light flooded the basement.

I looked around. The room was nearly empty, with just a lawnmower, some cans of paint, and a chair with a broken seat. Shelves lined one of the walls but they held very little as well—a few empty planters, a trowel, a naked baby doll. It was very cold, and I hugged myself to get warm.

Beatriz came down the stairs and stood beside me. "Where did that noise come from?" she asked, whispering.

"I don't know," I whispered back. "Nothing looks like it could have moved, does it?"

There were no tracks across the dirt floor. Dust covered everything, and cobwebs glittered from one of the walls like a ruined tapestry. The lawnmower, the paint, and the chair seemed like props in some sinister play, whose meaning would become clear only later.

Where had my father fallen? I looked for some sign, a bloodstain maybe, but I didn't see anything.

I felt reluctant to look at the stairs, to turn my back on the empty room. Finally I went to them and worked my way up, tugging on each of the steps in turn. "Nothing," I said. "Everything's okay."

"Well, maybe she fixed them later," Beatriz said. It was surprising how much we both wanted my theory to be true.

"It doesn't look like it."

I wanted urgently to leave, to run away and never come back. Instead I told Beatriz to go back to the kitchen, then started down the stairs to turn off the light. It was a sign of how frightened she was that she didn't argue, just passed me silently on the stairs.

I watched her until she was out of sight, then looked around at the basement. Had the doll moved? No, it couldn't have. I'd forgotten where it was before, that was all. I breathed deeply and pulled the cord.

I felt for the first step and started to climb. As I headed upward, the light from the kitchen came into view, and I kept it in front of me like a far-off beacon. Suddenly I heard Beatriz make a noise, a cross between a moan and a scream.

I stopped. "What is it?" I called.

"I felt something. Something—I felt it touch me."

"What do you mean?"

"They're getting out. They're leaving the basement. Ivy, hurry up—we have to close the door!"

I ran. I stumbled on a step and kept going, and finally broke through into the light. I could hear Beatriz now, mumbling softly to herself: "Oh my God, oh my God."

I burst into the kitchen. She slammed the door behind me and clicked the padlock shut.

"What happened?" I asked.

She leaned against a wall, breathing heavily. "I—I felt them leave. Like a wind, but dry, like dust . . . I think—I think we let them out."

I looked around. "So where are they?"

"I don't know. They left. They can't go through doors, maybe, or walls. Come on, we have to get out of here."

She was already heading for the living room. I followed her and opened the front door, and we hurried outside.

"What do you mean, you felt them?" I asked.

"For God's sake, close the door!" she said. She slammed the door shut. "What were you thinking? You can't let them out like that!"

"I don't . . . What do you mean? Let what out?"

"Those slithery things, the ones that made those noises. I felt them again . . ." She shivered.

I'd felt something too, just before she'd closed the door. The wind, I'd thought it was. There was no wind now, though.

She seemed on the verge of panic. I knew I had to pretend that nothing had happened, at least until we made it home. "I don't know what you're talking about," I said.

We started toward the bus stop. It was cold and the streets were getting dark; we'd been in the house for longer than I'd realized. I hadn't brought a coat because I'd thought of myself as a kind of ninja, ghosting silently down the stairs, and now I ran my hands up and down my arms, trying to get warm.

"And what about those—those noises?" Beatriz said.

This had to be hard for her, I thought. She was the most rational of all of us, someone who needed proof before she believed anything. "Maybe there was a tape recorder somewhere. In the basement."

She scoffed. "Did you see a tape recorder?"

"Well, I don't know then."

"Strange things happen," she said. I looked at her. "You said that, before."

We reached the bus stop. I remembered that I'd thought Ms. Burden had made up that story about the noises in the basement, that it had been a trick to get Philip over to her house. But it had turned out to be true, all of it.

I started shivering in short bursts, stopping and then starting again. I felt cold on the bus, too, and even when we got home, though Ms. Burden had turned the heat on. I kept remembering the way that thing had brushed past me, hurrying outside.

Strange things happen, I thought. But they aren't necessarily good things, or well disposed toward people.

CHAPTER 11

A few weeks later we were all sitting down for dinner, Esperanza's delicious lasagna. It was usually the only time that the five of us were together; otherwise we each went our separate ways.

But we didn't talk much even at dinner, not like we used to. So I was surprised when Amaranth said, "Can we go to the park again?"

Ms. Burden said nothing, just continued eating. "Kate?" Amaranth said. "Are we ever going to the park? Or we could stay here and play Murder again?"

She sounded terribly sad. She was too young to understand what was going on, but I should have tried to explain some of it to her. I'd been too trapped in my own problems to think about her, though.

"Oh, we can't do any of that now, Rantha," Ms. Burden said. "I have far too much work here as your guardian—I just don't have time for anything else."

"What kind of work?" Amaranth asked.

Ms. Burden looked up sharply. She'd thought Amaranth had been needling her, that the question was Amaranth's way of pointing out how little she actually did. Then her face changed as she realized that Amaranth really wanted to know.

"Well," she said. "I have to shop for all of you, and see to it that everything's going well at school, and take you for your check-ups and things."

Esperanza did most of the shopping, and Ms. Burden hadn't taken us to a doctor yet. "When are we going for check-ups?" I asked.

My question *had* been insulting, and she knew it. We'd fallen into this pattern over the months, a petty back-and-forth sniping. We might have even enjoyed it, or enjoyed some of it.

"I'm glad you reminded me, Ivy," she said. "It's time to make appointments with the dentist, for all of you."

A low noise came from beneath us, a sound like a rusty garage door opening, though we didn't have a garage. It was the same sad howl we'd heard in Ms. Burden's basement. There was something deeply wrong about it, like that feeling you get during an eclipse, when the sun should be shining but everything around you is in darkness.

I'd been looking at Ms. Burden, about to say something, so I caught the flash of fear on her face, a genuine terror that could not have been faked. Then, an instant later, the fright disappeared, and her expression turned smooth again.

The noise stopped, finally. "What was that?" Beatriz asked, her voice shaky. Her face was as white as the tablecloth.

"I don't know, dear," Ms. Burden said. "Could it be the house settling?"

Ms. Burden knew what the sounds were, though. So did Beatriz, and so did I. Those things we'd heard in the basement had not only escaped, they had followed us. And this time they were in our house, not Ms. Burden's; we couldn't run away from them.

Ms. Burden and I had become locked in a silent struggle to find Maeve first. She got Caller ID for the phone, in case Maeve tried to call us again. But Maeve must have guessed something was up, because we never heard from her.

One day I remembered how Philip would pick up Aunt Maeve's mail before we visited her. I even knew her box number, 369, from seeing it on all the letters. I sat down and wrote to her, feeling elated after I mailed it off; I thought I'd won the contest once and for all.

The letter came back about a week later. "No such holder at this post office box," someone had stamped on the envelope. Luckily it had been delivered on a Saturday, and I'd gotten to the mail first. God knows what Ms. Burden would have made of it.

I worried at first that something horrible had happened to Maeve, that she'd forgotten or been unable to pay for the box. Then I thought that maybe she'd hired someone else to answer her mail, and they'd gotten another post office. I hoped so, anyway.

I put the letter in a book I was reading and forgot all about it.

Meanwhile, the noises hadn't gone away. We all lived on the edge of terror, jumping at strange sounds and feeling anxious when we didn't hear them. Beatriz's face turned sallow and the skin under her eyes became a delicate shade of lavender, and Semiramis smiled less and less often. Ms. Burden pretended she didn't hear anything, but I saw her brace herself when the noises came.

Our house didn't have a basement, just a cramped crawlspace. I picked a day when the sun was shining and forced myself to go down there, but I saw nothing besides spider webs, not one abandoned toy or broken planter. Anyway, the sounds seemed to come from different places, upstairs when we were in the living room and vice versa.

Summer came, and school ended. With no homework and no after-school activities I had some time for myself, time to think about my sisters and their various unhappinesses. I'm sorry to say, though, that I was too wrapped up in my own problems to help them. Instead I did the same things I'd done in other years, reading and writing and wandering in the park.

Beatriz had moved Philip's computer into our room and was spending a lot of time on it. One day when she was out I got on the website Ms. Burden had told us about, ivoryorchard.com, the one dedicated to Adela Madden and her book. It turned out to be enormous, with sections for essays and histories and artwork and fan fiction, another about Madden herself, another with forums where people shared news and ideas.

Soon Beatriz and I were fighting over computer time. Finally I went to Ms. Burden and asked if I could get my own computer, but she said no, that she was not made of money. I left her, feeling mean and spiteful toward everyone, and I checked Beatriz's browsing history while she was out. But my anger disappeared when I saw what she'd searched for: "loud noises," "noises at night," "noises in basement," and other variations.

The next time I looked for her browsing history it was gone. And I realized I should erase mine too; the last thing I wanted was for Ms. Burden to see my fascination with ivoryorchard.com. I asked Beatriz to show me how she'd done it.

I read a lot of essays on the website, amazed that so many people had thought about *Ivory Apples* for so long. The book was more complex than I'd realized, and my admiration for Aunt Maeve grew the more I read. Those obsessives Philip had told me about were here too, with their theories and axes to grind. *Ivory Apples* was an allegory for the Albigensian Crusade, for example, or Adela Madden had secretly been a Theosophist.

By far the longest of the essays, by someone named Watchmaker, ran to about fifty pages. (A lot of the pseudonyms on the site were taken from the book, but I remembered the watchmaker only as a minor character.) Pommerie Town was real, they claimed; you could visit it and discover "the fount of creativity, the secret of the Muses." Madden had done this herself, which was why she had been able to write *Ivory Apples*. In fact she hadn't written it, the essayist said; it had been a gift from the Muses.

What Watchmaker wanted, of course, was to find the way in. The essay went on to quote the scene where a man named Fo'c'sle Flynn stumbled on Pommerie Town. "The chief alderman formed a committee, and five men, wearing their best suits and tallest hats, went to call upon Fo'c'sle Flynn at the tavern.

"'How did you get here?' one of them asked him.

"'I was lost in a forest one night,' Flynn answered. 'I came to a bridge across a river, and on the other side I saw two rows of pillars, shining like ivory in the moonlight. I walked between them, and so came upon the town.'

"The aldermen looked at him with interest. 'It was not your way that was lost, but yourself,' one of them said."

After this Watchmaker wrote, "I think that here Madden is speaking of actual places. The problem is finding the right forest, and the right bridge."

Too many of these essays were like this one, theories that the writers tried to prove with quotes from the book or historical events or equally unhinged ideas from other people. I clicked away from them and went over to the discussion forum.

I got caught up in the conversations immediately. They seemed like a long continuous party with dozens of friends, though some of the rudeness made me uncomfortable. Finally I exhausted the current topics, and I started going back through the archives. Something caught at me, some word or other, and I clicked on the thread.

"Important news, peeps," someone with the name of Eliza Woodbury had posted. (Eliza Woodbury was another character from the book, a woman with a parrot that spoke no recognizable language.) "I sent a letter with all my exciting new theories to Madden's publisher and then waited impatiently for 'David' to tell me that I was totally right and all the rest of you were complete morons. (Kidding!) But I didn't hear from 'him' for about two months, which was alot longer than my other letters took. Finally it came back yesterday, with a post office box number written on the envelope, and 'No such holder at this post office box.'

"I thought about this alot, guys. I guess the publisher used to forward our letters to this box, but why is it closed now, and who closed it? The only thing I could come up with is that, I'm sorry to say, Adela Madden might have died. I hope I'm wrong, I hope that someday we'll get the NB we've all been waiting for, but I don't think there can be any other reason. 'David' was Madden herself, obvs, and they closed the box when she died."

"NB" stood for "New Book." Everyone on the site hoped that Madden would publish something new, despite the fact that it had been over forty years since *Ivory Apples*.

I looked back at the date on the post. February 10, 2001, a month after Philip had died, so of course Eliza hadn't gotten an answer. But Philip wouldn't have told her that she was "totally right," I knew that much. Maeve had cautioned him never to discuss any of the theories about the book, and I don't think even he knew which ones were correct.

"And here's something else, fellow apple-pickers," Eliza went on. "The post office box number is P.O. Box 369, Eugene, Oregon. So congrats to everyone (including me!) who thought the letters came from Eugene because of their postmark. I know some of you thought they mailed all the letters to another city or state to disguise where 'David' lived, but that always seemed too complicated to me, even for Adela Madden. Any of you out there live in Eugene? What does the post office box look like?"

People started visiting the post office and writing about their experiences. The crowds grew, some of them coming from as far away as Los Angeles. Someone wrote an account of an argument between their group and some postal workers, a shouting match that ended when the workers threw them out of the building.

"Your so stupid I dont know how you can even read," a poster wrote, replying to Eliza. "David sounds nothing lik Adela Madden. Hes the one who died or got another job. Dont worry everone, Adela Madden is still alive."

Here was something else I hadn't known, that the posters were divided between those who thought David, or really Philip, was Adela Madden and those who were sure he couldn't be. The debate flared up again with Eliza Woodbury's post and went on for pages.

"You know what's really exciting though?" someone else wrote, a bit cold-heartedly, I thought. "If she is dead then maybe we'll finally get the NB. Her heirs or someone could publish it."

"I found out something really interesting, folks," said a man named Jedidiah Cabal, using another name from the book. "I read a bunch of obituaries from Eugene, and I found one about this guy named Philip David Quinn. He has to be the David who answered Madden's letters, right? And the letters stopped because he died."

"Congratulations," someone who called themselves Quentin Foxtree wrote back. "You put 2 and 2 together and managed to come up with 58. The man's name is Philip, not David. And I hope you noticed from the obituary that Philip (not David) Quinn was a professor of engineering at the University of Oregon. Do you really think an engineer could have written all those letters? Or were you in such a hurry to share your 'discovery' that you didn't even see that part?"

It was a shock to come upon Philip's name in the middle of these posts. Not just because Jedidiah had guessed correctly, but because I hadn't heard anyone mention him for a while. People were forgetting him, the way they had forgotten Jane. But Jedidiah never wrote back, maybe driven away by the tongue-lashing, and no one brought up his theory again.

Ms. Burden knew about the website, and I wondered if she could be Foxtree. Maybe she had written that insulting post to throw Jedidiah, and everyone else, off the track.

The thread dried up after that. It had been about David's letters, discussions and speculations about what he'd written, and when the letters stopped coming people seemed to have less to say. Still, there were enough other threads to keep me reading day after day.

Beatriz got interested in the website as well, and late at night, as we lay in bed, we would talk about what we'd found there. We both wanted to post on the forums but finally decided it was safer not to; there was a chance we'd give something away without meaning to.

I didn't want to talk about the noises, especially at night, didn't want to worry Beatriz any more than she already was. Once, though, she brought them up herself. "Do you think they followed us here?" she asked. "Those sounds?"

"I don't know," I said. "Maybe. But where did they come from in the first place?"

"She called them up. To scare us, to make us tell her what we know about Maeve."

"But she's afraid of them too. I saw her face that first time—she couldn't have faked that."

"Well, maybe she called them up and then couldn't get rid of them. That's why she locked them in the basement. And then when we opened the door we let them out, and they followed us home."

I shivered. "Called them up how?"

"How would I know?"

"Well, it was your idea. Anyway, she would have said something if she was trying to scare us. Like"—I put on a wavering, spooky voice—"'Tell me everything, and I'll make the noises stop.'"

I'd succeeded in making her laugh, and our talk turned to other things.

The long formless summer vacation ended and we went back to school. A few months later my birthday came around again, the first one without Philip. I was fourteen now, four years from coming of age and getting the money Philip's will had promised me. Or maybe I came of age at twenty-one; I'd asked Ms. Burden once but she hadn't known. I knew one thing, though—I was leaving home as soon as I could.

Much to my surprise, Esperanza brought out a chocolate cake for me after dinner, lit with fourteen candles. Beatriz had gone in with Amaranth and Semiramis and bought me a beautiful silk scarf patterned with stars—"Like the rain of stars in *Ivory Apples*," Beatriz said.

Ms. Burden glanced up at her sharply. Whenever any of us mentioned Maeve's book she got a certain look, something like a cop on the verge of wringing a confession from a suspect. We didn't say anything more about it, though, just talked about my birthday and the scarf and then fell back into our usual silence.

"Ms. Burden?" Semiramis said a while later.

Ms. Burden sighed. "I know Ivy calls me that, for her own abstruse reasons, but I would have thought the rest of you might use my first name, Kate. After all, I am your guardian, and we have to get along together."

"Kate?" Semiramis said. "Is Aunt Maeve dead?"

I turned to her, furious that she'd mentioned Maeve. Then I saw how young she was, how saddened and confused by everything that had happened, and a wash of pity swept the anger away. So many people had died in her short life that when she hadn't seen someone for a while, she just assumed they were dead.

I glanced at Ms. Burden to see what she'd made of the question. She had that eager cop look again. "No, she isn't dead," I said quickly. "We haven't gone to visit her for a long time, that's all."

"But we'll see her again, right?"

"I would love to visit your Aunt Maeve," Ms. Burden cut in. "Unfortunately I haven't been able to find out where she lives. I don't suppose you know."

"Of course we do," Amaranth said. "She lives in the woods."

I glared at her. Ms. Burden laughed. "Where in the woods?" she asked.

"She can't possibly remember that," I said. "She was seven or eight when we went there."

"I do so remember," Amaranth said. "This one time, Philip played that CD he liked, *Graceland*. And I said I liked it too so he played it again, and he told me it was African music. South African music. And when we got to Maeve's house it ended."

"What a smart girl you are, Rantha," Ms. Burden said.

Amaranth beamed. Ms. Burden stood and went upstairs, saying nothing. We looked at each other for a while, wondering what she was doing now, until she came back.

"Forty-four minutes—I looked it up." Her voice shook a little, a deep anger rumbling beneath her surface calm like an earthquake. "That's how long *Graceland* takes. And twice that would be about an hour and a half. You can't get to Bend in that amount of time, I don't think. Really, why would you want to lie about this, Ivy?"

I could have made up something, a lie shoring up another lie. But I felt impatient suddenly, sick of all our games. "Why is this so important? You don't even know Aunt Maeve."

Her eyes glittered strangely, like nailheads lit by the sun. "She wrote *Ivory Apples*, you stupid girl. And I need to ask her—"

"Maeve? Our aunt?" I was staring at her, facing her down, so I couldn't afford to look around at my sisters. I only hoped that Amaranth and Semiramis didn't understand what we were talking about. "No, she didn't—Adela Madden wrote that."

"You've never heard of pseudonyms, have you?"

"Look, I think I'd know if my own aunt—"

"All right, that's enough." She stood up. "We're going to take a drive, you and I, and you're going to show me where she lives."

"Aunt Maeve, you mean? I told you, I don't remember."

Semiramis looked up eagerly. "We're going to see Aunt Maeve?"

"No, we're not," I said. "For one thing, you and Rantha have to go to bed—"

"Oh, not yet, surely," Ms. Burden said. "Let's all go."

She sounded like she used to, wild and spontaneous, uncaring of what anyone else would think. It seemed grotesque to me, considering all the things she'd done since, but the others were already shouting with excitement and running to the door.

We piled into Philip's car and she made a circuit of all the freeway entrances near our house, asking me if I recognized them. Some of them did seem familiar, at least for a moment or two, but I said I didn't remember.

I stayed alert throughout the trip, ready to pinch any one of my sisters if they said anything, but none of them did.

CHAPTER 12

Ms. Burden took us on these drives a couple times a month, all over Eugene and across the river to Springfield. I made the others swear once again not to give anything away and they did, though Semiramis didn't understand why. "When are we going to visit Aunt Maeve, though?" she asked, and I had to tell her I didn't know.

It was around this time that Ms. Burden became crueler toward me, her punishments more frequent. She never said that this was because I wasn't telling her what she wanted, but she didn't have to. We both knew she would stop if I answered her questions.

It felt as if all the masks were off now, as if we'd stripped down to our innermost selves. She'd become the person I'd always known she was. The fact that I'd been right about her was no comfort, though.

So, for example, the next day she complained that I hadn't washed my dishes after breakfast. "But Esperanza does that," I said, puzzled. "When she comes to cook dinner."

"Oh, Ivy," she said. "Why should Esperanza clean up after you, especially when she has so much else to do?"

"It's only the dishes. And anyway, it's her job."

She sighed. "I just wish that for once in your life you wouldn't be so lazy."

"Really?" I said. "I'm not the one lying on the couch all day reading. And you don't wash your dishes either."

"That's enough. Don't you ever talk to me like that again. I'm taking away your allowance for a week."

Week after week, she found some excuse not to give me my allowance. I tried not rising to the bait, tried not saying anything at all, but nothing worked. She would always find some fault, usually one she'd never mentioned before, and my allowance would be gone.

It wasn't even all that much, just ten dollars a week. That's what Philip had given me, though I'd heard around school that kids were getting fifteen and even twenty dollars now. But it meant that I had to ask and sometimes beg if I needed new clothes or a book for school.

Beatriz saved me here, as she'd done so many times. She got ten dollars too, and she gave me half of it. But we both knew that Ms. Burden could start taking hers away at any time.

Her punishments became more clever, as if she enjoyed thinking them up. Maybe she did. Once she dropped me off in a sketchy part of town for a dentist appointment and then didn't come back to pick me up. The office closed for lunch, and I ended up sitting out front as men in old, torn clothes shuffled along the sidewalk, leering at me and making horrifying suggestions.

When the office opened up again I used their phone to call home. No one answered, and I left a message. Then I sat in a corner and pretended to read their dusty magazines, trying to ignore everyone's questioning glances. Sometimes that horrible drilling noise came down the hall, starting up with a whine and then fading in and out, like a fly buzzing around the room. Sometimes the door to the hall opened and the receptionist called another patient, bringing with her a bright chemical smell that was starting to make me feel nauseated.

I hadn't had lunch, and by afternoon I was starving. The only thing to eat was some non-sugar candy in a bowl on the receptionist's desk. I grabbed a handful whenever she left her station, but she caught me once and asked me when I thought my mother would pick me up.

I wanted to correct her about that "mother." Piper grinned within me, reminding me that he could unleash all the words I needed to put her in her place. I tamped him down, hard; I needed her on my side.

I hadn't felt him in a long time, I realized. Well, my life hadn't been very much fun, and I knew he didn't really understand sadness.

"I don't know," I said.

"Do you want to call her again? Or someone else?"

I tried her again but she didn't answer. A while later, two or three hours I think, it started to grow dark outside, and colder as well. I hadn't brought a coat, and I hugged myself to keep warm.

Some of the lights down the hall clicked off. The receptionist came out from behind her station, pulling on her coat. "Well, we're closing now," she said. "I guess I can ask the doctor . . ."

More lights shut off. The dentist and some assistants came out of a back room and shrugged out of their white coats. I stood up, feeling light-headed, from all the candy I'd eaten and from my worry about what might happen.

Ms. Burden hurried inside. "Oh, my goodness, Ivy!" she said. "I'm so sorry—I just got your message. But I told you to take the bus, I know I did." She turned to the receptionist and the dentist. "I did tell her, honestly! Oh, what you must think of me . . ."

"Well, you're here now," the receptionist said, looking relieved.

Ms. Burden was so convincing that I even wondered if she was right and I was supposed to have taken the bus—despite the fact that I had no money, and no idea which bus went to our house from here. But as things like this kept happening I realized that that was part of she wanted, to keep me confused and off-balance, to make me doubt things I knew were true.

Another time I noticed that I had outgrown most of my clothes. The last thing I wanted was to ask her for more favors, but finally, as my pants grew shorter and all my clothes became tighter, I had to say something. I'd expected we'd go shopping together, but instead she brought home bags of clothes and told me to try them on.

I started to unpack them. To my growing dismay I saw that she'd bought the kind of things she herself favored, long and loose, in pale colors like ivory or gray or light green. But the clothes that fit her so well were too tight on me, and the colors made me look worn out and drab.

And the shoes turned out to be a size too small. They pinched the first time I wore them, and within a week I'd developed blisters and then calluses. I started walking with my feet splayed out awkwardly, trying not to put weight on my toes. I asked her if we could take them back and get new ones, and she laughed lightly and said, "We can't possibly return them—they were on sale."

She "forgot" to pay our fees for the school cafeteria, and Beatriz and I went hungry for two days, until I remembered to pack some lunches for us. After the parent-teacher conference my history teacher would stammer in alarm whenever she called on me, and I was sure Ms. Burden had told her something about me, though I never found out what. This was horrible in a way Ms. Burden couldn't have imagined, because I'd had a fierce schoolgirl crush on that teacher, and after a while she simply ignored me, no matter how many times I raised my hand.

Ms. Burden left the house for two days, then three days, and these times always seemed to coincide with Esperanza's day off, and always when there was barely any food in the house, so we were forced to eat the bits and pieces we found in the kitchen. Esperanza saw what was happening and started making us extra meals, but there was nothing else she could do for us; I knew from something Philip had said that that she didn't have the right papers to work here, and that she avoided anything having to do with the authorities.

Only once did I cry, and Ms. Burden's response made me vow never to do it again. "And crying yet!" she said. "I'll give you something to cry about." That was one vow I managed to keep.

The worst stab to the heart was something I don't think she even knew about. I hope she didn't, anyway. Around spring break the next year ivoryorchard.com was full of talk about the Fourteenth Annual Adela Madden Conference, which would be held in Austin, Texas. Everyone seemed to be going, and I wanted nothing more in the world than to go too, to meet the people I had started to think of as my friends. I had about as much chance of traveling to Pommerie Town, though, so I tried not to think about it.

When we came down to breakfast on Friday, the first day of the conference, we saw that Ms. Burden was gone again. All that weekend, as she stayed away, I checked the website obsessively, reading about the panels and parties, the costumes and dinners and awards. No one ever mentioned her, but I was certain she was there. And when she came back Sunday night, carrying a bag stuffed with books and artwork related to *Ivory Apples*, I knew I'd been right. I never hated her more than at that moment.

CHAPTER 13

As the months passed Ms. Burden's strategy seemed to change, and she turned her focus on Amaranth and Semiramis instead of me. Of course we both knew that they couldn't tell her anything, that their punishments were really directed at me. If I wanted her to stop I'd have to answer her questions.

So she would tell Amaranth that she could have dessert if she finished her dinner, and then, when Amaranth had eaten everything on her plate, she'd swear that she had never offered any such thing. Or she would promise Semiramis that they could play Murder after school, and then deny she'd ever said it. She'd complain that they were too fat one day and too thin the next; that they read too much and should go out and play, and then that they should get serious about studying.

After about a month of this they began to act differently. Amaranth, who had always been so impatient, so eager to jump into everything, retreated into herself, turning quiet and sullen. Semiramis, who had always seemed younger and more innocent than her age, smiling at everything, now cried at every setback. And a new expression appeared on both their faces, a wary, suspicious look, as if they didn't know who to trust—or worse, as if they thought they couldn't trust anyone.

I'd been starting to think about going away, escaping Ms. Burden for good, but now I wondered if I could leave them behind. Beatriz was old enough to take care of herself, but Ms. Burden could still do a lot of damage to the other two. On the other hand, if I left there would be no one there who knew even as much as I did about Maeve, and maybe she would realize that and stop playing her games with my sisters.

The worst was when Semiramis went into Ms. Burden's bedroom.

She'd told us she could never be disturbed in there, but Semiramis had either forgotten or hadn't paid attention. A few minutes later she ran out into the hallway, screaming.

Beatriz and I hurried out of our own room, and I grabbed Semiramis and held her. For a long time I couldn't get any sense out of her; she was shaking against me and crying and saying something about monsters.

Finally she calmed down enough to talk. "She said—she said—she's going to put me in with the monsters."

"What monsters, Ramis?" I asked.

"The monsters in the closet." She started to tremble again. "She said she'd lock me in there."

That did it. I stamped down the hall and opened the door to Ms. Burden's room.

She was staring at her computer screen. "Get out, Semiramis," she said. "I told you I'd skin you alive if you bothered me again." She turned around. "Oh, it's you. What do you want?"

"Don't you ever scare Semiramis like that again," I said. "Or any of my sisters. The next time I'm going to the police, I mean it—"

"What on earth are you talking about, Ivy?"

"What did you tell her about monsters?"

"Monsters? Nothing. Why, what did she say to you?"

She sounded puzzled, concerned—exactly like someone who was telling the truth. If I hadn't heard her lie before, and hadn't seen Semiramis's terrified face, I might have even believed her.

"Well, for one thing, you told her you'd skin her alive. I heard that one myself. And for another, she said you were going to put her in with the monsters."

She smiled. "Well, of course I would never—"

Semiramis had come up behind me. She peered out around my shoulder and said, very softly, "You said you'd lock me in with them. Look, there's a lock on the door."

I went into the room, the first time I'd been there since Philip had died. A tide of clothes flowed from the closet and peaked into a wave at her bed, but otherwise very little had changed.

There was a padlock on the door of the closet, just as Semiramis had said, the kind that needed a code to unlock. It reminded me of the door we'd seen in her kitchen, of the sounds we'd heard, and I had to summon up the courage to ask her to open the door.

She sighed and pushed her chair away from the computer, then went to the closet and entered the code. "See?" she said, swinging the door open. "No monsters."

Semiramis ran into the hallway. I hesitated, then forced myself to go farther in and peer into the closet. There were clothes piled in heaps on the floor here too, with only three or four dresses hung up. I listened for noises but could only hear a few hangers chiming softly together.

Then I saw something standing behind the dresses, a square, bulky shape, and for a moment my head filled with angry, lurching monsters. I pushed the dresses aside. It was a filing cabinet.

"What's in the cabinet?" I asked. "And why do you need a lock for the closet?"

She brushed past me and opened one of the drawers. "It's just official papers, yours and your sisters. Here's your doctor's appointments, and your birth certificate—or no, it's Beatriz's."

"Why is the closet locked?" I asked again.

"I don't know. The lock was here when I moved in—I assume Philip put it there."

I didn't remember ever seeing it before. "So how do you know the code?"

"Ivy, really, I don't have time for this. Could you just do what I ask for once and not interrupt me when I'm working? And make your sisters stay out as well."

I stared at her. "I don't make my sisters do anything," I said, and walked as slowly as I could out of the room.

I went back a few times when she was out and tried her computer, but it was password-protected and nothing I could think of would open it. The padlock stayed stubbornly closed as well. By this time I was sure that those things, the noise-making things, lurked behind the closet door, so I never stayed very long.

Then my birthday came around again, my fifteenth this time. At dinner Beatriz gave me *The Art of Apples: Adela Madden and Pommerie Town*, a handsome book of paintings from *Ivory Apples*. Unfortunately I already had it; Philip had given it to me a long time ago. She looked so pleased, though, and had taken so much trouble, that I couldn't possibly tell her so.

"Wow," I said. "Thank you so much."

"What a thoughtful present, Beatriz," Ms. Burden said. "I suppose you didn't realize she already has it."

"You—you do?" Beatriz asked.

"Of course not," I said. "Anyway, how would she know? Is she sneaking into our room again?"

"Why are you lying, Ivy?" Ms. Burden said. "After all, it's easy enough to prove I'm right."

"I told you, I don't."

Ms. Burden got up and headed upstairs. "Stay out of our room!" I yelled after her.

She was taking the stairs two at a time now, and I ran after her. I'd lost this round, I knew, but I wanted to stop her from going through our things, and from making sarcastic comments about what she found.

I got to my room just as she took the book off the shelves. "Do you like lying for its own sake?" she asked. "Even when it's obvious you're wrong? Or have you just lost touch with reality?"

Beatriz came in, followed by Amaranth and Semiramis. Ms. Burden handed her the book. An envelope fell from between the pages. Ms. Burden caught it before it hit the floor and studied it.

"It's addressed to Maeve Reynolds," she said. "And look at this—Post Office Box 369. That's Adela Madden's box, if I'm not mistaken."

It was the letter I'd written to Aunt Maeve, what seemed like so long ago. The proof that Ms. Burden had been searching for all this time. I tried to grab it but she ran out of the room and down the hallway.

I hurried after her. She reached the bathroom and locked herself inside.

"Well, well, Ivy," she said from behind the door. "It seems you've been lying to me for quite some time."

I hit the door with my fists. "Give it back! It's mine!"

"'Dear Aunt Maeve,'" she read. I stopped banging on the door to hear her. "'It was good to talk to you . . .' blah, blah, blah . . . 'You were right not to trust the woman on the phone—she's a horrible person.' Oh, Ivy, really. Let's see—blah, blah, blah . . . Ah, here we are. 'She's a big fan of *Ivory Apples*. I think she somehow knows you are Adela Madden though I don't know how she found out. Please be careful' . . . blah, blah, blah . . ."

Ms. Burden opened the bathroom door and stepped outside. My sisters had joined me in the hallway and we stood in a half-circle around her, waiting for whatever she was going to do next, dreading it.

"Well," she said, folding the letter and hiding it somewhere among her loose clothes. "Why did you lie to me, Ivy?"

"Why do you lie to me?" I asked.

She reached out and slapped Semiramis in the face. Semiramis stood there a moment, too shocked to cry. Then she wailed and ran downstairs.

"I am so tired of this," Ms. Burden said. "You're going to start answering my questions. And every time you lie, every time you try to be clever, one of your sisters gets another slap. Maybe you don't care about yourself, but I know you wouldn't want to hurt them."

I stood there, uncertain. Why couldn't we tell her about Aunt Maeve, anyway? Maybe what she wanted was nothing very sinister, just to meet the author of *Ivory Apples* and discuss the book with her.

And if I told her, maybe she'd become the person we'd met in the park again, with her purse full of magic and her silly games. We'd have long talks about *Ivory Apples*, we'd go to Adela Madden Conferences together, we'd laugh at how stubborn I'd been. I was so tired of resisting, of playing her vicious games, of wearing shoes that pinched me at every step.

No, I had to keep the secret. Philip had made me promise.

Piper stirred, as if reminding me of his presence. Here was a way out, but one that might be worse than what I was escaping. I loosened his bindings carefully, one by one. I felt him stretch, felt him extend his body to fit mine. His shoulders touched my shoulders, his legs slipped into mine like putting on a pair of jeans.

He was offering me freedom. Freedom, finally, from Ms. Burden. I saw a picture of myself in his mind, running down the stairs, opening the door, slamming it behind me. I laughed with elation.

"I'm leaving," I said, or he did.

The word echoed within me like bells. *Leave, leaf, lift.*

"Leaving?" Ms. Burden said. "Don't be ridiculous—you just turned fifteen. Where would you go?"

"Oh, I'm far older than that. Older than the trees, younger than the moon."

She laughed uncertainly. "What are you talking about?"

"Nothing you'd understand."

Ms. Burden followed me to the stairway, shouting something about calling the police. I ran down the stairs and out the front door, just as Piper had shown me. The bells rang within me, became a song: *leave, laugh, live.* We danced to the melody, lightly, down the street and away.

CHAPTER 14

We sauntered through downtown Eugene. Downtown is near the university, and it held countless memories of Philip: eating out, going to movies, visiting the library. But Piper had no patience with sadness or nostalgia. Instead, as we walked through the streets, passing families, shoppers, students, he looked closely around him, searching for something.

I say "we walked" because Piper had changed my stride along with everything else. I moved like a young boy now, or the way I imagined a young boy would move—swift, confident, staking out my place on the sidewalk. My palms faced forward, as if I was open to anything. People got out of the way as I went, and I wondered if they saw me as a boy as well.

Piper found what he was looking for and went to stand behind some people stopped at a light. He studied them for a moment, and then lightly lifted a hat off a policeman. He took another hat, this one pink and laced with gauze and bows, from a woman. Then he exchanged them, his touch so gentle that neither turned around.

The light changed and they crossed the street, still unaware of what had been done to them. I started to laugh. Shhh, Piper said within me, and I tried to be quiet, but my hilarity escaped in a strangled cough. Fortunately no one seemed to notice.

Piper went into restaurants and switched people's drinks, he whispered something into a woman's ear and then darted away. When I got hungry he stole some food off plates at a diner.

We wandered around like this until the stores began to close. The streets became darker, and a few scary-looking people took to the sidewalks. It had been a clear day, warm for November, but now a chill wind started, and I hadn't brought a coat. For the first time I felt apprehensive.

Piper shook his head, and I saw he was searching for something again. We walked out of downtown and came to an abandoned lot. I'd seen some homeless people there once—I hadn't remembered them but apparently Piper had.

We picked out a place apart from the others and I lay down. I couldn't fall asleep, though; my mind raced with worry, and rocks and broken concrete dug into me no matter which way I turned. Whenever I started to doze off I'd hear a shout or a car alarm and wake up again, wondering where I was.

One question haunted me that night: Had I been right to leave my sisters? I told myself over and over again that they knew nothing, that Ms. Burden would have no reason to torment them. Still, I promised myself I'd go past our house every so often.

My time on the streets stands apart from anything else I've ever done. Everything was heightened, clarified, shining with its own light. Ordinary objects—streetlamps, cars, trees—seemed to have been invented just moments before, something new and astonishing.

Things were different for another reason too: I'd given myself over to Piper and could only follow his lead. I reveled in his excitement, the sense that I was risking everything at every moment. I told myself that I deserved some enjoyment for a change. Though enjoyment was a tame word for what he gave me—it was rapture, exhilaration, wildness.

The days unrolled like a dream, or like watching a movie and being a part of it at the same time. But unlike with a dream, I remember most of what we did. Sometimes I wish I didn't.

Piper's trick with the hats had impressed me, but he turned out to be even more dexterous than I'd thought. He could exchange jackets or watches, or slip a wallet from one pocket into another.

He set trash cans alight as we passed them, and built bonfires in empty lots. But he tired of this after a while and moved on to abandoned buildings, though I always made sure no one was inside before we struck the match. He loved to watch the flames climbing the walls, the changing colors, the black smoke and then bursts of red and gold like fireworks. And I loved it too after a while, the sheer destructiveness of it.

We broke into houses when their owners were out. Sometimes we stole from them, but mostly we'd do other things: rearrange the furniture, or leave something valuable that we'd taken from another house, or put a page of my poetry in the center of an otherwise empty table. Every so often I wondered what they made of the poetry, written with a dull pencil on a dirty scrap of paper.

We never kept any of the things we stole. They were unimportant to him, and he gave them away, as I said, or lost them. So I ended up living in shelters or falling-down shacks, under freeway overpasses or in one-room apartments with three or four roommates. I'd managed to find new shoes, but the soles had long since worn away, and I wore clothes I'd salvaged from dumpsters. One of my best finds was a blanket, to keep me warm through the cold nights, but I lost it when spring came.

I worked sometimes, illegal jobs since I hadn't brought any identification with me, and no one would hire a fifteen-year-old in any case. I worked at an ice cream parlor for a while, and as a cashier at a movie theater, but Piper always managed to get me fired sooner or later. He hated the boredom of going to the same place every day, doing the same thing over and over.

Once, when he tucked a fat wallet into the pocket of a homeless person, I wondered if I'd misjudged him, if his purpose was to right the wrongs of the world. But he didn't like that notion, and later that day we went to a bar where he switched around the patrons' drinks. One of the women, I'd overheard, had been sober for ten months and had had a Coke in front of her. I don't know what he gave her in exchange, but within a few minutes she was slurring her words.

He felt my outrage, but he wasn't in the least abashed. *I shake things up*, he said. *I slip between the rules, the heavy pillars holding up the world. I disturb, I confound.*

A few days later, during a rare quiet time, I thought about what he'd said. I'd had a similar idea about poetry, that I'd found a way through the words, through the very letters on the page. This was what tricksters did, I realized, this was what Maeve had been trying to tell me. They—we?—steal through the barriers of convention, of laws, and bring back fire from the gods. Not literal fire, but the fire of inspiration.

So was he right to switch drinks on that poor woman? I still didn't think so, but he grew impatient when I asked him about it.

And I was writing poetry, pages and pages of it. Setting Piper free had set something else free within me. In fact, I remember now that it hadn't been Piper who'd cost me my job at the ice cream parlor; I'd lost it because I'd set down my scoop in the middle of an order to scribble something on an old sales receipt, unable to wait until the end of my shift.

I remembered my vow to see my sisters, of course, but usually Piper managed to keep my mind on other things. Sometimes my longing overcame me and I started to head toward home, and he would suggest silly or funny or wonderful things to change my mind. And I felt that somehow I deserved to stay with him, that I'd been so unhappy for so long, and this was my reward.

After a few months we hitched rides to other cities, Corvallis, Salem, Portland. He'd gotten tired of Eugene, but I think he was also trying to keep me away from my old life.

We met dangerous people in our travels, thieves and drunks and violent men and women. Piper took part in most of what they did, stealing cars and robbing people lying in the streets, but there was one place where I refused to follow, and that was drinking alcohol or taking drugs. Not for any moral reason, but because what he gave me was so much better, so much more intoxicating. What I had, I thought, was what most of these people were searching for.

At first I felt afraid a lot of the time, worried about getting attacked or raped. A man did hit me once, but Piper helped me fight back, and after that I felt more confident. And no one ever raped me, though that might have also been due to Piper; he had a deranged way of acting that signaled to any rapist that I would do anything to get away. I did sleep with people when I wanted to, men and women both. Piper approved of this, the way he approved of any easy impulse. I told myself it was Piper, as a man, who was attracted to the women.

Two or three times I sensed someone following me, but when I looked around there was never anyone there. The next time I felt watched I slipped down an alley and waited. A man walked by, looking horribly familiar, though I couldn't remember where or when I'd seen him. He was short, chubby, with blond hair so pale it disappeared in a strong light, the color of weak lemonade. He wore wire-frame glasses, ovals that barely covered his eyes.

Piper was drawn to him, and urged me to leave my hiding place. I stayed where I was, the only time on the streets that I disobeyed him. He understood danger, but not the threat of it, the present but not the future.

Had Ms. Burden sent this man to look for me? Was that where I had seen him before? Where did she find them, these men like Ted-or-Ned who were willing to work for her?

Looking back on the whole experience now, I can see how hard it was. I was hungry a lot, and dirty and tired, and I remember always looking for a public restroom because I couldn't pee in public the way men did. I slept in the rain and had a sore throat that never went away. People shouted insults or set their dogs on me, though the dogs seemed to sense Piper's presence and wagged their tails with delight instead of attacking. I was nearly arrested several times. But in my memory even the worst parts are burnished with enchantment.

And once . . . once we went to an Adela Madden Conference.

At first, when Piper broke in to a house and urged me to take a shower, I didn't know what he had in mind. The shower was my first in a long time, and I stayed there even after the water had gone cold, trying to work the grime out of my skin.

After I finished, Piper set out some clothes from a wardrobe—a suit with black trousers and a black jacket, a white blouse with a frilly bow at the throat, black shoes with a slight heel. They felt somehow wrong when I put them on, too smooth, too whole. My clothing usually scratched and pinched in places, or hung badly, or had gaping holes.

I looked at myself in a full-length mirror, studying this person I hadn't seen for months. My hair was long and tangled, even after I had used the shampoo in the shower and most of a bottle of conditioner. My face had turned an unhealthy red, the color of a faded brick, from living outdoors. Something strange lurked within my eyes, as if I'd just woken from a year-long dream.

I asked him why I was dressing up, but he didn't answer. He stole a car and we headed north along Interstate 5.

A while later we came to Portland. He directed me off the freeway and through the city to a hotel.

A sign in front of the hotel said, "Welcome to the Sixteenth Annual Adela Madden Conference." I grinned, thrilled, and he caught my happiness and reflected it back to me, a feedback loop of delight.

We parked and went inside, where we registered for the conference with a thick wad of bills I didn't remember stealing. The man behind the desk asked for my name and I hesitated; I was certain that Ms. Burden was here somewhere, and that she would see my name if they published a list of attendees. "Jane Green," I said, my mother's maiden name.

I hadn't thought of Ms. Burden for a while, not since I'd seen that blond man. Now I looked around me, apprehensive, wondering what I would do if I ran into either one of them. But I was too overwhelmed to stay worried for long.

I couldn't decide where to go first. The crush of people seemed strange, and so did the hotel itself, which smelled like cleaning fluid and static electricity. I set off at random, caught up in the crowd.

I went past meeting rooms with names of the panels on the doors: "What Happened to Fo'c'sle Flynn?," "Comparing Apples and Oranges," even one called "Why Have the Letters Stopped?" I was too excited to sit through them, though, and I walked on to the Art Show, amazed at all the paintings and sculptures people had created from Aunt Maeve's book.

Then I wandered through the Dealers Room, past a spectacular array of books and posters, clothing and jewelry. I saw a new novel with "As extraordinary as *Ivory Apples*" on the front cover and nearly bought it, but by then I believed as Piper did about possessions, that it was better not to own anything, to travel light.

I turned away from the counter and saw Ms. Burden walking down another aisle. I hurried outside.

I looked behind me, making sure she wasn't following, then continued down the hall. A woman came toward me, and as she got closer I saw that her nametag read "Eliza Woodbury." She was one of those cute geeks, with over-large glasses and long hair falling down her back. Without thinking, I said, "Hey, I like your posts!"

"Thanks," she said, and kept going.

I turned to watch her. She joined a group of people and they greeted each other, laughing and shouting. Why had I expected anything else from her, after all? She was a kind of celebrity here, someone with a following, and I was nobody.

Never mind, Piper said. *Imagine what she'd say if she knew who you were. Who your great-aunt is.*

He was right, and I cheered up. It was too bad I couldn't post on the Adela Madden website, but if she only talked to people from the forums there, well, that was her loss.

Despite Eliza Woodbury I felt comfortable here, as if I belonged. Part of it, I realized, was that people no longer walked away when I approached, or talked about me as if I wasn't there. I must have accumulated a terrible odor before I'd taken that shower, but it had happened so slowly I'd never noticed it.

Eliza Woodbury and her friends went into a lecture room, and I followed them. A moment later the lights dimmed, and a man made his way to a podium at the front.

"I think we all know that Adela Madden's sister was Lydia Madden," he said. "Lydia died in 1993, at age 67. During her life she almost certainly kept up with her sister, and knew when her sister died, if indeed she had died. But, strangely enough, no one's ever looked into Lydia Madden. Who was she? Why didn't she tell the world what had happened to Adela?"

I was starting to feel uneasy, wondering where he was going with this. Had he researched Lydia's daughter? Her son-in-law, her grandchildren?

A slide appeared on the screen above him, a familiar-looking photo in black and white. "Here's the famous photograph of the sisters as children, the one Lydia Madden sent to a fanzine in the seventies," the speaker said.

Two girls were sitting on some rocks in a field, squinting into the camera. Their white hair frizzed outward and disappeared against the sun-bleached sky, as if they were dissolving into air. You could almost feel the heat, hear the monotonous chirp of the cicadas.

The slide changed to an official-looking piece of paper, with a lacy border and "Certificate of Marriage" written at the top in curlicue letters. "In 1953, Lydia married a man named Samuel Green," the speaker went on. "As you can see from the certificate, the marriage took place in Albany, New York."

I remembered Grampa Sam, a silly, funny man who'd played games with us when we were very young. He did all the usual things like pretending to steal our noses or hiding behind his hands and then peeking out again, but he could also blow smoke out of his ears, or somehow convinced us he could—anyway, I never figured out how he did it. They'd both smoked a lot, and Lydia had died of lung cancer when I was six. Sam had died when I was ten, so my memory of him was clearer.

"Samuel Green's father, Abraham Greenbaum, had come to the United States from Poland in 1924," the speaker said. "'Greenbaum,' perhaps appropriately for someone connected with the author of *Ivory Apples*, means 'green tree' in German. The name was shortened at Ellis Island.

"In 1959, Sam and Lydia had their only child, a daughter they named Jane. Jane's birth was registered in Eugene, Oregon, so they must have come west by that time. We don't know why they moved, but the usual reason for uprooting your family is to find work. In this case, though, there might be another explanation.

"Adela Madden's letters to her publisher show her living in Eugene by 1956." (Another slide, this one a letter signed "Adela.") "Of course it's possible that Adela and the Greens had come west at the same time, but I wonder if Adela had moved first, and if she had run into trouble and needed her family around her. As far as we know she never married, never held a job. The book she wrote, her only source of income, sold poorly in its first few years. She must have needed financial help, and perhaps she suggested to Sam and Lydia that they come to Oregon. Or maybe they came on their own, knowing that she needed assistance."

People were murmuring around me, impressed by the speaker's detective work. I didn't see why. None of this had anything to do with what had brought us all together, with *Ivory Apples*.

"She might have needed help for another reason at well," the speaker said. "Unfortunately, we know very little about Adela Madden, either before or after she wrote her book. The stories we do have, though, show her to be a somewhat unstable woman, a lost woman, someone who had difficulty making her way through the world. Perhaps, away from her family, she had run into trouble with the authorities. Perhaps she needed her sister and brother-in-law to keep her out of prison, or a mental institution."

"Lost?" someone muttered.

A number of people were turning against the speaker now. Most of her fans admired Adela Madden, even loved her. And I felt annoyed too, and then angry. He'd connected the few facts he had with links of "perhaps" and "maybe," but if you took those away you'd have no argument at all. And yet somehow by the end of it he'd made Aunt Maeve into a criminal, or a madwoman.

"If we turn to the daughter, Jane Green—"

That was enough. I stood up. My shadow fell over the slide on the screen, which had changed to a picture of a birth certificate. "Down in front!" someone shouted.

"What difference does any of this make?" I said, or Piper did. "When you eat an apple, do you wonder who grew it, or plucked it? And yet here you are, a peddler of impoverished drivel, turning conjecture into fact, clouds into dry land."

"Let him finish!" someone said.

"I'll be taking questions at the end—" the speaker said.

"Well, I have a question now," I said. "Why do you think Mae—Adela Madden needed to be kept out of jail? What crime did she commit?"

"I agree," someone else said, and to my surprise Eliza Woodbury rose from the audience. "Why is it that all women writers are—what did you say?—unstable and lost?"

"Exactly," I said. "As far as we know, Adela Madden was as stable as an omnibus."

Eliza Woodbury nodded in approval. Someone else stood up, and to my horror I saw it was Ms. Burden. She had turned toward me, squinting against the light of the projector.

"Let Dr. Chapman finish his talk," she said. "We owe him that much courtesy, at least."

"This isn't the first time Chapman's made these kinds of claims," a man said from the audience. "If you look at his paper on Emily Dickinson—"

"We're not here to discuss Emily Dickinson!" another man yelled.

Everyone was shouting now, their attention on each other and away from me. I made my way down the row of chairs and headed for the door. Out of the corner of my eye, I saw Ms. Burden moving too, coming after me.

I hurried outside and through the hotel corridor. Then I banged the hotel door open and ran out into the street. As I went I pulled my blouse out of my pants and tore off my jacket and threw it into a trash can, trying to change my appearance.

Then Piper did something extraordinary. He left me, left my body, and appeared out in the world beside me. I saw him for the first time in four years, a thing made of leaves and twigs, his elbows sharp as thorns. His skin was brown, tinged with green, and his eyes were lit with an ancient mischief.

"What are you doing?" I asked, alarmed.

"She's looking for one person, not someone with a child," he said.

"You don't look anything like a child!"

He grinned, enjoying himself. His mouth was longer than a human's, reaching almost to his ears.

"Ivy!" Ms. Burden shouted, sounding a long way behind me. "Ivy, is that you?"

Somehow I kept myself from turning around. Ms. Burden shouted my name a few more times, and then there was only silence.

Finally I felt brave enough to look back. Ms. Burden was gone. Piper's improbable plan had worked. I started laughing, and Piper grinned and then laughed as well. Then we were both overcome with hilarity, fighting for breath, unable to stop. Someone stared at us as from across the street, probably thinking we were drunk.

Just as I got control of myself I noticed that I was still wearing my name tag, the one that said "Jane Green." I'd wanted to be inconspicuous, but if I'd been trying to call attention to myself I couldn't have picked a better name. I showed it to Piper, and we started laughing again.

He stopped before I did. He turned to me, looking up with an expression I had never seen before, diffident, almost serious. His mouth was open, as if he wanted to say something.

Then he leapt, and I felt him land within me. He turned around several times, like a dog on a favorite bed, until he nestled down somewhere he felt comfortable.

We asked someone where the Greyhound bus station was and went toward it. We'd left the car in the hotel parking lot, I remembered, but I wasn't going back there to find it. Anyway, we'd stolen it in the first place.

Piper and I had grown so close that I could usually tell what he was thinking, and so I knew that he'd been about to ask if I wanted him back. The question confused me, even startled me. I'd thought that he'd be in my life forever, that I had no choice in the matter.

And if he *had* asked me, what would I have said?

CHAPTER 15

On the bus back to Eugene I thought about how much fun I'd had, how I'd enjoyed being treated like a regular person again. It was coming time to get off the streets, but I'd been gone so long I couldn't see any way back. I needed a phone number to get a job, but only a job would earn me enough money for a phone.

I started urging Piper toward homeless shelters, where I could get a bed and some food and maybe even a shower. But he didn't like those places; they were too regimented for him, and some of them required you to sign up earlier in the day, something he couldn't seem to manage.

I stayed with him for another year. We did what we had always done, confounding people, shaking them up, even teaching them something, though Piper always insisted that wasn't his intention.

Toward the end it sometimes seemed as if we were doing the same things over and over, to the point that I almost felt bored once or twice. When he found abandoned houses and set them alight I thought of the ending of *Ivory Apples*, when the town burned down and one of the children of Tabitha and Quentin Foxtree died. Wild revelry was fine in its place, Maeve seemed to be saying, but it had to stop sometime. But Piper was as manic as always, and I knew he couldn't understand how any of this could seem dull.

I was thinking about my family more and more, and finally I overruled him and went by my house. It seemed deserted, the lawn overgrown, a throwaway paper lying on the porch, still damp from the rain I walked around to the backyard, watching the windows carefully, but I still saw no signs of life. Philip had hidden a key there after Beatriz had locked herself out a few more times, and after a moment I found the fake rock he'd used to hide it in.

Should I take it and go inside? Piper shook his head, and I could feel his fear. No, I was the one who was afraid. I wasn't ready to confront Ms. Burden yet.

I left, telling myself that I'd come back later, or watch for my sisters at their schools. A few days after that I tried calling them from a payphone, but I got only voicemail.

Something else happened that should have made me leave the streets for good: I saw the blond man again. I turned and ran, but this time he spotted me and ran after me. "Wait!" he shouted. "I just want to talk to you!"

Of course he wanted to talk to me, I thought. Right before he'd throw me to the ground and tie me up, and then carry his prize back to Ms. Burden.

I kept running. Downtown Eugene is a grid of streets, with few places to hide. I knew a store that had another entrance in the back, and I darted through it and outside, leaving the man behind.

The weather turned cold again. My sixteenth birthday came and went, though I had lost track of time and wasn't sure exactly which day it was. Around then we stole another car, and Piper directed me out of the city. The drive looked familiar, though the name of the highway, 126, didn't mean anything to me. Then we started passing trees along the roadway, and I realized that this was the way to Aunt Maeve's house.

I asked him, astonished, if he knew where Maeve lived. Of course he did, he told me. He had lived in the grove near her house for years, maybe centuries.

"What the fuck?" I said, jolted into speaking out loud. It was something I rarely did, knowing that it made people stare at me and edge away. "Why the hell didn't you tell me?"

I'm telling you now, he said. *Anyway, I didn't think it was important.*

"Not important?" I was so angry I could barely catch my breath; it felt as if a band was constricting my chest, pulling tighter and tighter. "All I ever wanted was to find her."

He never felt guilty for anything, I knew, might not have even known what guilt was. I shouted at him for a long time, told him all about the hopelessness and misery of those years. He didn't seem to understand, though, and finally I gave up.

He lapsed into silence too, except to give me directions. We took the exit to the small town, which I saw now was called Woodbine. Why hadn't I noticed that when I was a child, or remembered the name?

Then we drove the rough road toward Maeve's house. As we came closer I started wondering how she had survived without Philip's help, and I felt a jumble of excitement and worry that crowded out my anger. Piper was pure eagerness, straining to see around the next curve.

The first thing I saw was her garden. Tall knotted weeds had choked off all her flowers and were spreading along the driveway and up the path to the house. I got out of the car and rang the rope of bells on her door.

No one answered. I rang the bells again, then knocked loudly. "Aunt Maeve!" I called. "Aunt Maeve, are you there? It's me, Ivy!"

I tried the door but it was locked, so I went around to the side. She'd never put curtains over her many windows, and I peered into every room, banging on the glass and shouting.

The back door was locked as well, and I started down the other side of the house. I came to what looked like her bedroom, a place I'd never gone into, and made out a lump in her bed. Was she sleeping? Or had she just left the bed unmade?

I returned to the back door, which had the smallest glass panes in the house, picked up a rock, and smashed out one of the windows. Then I reached inside and opened the door.

I hurried through the kitchen to her bedroom. There was a woman lying in the bed, but I didn't know who she was; she seemed far too small to be Aunt Maeve. The skin on her face was lax, and her nose jutted up like a blade. White hair lay spread against the pillow, and her gray eyes were open, staring blindly in front of her.

No, it was Aunt Maeve. She'd lost a lot of weight—even with the blankets over her I could see that. Her new thinness looked grotesque on her large frame.

"Aunt Maeve?" I said, rushing over to her.

She turned toward me, alarmed. "Who are you?" she asked, her voice a hoarse whisper.

"It's Ivy. Your great-niece."

"Ivy," she said, without recognition.

"Can I get you something? How about some food?"

"Drink."

"Drink, great. Just a minute."

I ran to the kitchen. The cupboards held very little; the first one I opened had an old box of pasta and a bottle of rice vinegar. The refrigerator was even worse, with celery so old it was turning liquid, and some other fruits or vegetables I couldn't identify.

Finally I found a box of tea and set her kettle boiling. I opened another cupboard to look for sugar and saw ants swirling around a bag of flour; a black line led there and back, like eager shoppers at a sale. As I turned away from the cupboard I realized how bad the kitchen smelled, of food that had gone moldy or rotten.

I poured the water and took the tea into her bedroom. She sat up carefully, displacing a sour, vinegary odor from somewhere within the blankets. When was the last time she had washed? I tried not to recoil, to hold the cup steady at her mouth.

"Who did you say you were?" she asked.

"Ivy. Philip and Jane's daughter."

"Philip." She closed her eyes and lay back.

"Are you tired? Do you want to go to sleep?"

"Why not? It's all gone, anyway."

"What's all gone?"

"All gone. No reason to stay."

I felt uncertain, hopeless. "Look—why don't you go back to sleep? I'll call a doctor."

Everything seemed harder than it had to be, and took longer. Part of that was because I hadn't done any work for a long time, I wasn't used to coming up with a plan and following it. The phone was dead, for example, probably because Maeve hadn't paid the bill, which meant that I had to drive to Woodbine and find a doctor. I took a quick shower in cold water (she hadn't paid the heating bill either, apparently), then looked through her clothes for something presentable to wear. I couldn't find anything that would fit me, though, and finally I just grabbed a dress at random. It billowed around me, and with its blue and white stripes I looked like a pool pavilion, but I couldn't take the time to change.

When I went to the front door I saw a drift of letters and packages piled against it, so many that I couldn't pull the door open. I bent down and started to arrange them, then realized that I could just go out the back.

And it didn't help that Piper laughed at everything, that he was constantly coming up with ideas for tricks and jokes. I told him firmly to shut up, but I had gotten out of the habit of resisting him and I felt him grin.

When I finally found a doctor in Woodbine he told me he didn't make house calls. It seemed like the last straw. I sat down, ready to give up, but the doctor said, "We can send an ambulance. Where does she live?"

That really was the last straw—I didn't know her address. But I was able to describe how to get to her house, well enough that the doctor said, "Sure, I know where that is. I'll go call them, and you can stay here, relax a bit. Would you like something to drink?"

It was the first time in years someone had been kind to me. I managed to thank him before I got outside and started crying, then drove back to Maeve's house.

I got there just as the ambulance was pulling up, and I took the crew around back and let them inside. They slowed to look at the broken windowpane and the dust and dirt and ants in the kitchen, whispering to each other. I didn't say anything, just led them to the bedroom.

It was too much like a repeat of the day Philip had died: a crowd of men and women in a room too small for them, voices talking, radios crackling. I found myself pushed into a corner, near her dresser. She had a group of photographs on the dresser, including the one Dr. Chapman had shown at the Adela Madden Conference, the light-haired children sitting in the sun.

For the first time I truly felt the connection between the two, Adela Madden and Maeve Reynolds. My great-aunt was Adela Madden, the woman who had written *Ivory Apples*. A national treasure, some people had called her. And now, just when I'd found her again, I was in danger of losing her.

"Miss?" one of the EMTs said. "Is this your —your grandmother?"

"My great-aunt," I said.

"Yes, well, we're going to have to take her to the hospital. She's badly dehydrated, she's malnourished, disoriented . . . Were you taking care of her?"

"No, I—I didn't know."

Aunt Maeve said something, a word as quiet as a sigh. "What?" I said. "What did you say?"

"No," she said. "No hospital. Anyway, there's a girl who comes in. I ordered her from the restaurant."

Two of the EMTs looked at each other, clearly thinking she was unmoored or delirious. "I'm sorry, ma'am, but you need to see a doctor," one of them said.

"I don't want to go to the hospital," she said, louder this time. She looked over at me. "What if—what if she takes care of me?"

"Do you know who she is, ma'am?"

Aunt Maeve said nothing. All of the EMTs had stopped what they were doing, as if everyone understood how high the stakes were.

"Of course," Maeve said finally. She sounded a little like her old imperious self. "She . . . she's my great-niece. I have four great-nieces. Her name is . . . her name is Ivy. Ivy Quinn."

"Is that right, miss?" the EMT asked.

I nodded, hoping they'd take my word for it. I hadn't had any identification for years.

"And what's your name?" the EMT asked Maeve.

"Maeve Reynolds."

"Do you know who's president?"

"Oh God," Maeve said.

Most of them laughed. She seemed to have passed the test. "Can you take care of her?" the EMT asked me.

"Yeah. Sure."

The EMT started listing the things I needed to do, but I could only give him half my attention. I was wondering if I was up to the job. I'd have to buy groceries, clean the house, straighten out her finances . . . Could I take all this on, after two years of frivolity?

No, Piper said.

I pushed back at him, as strongly as I could. But I thought of all the hard work ahead of me, and I felt the same reluctance as he did.

Everything seemed unreal at first, as if I found myself in a country where I barely spoke the language or understood the customs. I had to remind myself to pay for my groceries, for example, and not lift them from the market the way I once did. I had to get used to sleeping on Maeve's couch instead of out in the open, had to learn to relax at night, to stop listening for people creeping up on me while I slept.

I did all right, I think. I made a stab at cleaning up. I got rid of the ants, though Piper tried to convince me to write his name in flour and see if the black line of ants would spell it out. I got the heat turned back on; it was December, the dead of winter, and the cold crept in through all the windows.

But she had so many knickknacks, what Grampa Sam had called "tchotchkes," and all of them had gathered dust and cobwebs. It seemed an impossible task, like sorting seeds in a fairy tale. I wondered if we could afford a cleaner, someone like Esperanza, which meant looking through her finances, which meant opening her letters to see which ones had checks in them.

The pile blocking the front door turned out to be only a small part of her correspondence. She had stuffed a closet with letters going back at least a year; her publishers had probably started sending them to her when the post office box closed. And there was more coming every day, filled with questions, theories, requests, photos and paintings and jewelry, so many that I didn't see how anyone could finish it all.

Maeve got better, though slowly. A month later she was walking around a little. We'd been fined for the overgrown garden so I hired someone to cut it back, and the sigh of it razed to the ground depressed her so much that she usually stayed indoors.

She was different, though, sadder and less certain of herself. Her queenly manner, the way she had assumed that everyone would do her bidding, was gone. At times she seemed almost apologetic.

We settled into a routine, like an unmarried aunt and her caregiver niece in an old novel. In the morning I ran errands and did some chores around the house, and after lunch I settled down to her correspondence. I took it slowly, telling myself that I didn't have to do it all at once.

At first I had to ask her a lot of questions about the world of *Ivory Apples*, but as time passed it became easier. I hesitated over what name I should sign the letters with, and finally I settled on Dave. Jane and Philip had used David, and I liked to imagine heated arguments on the website over whether Dave and David were the same person.

And all the time I was working, I composed poetry in my head. In later years, reviewers would wonder why my earliest poems were so short, coming up with any number of ingenious explanations, but the truth was that I couldn't stop to write anything longer.

Every so often I drove back to Eugene, where I'd deposit Maeve's checks in the bank, and use Maeve's library card to check out books from the library, and pick up things I couldn't find in Woodbine. I rented a new post office box in Springfield, hoping to make the letter-writers forget about the Eugene address; the two towns were just across the Willamette River, but most people didn't know that.

I'd grown unhappy over having stolen the car, so I left it on the street somewhere. Then I bought a new one, with Maeve's money and her blessings, a four-wheel drive because of the rough roads where we lived. Piper was delighted by it. Different chimes and bells would sound depending on what you were doing—if you left the door open and the key in the ignition, for example, or you hadn't fastened your seat belt. He spent some time playing tunes by opening and closing the door, putting the key in the ignition, touching the seatbelt buckles to each other. I loved him then, and missed having his wild spirit with me all the time. I didn't know anyone else who could play a car.

One day, after we'd eaten dinner and I'd taken the dirty dishes to the kitchen to soak, Maeve said, "I think I'm well enough to hear about it now. Can you tell me how Philip died? And who was that dreadful woman at your house?"

"It's a long story," I said.

"I like stories," she said, smiling a little.

So I told her everything, all the long, hard tale of the past five years. It was good to share it with someone; I felt as if I had set down some baggage, some—yes—burden, as if I had been made free of something.

"I don't know why she's so obsessed with you, though," I said.

"I've seen it before," Maeve said. "Some people want—well, a source of creativity, let's call it. They want to make something, to bring something new into the world. Or they want the money and fame that come with it."

"But why is she stalking you like this? There are thousands of authors in the world."

"Well, because of Willa."

"Who's Willa?"

She laughed. "Oh, that's what I called her. I named her after my grandmother, because they were so much alike. Willa—Grandma Willa—was a strong woman, forbidding, tall and awkward, and her face looked like a slab of stone. I was always a little afraid of her."

Willa sounded like Maeve, though Maeve seemed unaware of it. "So, wait—Willa is the sprite you met in the grove?" I asked. "I thought women got male sprites, and men got female ones."

"Not in my experience. Anyway, Willa, my Willa, was very forceful. She felt like a sword of fire had run through me, or like drinking pure spirits. Far too powerful for the child I was then."

I hadn't felt Piper as a sword of fire, I thought. Well, perhaps they weren't all alike.

Then I realized something, and I shivered suddenly, as if my bones had turned to ice. "You talk about her in the past tense," I said. "Did she—is she gone?"

She shook her head, saying nothing for a long while. "Yes, dear," she said finally. "She left me."

"But why?"

"Well, she couldn't stay. I was too weak for her."

I thought about how I'd found Maeve, unmoving, close to death. "But you're better now. Can't she come back?"

"I'm not sure. It would be hard, very hard."

"And they can do that? Just leave?"

"I don't know about all of them, dear. She's the only one I ever knew."

"All gone," Maeve had said when I'd found her. I'd thought she was talking about the people she'd known who had died, and I'd been worried that she didn't want to live. But this might be even worse.

"I'm so sorry," I said. "Are you—how do you feel?"

"Well, it wasn't easy," she said. "But I've gotten used to it."

She was trying to speak briskly, I saw, to move on to more practical things. I fumbled around for something more to ask her. "So Willa—she helped you with your book?"

"I thought you would have figured it out by now," she said. "I asked you once how your writing was going, remember?"

"You mean my poems—I'm writing poems because of Piper?"

"Not because of him, not directly. You're writing poems because you want to write poems. But the sprites show us things, a way beyond this world. Like the muses, really."

Hadn't she told me they were tricksters? "But muses—aren't they those women in Greece somewhere, with long flowing dresses?"

She laughed. "Well, that's how the Greeks thought of them, I'm sure. Very decorous, those Greeks, with their 'nothing in excess.' Art isn't decorous, though—it's messy and dangerous, it takes you to frightening places."

I remembered my own thoughts, that I'd stolen past all the conventions and the rules, that I'd come upon a divine fire. The tricksters were connected to fire, Maeve had said.

And she was right—I should have realized all of this myself. I'd been too busy breaking in to people's houses to think about it, to understand how my poetry used some of the same skills. Breaking and entering into the realm of the gods.

"All right, so why am I writing poems and you wrote a novel? And why did you stop?"

"It takes people differently, I think. I met a musician once who had his own muse. Though I was pretty certain you'd turn out to be a writer, just from what I knew about you."

She hadn't told me why she'd stopped writing, I noticed. But she was being so helpful for once that I put that aside to ask later.

"How does Ms. Burden know about all of this? And how did she connect you to *Ivory Apples?*"

"That I don't know. There were always theories about the muses, people passing information along."

Suddenly I remembered something. "On the website— you know there's a website about you, right?" I said.

"What's a website?"

I sighed. She'd gotten a computer, finally, or I wouldn't have been able to write so many letters, but she never used it. "It's a place on the computer, where people go to share things that interest them," I said. "I'll show you later. Anyway, there's this site about you, and someone posted this whole long essay about how you went to Pommerie Town and discovered the secret of the muses and they gave you your book."

She smiled slyly, an old familiar expression. "There you are," she said. "Theories. Who wrote that, do you know?"

"They don't use their real names, mostly. This one just called themselves Watchmaker."

"Watchmaker?" She moved forward in her chair, looking apprehensive. "There's a watchmaker in *Ivory Apples.*"

"Yeah, but he doesn't do a lot, does he?"

"He does enough," she said.

I didn't remember much about him. I should probably read the book again, I thought. "You know what I wonder?" I asked. "I wonder if Ms. Burden wrote that essay. If she's Watchmaker."

Maeve didn't seem to be listening. Talk of the Watchmaker had disturbed her somehow. I tried another question. "Why don't you want anyone to know about them, those muses? Why did you and my father go to all that trouble to keep this place secret?"

"It isn't me, child. They're the ones who don't want discovery. I'm not sure why, really. They're vulnerable in some way, I think. They can be captured, maybe even imprisoned. And of course there would be people coming to bother them, from all over the world. They like their isolation."

"I wish I could have told Ms. Burden, though. It would have been so much easier if I could have just taken her to the grove."

"Really? What if she attracted a muse to her, and became a famous writer?"

"That wouldn't even matter," I said. Maeve studied me, and under her heavy scrutiny I was forced to admit the truth. "All right, I'd hate it. She doesn't deserve it—she's a horrible person. It would be like rewarding her for all the things she's done."

"Well, it isn't up to us. They're the ones who choose, who decide how best to bestow their gifts. I've seen people come to the grove hoping to be rewarded, to be burned in the muses' fire, and go away disappointed."

I had a sudden urge to bring Ms. Burden to the grove and watch her get rejected. But I couldn't risk it, not if she knew how to control them. "Those noises I told you about, in our house and Ms. Burden's—could they be muses, sprites, that she'd imprisoned? They sounded somehow, well, in despair. As if they'd lost everything."

Maeve shook her head. "I don't know, dear. I'd tell you if I did."

"Why are you answering all my questions? You never did before."

"Well, the best way to teach is for the student to learn by herself. That's how she comes to understanding. But the situation's changed now, and I don't have the luxury of waiting. We need to move quickly."

"What situation?"

"Well, where are your sisters?"

"Where?" Was she that confused, that she didn't remember where we lived? "They're at the house in Eugene."

"Oh." She sighed. "I was hoping you knew."

"Knew what?"

"I sent my companion to visit your house. To see how you were."

"Wait a minute. What companion?"

"The girl they sent me. I knew I needed help, you see, but I didn't know anyone I could call. The only place I could think of was that Italian restaurant in Woodbine that used to deliver our dinners. So I called them, and fortunately they knew someone who was looking for work, a high school student named May. She stopped coming a while ago, two months, I think. Or was it three?"

So that was what she'd meant by saying she'd ordered someone from the restaurant. I felt relieved; when I'd first heard this I'd thought that she'd left reality altogether.

"I told May to only talk to you or your sisters, not that woman," she went on. "I didn't know her name then, you see. And when May came back she said there was no one at home. Worse than that—she said it looked like no one had lived there for a while."

"They could have been at school. And Ms. Burden, well, she left the house sometimes."

"This was the beginning of August—there wasn't any school."

"They still could have been out."

"Did they do that? Go places together?"

"Not together, but they'd go out at the same time. Sometimes. But you think they—what?—That they moved away?"

"I don't know what I think. And you don't either, if you're honest."

I remembered my own visit, how uncared-for the house had looked, and I started to feel worried. No, I had been worried all along, and trying to ignore it. I'd felt able to leave home because I'd convinced myself that they'd be safe, that they couldn't tell Ms. Burden anything. Now I wondered if that was true, or even if it mattered. Ms. Burden had enjoyed her ingenious tortures, I knew that much. There was no reason to punish them, but she didn't need a reason. She might be hurting them even now.

I had to rescue them, had to bring them here, if Maeve would allow it. But I didn't know if I could, if I was able to defy Ms. Burden like that. She was their guardian, after all; she had all the force of the law on her side.

"All right," I said. "I'll go there myself."

"Do you think that's wise?"

"I'll be careful. But I have to get them away from her."

CHAPTER 16

The house looked more dilapidated than I remembered. It hadn't been special in any way, just a few rooms holding a few people, but the sight made my heart turn over, as if I had lost something I could never get back.

I walked up to the front door. A few browning newspapers sat on the porch, along with a flyer for a pizza place. I rang the doorbell, feeling anxious. I hadn't made any plans, though I had a vague idea that I might let Piper deal with Ms. Burden. No one answered.

I walked around to the backyard and got the key Philip had hidden, then unlocked the back door and went into the kitchen. It was very dim, the stove and refrigerator lurking like oversized animals in the darkness. I turned on the light but it was much weaker than I remembered, and I saw that only one bulb remained in the overhead lamp. The place smelled faintly of mold and unwashed clothes, and underlying that, even weaker, of rot.

I seemed to spend all my time breaking into places, I thought. Not just the houses Piper and I had gone into, but Ms. Burden's old house, and Maeve's, and now here. I could make a poem out of that, the outsider breaking in . . .

A hum started. I jumped, but it was only the refrigerator coming on. I told myself to relax.

Aside from that, the house was silent. I went through the dining room, the living room, the front hallway still hung with Ms. Burden's Photoshopped portraits. Everything seemed dirtier, shabbier. A path had worn down the carpet from the dining room to the kitchen, and a stain that looked like blood spread across the couch. Probably it was just coffee or juice, though.

"Beatriz?" I said. The house seemed to swallow my voice. "Beatriz!" I said again, shooting her name into the silence like an emergency flare. "Rantha! Ramis!"

No one answered.

I climbed the stairs and looked into the bedroom I'd shared with Beatriz. Clothes and books and paper littered the floor, all of them hers, while my stuff had been shoved into the corners on my side. Dust lay over everything, making my eyes itch.

If they'd gone away, why hadn't they taken their things? The pots and dishes in the kitchen, the television in the living room? I headed down the hallway to Philip's bedroom, feeling apprehensive. Not Philip's anymore, of course. Ms. Burden's.

This was the messiest room of all. The sheets and blankets on the bed were jumbled up like laundry, and plates and cups lay spread out on the floor within arm's reach, some still holding remnants of food and drink. Clothes were draped over the desk and computer in the corner.

The closet door was open. I peered inside carefully, ready to jump back if I heard noises. It looked the same as before, a few dresses hung up but the rest of her things on the floor.

Then I saw the filing cabinet, hiding behind her clothes. I pulled a drawer open and saw that she had been telling the truth for once: the cabinet had been Philip's, with folders for insurance, mortgage, our school reports, his contract from the university. Near the back was that puzzling will, a copy of the one the lawyer had shown us. "In the event of my death I would like my good friend Katherine Burden . . ."

What would Philip say about our family now? I couldn't bear to think about it. I moved on to the next drawer and took out the only folder there.

"Short Stories," the label said. Had Philip written stories? Well, there was a lot I hadn't known about him.

I opened it and saw a stack of paper, all more or less the same size.

"Dear Kate Burden," the first one said. "We're sorry, but your story does not meet our needs at the present time." It went on to thank her for submitting to their magazine, and it ended with the name of the editor sending the rejection slip. The rest were similar: all form letters, all of them rejecting her stories.

So this was what she had been doing with her time, writing stories and mailing them off to magazines. *The New Yorker*, *Harper's*, *Asimov's Science Fiction*, the *Magazine of Fantasy and Science Fiction* . . .

Halfway through the stack I found a rejection slip from *Asimov's Science Fiction* with a handwritten note. "This story shows some writing skill," it said, "but the plot and some of its characters and settings seem derivative of Adela Madden's novel *Ivory Apples*. As a writer, you should be working to develop your own voice, your own themes."

It sounded as if Ms. Burden had been trying to write *Ivory Apples* over and over again. It seemed a waste, a terrible lack of imagination, and I almost felt sorry for her. No wonder she was looking for a muse.

Apart from that file, I hadn't come across anything personal, or anything to say where she'd gone. I wanted to stay and look through the rest of her things, but I was feeling more and more anxious about her coming home, or hearing those noises. I hurried to clear the clothes off the computer and tried to boot it up, but it still needed a password.

I shut it down and left the house, taking the key with me.

In the weeks that followed I continued my search, tracking down people we'd known and asking them questions. Secretaries at both the grammar school and the middle school told me that Ms. Burden had said she was going to home-school my sisters, so they hadn't returned in September. At Ms. Burden's old house I found out that she had sold the place a while back, to a young couple. I asked them if they'd heard any noises from the basement, and although they looked at me strangely they said that no, they hadn't.

Philip's lawyer, Nate McLaren, hadn't seen Ms. Burden since she'd signed the documents making her our guardian. He looked doubtful when I told him some of the things she'd done, but he did have one positive suggestion: I could go to the police.

I didn't want to do that, though. I'd nearly been arrested a few times, and I was pretty sure the police had a long memory for those things. And if the police found my sisters, they'd just return them to Ms. Burden, as their guardian.

Esperanza told me that Ms. Burden had let her go over a year ago. Fortunately she'd found a new family to work for, one she liked a lot. "She was not agreeable, that Ms. Burden," she said. "A hard woman."

I still knew some people on the streets, and I offered them reward money for news of my sisters or Ms. Burden. I didn't expect anything, though.

"I can't be the only one who sees how horrible she is," I said to Maeve at dinner. "Well, Esperanza didn't like her, but she was there, she was a witness. But no one else believes me."

"I think it was Piper who recognized her," she said. "He knew from the beginning the harm she could do to him. Him and his people."

Of course. I'd thought of that before, but I'd forgotten it after everything that had happened.

"You didn't like her either," I said. "So did Willa say something?"

"Oh, I didn't need Willa. She tried to find me, to invade my privacy. I disliked her from the beginning."

I was walking in downtown Eugene when a man in a dirty overcoat came up to me. I reached automatically for my purse; since the time I'd been homeless I could never turn down anyone asking for money.

"You were asking about Ms. Burden?" he said.

I gave him a five-dollar bill. The sleeves of his coat hung so far over his hands that he had to push them up to take it. "Yeah—do you know her?" I asked.

"I know someone. This way."

I followed him through the crowded streets. His coat reached past his feet, and every so often he would trip on the hem and keep going.

He led me through an empty lot, a bus stop, the porch of a building where I used to shelter from the rain. I started wondering if he really knew anything or if he was just taking me somewhere to mug me. I had experience dealing with people like him, though, and my curiosity outweighed my fear.

"Where are we going?" I asked.

"Still looking for him," he said.

A few blocks later he stopped in front of the Whole Foods. "There you are," he said. A familiar-looking man leaned against the wall.

"Remember me?" the man asked.

I did. I'd called him Ted-or-Ned as a joke, and now I couldn't remember his real name.

"You were in that restaurant, with Ms. Burden," I said. "Helping her with something."

"Yeah." He laughed. "And you were one of those nosy kids, Aardvark or Guacamole or something."

"Yeah, no one's ever made fun of our names before. I'm Ivy."

"Ivy, okay. I'm Ned. Sit down, sit down."

The man in the overcoat left without saying goodbye, and I sat against the wall next to Ned. Now that I was looking at him I realized that he'd changed a great deal in the years since I'd seen him last. His clothes were torn and dirty and he smelled as if he hadn't washed in weeks, but it was more than that—his face was sunburned, and he had that expression, half angry and half stunned, that I'd seen on so many people who lived on the streets.

"That was pretty dicey, having you kids turn up just then," he said. "You almost gave the game away."

"What do you mean?" I asked. "What game? Weren't you talking about business?"

"A kind of business."

I started to get up. "If you're not going to tell me anything . . ."

"Sit down. You said there was a reward."

I sat again and got twenty dollars from my purse. "Oh, it's worth more than that," he said, taking the money.

"Tell me what it is and I'll see."

He scowled. "And I just have to trust you, is that it? All right, here it is, what I was doing for your friend Kate. I'm a forger. I was forging things."

"Okay . . ."

"Do I have to spell it out? I was forging signatures on a will. Your father's will, I gather."

"What?"

"Yeah, I thought you'd like that. She'd gotten his will somehow and copied it, except she'd changed a few things. And then she needed—"

"Wait—what?"

"She needed your father's signature, and she hired me to do that."

"You mean I was right—the will was a forgery? We should have gone to Uncle Len after all?"

He held up his hands, palms facing me. "Jeez, calm down. I was just doing a job."

"And we had to spend all those awful years with her, and now I don't know where my sisters are, she lost them somehow, and it was all because of you?"

"Hold on, hold on. She just wanted a small bequest from your father—she told me right up front that she wasn't going to take everything he had."

He hadn't understood anything I'd said, or hadn't been listening. "She was lying to you. I'll tell you what she did, why she changed the will. She made herself our guardian."

He laughed.

"Right, very funny," I said.

"Sorry. It's funny if you know her. She would have made a terrible guardian."

"What do you mean, would have? She *was* terrible at it."

"But I thought—well, your father was pretty young, wasn't he? I saw him that night at the restaurant. Did he—did he die?"

"Yeah. And she was worse than you could possibly imagine."

"But why did she want to be your guardian?" Ned asked. "She hated the idea of settling down, of having a family."

"She wanted to know something about us."

"What?"

"Like I'd tell you."

"Okay, fair enough. She always did have some weird angle going."

His revelation had blown apart a lot of what I thought I know, and I was still sorting out the debris in my head. She *had* been sneaking around our house—she'd even gotten into Philip's bedroom, into his computer files. "What did you get out of all of this?" I asked Ned. "How much did she pay you?"

"Well, that's a funny thing." He wasn't laughing this time, though. "She paid me the first half, five thousand dollars, but not the second. She said she hadn't gotten what she wanted yet. And I can't, you know, go to the police about it."

"So that's why you're telling me all of this. Because she didn't give you what she promised."

"Well, yeah," he said, sounding surprised that there might be any other reason.

"Where did you get those witnesses?"

"On the will? I just made them up. The signatures were pretty illegible, in case anyone wanted to track them down."

I thought about what he'd told me, trying to work out when and how everything had happened. We'd seen Ned at the restaurant just after Ms. Burden had gotten back from her trip. "Were you the one who went to Europe with her?"

"One of your sisters already asked me that, Cuisinart or somebody. She went to Europe alone, actually."

"No, she said—oh."

"Yeah, oh. She lies a lot. You might have gathered that."

"So why did she go? Do you know?"

He laughed again. "Yeah, I do. You know she's crazy, right?"

I didn't much like the word "crazy," maybe because people had used it about me. I just nodded, hoping he'd continue.

"She has this idea about muses. You know what a muse is?"

Piper laughed soundlessly within me. I nodded again.

"Well, she thinks you can, I don't know, capture one somehow. That's why she was so interested in your family, because for some reason she thought you had one. And I bet that's what she was asking you about—where it was, if she could see it, something like that."

I said nothing. It alarmed me that he had gotten this close, though.

"Anyway, like you said, you never told her anything. Finally she got so frustrated she decided give up on you and try to find one herself. They're supposed to live in Greece, mostly, on mountaintops. So she went off to Europe, to all kinds of mountains, Olympus and Parnassus and another one called—called Mount Hell-I-Can, or something like that. That didn't work out so well, though, big surprise, so when she came back she asked me to forge those signatures."

He paused. "You know, it's weird. Something happened in Europe. She seemed worried when she got back, or scared, maybe. She wouldn't tell me what it was, though."

"How'd she find you in the first place, though? I mean, how do you go about getting a forger?"

"We worked at a bank together."

The bank he named was very familiar. It was the same one that Maeve and I used, that Philip had used. The last piece of the jigsaw puzzle fell into place with a satisfying click. Ms. Burden had seen Maeve's account at the bank, had seen checks that were made out to Adela Madden and deposited by Philip Quinn, and then money withdrawn by Maeve Reynolds. For an Adela Madden fan it would have been like finding the Holy Grail, or an ivory apple.

She'd known Maeve's name all along, then. The address on the account had been Philip's, though, which was why she'd attached herself to us—she still needed to find out where Maeve lived.

"Funny thing," he said. "We were both fired around the same time. She'd looked up confidential information about one of the bank's clients, your family probably. And I'd forged a few signatures, people who never looked at their bank statements from one year to the next. People with enough money for everyone in Oregon, so you'd think they wouldn't miss a few dollars here or there. Anyway, we got together after we left."

"Why didn't the bank have you arrested?"

"They did, actually. I got a year inside. And of course they never gave me a recommendation."

"You could forge one," I said, half sarcastically.

"I did. But human resources departments don't trust letters for some reason—they want to talk to actual people these days. So that's why you find me here, in these illustrious circumstances. And now I suppose I won't get that reward you promised."

I didn't want to give it to him, of course. He'd ruined years of my life. Still, I had promised. And, as he said, he hadn't known what she was doing.

On the other hand, if I gave him money I'd be rewarding a criminal. But there was still another hand, which was that no one ever lived a perfectly blameless life. I'd stolen things too, though not out of greed as Ned had. And there was that woman in the bar, the one who had been sober for ten months, and whose glass we had exchanged for something alcoholic. I still thought of her sometimes, of the way she'd nearly fallen off her stool at the end.

I could feel Piper objecting, but I ignored him. I opened my purse. How much did you give the man who had destroyed a part of your life?

In the end I gave him thirty dollars more, hoping he'd think of it as an incentive. "Let me know if you see her again, or hear from her," I said.

"Sure," he said. "I don't suppose you'd do the same for me? She still owes me money, you know."

"I don't suppose you'd testify against her, tell the police you'd forged the will?"

"Sorry."

"Okay, then," I said.

CHAPTER 17

A few days later I went back to my old house and looked around again, but nothing seemed to have changed. I'd come prepared with a few large shopping bags, and I packed away our birth certificates and other important documents.

As I was leaving, locking the front door, someone behind me called out: "Hey, can I talk to you?"

I turned quickly. It was the blond man, the one I'd thought had been following me on the streets. Now he was standing on the front path to the house. I looked left and right, but the lawn was too overgrown to escape through.

"I just want to ask a few questions," he said. "I promise."

Ms. Burden had promised things too. Still, I thought, I might as well talk to him, as long as I took precautions. Maybe he could tell me where she was, what she was doing.

"Okay," I said. "But out in public somewhere. A coffeeshop or something."

"Sure," he said.

We went to a place where I used to go with my family. The moment we walked in I realized I should have picked somewhere else. I was surrounded by old memories: the first time Philip let me have a taste of hard cider, the time Beatriz had fallen and knocked out two of her baby teeth.

We got coffee and found a table, and I settled all my shopping bags around me like a bag lady. "So," I said. I was determined to go first, to take the advantage and keep it. "Where is she?"

"Who?" he asked.

"Who do you think? Your friend, Ms. Burden."

He looked puzzled at that. "She isn't my friend. In fact, I'm looking for her too."

"What? Why? Who are you?"

"Who are you?"

"Oh, no—you first," I said. "You're the one who wants something from me. And why do you look so familiar? Where do I know you from?"

"Very well. You don't know me, not really."

"Oh, yeah? Then why do I—"

"It's your muse. He recognizes mine."

I sat back. All the advantage had passed to him effortlessly, as if he'd won a chess match while I was still admiring the pieces. "They—they can do that?"

He nodded.

"How did you find me?"

"Let me tell it, all right? You can ask questions later. I'm Craig."

"Ivy."

"Well, then. I met Ms. Burden, Kate, in Greece. This was—let's see—I think five years ago. I was at a hotel in Athens, and we were the only people eating breakfast by ourselves, so we started talking. There was a lot of back and forth, each of us feeling the other out, but finally she told me why she was there. She'd rented a car and was going to drive to Mount Helicon and make an offering to the muses."

"An—an offering?"

"Yeah. Some people think that helps, that they'll pay more attention to you if you give them something."

"But—I never did that with Piper. I didn't even know about the muses then, about what they do. He just slammed into me, took over my life. Anyway, I don't think they're interested in things, in objects."

"Yeah, I never gave Alonzo anything either. They just—they feel a kinship with some people. I think that whole offering thing is something people tell themselves, a way of making them think they're in control."

The idea of kinship warmed me, made me feel closer to Piper. And I could sense Piper grinning within me as well.

"Anyway, there was something odd about her," Craig went on.

"Maybe it was that she'd brought an offering, that she didn't seem to have faith in herself as a candidate. Or maybe Alonzo had picked up some strangeness.

"I'd visited Mount Helicon before, and I'd met a muse named Claudio. He told me he'd lived there a long time, and that hundreds of years ago he'd fallen in love with another muse named Talia. She was very powerful, more than any muse he'd ever seen or heard of, and, well . . . I know this is fanciful, but the original Greek muses were supposed to live on Mount Helicon, nine of them, the inspirations for poetry and art and history. And I wondered if she could be one of the Nine, Thalia, the muse of comedy and idyllic poetry. It would explain the way he described her, his feelings toward her. A fire in the shape of a woman, he called her.

"They aren't monogamous—well, they can't be, they go wherever their fancy takes them. But these two stayed together for a long time, even by their own count.

"Claudio was old and powerful in his own right, and the others listened to the two of them and went to them for advice. They weren't what we would call leaders, though—they don't allow anyone to rule over them, or to give them orders.

"Then someone came to the grove, and Talia accepted him, took possession of him. They can't leave without a person, they have to stay where they are until someone comes to petition them. But when they go they can take others with them. Talia's new person wanted to go back to his home in Oregon.

"So Talia asked Claudio to come with her, but he said no, that he'd started a dalliance with someone else. Talia left without him, and others went with her, enough to found a new grove over here. Didn't you ever wonder how they came to be in this obscure spot in Oregon?"

I shook my head.

"Some years later, fifty or a hundred or so, Claudio began to think about Talia again. All he knew was that she'd gone to Oregon, and that it had been long enough that the person she'd left with was probably dead. He waited for someone to come to the grove and petition him so that he could leave, but the world had changed in those years and people had forgotten the muses.

"Then I met Kate in Greece. And Kate was from Oregon, coincidentally. Well, not so coincidentally, as I found out later.

"Kate left for the grove the next morning, early, so I didn't see her go. I waited for her that evening so I could hear how it went, but she didn't come back. I asked at the reception desk, and they told me that she'd called to check out.

"So the next day I rented a car and drove to Mount Helicon. It takes about two hours to get there, and then you park in the village of Agia Anna and hike up the east side of the mountain. You go through these old trees, big shaggy firs, and then you follow the trail to the Valley of the Muses—the real one, not the one the tourists go to. There's a spring there, flowing into a pool, and near it—well, it looks like an old brick building, a shed, but it's really a temple to the original Muses. It's been there in some form or another for thousands of years.

"I looked around for Claudio, to ask him what had happened with Kate. But he wasn't at the grove, and a lot of the others were gone as well. The ones who had stayed seemed frightened about something, so it took a while before they calmed down enough to talk to me.

"Kate had gone to see them, but none of them thought she was a worthy candidate, none of them wanted to leave with her. She started talking to them, asking them to become her muse, even begging them. But still none of them would accept her.

"She got angry at that. She started yelling, ordering them to come with her. The muses I talked to had become bored by then and wandered off, but Claudio and some of the others stayed.

"Some of them saw Kate say something, but they were too far away to hear what it was. The ones closest to her—well, something happened to them. She spoke to them and raised her arms, and they came up out of the lake and went toward her. Then they disappeared, or that's what it looked like, but the ones I talked to said they could still sense them around her, like a cloud. They said it looked as if she had put them under a spell, or trapped them somehow. They became terrified of her, of what she could do, and they ran away. So they didn't see where Claudio and the others went, where Kate had taken them.

"The next day I flew to Oregon. And then, well, I just traveled around the state. I saw you downtown and my muse called to yours, but I didn't know you had anything to do with Kate. Finally I checked the property records and found out that Kate owned a house. But when I went there it was empty—she'd already moved on."

Kate had gone to Europe in early 2000, and it was now January, 2005. "You spent five years looking for her?"

"Well, I did other things too. But I didn't like the idea of Claudio and the others being forced to do Kate's bidding. They'd given me so much, all this talent and ability, I might as well do something for them. And they made me independently wealthy, so I can afford to do it."

He didn't look wealthy; in fact I'd thought him another street person when I'd seen him before. He wore faded jeans and running shoes, and an old T-shirt with the words "Gogol Bordello" on it, which I guessed was a band.

I wanted to ask him what they'd given him, how he'd become wealthy. I was starting to understand that whatever joys poetry gave me, it wouldn't help much in earning a living. But I didn't want to interrupt his story.

"Another thing I learned from the muses was that Kate had left the offering she'd brought them, and they took it out to show me. I thought—well, I thought it was a ball at first, a white ball. But really what it was—"

I looked up sharply. "Do you know what I'm talking about?" he asked.

I nodded. "I'll tell you later," I said.

"Anyway, it was an apple, a white apple. They liked the gift, I think, but they still wouldn't accept her.

"How did she trap them, do you know?"

"I don't, unfortunately. There have always been stories about people coercing the muses, making them do their bidding. One of those stories says something about 'turning them inside-out.' I don't know what that means, but I don't like the sound of it."

I didn't either—and I could feel Piper curling up in fear within me. "Did they tell you all of that? The ones you talked to in Greece?"

"Not all of it. I went to other places around the world and talked to the muses there. In fact, that's one of the things I'd like to ask you about. You found your muse around here, right? So you probably know where Talia ended up. I wonder if you can take me there."

I wondered that too. I'd become an expert at lying, and I'd noticed that both Ms. Burden and Ned would pause an almost imperceptible amount before coming out with a lie, that they needed that time to make something up. As far as I could tell Craig had told the truth throughout, but I still wasn't completely sure of him. And I didn't want to introduce him to Maeve, who was still so fragile, who hadn't yet recovered from her illness.

He saw my hesitation. "Or, well, you can tell me *your* story. Why were you in Kate's house?"

"It's my house!" I said.

"All right. So how did it come into her possession?"

I liked the way he talked, his use of words and phrases like "dalliance" and "wherever their fancy takes them." That wasn't reason enough to take him to Maeve's grove, though. But I could tell him what had happened, the way I'd told it to Maeve, and see if he had any ideas.

"All right," I said. "Have you ever read *Ivory Apples*?"

It took hours to tell our stories in full. Meanwhile people came and went, and in the background we heard plates clattering, and steam hissing from the coffee machine. The proprietor came by a few times and flapped his dishrag at us, as if he wanted to sweep us away along with the crumbs and napkins, but we ignored him.

I had to start my account with Adela Madden, since he had never heard of her or her book. That surprised me: for one thing, he'd mentioned an ivory apple in his story, and for another, I'd always associated the book and the muses together.

Oh, and he had gotten rich by writing a rock song, of all things, something called "Grasshopper, Fly Away." I'd heard it on the radio in what seemed like a bygone era, a time before Piper and Ms. Burden.

He looked horrified by the things Ms. Burden had done, which was gratifying. We exchanged email addresses and promised to write if we discovered anything. I was feeling more and more discouraged, though. If even he, with all his knowledge of the muses, hadn't managed to find Ms. Burden, I didn't see how I could.

I repeated his story to Maeve, telling her about Talia and Claudia, about the captured muses. In response she gave me Hesiod's *Theogony*, but she had nothing to add, no advice to share.

I saw why she'd suggested the book right away, "And one day they taught Hesiod glorious song while he was shepherding his lambs under holy Helicon," it says about the muses. And later Hesiod says that they "breathed into me a divine voice to celebrate things that shall be and things there were aforetime," which was as good a description of their coming as anything. Aside from that, though, it didn't seem very helpful.

I realized something after I finished it. I had never felt that recognition with Maeve that I'd had with Craig, had never sensed the muse within her. But she was just my aunt, someone I'd known all my life, and there was already a bond between us.

Craig emailed me a few weeks later. "I've read *Ivory Apples* and gone on the website, as you suggested. Have you looked through the archives? Someone posted a story that uses the phrase 'ivory apple.'"

I clicked on his link. "How common do you think the words 'ivory apple' are?" someone with the name of Dr. Spottiswood had written, eight years ago. I'd never seen this post; I'd never gone back that far in the archives. "Because it's mentioned in this story I read, 'The Woman and the Apple.' The story isn't online, but the book it's from, *Folktales from All Over*, is old enough that it should be in the public domain. So here it is:

"A woman once let her dog out at night and stopped to look up into her apple tree. An apple of the purest white, like ivory or alabaster, shone down from the topmost branch. Immediately she felt a great longing for it, a longing that drove all other thoughts out of her mind.

"She brought out her ladder and laid it against the lowest branches, then stepped out onto the tree itself. But she had only gone a little ways when her breath started to come faster and the branches seemed to sway beneath her, and she had to return to the ground. She tried several more times, but always when she rose above a certain height she grew faint and dizzy and had to stop.

"She climbed at night, because the apple seemed brighter then. Sometimes it dazzled her, shining out against the darkness, and sometimes its light seemed weaker, but her desire for it remained unchanged.

"She thought about it constantly, as she milked her goats and churned her butter and harvested her fruits and vegetables. She felt she would never be happy unless she had it, that she would sicken and die for lack of it.

"She no longer talked to her dog, or threw sticks for him, or took him on long walks. His fur grew matted and he became thinner, and he followed her with his tail down, knowing that there was something wrong with her but not what it was.

"A man who lived in her village, a cobbler, began to court her but she turned him away, having no interest in anything but her apple—for she had already begun to think of it as hers. Finally the man said, in frustration, 'What would it take to win your hand? I will do anything for you, anything at all.'

"At that she brightened and said, 'Will you pluck an apple for me?'

"'Of course,' the man said.

"So that night the man climbed the ladder set against the tree trunk and then stepped out onto the branches. At first they were thick beneath him and he went quickly; then they began to thin, to bend under his weight. Still he continued climbing, higher and higher, and when he looked up he saw only more boughs and more, and the leaves and apples they bore.

"Finally he caught a glimmer of white ahead of him. He clung tightly to a branch and looked down, wanting to tell the woman what he had seen, but she had dwindled to the size of a cat, and his fear at how high he had climbed stopped the words in his throat.

"He went on. The gleam of the apple grew stronger, and once again he wanted to call down to the woman, but this time when he looked at her she was the size of an ant. He hurried ahead, certain that he would reach his goal soon.

"As he climbed a suspicion grew within him, and when he saw the apple just above him his suspicion turned into a certainty. He looked down, and this time he could not see the woman at all. Still, he knew he had to tell her what he had discovered, and so he shouted, 'It isn't an apple!'

"And very faintly, her voice came back. 'What is it, then?'

"'It's the moon!'

"And her voice came back to him: 'Then pluck me the moon.'

"And so the man reached up and took hold of the moon. It felt cool and smooth to his touch, and it was very heavy. But although he tugged at it with all his might he could not pull it free.

"Then a face appeared on the moon, two wide eyes and an open mouth. 'Are you certain you want to take me from the night sky?' she asked.

"'Yes,' the man said.

"'Then on your head be it,' she said. She came away from the branch so suddenly that the man lost his balance and tumbled downward. Down and down he fell, still holding the moon, the branches whipping him as he went. Finally a branch caught him and he lay still.

"The moon, you know, has her friends, or some say her children. They come to her from all over, and she hosts their nightly revels. They dance and sing, they laugh and play games, they celebrate her presence in their own way. And because she is changeable, because she moves from one shape to another and never stays still, they are changeable as well. They come and go as they please, and they believe in nothing.

"These friends heard the moon cry out, and they climbed the tree to where the man lay. They took the moon from his hands and tried to return it to the sky. But they laughed as they worked, and one of them began a game where they tossed her back and forth. Another had stopped to look at the night sky without the moon, to marvel at the garden of stars like white roses, and when they tossed the moon to him she slipped through his fingers and fell to earth.

"The woman saw the moon fall, and she reached out her hands to catch her. Then the woman felt something hit her, and she dropped senseless to the ground.

"As the sun rose the next day the man woke and found himself held within the branches of the tree. He did not remember anything of the night before, but he felt a strange loss in his hands, a lightness, as if he had once held something very precious.

"The man climbed slowly to the ground, feeling aches in every part of his body. He saw the woman lying there and he remembered that she was something to do with him, but he could not remember why. He worked gently to rouse her, and finally she opened her eyes and looked at him.

"He asked her who she was, but she only babbled nonsense. He put her to bed in the house and stayed with her for several days, but although he spoke patiently to her she would only ever answer him in gibberish. Sometimes he thought that he could understand her, or almost understand her, that if he could just listen in the right way her words would make sense.

"At nights he felt drawn to go outside, and several times he found himself looking up at the star-filled sky, with no memory of waking up or leaving the house. Once he saw the round moon hanging like a ripe fruit, and he thought to himself, Ah, so they've put her back. But he didn't know why he had thought that, and he shook his head at his foolishness. From then on, though, he understood that the moon had something to do with him, and he found himself going out more on the nights when she was full.

"The people of the village still needed new shoes, and wanted their old shoes mended, and the man began to remember his house and his shop. The woman's neighbors told him about some distant cousins of hers in the next village, and he left her with them and returned home.

"He had not escaped the moon's influence, though. He found himself singing and dancing more, and he composed songs for the village's festivals and celebrations, and for their more somber occasions. His neighbors grew fonder of him, and from that time on he never had to buy his own beer.

"The dog enjoyed his company as well. He had followed the man to his house and had grown fatter under his care, and at night he slept curled up at the foot of the man's bed. Sometimes the man would dance under the full moon, and sometimes the dog would dance with him.

"And the moon's friends? She rarely grew angry, but she could not forget how they had tossed her like a ball and then let her fall to the ground. They were playing at their games when they heard the moon's voice, coming from above them:

"'Sound the tocsin, roll the bell,

Down and down the children fell.'

"They looked around and found themselves on earth, on stony ground. They saw that she had exiled them, and that they would stay where she had sent them until she pardoned them.

"In time they came to live on mountaintops, where they are closer to her and can see her more clearly. They look up at her on dark nights, and they sigh for their old friendship. But they know that she is changeable, and they hope that someday she will reverse her decree and take them back."

I took a breath and read the story again. Of course the muses hadn't been friends of the moon, and they hadn't dropped her to earth like a basketball, I knew that much. But there was something there, something I could almost understand, the way the man in the story had almost understood the woman. It wasn't my story, but it rhymed with mine.

I left the computer and went to find Maeve. "Where did you get the name *Ivory Apples?*" I asked.

She had that foxy look again. "Is one of the letter-writers asking that question?"

"No, just me. The thing is, there's this folktale with an ivory apple in it, and I'm wondering if you read it."

"I don't think so, no."

"The apple turns out to be the moon, in the story. So does that have anything to do with your apple, the Watchmaker's apple?"

"Oh, I can't remember—it was all so long ago. I wrote most of the book by moonlight, I remember that much."

She didn't want to discuss it, I saw. I remembered that someone had used the pseudonym "Watchmaker" on the website, and that she had seemed disturbed when I told her about it.

Later, when I was alone, I asked Piper if he'd ever heard the phrase. *Sure*, he said.

Really? I asked. *Where?*

Just now. When you read that story.

I gave up talking to him and skimmed through *Ivory Apples* instead. In the book, the apple had been ivory or a muted white. It was owned by the Watchmaker, and it stood on a shelf behind the counter. Several of the characters wanted to buy it, but the Watchmaker always told them it wasn't for sale. Some of them begged to be allowed to touch it, but he refused them even that. They would come into the store whenever they passed his shop and look at it, and they would resent him for teasing them with it and yet refusing to sell it to them.

CHAPTER 18

And then, amazingly, Ned came through. A few weeks after I met Craig, Ned stopped me in downtown and told me he'd run into Ms. Burden, and that she'd given him her new address. Of course he wanted a reward, but this time I was happy to give it to him.

I got in my car and drove toward the address. I thought of my sisters, alone with her for all this time, and I wondered what new miseries she had conjured up. I felt jittery, sick to my stomach, my hands sweaty on the steering wheel.

I found myself in a part of Eugene I'd never seen before, block after block of warehouses, some of them empty. I grew more and more apprehensive as I went on, as the numbers counted down: 319, 317, 315. And then I saw it—313.

She couldn't possibly live there, I thought. It was one of the abandoned buildings, with painted-over windows, some of them broken, and graffiti on the walls. A sign at the top said "For Lease," the words striped white with pigeon shit.

I parked the car and got out. There was a massive gate at the front but it was locked, and so was a smaller door within it.

I went around the warehouse and found an open window with a steel grate pulled more than halfway down. I squeezed myself through the gap and stood in the building, looking around.

I was in a huge echoing space, with light and dust lancing through a few small high windows. A patchwork of windows painted white lined one wall, some new, some broken or faded to gray. A stairway hugged another wall and stopped halfway up, its last step poised out over the air. Steel shelves and broken machinery littered the corners.

I'd slept in places a lot like this when I'd been on the streets, and I sniffed for the old familiar odors, shit and spoiled food and unwashed bodies. But I could smell only damp wood, gone rotten from the rain.

Were people avoiding this place? I would have been grateful to have found it, somewhere to get out of the rain, or most of it. But no one had ever mentioned it to me, not even to warn me away.

I set off into the building, skirting the light from the windows. The echoes of my footsteps seemed weirdly loud, as though the walls were amplifying them. I went more carefully and the echoes diminished.

A light appeared up ahead, illuminating a scene like a stage play. I came closer and saw my sisters eating at our dining table. They weren't talking and laughing and bickering as usual, though. Instead Amaranth was staring off into the distance, scowling, and Semiramis looked afraid. Only Beatriz seemed aware of her surroundings, but her attention came and went, like a light flickering on and off.

Everything seemed blurred, as though I was seeing through gauze. Was I crying? I blinked, but the haze didn't go away.

Then I heard Philip's voice, and saw him sitting at the head of the table. And Jane was there too, saying something to Philip over the heads of my sisters.

I don't know how long I stood there watching them. They finished dinner, and then Jane and Philip urged my two youngest sisters to bed. They protested, and my parents joked with them, and finally they were allowed to stay up for another hour.

I felt a yearning that threatened to swallow me whole. I knew my parents were dead, of course I knew that, and that we weren't at home but in a warehouse. It didn't seem to matter. All I could think was that I had found them, that we could be a family again.

I started toward the light, my arms already opening to hold them. Piper pushed hard at my ribs. Get out! he said. Move!

Loud footsteps sounded, and I saw Ms. Burden coming toward me across the warehouse floor. I stood taller, trying to look unafraid. A hundred questions passed through my mind. Why were my sisters here, in this abandoned warehouse? Or were these illusions, the way Philip and Jane had to be? I knew that my parents were dead, so was it possible that my sisters . . .

Ms. Burden started talking before I could think what to ask her.

"I don't want them, not really," she said. "Just tell me where Adela Madden lives, and I'll give them back."

She muttered something I couldn't hear, though I thought I caught the word "bell." The haze around them thickened and grew, until it became the size of a room, a cloud.

I tried to back away and found that I couldn't. Instead the cloud came closer, or I moved toward it. One step more and I would join it.

Piper danced within me, his knees and feet and elbows striking a painful percussion against my ribcage. *Once she has you she'll never let you go,* he said.

"Ivy!" Philip said, from somewhere inside the cloud. "Why didn't you come down for dinner? Come and join us!"

I took another step toward them. There would be someone else to make all the decisions now, someone who understood things the way an adult did. I could stop working so hard. I could rest, finally.

The mist parted, and I saw the Oregon Zoo in Portland, a place we'd visited once with Philip. My family was at the elephant exhibit, looking enthralled.

They continued on, down a path past the other animals. The path led them away from the zoo, into a dark, thick forest. They looked around uneasily. Someone leapt at them from between the trees, and then two more people, five, ten. Witches shrouded in black, shadowy terrors from a child's nightmare. My sisters screamed.

The witches dragged them to an open space in the forest. A huge iron cauldron stood there, filled with water. Fire blazed up beneath it, and as I watched the water began to boil.

Philip and Jane were gone now, returned to whatever dreamland they had come from. My sisters were still screaming, the sound echoing throughout the warehouse. The witches bent and lifted them like sticks, then tossed them into the cauldron.

Get out! Piper said again.

No, I said. *I have to rescue them.*

Go! It isn't real.

Are you sure?

You can't rescue them. Just go, before it's too late.

He was right, I couldn't do anything. I tried to wrench my gaze away from the cauldron, but once again I was caught, unable to move.

With my last strength, I let go of Piper. He rose within me and took control, then tried to force me to move. I stumbled back a few steps. He grew stronger, and we continued to back away.

"Help us!" Beatriz called. "It's getting hotter!"

Hurry! Piper said.

I wanted to look at them, but Piper made me stagger toward the window. I heard footsteps, heightened thuds as if a giant was walking behind me, and I ran faster. I made it to the window and got my head and torso through it.

Hands clutched my ankles. I kicked out and the hands slid to my shoes.

"It doesn't matter," Ms. Burden said behind me, sounding satisfied. "You'll be back."

I twisted out of my shoes and dropped to the ground below.

I spent the drive back to Maeve's trying to convince myself that none of it had been real. I hadn't seen my sisters, they hadn't nearly been cooked to death in a pot by witches. It was all a play, scripted by Ms. Burden. And, if Craig was right, acted out by the muses under her control.

I couldn't stop shaking, though. What if I was wrong, what if Ms. Burden was holding my sisters prisoner, waiting for me to come rescue them? I should assume the worst, I knew—that was always the best way to deal with her.

I remembered Ned, how he'd searched me out and given me Ms. Burden's address, and I realized that that had been part of her plan. She had created the trap, and I had walked into it with no more thought than a bird hopping into a cage.

I started imagining all the things she could do now, the new and clever punishments she could devise. Even the good moments she allowed my sisters would become a kind of torture; they would relax, would start to think themselves free, and then be brought face to face with the next horror. How many times had Ms. Burden made them dance between those two poles?

And what about the nightmare she had created? At first glance it was too ridiculous to take seriously; that cauldron, for example, had come out of a cartoon or a comic book. I had met a woman on the streets who claimed to be a witch, and I would swear to it that she had never boiled anyone in a pot.

Yes, I thought, but you saw the cartoon as a child and it went deep, and your sisters did too. Still, I couldn't help but think, once again, what a poor imagination Ms. Burden had, how much it relied on shopworn clichés.

And I would have been trapped there with them if not for Piper. I would have kept walking toward the fantasies Ms. Burden had conjured for me, and then, when it was too late, I would have boiled in that cauldron along with my sisters.

The thought terrified me so much my hands shook, and I veered into the opposite lane. I might have done anything to get out, given up any secret with barely a qualm.

When I got home I told Maeve about what I'd seen, and I emailed Craig. Craig agreed with me that Ms. Burden's muses must have created those scenes, though, like me, he didn't know whether my sisters had been real or illusion. But neither he nor Maeve had any ideas for me—and that too was part of Ms. Burden's plan, I knew, that I should feel this powerless, this anguished at being unable to do anything.

Several weeks passed, but they seemed like years, centuries. I thought of my sisters at every waking moment, and they came into my dreams as well. Amaranth had looked so unhappy, so bitter—what was this ordeal doing to her? Or to Semiramis, who'd seemed so terrified?

I thought about calling the police, but I didn't want to risk anyone else getting caught in her web. And if the police did rescue my sisters they'd almost certainly involve Child Protection Services, and we'd all be placed in different homes. Still, I kept the thought at the back of my mind, as a last resort.

I did nothing during those weeks, no housework, no correspondence, none of my own writing. I heated up frozen dinners instead of making my own, and Maeve and I ate them in silence. I walked through the house listlessly, turning over plans in my head, none of them with any hope of succeeding.

Now that I'd seen that Ms. Burden controlled the muses, I was more and more certain that she had killed Philip. She had once seemed to have the perfect alibi—she hadn't even been in the room when he'd died—but now I realized she could have given the muses their orders before we ever got there.

And I wondered about what she had said in the warehouse, the spell she'd used to make them do her bidding. I'd heard the word "bell" when she'd spoken, or I thought I had, and I remembered that story Craig had sent me, "The Woman and the Apple." It had contained something like a spell, the moon's rhyme that had sent the muses into exile: *Sound the tocsin, toll the bell,/ Down and down the children fell.* Could those words control the muses in other ways? What would happen if I recited them back to her?

It was a slim hope, as thin as a new moon. Still, I read and reread the story, and I memorized the poem. I looked up "tocsin"—"an alarm bell," my dictionary said—and added it to my list of words.

Did I have to ring an actual bell or just recite the poem? I hadn't heard any bells in the warehouse. Probably the word "bell" was there because it echoed the "l" in "toll" and "children" and "fell" . . . and I got lost in the sounds of the rhyme and had to force myself to climb back out into the real world.

Finally I came up with a plan, one cobbled together out of hopelessness and cunning. I remembered that Piper had been unaffected by Ms. Burden, and I thought that he might be free to act against her even if I couldn't. (And I wondered in passing why she hadn't been able to influence him. Was it because she hadn't been aware of him, and hadn't included him in her spell? Or because he wasn't human, and so outside her influence?)

I didn't know if he was reliable enough to follow my directions, or even understand them. But I couldn't come up with anything else, so it would have to do.

I need you to do something for me, I said to him. *Do you think you can be brave?*

Of course, he said.

We'll have to go back to the warehouse.

Instead of an answer, he curled up tightly within me. *I know you're afraid of her,* I said. *I'm afraid too. But I have to rescue my sisters, and I want to make sure she can't say anything, that she can't speak that spell. What I want you to do is, well, I want you to Leave me.*

What? he asked, startled.

Leave. And then go after her, knock her down, put your hand over her mouth, whatever it takes to stop her from saying anything. And if I fail, if I can't rescue them, you keep her there. Tell her that you won't let her go unless she does what we want.

I'd felt his wiry strength and was certain he could overpower her. Just to make sure, though, I asked, Do you think you can do that?

I felt him nod. I got in the car and drove up to Eugene. Neither of us said anything on the journey over. I was going over my plan, and he—well, I didn't know what he was thinking.

We pulled up at the back of the warehouse. The window I had climbed through was still open. Of course it was, I thought. She wouldn't have closed it, any more than a hunter would close a bear trap.

I walked around the warehouse, looking for other entrances. There weren't any, though, so I came back to the open window, took a deep breath, and climbed inside.

I set off with my back to the wall, hoping the echoes of my footsteps would be quieter there. To my dismay they sounded out across the warehouse, and a door opened on the other side.

Ms. Burden stepped out of a room and looked around. She hadn't spotted me, not yet. My sisters came out behind her. She said something to them and they started across the vast floor, their footsteps pounding like a heartbeat.

Beatriz saw me and called my name. Ms. Burden turned toward me. Our glances met and I felt a shudder, like two swords scraping against each other.

She began to speak. I could hear a few words, and I realized that I'd been right, that she was reciting the poem from the book. I felt stronger. I could do this.

A mist began to rise up near my sisters. *Go!* I said to Piper.

Nuh-uh, he said.

Dammit, you said you would! You have to stop her!

No.

You said you'd do it! You said you could be brave.

It's too dangerous out there to be brave.

Goddamn it! That's what bravery is.

He curled in on himself, shaking his head. I nearly fled back out the window, leaving my sisters behind for a second time. But I had one last chance, the moon's spell.

I spoke the words. The mist didn't dissolve, though; instead it thickened, became a cloud, stretched itself outward. It reached my sisters and flowed over them, erased them.

Something had gone wrong. Ms. Burden could use the poem, but for some reason I could not.

Maybe I'd said it incorrectly. I tried again, shouting this time, but nothing happened. Should I have brought a bell after all?

Something dry as dust brushed against my hand, and I looked down. A tendril of mist circled my arm and dragged me toward the cloud.

I tried to jerk away, but it was too strong. At the same time, the cloud swelled outward, folding me within it. Everything blurred. Whiteness formed around me, thick as a marshmallow. I couldn't see, couldn't think, could barely move.

Then the mist cleared, and I could take in my surroundings again.

I was in the warehouse, but this time my sisters were standing with me. I smiled, glad to see them, glad to be out of that thick, feature-less white. They didn't smile back, though. They looked uneasy.

I glanced around for Ms. Burden but didn't see her anywhere. "Come on!" I said. "We can go out the window."

They stared at me, not moving. "What are you doing?" I asked. "Hurry!"

I grabbed Semiramis by the arm and headed toward the window. She shrank back, shaking her head. I pulled her, harder this time, and she stumbled after me, her steps slow and reluctant. The others followed, moving at the same sluggish pace.

I wanted to shake her. What was wrong with everyone? "Come on!" I said.

Finally we reached the window. I tried to lift her, but she squirmed away. "Help me here!" I said to Beatriz.

"Look," Beatriz said, her voice flat.

"What?" I said.

"Look." She pointed out of the window.

The streets and cars and warehouses had disappeared. Instead, an expanse of dry grass stretched out to the horizon. A lion stood there, about a house's distance from us, watching us closely. A cluster of flies buzzed around it, and a bright sun shone in the sky, turning the lion and the grass to hot gold.

"It isn't real," Beatriz said dispiritedly. "None of it's real. And she does it over and over."

I'd been an idiot. None of my plans had worked. As if to prove to myself how stupid I'd been, I tried reciting the spell again.

The scene in front of me didn't change. The grass still rolled on before us, and the lion still stood there, its tail twitching lazily at the flies. And now I noticed that everything was surrounded by a slight haze, a glimmer of white.

"Is that a real lion?" I asked.

Beatriz said nothing. Probably it didn't matter. Nothing seemed to matter here.

I tried to talk to my sisters some more, to ask them questions or come up with some kind of plan, but they spoke very little. I could see why, of course; there was no point in talking to someone who might turn out to be a phantom. For that matter, I had no way of knowing if they were real or not.

After that escape attempt we mostly stayed separate, wrapped in our own thoughts. We ate and drank, and sometimes our parents ate and drank with us, and we went to our separate beds to sleep. I think the food and drink really existed, though I'm not sure about the beds.

I went back to look at the window, but it had disappeared. The entire wall felt like rough concrete, with no break where the window might have been. I returned to it several times, running my hand over it, but there was only the wall.

It was hard to measure time there. A day after I'd been trapped—or maybe a few days, or a week—a river of water began flowing across the floor. The river broadened out to a lake and the water rose higher and higher, reaching my knees, my waist.

There was no time to ask my sisters what was happening, or to try to help them. The warehouse filled quickly, and I started swimming. I swam for a long time, my arms and legs growing tired, and then suddenly I felt something overhead.

I looked up. I'd reached the ceiling, with only a thin gap of air between it and the water.

I swam frantically, looking for a way out. Then I saw someone falling away from me through the water. Semiramis.

I kicked down to reach her. My lungs grew desperate for air, and I surfaced again and hit my head on the ceiling. I took a deep gasping breath and dove into the water once more—and found myself flailing on the ground, my arms rising and falling.

I coughed, still feeling water in my lungs. Then I got to my knees and called out for Semiramis. She was lying near me, pale and still. I ran to her and grasped her shoulder, not sure if she was alive or dead. She rolled away from me and sobbed.

I looked at Beatriz. "What just happened?" I asked.

She shrugged. I twisted my hair to wring it out, but it was as dry as if it had never touched water. She'd been right—none of this was real.

"Where's Ms. Burden?" I asked. "Isn't she going to come out and gloat now? Tell us she'll stop all this if we do what she wants?"

"Sometimes she does. Sometimes she leaves us alone."

"She's having fun, I bet. She wants answers, but she likes torturing us in the meantime."

Beatriz shrugged again. I'd thought before that Ms. Burden enjoyed what she was doing. It would explain a lot: her ingenious punishments, the way she smiled at the wrong moments. It meant that she would probably never kill us, that she liked keeping us alive, playing with us. But it also meant that she might hold us here forever, whether we told her what she wanted or not.

The next day I heard that familiar sad, shivery cry, coming from nowhere and echoing throughout the warehouse. I looked around, startled, but the others seemed used to it.

The cry rose and then broke into a sob. "They're crying," Semiramis said.

"Who's crying?" I asked.

"Those—those things she captured. They miss where they came from—they're homesick."

"How do you know?"

She drifted away without answering, and it was left to Beatriz to explain, "We don't know, not really. But it makes sense."

So Ms. Burden had bound them to her, but she hadn't expected those sounds of grief, she'd had no idea what else they might do. No wonder she'd been frightened, along with the rest of us.

The cries would come at odd times, usually when I'd forgotten all about them. Piper hated them, and he would put his hands over his ears until they stopped. I still tried to get him to leave me, to go out into the warehouse and help us somehow. But he had grown more terrified, not less, since we'd gotten there, and he would shake his head and shiver, or promise to do it and then refuse at the last moment. I found myself wishing for a spell like Ms. Burden's, something to force him to obey me.

I don't know how long I was trapped in that place. I began to hope for something to break the monotony, and then, when Ms. Burden called up one of her illusions, to want nothing more than monotony again. Most of the time I was able to remind myself that it wasn't real, that she wouldn't harm us too badly. But sometimes fear overwhelmed me, and no amount of explanation would help.

One day we heard her footsteps heading toward us, heard her speaking her spell, and we braced ourselves for whatever horror would come next. The mist rose up, and a tall dim form with a lot of ropy arms shambled toward us, dragging some of its many legs behind it. Semiramis ran to hide behind me, and Beatriz moaned softly. Amaranth just looked at it and said, "Huh."

It came closer. It still seemed blurred, though I could see that its head looked wrong, cratered in on one side. Something like tendrils swam around its mouth.

"It isn't there, Ramis," I said. Then, as it came closer, I repeated that over and over. "It isn't there, it isn't there, it isn't there."

Ms. Burden said something, a sound of disgust or disappointment. The creature turned and stumbled away. The mist receded, leaving only thin gauze.

"What—what happened?" I asked.

No one answered. It didn't seem to matter to them. To me, though, it seemed like Ms. Burden had started something and then given up in frustration.

I looked around and realized that I couldn't see her anywhere. Maybe she'd finally understood that her illusions weren't working, maybe she'd gone away to think, or to figure out something else.

The warehouse looked brighter. The wall was broken up now, and light streamed through the window onto the floor. I went closer. My eyes watered from the sun. I squinted and made out some warehouses across the street, their windows glittering in the light.

"Beatriz," I said. She didn't say anything. "Beatriz! Look at this."

"What? Don't tell me you're going to try the window again."

"Look—the street's back. The street and all the warehouses."

"You know that isn't real."

"Yes, it is. It is! That's the way it looked when I got here."

She came over and joined me at the window. "What month is it?" she asked.

"What?" I realized I didn't know. "It's February. Or March, maybe."

"Isn't that too sunny for February?"

"I think she left," I said, ignoring her. "She left, and all her spells stopped working. We have to move fast—she might come back at any moment. Get the others over here."

I squeezed through the window and dropped to the other side. Then I stood there, feeling the sun on my skin. It smelled like spring, like new leaves and unfolding flowers. How long had it been since I'd smelled anything but stale air?

But I had to hurry. Beatriz had shepherded the others to the window, and now she handed them down to me and then jumped to the ground herself.

"Come on!" I said.

We ran for the car. It was where I'd left it, and my keys were still in my pocket. We got inside, and I sped away from the warehouse.

I was still having trouble seeing. There was too much to look at, and for a while I could only pay attention to small things, especially as we got closer to the center of town. I heard cars honking and people laughing and planes flying overhead, saw traffic lights and houses painted in different colors and leafy trees swaying in the air. Everything seemed clothed in brightness after the dim light of the warehouse. I laughed out loud.

When I finally looked at the road I saw that I was heading toward our old house instead of Aunt Maeve's. Well, that was all right, I thought. We could stop there and pick up some things for my sisters.

I turned around to look at them. "How are you doing?" I asked.

They said nothing. They each had the same expression, blank

and uncaring. Probably they hadn't realized yet that we'd left the warehouse, that they were free.

I followed the familiar turnings and pulled up in front of the house. We got out and walked up the path, and I unlocked the door. The Photoshopped portraits in the hall seemed to shine out from their places on the wall.

I went farther in, going carefully. "Hello!" Beatriz called out.

"Quiet," I said. "There's no one here."

"We're home!" Beatriz said.

A creaking sound came from inside the house, someone walking toward us. "Who—who is it?" I said.

"Oh, come on, Ivy," Beatriz said. "Don't be so stupid. You know who it is."

She started laughing. Philip came toward us down the hallway. Then they were all laughing, Philip and Beatriz and Amaranth and Semiramis, overcome with hilarity.

"She believed it!" Beatriz said. "She believed all of it!"

Tears shimmered on my eyelids. How could Beatriz be so mean?

"Like Kate would really let her go like that," Amaranth said.

"Fell right into the trap," Philip said.

"I mean, we knew she wasn't very bright," Beatriz said. "But I never thought she'd fall for this."

I was really crying now. "Come on, Beatriz, that's not fair," I said.

"And now she's crying," she said.

But it wasn't her speaking. She wavered in the air, growing more and more transparent, and then disappeared. The house vanished, and I was back at the warehouse. No, not back—I'd never left it.

Ms. Burden stood in front of me. "I'll give you something to cry about," she said. Then she too disappeared.

CHAPTER 19

A lot of things I'd wondered about made sense now. I'd driven to our old house and not Maeve's because Ms. Burden didn't know where Maeve lived, and hadn't been able to create an illusion of the place. And she wasn't that familiar with the streets from here to our house, so she could only show me one distinct thing after another, a car, a tree. And of course the Photoshopped pictures had stood out from everything around me—she had created them, after all.

The more I thought about it the dumber I felt. I'd missed so many clues. There had even been a halo of light around everything, like all of Ms. Burden's illusions, but I'd thought it had come from the bright sun or the joy of freedom, some idiot thing like that.

I'd been trying to get my sisters to open up, but now I stopped talking to them completely. How could I, after all the cruel things they'd said to me? It took me a stupidly long time to realize that they probably hadn't even been there, that they'd been conjured up along with everything else.

I asked them, of course, but they looked at me with dull incomprehension, as if they had no idea what I was talking about. Probably they didn't, I thought. One day was the same as all the rest to them. I'd ask them when we got out of here, if we ever got out.

I even felt desperate enough to try Piper again, but he refused me as he always had. More than ever I wished I had a spell like Ms. Burden's, something to make him do what I wanted. To turn him inside-out, as Craig had said. Reverse him.

Reverse him. Where had those words come from? Something I'd read recently, but what? I thought about them over and over, sure they were important somehow.

Finally, one day, I remembered. They'd been in "The Woman and the Apple." At the end, after the muses had been exiled by the moon, they "hope that someday she will reverse her decree and take them back."

"Reverse" was a strange word to use there, I remember thinking that when I'd read the story. The moon could cancel her decree, or revoke it. If she reversed it it would, well, it would be backwards, or upside-down.

Semiramis cried out, and I heard footsteps booming out across the warehouse. I looked up quickly to see Ms. Burden coming toward us, calling the mist as she went. I moved in front of Semiramis, bracing myself for her next attack.

But at the same time I knew that I was close to something, that I had to follow my thoughts to the end. I had to hurry, though. Ms. Burden was coming closer. The thing we'd seen before, the one with all those arms and legs, formed out of the mist and shuffled toward us, and I could feel Semiramis shaking.

"Fell children the down and down," I said, working it out as I spoke. "Bell the toll, tocsin the sound."

The mist around Ms. Burden thinned, then blew away like smoke. I turned quickly to the window. The illusion covering it had disappeared, and I ran over and peered out. A dull sky, as gray as oatmeal, looked down on a street filled with warehouses.

It had worked. I'd reversed the spell, said it backwards.

"Over here!" I called out to Beatriz. "Look! This time it's real, I swear to you."

Beatriz didn't move.

"Come on! Her spell's useless—I know how to fight it now. Hurry up—we have to go!"

I went back to my sisters and tried to lift Semiramis. "No!" she said, pulling away from me. "No, I don't want to go. There's—there's spiders!"

I hesitated. I'd thought I'd escaped before, after all. I was losing my ability to tell truth from falsehood. What if Ms. Burden was creating all of this as well?

She was almost upon us, so close I could hear her saying the words of the spell. I recited the counter-spell. What would happen now? Would we go on like this, spell and counter-spell, until one of us dropped with exhaustion?

I gave up on Semiramis and started pulling Amaranth toward the window. Then, for the second time, I felt Piper leave me. He darted toward Ms. Burden, moving faster than I had ever seen him, and he knocked her down and sat on her. She was still speaking, and he pinched her lips together with his long greeny-brown fingers.

I looked back at my sisters. Beatriz was staring at Piper. Whatever she saw must have convinced her, because she hurried over to help me. We wrestled Amaranth over the windowsill together, and I went back for Semiramis.

"No!" she screamed, backing away from us. "No!"

"There's nothing out there, Ramis," I said. "I made it all go away. Come on, Rantha's waiting for you."

Semiramis went limp. She still didn't trust us, I could tell, but she had given up, had decided to accept whatever happened next. We led her to the window and dropped her into Amaranth's waiting arms. Beatriz climbed out after her.

"It's the green car!" I shouted after them. "It's unlocked!"

I turned back to Ms. Burden. She raised herself up to struggle with Piper, but he forced her back down with his wiry strength. Then he pulled and prodded her until she stood up, pinning her arms back and shoving her through the warehouse so that we stood face to face.

There she was, this woman I'd searched for for so long. Who had torn my family apart, who had terrorized us, who had killed our father. Who'd lied and cheated her way into our lives.

I had never felt anything like the rage that overtook me now. I trembled with the force of it. I wanted to beat her, kick her, knock her senseless. I couldn't do any of that, though. I had to get back to Semiramis, to the rest of my family.

I spat on her. I said, "If you ever come after any of us again, I promise I will kill you."

Piper jumped into me. Ms. Burden's eyes widened. "You—you had—all this time—"

"Shut up," I said. "Remember what I told you."

I climbed out the window. I could hear Ms. Burden coming after me, ignoring everything I had said to her. I dropped to the ground and hurried to my car, taking the keys out of my pocket as I ran. I made sure that all my sisters had gotten inside the car, and leapt into the driver's seat.

I turned the key. The engine groaned a few times and then fell silent. How long had the car sat out on the street, while I was trapped inside the warehouse?

I tried again. The noises from the engine went on for longer before finally trailing off. A whimper of fear came from the back seat, one of my sisters. I swore and slapped the steering wheel. I should wait, I knew, or I'd flood the engine.

In the rearview mirror, I caught a glimpse of someone getting into the car behind us. I turned the key and slammed on the gas pedal. The engine caught and I pulled away.

The other car started up. I glanced up at the rearview mirror and saw a gold Toyota, with a windshield so dark I couldn't see who was driving.

I knew who it was, though. I couldn't let her follow me to Maeve's house. A plan came to me, a very dangerous plan, but I couldn't think of anything else.

All right, I said to Piper. *You can drive.*

Piper drove faster than I'd ever dared. He darted into side streets, spun in circles in intersections, ran red lights. Once he took a turn so fast, the car went up on two wheels. And all the while he was laughing and shouting triumphantly inside my head.

He made so much noise that it took me a while to realize that Semiramis was crying in the back seat. I glanced away from the road to look at the others. Amaranth sat without moving, clutching the seatbelt where it crossed her chest. Beatriz, next to me, was hanging on to the armrest.

"What are you doing?" Beatriz said. "You're going to get us killed!"

"We have to get away from her," I said.

Piper careened into the opposite lane to pass a slow-moving truck. "Get back!" Beatriz said.

I did it! Piper shouted, moving back into our lane. *I'm brave, yes I am! I stopped her! Let's see her say that spell with my fingers clamping down on her mouth!*

Quiet, I said to him.

You said I wasn't brave, but I am, yes I am! You saw me, I made her stop talking!

Yeah, when I didn't need you anymore. I reversed her spell, you saw that. It isn't brave if the danger's already gone.

He took no notice. *I faced her down and fought her, knocked her to the floor! An epic battle, to be sung throughout the ages!*

The sign for the highway came up in front of us "Is she still there?" I asked Beatriz. "Ms. Burden. It's a gold car with a dark windshield."

She turned around. "No."

I took one last look behind me. Then I took control of Piper and got on the onramp, slowing the car to the speed limit.

Semiramis had stopped crying. "It's all right," I said to her. "You're safe now."

She didn't say anything. Then, after a long while, she stirred in the back seat and asked, "Is this real?"

God, I thought. I felt so sad for her, thinking about what she'd endured. I was asking the same question myself, though. It seemed real, or more real than the last time I'd tried to escape. Semiramis had weighed a lot more when I'd lifted her up, for one thing. I was seeing everything whole instead of in parts, and the haze that had clung to Ms. Burden's illusions was gone.

But I couldn't escape the thought that we were still doing her bidding. No doubt my sisters felt the same, only much stronger. Could they even come back from where they'd been, return to the real world? Semiramis was—I had to think a while—eleven years old now, Amaranth thirteen, Beatriz fifteen.

"Oh, Ramis," Beatriz said, turning toward her. "Of course it's real."

"Is that really Ivy?"

My eyes filled with tears, but I tried to keep my voice steady. "Yeah. Yeah, I'm Ivy."

"Where were you?" Semiramis asked. "Why didn't you get us before this?"

Guilt speared my heart, and I looked at her in the mirror. She was staring straight ahead, blinking like someone who had come out of a dark room into sunlight. Amaranth seemed to be asleep, and Beatriz was still holding on to the armrest.

They weren't ready to hear the whole story. I'd have to get them settled, give them some food, let them get used to being back in the real world.

"I couldn't find you," I said. "I'll tell you everything when we get to Maeve's house."

Beatriz looked at me, interest showing on her face for the first time. "Maeve? Did you find her?"

"Yeah," I said.

"Why didn't you say anything?"

"She might have heard me," I said. "Ms. Burden."

Amaranth and Semiramis were both asleep by the time we reached the house. Semiramis came awake with a gasp, and Amaranth opened her eyes and looked around sullenly, as if all places were alike to her, and there was nothing to be hoped for from any of them.

Then they saw Maeve's house. They each managed a tiny smile, and I felt my heart lift for the first time since I started looking for them.

Maeve came to meet us as I opened the door. "Oh, my goodness!" she said, putting her hand to her chest. "Where on earth were you? I was so worried!"

"I'll tell you later," I said. "I have to take care of my sisters first." I turned to them and asked, "What do you want? Are you hungry?"

"Sleep," Semiramis said.

They all felt the same way. Beatriz took the couch, my old bed, and the other two slept in Maeve's bed. We were going to have to move things around, buy some new furniture—that was, if we were going to stay here.

I felt tired as well, but I had to talk to Maeve. "How did you manage while I was gone?" I asked, as we sat at the dining table.

"Not that well, really. I ran out of microwave dinners, and that other food you bought—well, I didn't know how to put any of it together. You can't go away like this and not tell me, Ivy."

She didn't want to reveal how much she depended on me, I saw, and her weakness had made her angry. "I didn't mean to," I said. "She trapped me—Ms. Burden. Trapped me with my sisters. How long was I gone?"

Maeve thought a while. "A week, I think."

A week? It had seemed much more than that, an eternity. I told her what had happened at the warehouse and how we'd gotten free, and at the end I asked her if my sisters could stay here for a while.

"Well, of course you can. But you can't just go away like this, you know. I was nearly out of my mind with worry."

"I won't," I said. "I promise."

My sisters all slept for a long time. Semiramis cried out once during a nightmare and I went and sat by her, talking to her softly and stroking her hair.

Over the next few days they moved as if in a dream. They wandered through the house, looking at each other in amazement, reaching out to touch a book or a chair as if they thought it would disappear.

At times I felt the same way. I'd be cleaning, or cooking dinner, and I'd stop and wonder if this would be the moment when it all dissolved around me, the walls and stove and lamps and chairs, and the true nature of my surroundings would be revealed. Or I'd brush against something, and I'd feel that dry, smooth tendril sliding along my arm, like something ancient made out of dust.

Sometimes, though, I wondered if I could ever understand what my sisters had gone through. I'd only been there a week, after all. And they'd been trapped for how long—a month, a year?

Finally, one evening at dinner, Semiramis felt strong enough to speak up. "Why didn't you come get us?"

"And where did you go when you left?" Beatriz asked.

"All right," I said. "Let me start at the beginning."

I told them about Piper first. I was prepared for disbelief, but even Beatriz seemed to accept everything without question. Well, they'd seen him at the warehouse, and they'd met those other muses, however corrupted those muses had become.

"Why didn't you tell me?" Beatriz asked. "I knew there was something different about you around then."

"Would you have believed me?" I asked.

"Sure. You were acting pretty weird."

I expected her to go on, to say, "weirder than usual." She didn't, though. We still hadn't found our way back to our old habits, our own rhythms.

I explained why Ms. Burden had wanted to know where Maeve lived, how she'd been desperate for her own muse. Then I took a deep breath and told them why I'd had to run away.

"No, you didn't," Amaranth said when I had finished. "You didn't have to. You should have stayed with us. You knew what she was like."

"Well, but I thought you'd be okay, that she'd leave you alone. I was the one she was interested in, and I thought that if I left she'd just give up. And I was tired of always being the responsible one. I wanted to have some fun for a change."

"And look what happened!" Amaranth said. "We needed you, and you—you just went away. You left us."

She was right, of course. I'd abandoned them over and over, ever since the beginning, when I'd left them at Maeve's house and found Piper in the grove.

"Well, was it?" Beatriz asked.

"Was it what?"

"Fun."

"Yeah," I said. "Sort of."

I skipped that part, though; I didn't think they were old enough for it. And I didn't tell them how Ned and Ms. Burden had forged Philip's will. If they knew about that they might realize that Ms. Burden had caused Philip's death, and I wanted to keep them ignorant of that a while longer. They'd had enough unhappiness already.

It only remained to tell them Craig's story, how he had met Ms. Burden in Greece, how she'd trapped the muses, how she'd realized she could use them even though they terrified her. As I spoke I looked at Beatriz, trying to bring her with me into our shared past.

I'd lost her, though; I'd lost all of them. Now that they'd escaped the warehouse they were only interested in putting as much distance between themselves and her as they could. They didn't care how she'd worked everything out; they wanted to forget all of it, everything they'd had to endure.

I sent an email to Craig, telling him about the escape from the warehouse. "That's fantastic," he wrote back. "And pretty brave, I have to say. Do you think you freed the muses or did Kate have time to trap them again?"

I hadn't even thought about that. I wrote him back, saying I didn't know, but that I was pretty sure they hadn't gotten away.

"It would be good if Claudio was free again, and the others with him," his next email said. "I'm going to go to Greece and see if they're back at Mount Helicon. Do you want to come with me? I have enough frequent flyer miles to pay for your trip."

Of course I wanted to come with him, to visit Greece, see the Valley of the Muses Craig had talked about, the pool and the temple. But I had to stay with my sisters, and I said no, reluctantly.

A week later I got another email from him. "They aren't at the grove, unfortunately. Even worse, two of them have died since the last time I was there.

"I don't know how much you know about them, so forgive me if I'm telling you things you've already heard. They have children very seldom, so whenever two of them form a pairing the rest of the grove rejoices, because they're more likely to have a child if they stay together, do what we would think of as settling down. The muses here had hoped for a long time that Claudio and Talia would find each other again, and now that both of them are gone, along with so many of the others, they seem to have lost heart.

"Their deaths aren't like ours—they can somehow will themselves to die, if they want to. I think that's what happened here. And I think—I fear—that there will be more deaths. Their population has been dwindling over the years—fewer and fewer people know about them and seek them out. And what will happen if they're gone?

"So it's more important than ever that we find Claudio and free him, and that he joins Talia again. Claudio told me once that he and Talia never had children, but that doesn't matter so much—their union had animated the others, and that seemed to make them more fertile.

"Maybe we can figure something out together when I get back."

For the first time I wondered how the muses had worked throughout history. They couldn't have helped everyone who'd written a book or composed a symphony; there would have to be thousands of them to do that. But some people had soared so high above the rest that they must have been inspired: Shakespeare and Bach and Dante and Tolkien, maybe. And the presence of a grove would explain why geniuses sometimes ran in families, and why creativity had flourished in some places, Renaissance Florence and Elizabethan England, for example. Had Lennon and McCartney each recognized the muse in the other?

I remembered the book Maeve had lent me, the *Theogony*, and how the muses had appeared to Hesiod while he was shepherding his lambs. No one back then had thought how strange it was that a mere shepherd had started chanting poetry about the gods; maybe people knew more about muses in those days. And of course there had been all those poets and artists and playwrights in ancient Greece.

I read Craig's email again. He seemed so sure I'd help him, and he'd certainly put enough pressure on me to do so: if we couldn't find her we'd only be responsible for the loss of genius around the world. But I couldn't do anything about that; my focus had narrowed down to staying home with my sisters, and keeping Ms. Burden from finding us.

And I was far too busy to do anything else. I bought beds and towels and clothing, and I moved things around so we all had places to sleep, Maeve in her bedroom, my sisters in her study, me on the couch in the living room. I learned how to make dinners for more than two people, and got up at night when I heard Semiramis cry out. I got them to a doctor, wanting to make sure they hadn't suffered any physical trauma along with all the mental ones.

Every so often I'd come across my sisters sitting together in silence, each of them staring with unfocused eyes at a different spot. It had horrified me at first, seeing them like that, but after a while I almost got used to it. I had to let them be, at least for a time: they were retreating into their own worlds, afraid to walk the paths back to reality in case those paths disappeared beneath them.

I'd asked Maeve again if she minded having us here, and assured her that we could leave as soon as we found somewhere to go. "No, it's all right," she said. "I enjoy having you, all of you. It reminds me of when I was young, when your grandparents came out from Albany, and what a great help they were to me. The authorities had found me wandering naked in the streets, you know." She saw my expression and laughed. "Don't worry—I won't do it again."

I hadn't been worried about that, though. What I'd thought was, Damn, so Dr. Chapman had been right all along.

"Well, but we're spending a lot of your money," I said, wanting to make sure she knew what she was getting into.

"Oh, that's all right. I certainly have enough. And the work you're doing for me would cost me twice as much, if I had to hire someone."

She didn't really understand her finances, though. She had a lot for one person, but the four of us would cut things very close. Still, I thought I could make our life here work, if we were careful.

There were other problems I couldn't solve as easily. One day I came home from grocery shopping to find that someone had torn through the study, ripping the bedsheets, breaking vases, emptying out all the drawers and throwing everything on the floor. Pages from different books were scattered across the room, some of them lying in puddles of water from the vases.

I'd seen my sisters in the living room, sitting and staring at nothing, and I went back there. "Did someone break into the house?" I asked.

Beatriz wrested her eyes away from her spot and looked at me. "What?" she said.

"Did someone break in? Because the study's been completely trashed."

"Oh, yeah. Rantha did that."

"Rantha? Why?"

Now it was Amaranth's turn to break eye contact with whatever she was looking at. "I don't know," she said.

"What do you mean, you don't know?" I said. "You must have had a reason."

"Okay. Because I felt like it."

I didn't know what to do. Should I punish her? But I wasn't her parent, and she had already been through enough . . .

"She was screaming when she did it," Beatriz said. "Really loud."

I actually felt encouraged when she said that. She was tattling on her sisters again, a good sign.

"Well, go clean it up," I said to Amaranth. "And don't do it again."

She sighed and stood up. Another good sign—a few weeks ago she'd ignored me completely.

Why had she done it, though? Had she wanted to reassure herself that the things around her were real? Or had she just gotten so frustrated she couldn't think of anything else to do? They'd been in the warehouse for so long . . .

How long *had* it been? Enough time had passed that I thought I could ask Beatriz, but she didn't know. Ms. Burden had told them she was taking them for an outing and they'd piled in the car, and the next thing they knew they were back at home with our parents, or so they'd thought.

That was all she could remember for a while. Slowly, as we talked it over, we figured out that they'd been taken to the warehouse sometime in June, after school ended. The "girl" Maeve had sent to visit the house had gone there in August.

They'd been there for nine months, then. Nine months of hope, of coming home to Philip and Jane, and then crushing disappointment. Over and over, until finally they came to disbelieve everything, reality itself. I couldn't imagine it.

The mention of school reminded me that they'd have to go back when they felt up to it. How would I explain their long absence? Would Ms. Burden be able to find them somehow, if the school had a record of them? And what about college? Even if they wanted to go, I knew we couldn't afford it.

Then I remembered that we did have money for college; Philip's lawyer, Mr. McLaren, had told us so. And I realized that I was about to turn eighteen at the end of this year, and might be coming into my inheritance.

So I made an appointment and set out for his office. I knew this could be dangerous, that he could still be in contact with Ms. Burden, but I wasn't planning on giving him more information than I had to.

CHAPTER 20

Mr. McLaren seemed wary of me at first, and I couldn't really blame him. We sat around the small table, and he asked, "How is Ms. Burden? Are you settling in with her?"

"She's—well—she isn't our guardian anymore," I said. "In fact, I don't want her to know I was here."

He frowned. "I don't know about the legality of that. Your father's will was very clear—"

"The will was a forgery."

He sat back, clearly disappointed in me. "I know you were unhappy with the choice of Ms. Burden as your guardian, but I doubt very much it was forged. I showed you those signatures, didn't I, your father's and the witnesses?"

"I met the man who forged them, actually."

He took his glasses off, put them on again. "You did? Can you produce him in court?"

"Well, no. I mean, of course not. If he admitted to the forgery he'd go to jail."

"I see."

I felt sorry for him, a bystander caught up in something he wouldn't understand, or even believe. "Look," I said. "I'm not here to talk about that. What I want to know is, well, last time you said that Ms. Burden would be my guardian until I came of age. So when is that?"

He had our folder in front of him, and he took out the will and shuffled through it. "So the inheritance comes to you when you turn eighteen, it says here," he said finally. "A fourth of the money in the account."

"Great. Do you know how much it is?"

"I'm named as an executor of the will, so I could find out if you like. Though it'll be less than it was—Ms. Burden had access to that money for necessities, the upkeep of the house and your clothing and education and so forth."

"Yeah. Please."

He went to the desk and dialed a number, the bank probably, and spoke on the phone for a long time. I couldn't get much from his side of the conversation, only that he was being shunted from one employee to another, and growing increasingly angry. "Do you have records of those transactions?" he said. He paused, then said, "Yes, well, I hope you held on to everything you have in connection with this account. I'm going to want copies of every email, every record, every piece of paper."

He hung up. He'd written something on a legal pad, and he brought it with him to the table and sat down. "So the amount in the account is now forty-seven dollars and fifty-six cents," he read.

He looked up at me. I think he expected me to become outraged, or hysterical, but this didn't even seem as bad as some of the things Ms. Burden had done.

He took off his glasses. He put his elbows on the table and pressed the heels of his hands to his eyes, and he sat without moving for a long time. "Oh, God," he said finally. "Oh, my God."

"I'm not blaming you," I said. "That's what she's like. I did try to warn you."

"Oh, God," he said again. He lifted his head from his hands and looked at me blearily. His mustache was trembling like a frightened animal. Then he seemed to think of something, and his expression brightened. "There's one positive thing, though—this ends her guardianship for good. So that solves your problem, doesn't it? You never have to see her again."

"Not really. She's still looking for us."

"What? Why?"

I shook my head. "I can't tell you."

"Look, Ivy. She's committed a crime here, and I have to report her to the authorities. So the more I know about this the better." I said nothing, and he went on. "Or, well, you could report her."

I felt briefly optimistic at that. Then I remembered her cleverness, her ability to get people on her side. She would lie about why she'd had to spend all that money, and they would believe her.

I probably looked miserable, so he continued, explaining what was going to happen next—or what would have happened if we were a more normal family. "And when she's gone, the court will appoint a new guardian. Not for you, because you're eighteen, but for your sisters."

They already had a guardian, of course—Aunt Maeve. But I couldn't tell him that either: Ms. Burden was looking for us, and I couldn't give him or anyone a way to find us. Well, I'd worry about that when it came to it.

Then I remembered that we were looking for her too, or Craig was, trying to find Talia. I decided to take a chance. "Do you have Ms. Burden's address?" I asked.

He hesitated. Had I asked him to do something illegal? "I have to find her if I'm going to report her," I said.

"Oh, what the hell," he said finally. He took a page from the folder and showed it to me, some official paper she had signed to become our guardian.

I shook my head. "That's our house, that address. She isn't there anymore."

He rifled through the folder. "That's all I have. I'm sorry."

"It's all right."

"So I'll look into what you have to do next and get back to you. Just leave your information with my secretary."

I tried not to show my relief. He'd given me a way to disappear again, to break loose from the whole sticky web of the law. Of course I wasn't going to tell his secretary where we lived.

"Sure," I said. "And thanks a lot."

"Well," he said. "I wish I could have done more for you."

I left the room, sauntered past the secretary, and waved her a cheery goodbye.

I felt more pessimistic when I got outside, though. I hadn't found out where Ms. Burden lived, and now we were hundreds of thousands of dollars poorer. I felt more upset about not having gotten her address, though. You could always make more money, but I'd wanted to tell Craig where she was.

Then I remembered something Craig had said, a comment I hadn't paid attention to at the time: that he had found her by looking up property records. Somehow she had gotten a hold of our house, along with everything else. I could sue her for that, maybe . . . But all I wanted was to live a peaceful life, and stay as far away from her as possible.

A few days later, on April first, I got a letter telling me I'd sold my first poem. I remember the date because I thought it was an April Fool's Day prank at first, but also, and more importantly, because it marked the day that I got validation from an editor, that I became a writer.

I'd used a pseudonym on the unlikely chance that Ms. Burden read obscure poetry magazines, and I'd gotten a post office box near Maeve's for my submissions. They offered me ten dollars for the poem, and I had the rueful thought that I'd only have to sell tens of thousands more to make up for what we'd lost. I didn't tell my sisters anything about our finances, though. I didn't want them to worry, just rest and recuperate.

We went out to celebrate at a restaurant in Woodbine, spending far more than the magazine had given me for the poem. For once I didn't care. It was an exciting day for me, as I said, and I wanted to indulge myself.

My sisters still seemed a little shaky, looking around them with worried expressions, stopping in the middle of sentences. For the most part, though, we appeared to be a normal family, talking and . . . well, they weren't yet laughing, but they'd smile every so often, especially Semiramis. Even Maeve had come out with us, and seemed to be enjoying herself.

Then everything in front of me skewed somehow, and I had the horrible thought that none of it was real. The people around us, the food we were eating, the music playing in the background—all of it was an illusion. A waitress called out to someone in the kitchen, and

I waited for her to vanish, for everything to drop away like a mask and reveal the reality of the warehouse beneath it.

Nothing happened, though. I reached out for my soft drink and held it tightly, feeling the cold condensation on the outside of the glass. Beatriz said something, and everything seemed normal again.

Mostly normal, anyway. Amaranth looked sullen, though I couldn't remember if she'd been that way all through the meal or if it was a response to something someone had said. Of all my sisters she seemed to be having the hardest time returning to life outside the warehouse. She rarely spoke, and when she did it was one or two words only, mostly answers to questions.

The next morning at breakfast she seemed more civil, actually talking to the rest of us. After a few minutes of conversation, though, she got to what she really wanted. "Can we go see that grove?" she asked.

"What grove?" I said.

"You know, the one you told us about. Where you met Piper."

I'd never gone back to the grove, not since that first time. I'd had a lot of work to do, of course, but there was another reason for not returning, one I didn't like to think about. I still had a vivid memory of Maeve swimming naked in the lake, all these years later. I was afraid that I'd be taken by the same compulsion, that I'd strip off all my clothes, all my decorum, and dive headlong into the water. I'd finally come to a solid place after years of living like Piper, and I no longer wanted to give myself up to every impulse.

And, I had no desire to expose my sisters to the muses. I didn't want to take the chance that one or more of them would find themselves taken over, their lives utterly changed.

"Maybe later," I said, hoping she'd forget about it. "When I have some free time."

"Why not now?"

"Because I'm busy. Maybe you haven't noticed, but someone has to clean up around here, and shop and cook for you, and—"

"You know what I think? I think you don't want any competition."

"What?"

"You want to be the only writer around here, the only one who does anything fun."

"Fun?" I said, disbelieving.

"Maybe someone else wants to be creative too. Ramis told me she wants to be a painter."

"You do?" I asked Semiramis.

Semiramis nodded. She seemed about to say something, but Amaranth spoke over her. "And I want to be a dancer," Amaranth said. "And I want to go to that grove."

"Later, I said."

Her face turned hard, and I knew she was about to say something hurtful. "Did you ever think that you don't really have any talent at all?" she said. "That the poem you sold wasn't even yours, that Piper wrote it for you? That you wouldn't be anything without him?"

"It doesn't work like that," I said. How could I explain to her about breaking in, breaking through, stealing divine fire? "I write those poems, and I work damn hard on them. A muse takes your strengths, the things you can do, and shows you how to go beyond, how to see—"

"So you admit that the poem wouldn't have been as good without his help," she said. "That you might not have sold it without him."

"I never said anything like that."

"Yes you did, you said—"

"I'm not going to discuss this. And you're just going to have to wait to go to the grove, until there's time."

"What if I look for it myself?"

"Go right ahead," I said. "Don't fall in the river."

After that conversation I began to think more and more about the grove. One afternoon I left the house without telling anyone and took the path through the woods. I was worried that I wouldn't remember the way, but of course Piper still knew it and could lead me there.

After all these years it seemed barely changed. It was still autumn there, the leaves fluttering like a shaken cloth of gold. The sprites—the muses—still capered through the trees, still made music on their pipes, still spun down the waterfall into the lake. Several were running and laughing, their hair and scarves trailing out behind them.

I had no desire to take my clothes off, or to go swimming in the lake. It takes everyone differently, Maeve had said. I sat down on a rock and looked out across the water. The others looked at me sidelong from their long eyes, even seemed to approve of my presence, but they kept to what they were doing.

"Is Talia here?" I asked Piper.

He shrugged. Did he know her by another name?

One of them came closer to me, looking shy. Her skin was a greeny-brown, like tree bark, and her dark hair shone green where the sun touched it. She wore a tight red cap dotted with white, the colors of a mushroom, and a necklace of leaves and red berries hung from her neck.

Craig had said he'd talked to them and so, feeling foolish, I said hello.

She looked sidelong at me, then laughed and said, "Hello."

"Should I bring my sister Amaranth here?" I asked.

She laughed again, and skittered away like a leaf blown in the wind. But she pushed someone else closer, and I repeated my question.

"Well, does she meet the qualifications?" this new one said. It might have been male or female; it wore a green and yellow striped knitted cap, like a nightcap, that fell to its feet.

"What qualifications?" I asked.

"Does she like strawberries?" one of the others asked. Her pointed ears lifted, like an alert animal's.

They crowded around me now, shouting out questions. "Does she have a cat with six toes?" "Has she ever dreamt of a train station?" "Can she touch her nose with her tongue?"

I gave up. But now that I'd started them talking they kept on, making more suggestions and laughing. The subject changed and changed again, to the music, to something that had happened a year ago, or a hundred years, to whether there was a word for a leaf that had changed overnight from green to bronze.

I listened to them, fascinated, hoping to learn something more about who they were and how they chose the people they did. They never said anything serious, though, and after a while I thought about my chores and headed home.

I went back to the grove a lot after that, whenever I had a free moment, always making sure that no one could follow me. They didn't seem to talk much among themselves, and sometimes I just sat there without saying anything. It was calming to watch these creatures who lived for the moment, who never worried about what to make for dinner, or how to pay for college.

One day, when I'd just come into the grove, I heard a branch crack behind me. I looked back into the woods, alarmed, thinking that Ms. Burden had finally found us. The woods stayed as they were, unmoving. Then someone giggled.

I hadn't heard my sisters laugh in a long time, but despite that I knew it was Semiramis. "All right," I called out. "Who's there?"

Another, louder giggle. "I know you're there, Ramis," I said.

Some branches shook and a few leaves dropped to the ground, like falling gold. Semiramis stepped out, laughing. "You never even saw us!" she said. "We were behind you this whole time."

"Us?"

Beatriz came out after her, and then Amaranth. "I told you I'd find it," Amaranth said.

"Wow!" Semiramis said. "Look at them!"

Beatriz and Amaranth were staring as well, their eyes wide. One of the sprites was playing a set of bells shaped like flowers, and another stamped his shoeless feet in time to the music. Still others had picked up the rhythm and were dancing.

And nothing had happened to any of my sisters so far. It might even have been good for them to come here, I thought.

"So how do you do it?" Amaranth said. "You just stand here and let one of them choose you?"

"That's what happened to me," I said. "Or you could leave them a gift—some people do that."

"Well, you should have told me that before I came here," she said. "I would have brought something. What do people usually give them?"

"I didn't know you were going to follow me, did I?"

One of the muses jumped down from a branch and danced toward us, smiling, her tangled hair streaming out behind her. Her smile grew wider, became a grin that nearly reached her ears, and the circlet of flowers on her head slipped over one eye. I couldn't help laughing myself as she came, at the giddy joy that seemed to radiate out from her. Piper laughed too, within me.

She flipped over into a somersault and leapt back to her feet. She landed in front of Semiramis, and they stared at each other, standing as still as mirror images. The sprite reached out cautiously, and Semiramis did the same.

Amaranth pushed herself between them. "No, wait!" she said. "It's supposed to be me, not her!"

The sprite looked at Amaranth. Then she laughed and somersaulted backwards toward the trees, and soon became lost among the leaves and branches.

Semiramis blinked as if waking up. "No, she was—she was mine," she said. "She was going to choose me, she said she'd show me things . . ." She looked out into the trees, searching for her.

"You!" Amaranth said scornfully.

Semiramis turned back to Amaranth. "I told you—I want to be a painter. And she was going to do it, she was going to pick me, and then you came over and spoiled everything—"

"She wasn't—"

"I hate you! I'm never talking to you ever again! You ruined everything, just because you're jealous. And they're never going to pick you, never ever, because you're stupid and none of them like you."

"That's enough," I said, speaking loudly to drown out whatever Amaranth was yelling back at her. "See, this is why I didn't want to take you—I knew there would be trouble. We're going home now."

"I'm not going anywhere," Amaranth said.

"Me either," Semiramis said.

"Fine," I said. "Don't be late for dinner."

Life at home became a maze of difficulties. Amaranth and Semiramis had been very close, but now they each nursed a feeling of betrayal and stopped speaking to each other. Whenever they had something to say they pretended they were really talking to one of us: "Ramis forgot to clean up her room again. It's really hard living with such a pig."

Amaranth went to the grove every day. She took her prized possessions and laid them out on the shore of the lake; I saw them when I visited, looking like the sad remains of a shipwreck. She stole one of the apples someone had given Aunt Maeve, not ivory but wood painted white, with a minutely carved scene of a town hall meeting within it. The muses rejected it along with all her other gifts, and I quietly took it back to the house.

About four months after they first visited the grove, Amaranth told me she wanted to leave home. "Really?" I said. I tried to treat her gently, to avoid making fun of her, but I failed as often as I succeeded. "Where would you go?"

"Where did you go?" she asked.

"Nowhere you'd want to live."

"How would you know?"

"All right. Could you go two or three days without food? Could you sleep out on the street in the rain, with a blanket about as thin as a sheet of paper? What would you do if someone beat you up and took all your money?"

"Well, I'd be smarter about it than you were. I'd get a job, an apartment."

"How? You're thirteen years old."

"That's almost as old as you were when you left," Amaranth said. "When you abandoned us. Wasn't it?"

"I was fifteen. And even then I could barely get a job." That had been because of Piper, because he hated to work, and not on account of my age. I didn't tell her that, though.

As the days passed, she seemed to drop the whole idea. But I knew she was still thinking about it, and that I had to do something to keep her busy.

It was nearly September, when the new school year started. I checked the internet and found out that Woodbine had a middle school where Beatriz and Amaranth could go, and a grade school for Semiramis. I sat them down and asked them if they thought they were ready.

"Sure," Beatriz said. She had been wandering around aimlessly for a month, grumbling about having nothing to do; out of all of them, she had made the quickest recovery. But even she hadn't come all the way back.

"I won't have to be in Ramis's class, will I?" Amaranth asked.

"No, of course not," I said.

"Okay, I'm in," she said.

"What do you think?" I asked Semiramis.

She didn't say anything for a long time. Finally she shook her head.

"You mean—no? You don't want to go?"

She nodded.

I tried not to sigh. Of course she shouldn't go if she didn't think she could. Her encounter with the sprite had changed her—she stayed in her room for hours drawing picture after picture, mostly of the grove—and it looked like she still wasn't ready to return to the world.

Everything I had to do seemed more complicated than it should have been. I filled out forms for Beatriz and Amaranth, but they had to be signed by an adult guardian and so, despite the fact that I felt more like their guardian than anyone, I got Maeve to do it, and had the forms notarized.

They had missed a year, of course, and I explained that by saying they'd been home-schooled. The school gave them some tests and decided that they could be placed with students their own age, which was a relief. I didn't want them in a class where everyone was a year younger. The other students would make fun of them for failing a grade, and they had enough problems already.

Most of the forms asked for our address, to make sure we lived in the right district for the schools they were going to. I didn't want to give it to them, of course, but in the end I told myself that even Ms. Burden couldn't find us here, in this tiny town at what seemed like the ends of the earth.

When school started I finally had more time to myself, to sit and write, or just think. Beatriz and Amaranth did well in their classes, though Amaranth's teachers complained to me that she barely spoke. I told myself I'd talk to her, but somehow I never got around to it.

Then, a few days after her birthday in April, she ran away from home.

CHAPTER 21

I didn't notice she was gone until we were all gathered at dinner. "Where's Rantha?" I asked.

"At the grove, probably," Beatriz said.

"Well, we're not waiting for her."

But she hadn't returned by the time we finished, and I was starting to get worried. It was still light outside, but darkness was closing down on us like the lid of a box. I remembered my own homecoming, when I had dawdled in the forest and made Philip so anxious. Had Amaranth finally gotten what she desired?

It grew darker, and there was no moon to see by. Beatriz and Semiramis and I got out some flashlights and headed to the grove. We called Amaranth's name as we went, shining the light through the trees. We'd never come here at night, and the shifting shadows made it seem like a different place, a stranger one. Rustling noises sounded, first from one spot and then another. Then we left the woods and came out into the grove.

Pinpoints of light shone from the trees. I looked at them, alarmed, wondering what they were. Then, as I saw the lights wink in and out, I realized that they were eyes, sprites peering out from between the branches. Other sprites were sleeping, curled up near each other or splayed out across the branches.

Are they all here? I asked Piper.

I don't know, he said.

Well, count them.

I don't know how many of them there are, he said. *So I don't know how many there should be.*

I sighed. *All right then—what do you think? Did one of them leave with Rantha?*

I don't think so.

That was reassuring, at least. Or maybe not, since we still didn't know where she was.

We searched for hours, circling through the woods, going farther than we'd ever been. The creek became a rushing river, with a bridge spanning the two shores. A chilly mist or fog settled around us, working through our clothes and making us shiver, turning the beams of our flashlights to cobwebs. Our voices grew weaker, hopeless, like lost birds peeping for their mother.

Semiramis seemed apprehensive, and I finally realized that the fog reminded her of the warehouse. We were too cold and exhausted to continue on, anyway, and we headed back to the house. I tried not to think of Amaranth still out here, tired, freezing, maybe lost.

Maeve was asleep when we got back, so I waited until the next morning to tell her what had happened. "What are you going to do, dear?" she asked.

"I don't know," I said. "Keep looking, I guess."

"You'll have to tell the police, you know."

"What? No."

"The school's going to wonder where she is."

I was still suspicious of the police, and living with Piper had given me an even deeper distrust of authority. Look how much work it had been just to get my sisters registered in school, for example. Still, I knew Maeve was right, that I would have to go there sooner or later.

Amaranth didn't come back the next day, so I put aside my misgivings and went to the police in Woodbine. They assured me that she'd probably just run away, that she would come back when she missed the comforts of home. Still, they asked for some information and borrowed a photograph of her, and they promised to get back to me if they found anything.

Then I drove on to the school. I asked the officials there to keep her disappearance to themselves; our family had suffered so many gothic tragedies already, and if the kids knew about his new one they could make Beatriz a complete outcast.

Days passed, and then weeks, and we still didn't hear from her. I found myself wanting to tell her something, or about to call her for dinner, and I would feel a fresh sadness that she was still missing. And a piercing guilt as well—how could I have forgotten that she was gone?

I did everything I could think of to find her. I talked to the police as often as I could, and I called her old friends in Eugene, though none of them had heard from her in years. I visited the grove and asked the sprites if one of them had left with her, and their answers, though confusing, seemed to say they hadn't seen her. I went to other places I thought she might be: our old house, her favorite restaurant, Amazon Park where we used to meet Ms. Burden. I even thought about asking Ned if he'd seen her, but I knew that if I did, her disappearance would get back to Ms. Burden.

At the same time, though, things around the house seemed to settle down for a while. Beatriz went to school, and worked in the afternoon to save up for college, and Semiramis stayed in her room with her drawings. She seemed to have some talent, but nothing about her work stood out or caught fire, and I wondered how much better she would be if that muse had chosen her. Mostly, though, I was just glad she'd found something to do.

I was able to sit and write, and I sold more poems. I even had time to go to ivoryorchard.com. I hadn't looked at the site for years—I hadn't had a computer when I'd run away, of course, and then when I got to Aunt Maeve's I'd been too busy. I'd surfed over once to read "The Woman and the Apple," but that was because Craig had sent me the link.

So I snatched moments here and there to catch up. I went deep into the archives and started from the time I ran away, 2002, on my fifteenth birthday. The posts had slowed even more in the years I'd been gone, when it looked as if the letters from David had stopped for good. But people still wrote about other things, and about their concern, even distress, over what might have happened to Adela Madden and/or the letter-writer.

Then, when I took over the task of answering the mail, the site exploded with activity. People wrote excitedly about getting answers to letters they had sent years ago, and they speculated about what had happened during all that time. Had David been ill, or had he become exhausted from the amount of writing he'd had to do? Watchmaker wrote an essay claiming that he'd lived in Pommerie Town for those years. And of course there were endless arguments over whether David and Dave were the same person, just as I'd hoped there would be.

I came closer and closer to the present day, reading posts from three months before, two months before I stopped at one from Eliza Woodbury, who wrote about how much she'd enjoyed the letter she'd gotten from Dave. I was pleased to see it; I'd had a soft spot for her ever since she'd spoken up for me at the Adela Madden Conference, and when I found a letter from her I'd spent more time on it than usual.

After Eliza's post came a message from someone with the name Seeker After Truth, asking Watchmaker to get in touch with them. I frowned. Philip had called one of my sisters by that name, but I couldn't remember which one. Someone who had asked question after question, trying his patience . . . Amaranth?

That's right, it was Amaranth. And I remembered I'd thought that Watchmaker was Ms. Burden, but only because they seemed obsessed with the muses, with inspiration and creativity.

If both these things were true, then it meant that Amaranth wanted to find Ms. Burden. And she'd written her post in January, a few months before she'd run away, so she'd been looking for her for a while.

I didn't see any more posts from Seeker After Truth, but ivory-orchard had an internal mail service and the two of them could have gotten in touch that way. But why would Amaranth want to talk to Ms. Burden, after everything she had done? Was it because she knew that Ms. Burden was also looking for muses, because they'd both been disappointed in their quests?

I showed the post to Beatriz and asked her what she thought of it, but she shrugged and didn't answer. Still, I made time to look at the site every day, but Seeker After Truth never came back.

CHAPTER 22

I started having nightmares about Amaranth. I had a dream where she met Ms. Burden, ran into her on the streets of Eugene somewhere, and that Ms. Burden imprisoned her in the deadening fog again. And then somehow I was there too, trying to rescue her and failing.

I woke from these dreams fighting my sheets and blankets, certain that I was still trapped with her. I lay there until my pulse slowed and my sweat cooled, trying to convince myself that Amaranth was all right. But even when I woke up completely, when I was cooking or cleaning or paying bills, I felt apprehensive, as if something was about to happen, some catastrophe lying in wait just around the corner.

A month after Amaranth left, I picked out a private investigator at random from the phone book, someone named Judith Reinhart. I called her and gave her a few details about Amaranth's disappearance, and we made an appointment. She had trouble spelling Amaranth, like everyone else.

I drove to Eugene on a pleasant day in May. The sky was the color of my old math teacher's hair, a pale white tinged with blue. I felt a little foolish going to a private detective, as if I'd wandered into a cheap mystery novel. I'd been reading a lot of mysteries lately, though I'd never liked them before. Then I realized that mysteries, unlike other fiction, give the reader an explanation for death.

The office didn't look like any of the ones in the books, though. The waiting room could have belonged to a lawyer, Mr. McLaren for example, though it was smaller and didn't have a receptionist.

A woman came out of another room. Her hair was somewhere between blond and brown, and her eyes, unusual for her coloring, were a dark brown, almost black. She was about my height but thinner, almost gangly. She wore a light tweed jacket, a white button-down blouse, jeans, and, incongruously, red high-top tennis shoes. At first glance she seemed only a few years older than me, much too young for her job.

The room she led me into was just as dull as the outer one, with a desk and a computer, a couch, and a chair. A door to a closet stood half open, and I could see some books and filing cabinets inside. A Matisse print hung over the couch, some women dancing in a ring.

We shook hands. The handshake was brisk, her hand dry. For some reason I felt reassured, as if this firm, businesslike gesture extended to her working habits as well.

Judith Reinhart sat behind the desk and I took the chair. "So," she said. "You want me to find your sister." She looked down at some notes on her desk, her straight hair falling over her face. "Amaranth, is that right?"

I nodded.

"Did you bring a photo?" she asked.

I took out the picture I'd brought. Judith had also asked for lists of Amaranth's friends and of places she liked to go, and I gave her those as well.

She studied the photo a while and then said, "How old did you say she was? Fourteen?"

I nodded again. Why wasn't I saying anything? I cleared my throat and said, "That's right."

"She looks older than that."

"Is that a problem?"

"Well, people remember young kids on their own, but she could be sixteen or seventeen. Still, I don't think it matters."

We went over some of the details of her disappearance, and then she said, "I'm going to have to ask you some questions, painful questions, maybe. How sure are you that she ran away, that she wasn't kidnapped?"

"Well, she talked about running away a lot," I said. "And we would have gotten a ransom note if she'd been kidnapped, right?"

"Not necessarily. People take girls like her for all kinds of reasons, I'm sorry to say. Sexual slavery, or sex trafficking."

"Oh, my God."

"Well, but you said she talked about running away, so let's concentrate on that for now. Why would she do that? What's going on at home? Why didn't your parents come talk to me, for one thing? Are they too busy, or not involved in your lives?"

I sighed and told her about our parents, about living with Maeve. "But really, there's nothing like what you said at home. Amaranth was just—she was just unhappy with her life."

She'd been writing something on a yellow pad of paper, but now she stopped to look up at me, her dark eyes steady. "There's usually something more, in my experience," she said. "Did she have a boyfriend that you know of? Or girlfriend?"

Why had I come here? I'd been warned all my life to keep my family's secrets, and now I was spilling them to a complete stranger.

"Well, there was this woman," I said cautiously. "Ms. Burden. She—she forged my father's will and made herself our guardian."

"Wow." Judith seemed startled, diverted from the well-worn path she'd been following. And I have to say I liked it, liked her looking at me as if I was something different from her usual run of clients. Maybe she'd put more effort into searching for Amaranth. "Why did she do that?"

"I'm not sure," I said, coming up with the lie as I spoke. "She wanted a family of her own, maybe. Anyway, Rantha might be trying to find her."

"Okay. What's Ms. Burden's first name? And do you know where she lives?"

"Kate. Katherine, maybe. I don't know her address—she used to live with us, in our old house, but she's not there anymore."

I felt a brush of fear at the thought that we might find Ms. Burden along with Amaranth, and I pushed it away. I'd deal with that if it happened.

"Okay. I'd like to have a look at your sister's bedroom, if I can."

"Why?"

"Well, I might find something there that could tell us where she went. Some notes or a journal, maybe."

"We live pretty far away."

"Okay, maybe we'll do that later. What have you done so far? Did you print up posters with her picture on them, saying that she's missing? And what about going to the police, talking to her friends, things like that?"

"No on the posters. I know it sounds ridiculous, but I don't want Ms. Burden to know she's gone. But I did talk to the police, and they looked for her for a while and didn't find anything. And I called her friends—I've been calling—but they haven't seen her. They're on that list there."

She picked up the lists I'd given her and studied them, then looked up at me. "Okay, here's what I'll do. I'll follow up on these lists, of course, and check with shelters and programs for runaway kids, things like that. And bus stations and train stations, in case she left town. And, well, I have to bring this up—there's always a possibility she's in the hospital, or the morgue. I have her picture now, so I can show that around."

I nodded, trying not to show any reaction to that dreadful word "morgue." I signed a contract, using the post office box as my address, and gave her a retainer. There was enough money in the bank to cover it, though just barely.

She led me back to the waiting room and opened the outer door. Please shake my hand again, I thought. The room grew hotter. No, I was blushing. Oh, God, I was interested in her. I told myself to cut it out. I had to find Amaranth; I didn't have time for this.

I tried to put Judith out of my mind as I went about my other errands. I kept seeing her face in front of me, though, that final smile as she held the door open.

I'd had the idea that I'd slept with women because of Piper, that he was the one interested in them, not me. Piper grinned at that thought. *We like them all, you and I,* he said. *Men and women both.*

I scowled. I already felt so different from other people that this seemed like the final straw. Still, I wondered how long it would take before she got back to me.

She called three weeks later. During that time I wrote a poem about Amaranth's disappearance, and then felt guilty about using her troubles this way, for my own benefit. I learned later that every writer did this with people they knew, that we were all vampires, feeding on other people's experiences. I never felt good about it, though.

"Hello, it's Judith," she said when I answered the phone.

"Hi!" I said, not sure if my excitement came from hearing her voice or from the thought that she might have learned something. I decided to pretend it was the latter. "Any news?"

"Nothing yet, unfortunately. Some people thought they saw her but they weren't sure. That's the way it goes, though. People are pretty unobservant, most of the time. Most of the answers came from downtown, so I'm going to keep trying there."

"So you think she's still in Eugene?"

She sighed. "I don't know, Ivy. I'm sorry, I wish I had more to tell you. I can't guarantee anything, though."

I thought I felt Piper frolicking. Then I realized it was me, my first experience of that old cliché—my heart was dancing. Or maybe all my organs were dancing together, standing face to face and skipping toward each other. And all this just because she'd said my name.

The next instant, of course, I felt disgusted with myself. Amaranth was missing, and here I was thinking about myself. "Okay, Judith," I said, trying out her name in return. "Let me know if you find anything. And thanks for calling."

She called again a few weeks later. All right, it was fifteen days, not that I was keeping track or anything. "Two people told me they saw her at a movie theater, the Four Star, working as a cashier," she said. "I talked to the manager, someone named Mr. Morris, but he didn't know Amaranth and he didn't recognize her from the photograph. What's so funny?"

"Sorry," I said. "I used to work there too—that's why I was laughing. I should have thought of it myself. Mr. Morris doesn't ask your age, so a lot of kids get jobs there. And he doesn't answer questions about his employees."

"Well, what I thought I'd do is watch the place, see if she shows up. I'll let you know what happens."

Her next call came six days later. "All right, it is her at the movie theater," she said without preamble. "So what I thought we'd do—"

"Wait. You found her?"

"Yeah. Sorry, I should have been clearer. So I thought we could go to the theater together, the next time she's on, and you can decide where to go from there. I got her schedule from one of the other employees."

I didn't listen to much beyond "go to the theater together." Put that way, it sounded like a date. I told myself firmly to keep things professional.

"Sounds good," I said.

"Okay. Should I pick you up?"

"Oh. Um, well, I live pretty far away. Why don't I meet you at your office?"

"All right. See you then."

We drove together to the Four Star Theater, a large place near downtown showing *The Da Vinci Code*. She parked down the street, and we sat in her car and waited for Amaranth to start her shift.

"So," she said, "where do you live, exactly?"

"Well, pretty far away."

"Yeah, so you said. You know I'm a private investigator, right?" She laughed to show she was kidding, that she wasn't really planning to track me down.

I wanted to tell her everything, of course. "Okay, well, we're sort of in hiding. Me and my family. I didn't tell you everything about Ms. Burden, what she did to us. And she's still looking for us."

She turned her level gaze on me. "But—I don't get it. She's just one woman. Why are you so afraid of her?"

"It's hard to explain. She's sort of, well, obsessed with us."

"You can get a restraining order against her, you know."

"But they don't help all that much, do they?" I asked. "They're just pieces of paper. Husbands still beat their wives, and—and even kill them, even with restraining orders."

"You think she's going to kill you?"

"No, but she got pretty good at terrorizing us."

"Well, but you have two sisters, right?"

"Three."

"Three sisters, and an aunt. So what can she do against all of you?"

"A great-aunt. She's pretty old, pretty out of it. And my sisters are too young to take care of themselves."

"How long did you live with her?"

"Two years. Well, my sisters stayed for four years, but I ran away after two."

She looked at me with sudden curiosity. "Really?" she asked.

Then, somehow, I was telling her about my time on the streets. Not only that, I was taking events and spinning them into gold, turning the cold and rain and poverty into stories filled with chases and narrow escapes, dogs and police, terrible jobs and unexpected good fortune. Anything to keep myself in the spotlight of that dark, thoughtful gaze.

"You should have told me all of this before," she said when I finished. "It looks like Amaranth's following in your footsteps."

She was right, of course. I nodded.

"Why didn't you just go to your great-aunt for help?" she asked.

"Well, we were too young to remember how to get to her house."

"Is she together enough to take care of all of you?"

"Not really. I'm doing a lot of it, pretty much."

She looked impressed. "How old are you?"

"Eighteen."

"Really? You seem older."

"All right, how old are you?"

"Twenty-five."

"Really? You seem younger."

We laughed. I had a lot more questions, and I expect she did too. And at the same time I was doing subtraction in my head: twenty-five minus eighteen equals seven. That wasn't too much older, was it? Should I have said nineteen, or twenty?

"They're changing shifts now," Judith said, nodding toward the theater.

I looked up. A girl carrying a coin tray came into the ticket booth and said something to the cashier working there. The cashier took her tray out of the drawer and left.

"Is that her? I can't tell," I said.

Judith reached for a pair of binoculars in the back seat and handed them to me, and I put them up to my eyes. "It is—it is her!" I said. "Oh, my God!"

She'd been gone for only two months, but already she looked different. Her auburn hair had dulled to brown, and her print blouse had wrinkled and faded until it barely looked presentable. Acne had broken out on her cheeks and forehead. The biggest change, though, was in the way she acted. She moved slowly, unsmiling, as if she was working through a heavier gravity. Her great adventure had turned into a struggle just to survive.

My heart turned over to see her. At least I'd had Piper, to help me through the hard parts.

We left the car and headed to the theater. Judith got to the ticket booth first. "Hello," she said. "I'm looking for Amaranth Quinn."

"Who's Amaranth?" Amaranth said.

"Well, I thought you were," Judith said. "Your sister Ivy's been looking for you."

I stepped up to the cashier's window. "Hi, Rantha," I said.

"Oh, God," she said, sounding resigned. "What do you want?"

"Well, I want you to come home. We miss you."

"Yeah, I bet you do."

"We do. And this can't be any fun for you—working for a pittance, living in some god-awful place you can barely afford."

"You don't know anything about me, or where I live. And you have some nerve, talking about work. You left us and had fun for two years—you never did any work in your life. And now you're sponging off—"

She stopped before she gave away Aunt Maeve's name. At least she knew enough not to say it in front of a stranger. I didn't have time for relief, though, because she was still talking.

"Anyway, you think you're so clever. I found out some things even you don't know."

"Yeah, like what?"

"Like where Kate is."

"Ms. Burden? Why would you do that? After what she did to you, and Beatriz and Ramis? Did you talk to her?"

"Yeah."

"God, Rantha, you know you can't trust her." I tried to speak evenly, without letting her see how worried I was. Though she couldn't have told Ms. Burden where we lived or we'd have gotten a visit, with her trail of spooks following along behind her. "What did you tell her?"

"It's not what I told her. It's what she told me."

"Okay, what did she tell you?"

"Things. Things about *Ivory Apples.*"

Judith, standing next to me, looked startled. "What about it?" I asked. "I didn't think you were even interested."

"Of course I am. I only read it like three or four times. And we talk about it all the time, and Kate even said I had some good ideas. But you wouldn't know—you never paid any attention to me."

"Well, I'm sorry. You never said you'd read the book, or that you wanted to talk about it. Why don't you come home and we can discuss it?"

"I'm not going anywhere. You can't make me."

"Sure I can. You're too young to be working, for one thing. All I have to do is call the police and tell them where you are, and they'll come get you. And they'll bust Mr. Morris, too, and make him pay a fine, or even close down the theater. Are you sure you want to do that? I remember him as a pretty decent guy."

She said something, and ribbons of mist began to twine up around us. God, she'd learned Ms. Burden's spell, the one that brought that horrible whiteness. But it was those enslaved creatures who created the mist, so at least one of them had to be nearby, following Amaranth's orders.

I said the counter-spell and the mist disappeared, then gusted up again. "Rantha," I said. "Just come home, please. We can do—do whatever you want together. I'll help you as much as I can, I promise you."

I'd been talking for too long, though. The whiteness became thicker. Shapes swirled up within it, an old cat we'd had once; Philip and Jane talking in the kitchen, too far away for me to hear them.

I pushed against it with the counter-spell. The fog turned to gauze, to cobwebs, and then frayed apart into air.

This was ridiculous; we could be doing this for hours. Then a dreadful possibility occurred to me, that Ms. Burden was somewhere nearby, with her creatures.

"We should go," I said to Judith.

She stood still, looking stunned for the first time since I'd met her. I grabbed her hand and pulled her away.

We reached the car and got inside. "I—what was that?" she asked.

"I'll tell you later. Come on, let's go."

"Why?"

"Someone could be following us."

Judith started the car and we headed away from the theater. She drove steadily; I was glad to see it.

She left downtown, then got on the freeway and continued for a while, crossing the Willamette River. "There's no one there," she said, looking in her rearview mirror. She took an exit and pulled over. "No one's following us. What just happened?"

"It was . . . Okay, you're not going to believe this."

"I already don't believe it."

"Well, what Amaranth said—it was a kind of spell."

"And then what you said?"

"That was just the spell backwards. To stop it."

"Just."

"Look, I know it sounds impossible—"

"No, that's the thing. It doesn't. I mean, it would, if I hadn't seen it for myself, but I can't think of any other explanation. You and Amaranth could have planned it all together, I guess, set up some kind of, I don't know, a fog machine or something, but I don't see why you would. How—where did she learn something like that? Where did you, for that matter?"

"Well, I read it in a book. She must have gotten it from Ms. Burden."

She sat back. "You know, you keep telling me Ms. Burden is behind this or that, but you never say why, just that she's obsessed with your family. But it has to be more than that."

"Well, she thinks we know something about—about some other spell," I said.

"And do you?"

"Sort of."

"What kind of spell?"

I didn't say anything.

"Okay," she said. "Amaranth mentioned *Ivory Apples*, so I'm guessing it has something to do with that. And you said you live with your great-aunt, who could be the right age for Adela Madden, and there were always rumors that Madden was still alive. How am I doing?"

I shook my head miserably. It was just my luck to have found an investigator who was good at her job.

"I can't help you with this unless I know what's going on," she said.

Once again, I wanted to tell her everything. But I thought about Maeve, who was still coming to terms with the loss of Willa, and about everyone who had kept the family secret for so long, Philip and Jane and my grandmother Lydia. I thought about Ms. Burden, who had been liked by nearly everyone, at least at first, and how it was impossible to know who to trust. Maybe I'd never believe anyone ever again—or maybe it was only women who would raise my suspicions. Just my luck, I thought again.

I felt for Piper to see what he thought, but he shrugged and shook his head, leaving it up to me. "I'm sorry," I said finally. "It isn't my story to tell."

"All right," she said. She started the car again and pulled out into traffic.

"Where are we going?"

"Back to my office. I can't do anything more for you."

"Oh." For the first time I realized that if she stopped working for me I'd never see her again. "Do I still owe you anything? Or is there some paperwork or something I have to sign?"

"Nope. We're done here." She let a few moments go by, and then said, "Look. Everything you told me, everything I learned on this case is confidential. Even if your aunt is Adela Madden—well, it's not just that I won't tell anyone who she is, it's that I can't. It would be unprofessional."

I felt my scruples melt away. Anyway, she pretty much knew everything anyway. "All right. Yeah, she is. She's Adela Madden."

"Wow. *Ivory Apples* was my favorite book when I was a kid. I read it about once a year—I practically had it memorized. I still read it every so often."

"Yeah, me too."

"What was that like, growing up with her as your aunt?"

"It didn't seem like anything special. I mean, she was just around, you know? But then, after I read her book a few times, I realized how amazing she is."

"Why did she stop writing, do you know?"

I had a few guesses, but nothing I could tell Judith. "No, I don't. She's very good at not answering questions."

She looked at me and smiled. "So are you," she said.

We talked about *Ivory Apples* until we got to her office. I pictured her as a child, solemn and practical even then, yet still lost like so many others in Pommerie Town.

We reached her office building and parked in the lot behind it. "Well," she said. "It was fun working with you. Give me a call if you need anything."

"Okay," I said.

I put out my hand for her to shake. She hesitated a moment and then took it, and I got out of the car.

I thought about her nearly all the way home, wondering what I could have done differently. Then, as I took the exit to Woodbine, my worries about Amaranth returned. What had Kate told her about *Ivory Apples*?

I could hire Judith to look into it. I let myself dwell on the possibilities for a while, then shook my head. I was pretty sure that I'd never see her again.

CHAPTER 23

Even though I'd found Amaranth and had seen that she was safe, I still had nightmares about her. One night, about four months after she'd run away, I woke up suddenly, grasping the blankets, thinking

I'd heard a noise.

The full moon shone through all the house's windows, so bright I could almost read the titles on the bookshelves. I heard the sound again, coming from the back of the house. I got up and went toward it.

I looked into the study first. The moon's light picked out the one empty bed, Amaranth's. Beatriz and Semiramis were in shadow, but I could tell they were asleep. The door to Maeve's room was closed as usual, and I decided not to bother her, to check on her only as a last resort.

Something moved in the kitchen, heading toward the back door. I hurried toward it. The figure turned at the sound of my footsteps, and Amaranth looked back at me.

"What are you doing here?" I asked.

She glanced toward the door, no doubt wondering if she could outrun me. I closed the distance between us and glared down at her. I was still taller than her, I was pleased to see.

"Maeve gave me this," she said.

Now I noticed something in her arms, a round shape covered with a towel she'd taken from the bathroom. "What is it?" I asked.

"Never mind. Maeve said I could have it."

"It's an ivory apple, isn't it?" I said, remembering the offerings Amaranth had left on the lakeshore.

"So what?"

"Let me see."

She unfolded the cloth. An apple lay there, the one she'd brought to the grove, showing a town hall meeting in Pommerie Town.

"Are you sure that's the one she gave you?" I asked.

"Of course I'm sure. I asked for it, and she gave it to me."

"And you're going to do what with it? Hand it over to Ms. Burden? That's the last thing Maeve would want."

"No, of course not. It's mine."

I was completely awake now, and remembering everything Ms. Burden had done. "Why on earth are you even talking to her? She's a horrible person—you of all people should know that."

"She taught me some things. And you never tell me anything."

"She's going to want something in exchange. Like an ivory apple, maybe."

Amaranth said nothing. I took advantage of her silence to ask more questions. "What did you talk about? Those ideas you said you were so impressed with?"

"Why should I tell you? You never tell me anything."

Now I noticed how thin she was, how sallow her complexion looked. She seemed worse than last time, maybe even sick. Just as I thought that, she coughed, the kind of loose, rattling cough that comes at the end of a long illness.

"Can I get you something to eat?" I asked.

She hesitated, then edged toward the back door. The small window was broken again; she'd probably gone through it to reach the lock. "No, thanks," she said.

"How about giving me your address? A phone number?"

"I gotta go."

"She's using you, you know. She has some plan, she's going to take advantage of you somehow."

"No, you're wrong. We're on the same side. We both want the same thing." She opened the door, and I heard her run around to the front of the house.

How had she gotten here? Had Ms. Burden dropped her off? No, even she wouldn't tell Ms. Burden where we lived. She had to have gotten someone to drive her. I ran through the house to look out the front windows, but all I could see were two red taillights, growing smaller in the distance.

It rained hard at the beginning of December, the sky turning the same gray as the sidewalks, and I worried about Amaranth more than ever. Still, she'd seemed so determined to stay away that I had no expectations of her ever returning. So when she showed up on the doorstep, her thin parka and knapsack drenched with rain, she took me completely by surprise.

I wanted to laugh at her, to say "I told you so," or ask why she hadn't broken a window this time, but I knew she'd leave again if I did that. And another part of me wanted to hug her, to hold her there, to keep her with us for good. The best thing, I decided, was not to make a big deal out of it.

"Hi," I said. "Come on in."

She followed me through the living room, looking around at the books and knickknacks. I remembered this part, when normal life seems like visiting a foreign country, when you have to relearn ordinary objects one by one.

"Are you going to stay for a while?" I asked.

"Yeah," she said. "Sure."

"Great. Do you want your old room back?"

She nodded and we went down the hallway. "Ramis is in there," I said. "She stays in her room a lot now."

She shrugged. Semiramis looked up as we came inside, and then returned to her drawing.

A small smile appeared on Amaranth's face, a brief muscle tug, there and gone. "Hi, Ramis," she said.

"Hi," Semiramis said. "Where were you?"

"Lots of places," Amaranth said, sitting on the edge of her bed.

"Like where?"

It was time to pick up Beatriz at school. I said goodbye and set off, hoping I wasn't making a mistake by leaving the two of them together. They'd been deadly rivals when Amaranth had left.

Beatriz and I could barely hear each other on the drive back, over the pounding of the rain and the swish of the windshield wipers at their highest speed. Still, I managed to tell Beatriz that Amaranth had come back, at least for now. When we got home, we found her and Semiramis sitting across from each other on their beds, their heads together, talking in low voices.

"Hi, Rantha," Beatriz said.

They looked up, startled. "Hi," Amaranth said. Semiramis giggled. They moved apart and stared at Beatriz, saying nothing.

"Okay, then," Beatriz said. "I know where I'm not wanted."

"At least they're not fighting," I said.

A few days later I asked Amaranth, "Where's that carved apple?"

"I, um, I haven't unpacked it," she said.

I went through her knapsack while she was out somewhere with Semiramis. I know I probably shouldn't have, but no one had given me the *How to Parent* manual and I had to make it up as I went along. I didn't find the apple anywhere, though.

She and Semiramis continued to spend long hours in their room with the door closed, speaking too softly for me to hear them—though once in a while a high musical giggle would come from behind the door, Semiramis laughing. But with everyone else, Amaranth acted the same as she always had, still angry, still surly and resentful. I hoped she wasn't telling tales of Ms. Burden to Semiramis, getting her interested in the grove all over again.

Beatriz made some friends at school, and she started having dinner with them and even sleeping over. She had begun to put her experiences in the warehouse behind her, and was even revising some of her rational view of the world, making room for everything she had seen there. I was pleased to see it, but at the same time I envied her for having such a normal life.

Finally, one evening, I couldn't take Amaranth's stubborn silence any longer. Beatriz was eating at a friend's house and dinner was muted, with Amaranth saying nothing and the loud rain nearly drowning out any conversation.

Amaranth finished dinner and started to get up. "Did you unpack yet?" I asked. "What happened to that apple?"

She glanced at Maeve, and at that moment I knew that she'd lied, that Maeve hadn't given her the apple after all. "I gave it to Ms. Burden, if you have to know," she said.

"You're kidding me. After everything she's done, to you, and—and our family . . . What does she want with it? Does it have some kind of power or something? What if she comes after us again, and I can't stop her this time?"

"It doesn't have any power, as far as I know," Maeve said.

"Well, but she shouldn't have—" I said.

"Yeah, well, Kate thinks it does," Amaranth said. "It does have power. She knows things, she knows a lot more than you do."

"Yeah, you keep saying that," I said. "Like what?"

She was silent a moment. Then she said in a rush, "Like, well, you can lend Piper to other people."

I sat back. The rain had stopped, I realized, and her words had sounded loud in the small room. "What?" I asked.

"Kate told me so. She said that if your—your muse trusts you, you can ask him to leave, to visit someone else. Just for a while, she said."

"She said that, did she? How does she know?"

"She read it somewhere. So you can, you know, tell Piper to visit me every so often."

"I can't tell Piper anything."

"You know what I mean. Ask him. Ask him to leave you, just for a few minutes."

I asked him. I felt him grin, as though he thought it might be fun. I hated the idea, though. For one thing, Ms. Burden had suggested it. For another, Piper was mine, just as I was his. He didn't belong to Amaranth, or anyone else.

"Why should I?" I asked.

"Why? Because everyone in this goddamn family has a muse, everyone except me. It isn't fair." She glared around the table at the three of us, speaking faster and faster. "So you're all geniuses, everyone loves you. That letter from that poetry magazine, about how brilliant you are—"

"Wait—you saw that?" I asked.

"Of course I saw it. That's why you left it out, wasn't it? I'm just surprised you didn't frame it. And everyone ignores me, or feels sorry for me. I'm like the ugly duckling."

She'd gotten the fairy tale wrong, but it would have been the height of cruelty to tell her so. All I could do was let her talk.

"Just once, just one time, I'd like to get noticed like that," she said. "To be the one everyone thinks is so special. And you didn't even do anything to earn it—it all comes so easy for you. It's not fair."

"I don't think—" I said.

"Right. You never want to help me with anything. Remember what Philip used to say about sharing?"

"It isn't about that. I just don't think I can do it, or Piper can."

"But you said he left you, that one time in the warehouse. So if he can leave, he can visit someone else. Right?"

"It doesn't work like that."

"So find out how it does work. And you said you'd do anything I want, when you saw me at the theater."

"If the child wants to see what it's like, maybe we should help her," Maeve said.

I turned to her, startled. Amaranth's eyes lit up. "Help me how?" she said.

"Oh, I don't know. I'd give you Willa, if I still had her."

"Could you, well, call her back?"

Maeve said nothing, though I thought I saw the shine of tears in her eyes.

"Maeve nearly died," I said. "I don't want her to take any more chances."

"All right, then, you do it," Maeve said.

Oh, God, I thought. But Amaranth spoke up before I could say anything. "That's what I said the first time. You're pretty healthy, aren't you?"

I was more worried about Piper, though. The sprites were tricksters, tricky. They liked us, maybe even loved us, but they would mislead us for a good laugh.

Still, I didn't want Maeve to put herself in danger. And if I agreed, it would placate Amaranth, would keep her from running away again.

Piper danced within me, excited. I tried to ignore him. "Well, maybe we should, I don't know, go to the grove or something," I said. "Maybe that would be a better place for it."

Amaranth was grinning. "Come on, we don't have time for that," she said. "And it's raining outside. Just do it."

We had plenty of time. She was thrumming with impatience, though, and for the first time I let myself understand how she felt. I might have felt the same, if I didn't have Piper.

"All right," I said. "Just for a minute, though. Piper, go to Amaranth."

He left before I finished speaking. I didn't even see him go; one minute I felt him within me, and the next Amaranth changed subtly, her eyes bright, her head raised to greet him.

"Hi there, Piper," she said. She looked around at the rest of us and said, "Good evening!"

"Did it work?" I asked. "How are you?"

"Or is it morning?" she asked. "They shouldn't look so much alike—it throws you off. Maybe it's fireplace. Or herring."

"Rantha?"

"I think it's herring, don't you? Good herring—that sounds right. And here I've been saying it wrong all these years."

"Rantha, stop it. Look at me."

"No, what am I saying?" Her head lurched back and forth, her eyes wide. Her mouth worked, and she said, "Evening, morning, morning, evening . . ."

"Amaranth! Piper, come back! Come back, do you hear me?"

"Piper says to say goodbye. Goodbye, goodbye. The moon jumped over the cow."

Semiramis looked at her, worried. "Rantha, what's going on? Can I get you something?"

"The moon. The moon and some rubies. And a good pair of socks, and a bus pass. No, I need to sleep."

I looked at Maeve. "Oh, God. What do I do now?"

Her hands were pressed against her mouth, and she took them away to speak. "I don't know," she whispered. "If she wants to sleep, I suppose we could put her to bed."

"I can't sleep, though," Amaranth said. "My heart's racing so fast. If my heart raced your heart, my heart would win."

"She'll have to sleep sometime," I said.

God, I was talking about her as if she wasn't there. "Piper!" I said again. "Piper, come back!"

The understanding of what we'd done washed over me in waves, one after the other, each more terrible than the last. She'd lost touch with reality. Her quickened heartbeat might kill her. She'd die anyway, if she couldn't get to sleep. And I'd lost Piper. My muse, my lodestar, my friend.

I had some sleeping pills left over from when I'd taken care of Maeve, and I suggested that we give her one. No one else had a better idea, so Semiramis and I took her hands and walked her to bed, while Maeve got a pill and a glass of water.

"Here, take this," Maeve said.

"I want a piccolo, not a pill," Amaranth said. She sat up straight in bed, showing no signs of sleepiness. "Didn't I say so? Maybe not. Peter Piper picked a peck of pickled piccolos."

Together we managed to get the pill into her mouth and the glass up to her lips. "Drink some water," Semiramis said, her voice gentle. "Go on."

"Peter Piper wants to play," Amaranth said. She took a sip, then another. "He wants to play but he can't. He's trapped in here forever."

I felt a horrible shivering sorrow. Piper was caught, lost. Was he terrified, hurt, angry? Did he hate me for asking this of him? I'd never sensed anger from him, could barely imagine it.

"Forever and ever and ever and ever . . ." Amaranth said. Finally the stream of words slowed, then stopped. She closed her eyes and fell back against her pillow.

Sometime during the night I heard a voice from the study, and I dragged myself out of bed to check on my sisters. Amaranth had woken up and was talking nonsense again, her voice loud in the darkness.

Beatriz had come home, and both she and Semiramis were awake now. "God, this is horrible," Beatriz said.

"Did Ramis explain what happened?" I asked.

"Yeah," Beatriz said. "Can you—can you help her somehow?"

"I don't know."

"I hate to say it, but I have to get to sleep. Can't she go to another room?"

"What room? We're already using every room in the house."

"Well, you can change places with her. She goes on the couch and you come sleep with us."

I didn't want to do that, though. I was still struggling with this strange new place I occupied, not a parent but more than a sister. "I'll go to the dining room," I said.

"Where? Under the table?"

"Why not?"

"Are you sure?"

"Yeah."

Amaranth showed no signs of slowing down. I moved her to the living room and changed the bedding on the couch, then gave her another pill. We'd need a new prescription at this rate, but I wasn't going to worry about that now.

Then I dragged my blankets into the dining room and spread them under the table. This responsibility thing was the pits, I thought, crawling into the blankets and lying down.

CHAPTER 24

Amaranth ate and slept very little, and she grew thinner than ever. Her eyes turned a hectic traffic-light green, and she talked and talked, a nonstop babble of nonsense.

Even this stream of words was better than the times when she seemed to come to herself. Then her eyes would grow wide, and she'd make a heartwrenching effort to break out of her madness. It was never enough, though, and she would sink back helplessly into gibberish.

The worst for me was when she talked about Piper. "He misses you," she said once. "He wants to know why it's so dark where he is."

I missed him too, terribly. I missed his observations, his strange, funny way of looking at things. The world was uninteresting without him, and my poems seemed uninspired, like ads for toothpaste or cell phones.

I tried to ignore Amaranth's prattle, to let it flow over me like background noise. But just when I managed to stop listening she'd come up with a startling word or turn of phrase, and I'd find myself paying attention again. I renewed Maeve's prescription for sleeping pills, but I felt horrible every time I gave her one, as if I were sedating her for my own convenience, just to keep her quiet.

I did everything I could think of to help her. I wrote Craig for advice, and searched the ivoryorchard website. I went back and forth to the grove, though the ground had become muddy with rain and was once covered by a thin layer of snow. The sprites no longer talked to me, though. Maybe they couldn't, without Piper there. Maybe they didn't even recognize me.

I took Amaranth to the grove, choosing a day when she seemed more docile than usual. "Who's there?" one of them asked as we stepped out of the forest.

"It's Piper!" said another.

A crowd flew over and formed a circle around Amaranth, two or three deep, and looked at her solemnly. She seemed more serious as well; her eyes had a pinprick of intelligence within them, and she was silent for the first time in days.

"It's Piper's knot," someone said.

"He's caught fast," another said.

"And slow, too."

"She's quick, though. Or at least not dead."

"Not yet, anyway."

Finally the flow of nonsense ended and I could ask my question. "What can I do for her?" I asked. "How can I help her?"

"Do?" one of them asked. Unlike most of the others he had a

long white beard, with twigs and leaves and even a green caterpillar caught within it. "You should never have allowed it."

"How was I supposed to know?" I asked angrily. "Even Piper didn't know. You should have warned me."

The sprites turned away, losing interest. They dove into the lake in one swift motion, and the one I was talking to followed. "No, wait!" I said, calling after him. "Please! How can I get him back?"

Finally they were all gone, and we stood there alone. I shouted to them again and again, but no one paid me any attention. I took Amaranth back through the forest, a hundred thoughts flying untethered through my mind.

It was late by the time we got home. I put Amaranth on the couch and sat down next to her. I'd asked her questions before, of course, and gotten only nonsense, but I wanted to try again.

"Is there a way to get Piper back?" I asked.

"Of course there is. You have to wear an apple on your head."

"What? What about apples?"

"No, wait. You don't wear apples on your head, do you? That's hats. Or cats? No, I'm pretty sure it's hats. Oh, I can't remember. Why do you ask me all these questions if you know I can't remember?"

She was growing agitated now, her voice rising. I should stop, I knew that, but I tried one last time. "Think, Rantha, it's important. Are you talking about Maeve's apple, the one you stole? Did you give it to Ms. Burden? Kate?"

"Kate." She frowned. "I know that name. I have to ask her something."

"What?"

"Garibaldi! That's the answer. Or is it? I forgot the question."

It was impossible. I left her and went to make dinner.

When I finally got to my nest of blankets that night I was unable to sleep. Was her talk of apples just more foolishness, or did it mean something? Had she given Maeve's apple to Ms. Burden?

Of course I could ask Ms. Burden myself. But the idea of talking to her made my heart race as fast as Amaranth's. Instead I could break into her house; I'd done it before, after all. If she had the apple there I could steal it back.

My pulse slowed, and I felt myself relax. That's what my life had come to, I thought—burglary was easier for me than actually talking to someone.

The whole thing was probably just more of Amaranth's nonsense. But I had to do something. Amaranth was visibly worse, so thin now that we could see her bones, the hills of her ribs, the knobs of her wrists and elbows. She was getting used to the sleeping pills and woke up earlier and earlier, and she had started hurrying through the house as if searching for something, like a wind-up toy that had lost some important gear and sped up beyond all reason.

The problem was the same as always: I didn't know where Ms. Burden lived. How did you go about finding people, especially when you didn't want them to find you?

I'd known from the beginning what I had to do, of course. I just hadn't admitted it to myself. You find people by hiring a private investigator.

This time, though, I'd have to tell Judith everything, or most things. But I needed Maeve's permission to do that, and I knew how she felt about giving up her secrets.

I sat down with her the next day after dinner, prepared with a whole host of arguments. But she ended up surprising me; she understood that we had to do something about Amaranth, and she gave me her blessing.

I called Judith, trying to ignore the little fireworks of excitement going off within me. "Hi, it's Ivy," I said when she answered.

"Ivy!" she said. I thought she sounded pleased to hear from me, but that could have just been wishful thinking. "What's new?"

Now that it came to it, I felt reluctant. Not because I didn't trust her with our secrets, but because the whole story was so far-fetched. "Listen," I said. "Could you come over? I have some things I want to show you."

"Well," she said. "I don't know. Are you going to tell me where you live this time?"

We made an appointment for the next day. Before she came I folded the sheets and blankets under the table and threw them into the study, then dusted the bookshelves and swept the floor. We'd never had any visitors, and I wanted the house to look its best.

Then I gave Amaranth a sleeping pill, to keep her from disturbing us. She was becoming so habituated to the pills I thought about giving her two, but I didn't want to make her even more dependent than she was.

The bells rang, and I ran to open the door. I'd been so busy I hadn't noticed that it had rained all morning and then cleared up, so that everything was sparkling with water drops. Even Maeve's ruined garden shone, as if all the plants had budded with jewels.

It seemed a good omen. I let Judith in and took her through the living room, to where Amaranth was asleep on the couch. "She came back, then?" Judith asked. "How is she?"

"Well, that's part of what I have to tell you. Come on, let's go to the dining room."

She kept looking around her, though—at a painting of the town founders and their dog Oscar from *Ivory Apples*, at all the bookshelves, at a four-foot-high coach someone had built, with a little man made out of stuffed cloth on the driver's seat. "I remember him from the book," she said, talking quietly so as not to wake Amaranth. "God, this is amazing. Do you think—can I meet your great-aunt?"

I'd never seen her so impressed. Part of me was enjoying it, preening under her interest, but another part was anxious to talk to her. "Maybe," I said. "It depends on her."

We came to the dining room. I made some tea and sat down with her, then took a deep breath and started in on the story. As I talked I stared at the table or gazed out a window, holding my tea mug for comfort. I wasn't ready to find out if she believed me, didn't want to see her look incredulous, or worse, pitying.

When I reached the end I gathered up my courage and looked straight at her. Her expression gave nothing away. "Well," I said, "what do you think?"

"I don't know," she said. "I saw what Amaranth did at the theater, so I have to believe some of it, at least. But it doesn't really matter what I think. If you're hiring me to find Ms. Burden"—she raised one eyebrow in a question, and I nodded —"then I can do that without having an opinion on the rest of it."

I wanted her to believe me, of course. If she didn't, there were only two choices left to her: I was either a liar or deluded. Neither one put me in a very good light.

"Although, you know, *Ivory Apples* is so good it only makes sense that there was a muse involved," she said, smiling.

I tried to smile back. "How would you find her?" I asked. "Ms. Burden."

"Well, it's different for an adult. There's more of a paper trail— drivers' licenses, work histories, credit cards, mortgages. Do you have anything from the time you spent with her? Any photographs?"

I shook my head. Ms. Burden had removed everything that could identify her from the house, and I'd never had a reason to take a picture of her. "One of my sisters might be able to draw her," I said, thinking of Semiramis and her reams of paper.

"All right. And I'll see what I can do. I brought another con- tract—"

Amaranth came running into the room, then stopped when she saw us. "Who are you?" she asked Judith. "Are you here to teach the rabbits to read? A is for Apple, B is for Broccoli, C is for Carrot, that kind of thing? You have to use fruits and vegetables, otherwise they won't get it."

Judith looked at me, uncertain. No one knows how to respond to madness; it's frightening, like a bomb that could go off at any moment. "How are you?" I asked Amaranth.

"I'm fine. Well, fine except for Piper. He keeps twisting and poking and kicking and trying to get out. Okay, not fine. Not fine at all."

"Do you want to go back to sleep?"

"But I'm asleep right now, aren't I? And I'm dreaming that I'm in the dining room, but there's a stranger there. And you know what's funny? When you give me a pill, I don't dream at all. So I know I'm not sleeping then. Only now."

"This is Judith Reinhart. She's going to help us."

She opened her mouth to speak, then ran away into the kitchen. I got up, sighing. "Sorry, I have to keep an eye on her," I said to Judith. "Make sure she doesn't hurt herself."

Judith followed me. Amaranth was opening and closing all the cabinets. "Is this what it's like all the time?" Judith asked softly.

"Yeah, more or less. Except when she's sleeping."

"Have you tried, I don't know, taking her to a doctor?"

"And saying what, exactly? That she's been infected by a muse?"

"No, I thought—"

"You think she has mental problems." I was speaking louder now, not caring if Amaranth heard me. "You think I should take her to a doctor, that I'm in denial and made the whole thing up."

"No. No, wait. Look at me." I'd been avoiding her eyes, and now I looked directly at her. "I've learned a lot about people over the years, and I don't think you're making this up. And I can tell other things about you—that you face problems head-on, not just your problems but other people's. You could have given up, moved away and left all of this for someone else to deal with, and instead you took on this huge job, looking after your aunt and your sister, and your other sisters too. That's why I accepted you as a client. Like you said to Amaranth, I think I can help."

A slow warmth rose up through me, a kind of happiness I'd never felt before. Piper's happiness was wild, unstable, whirling from one thing to another. This was more like contentment, like a fire, and I was the fireplace. Was that really what she thought about me?

Amaranth opened the oven door. "Why is this cabinet empty?" she said. "Do we need to get some more food? Dandelions—we're out of dandelions, aren't we?"

"How is she?" Maeve asked, coming into the kitchen. "Oh. You are—I'm sorry, I forgot your name."

"This is Judith," I said. "And this is my aunt, Maeve. Adela Madden."

Judith actually blushed; it was astonishing to see. "Hello, Ms. Madden. I love *Ivory Apples*—it's my favorite book in the world."

Maeve looked pleased too. Well, she hadn't heard anyone praise her book for a long time, nearly fifty years. I'd shown her some of the more interesting letters, of course, and Philip had too, but it was a different thing to meet an excited fan in the flesh.

Amaranth hurried into the dining room. "I'll try to keep her out of trouble," Maeve said. "It was good meeting you, Judith."

Judith watched her go. She looked as if she'd seen some fabulous creature, a unicorn maybe. This is what Maeve does, I thought. She brings wonder into even the most practical lives. I had a flash of empathy for Ms. Burden, just a tiny bit. I understood why she had devoted her life to getting that ability, that magic, for herself.

Judith seemed to force herself back to the practicalities of her job. "Okay, well, let's go sign the contract," she said.

We went back to the dining room and sat down. She didn't leave after we finished our business, though; instead we talked about all kinds of things—other books we'd read as children or as adults, her family (mother and father, one older brother, no hidden groves or muses), the private investigator who'd trained her, the poems I'd published. She wanted to read some of them, but I felt shy suddenly and promised to email them to her instead.

I got a glimpse of her watch and realized it was past time to go. "Oh, God—I have to pick up my sister from school," I said, standing up.

"Is it that late?" she said. "Damn, I have to go. Meanwhile, can you get your sister to draw a picture of Ms. Burden? And send me a scan of it?"

"No scans, sorry—we're pretty primitive out here. I can mail it to you, or drop it at your office the next time I'm in Eugene."

"I need it pretty soon. I'll tell you what—if you find something, come to Eugene and we'll go out for coffee."

"Sure," I said, and we both left, heading back to the world and our obligations.

It was funny, I thought as I drove to Woodbine, how much you had to pretend, even lie, at the beginning of a relationship. I couldn't just say that I wanted to know her better, or that I'd like to get her to bed and unwrap her like a birthday present, which was how I really felt. We had to follow a ritual, act out a play about meeting for coffee, while we both kept up the pretense that it was the picture of Ms. Burden that was important.

Maybe she wasn't acting, though. Maybe she really just wanted coffee. But she'd been the one to come up with the invitation . . .

I seesawed between these two choices all the way to the school. Was it me or the picture she was interested in?

All this worry turned out to be unnecessary, though. Judith called that evening and told me she'd already found Ms. Burden's address in Eugene.

"Really?" I said. "How?"

"Actually it was easy," she said. "It was on her driver's license."

"How'd you get her driver's license?"

"I have a source in the Driver & Motor Vehicles Services office. But if you want me to give up his name, forget it."

"No. No, that's great."

"What are you going to do now?"

"I—you know, I don't know. I didn't think you'd find her so quickly."

"Hey, we do good work."

"Absolutely. Well, I guess I'm going to break into her house and get the apple back. Do you want to come with me?"

There was a long silence on the other end. Finally she said, "I can't do that, Ivy. I can't do anything illegal, or I'll lose my license. I can't even plan anything illegal, so I'm going to pretend you never said that."

It was a rebuke. I hadn't cared about criticism for so long that I'd forgotten how bad it could feel. And did this mean our business together was over?

I blurted out the first thing that came into my mind. "So, do you still want to go out for coffee?"

"Sure," she said. "I'll let you know when I'm free."

A huge heavy stone came crashing down on the seesaw, on the side that said that all of this was just business, and the person at the other end, the relationship end, went flying off into space, never to be seen again.

CHAPTER 25

Beatriz slept over at our house several days later, one of the few times she stayed with us and not with her friends. I took her aside and told her what I wanted to do.

She looked apprehensive, but the old excitement shone in her eyes as well, and maybe even a longing for our former closeness. "How come you didn't tell me this before?" she asked.

"You're never here," I said.

"Yeah, I guess that's true. You know, I gotta say that it feels good to be normal for a change. To have normal friends, and go over to normal houses for normal dinners . . ."

"I wouldn't know."

She looked stricken. "God, I'm sorry. I know you do a lot of work around here, and I guess you gave up college for us—"

"No, it's okay. Don't worry about it. So, what do you think? I'll watch her for a while, and then when school ends you can come with me."

"She still has those—those things, right?"

"Yeah. But I told you—I know how to stop them. Or I could teach you how to do it."

She shuddered. "That wouldn't help," she said. "I don't want to go anywhere near them. You can't know how—what they're like."

"I do, sort of. I was trapped with you for a while, remember."

"Not long enough."

"No, I know. Look—I can go myself."

"No, wait. I didn't say I wouldn't do it. I want to help Rantha as much as you do. I just think I'd hold you back, that's all."

"It would help me a lot if you came, actually."

We'd grown close in the past couple years, but I'd never said anything so supportive. She hurried on as if she hadn't heard me. "I'll think about it. I can't do anything until school's over, like you said."

The mention of school reminded me of something. "God, I forgot to ask—did you hear back from those colleges you applied to?"

She nodded. "Some of them."

She was right, we were nothing like a normal family. Philip should have been helping her get ready for college, or Jane. I'd worked on the applications with her, but I should have been more involved, should have asked more questions. I'd been so worried about Amaranth, though, that I hadn't given Beatriz much thought.

I felt the dull pain of missing my parents, and guilt at how badly I was doing as a substitute. I made myself sit and talk about colleges for a while, hoping it would be enough.

Maeve assured me she could keep an eye on Amaranth, so I drove to Ms. Burden's house in Eugene. I parked down the street from her house and put my new binoculars on the seat next to me. Who needed a private investigator anyway?

It was the warmest May anyone could remember; the car felt hot enough to grow orchids in. I cracked open a window and waited.

Ms. Burden's new house seemed in better repair than the old one. It had been freshly painted in pale purple, the color of grape gum with the flavor chewed out of it. The lawn, unlike most of the lawns on the street, had been watered regularly, and the bright green stood in contrast to the neighbors' patches of straw. It looked not so much trimmed as cultivated, so neat it might have been planted in rows, like crops. Even the brass doorknocker (a wreath of flowers, I saw through my binoculars) had been polished. Curtains covered the few windows, giving the house an inward, secretive look. A late-model Camry with a tinted windshield was parked in front of the house, probably the car that had followed us from the warehouse.

At the beginning I'd braced myself for my first sight of her, but after a few hours I'd turned listless, all my emotions submerged in the heat. Then she stepped out the door and I felt a sudden chill at the back of my neck, as if someone had touched me there with an ice cube. She looked to the right and left and I ducked below the steering wheel, even though I was too far for her to possibly see me. When I straightened up, the Camry was driving away, fortunately in the opposite direction.

She returned about an hour later. I waited until I had to pick up Beatriz from school, but she didn't leave again.

I watched her house for several weeks. I couldn't bring a book because I'd get caught up in it, so I had only my thoughts for company, a dreary jumble of household chores and worries about Amaranth. A boring middle-class neighborhood stretched out in front of me, and the sun never relented, beating down on the houses, on the grass, on the car I sat in. Heat mirages wavered on the street.

May slipped into June, and school ended. I could bring Beatriz with me now, but I still hadn't found a pattern to Ms. Burden's comings and goings, and it would be dangerous to break in without knowing when she might come home. Finally I decided to pick a time and hope for the best.

It was just our luck that Ms. Burden never left the house while we were watching. The hot weather hadn't broken, and we both usually wore shorts, our legs sticking uncomfortably to the plastic seats. Finally, about a week after Beatriz joined me, we saw her get into her car and drive away.

I left the car quickly, feeling the cooler air with relief. Beatriz was still sitting on the passenger side, and I tugged her door open. "Come on!" I said.

She seemed to make an effort and pulled herself out of the car. I hurried to the side of the house, trying not to look as if I was running.

As I turned into the backyard I realized that Beatriz hadn't followed me. I ran to the front of the house and saw her still on the sidewalk, staring up at the house with dismay.

"Come on!" I said again. "Or go to the car and wait for me, one or the other."

She started around the corner. I grabbed her hand and pulled her along into the yard. The rear of the house stood before us, nearly blank, with no windows and one small door.

"Now what?" Beatriz said.

I didn't know. I'd learned a lot about breaking into houses, but on the other hand Ms. Burden had probably learned a lot about security. I went to the door and turned the knob. It opened under my hand.

"What did you do?" Beatriz asked, whispering.

"Nothing," I said.

We stood still a while. Beatriz clearly didn't want to go inside, and I was thinking that it was obviously a trap, like the gingerbread house in "Hansel and Gretel."

I had to do it, though. I stepped inside, quickly so I couldn't change my mind, and Beatriz followed.

I closed the door behind us, then fumbled for the light switch and turned it on. We were in the kitchen. It looked a lot like her last place, stark and uncluttered; the main difference was that the countertops had been upgraded from Formica to tile. A thin layer of dust covered everything, with smudges where she'd set something down or moved it. No doubt any cleaner she hired would run screaming when they heard the noises.

At that thought I looked for a door leading into the basement, but I didn't see one. Well, most houses in Eugene didn't have them.

A man's voice sounded behind me. Beatriz screamed and I whirled around, my heart pounding so hard I couldn't breathe. There was no one there. A light glowed on the counter. A boom box.

I must have pressed the power button with my elbow. I turned it off and stood there awhile, feeling my pulse slow to normal.

"God," Beatriz said, trying to laugh.

"God," I said. It was stuffy in here as well; she must have never opened a window or turned on a fan.

Beatriz left the kitchen. I wanted to take my time, to go through every drawer and cabinet, but I knew we had to hurry.

I followed her down the hallway. She had already turned on the light in the next room. A bed stood against one wall, and there was a dresser holding a television and a computer on the opposite side. I went in and looked in the corners and under the bed, but I only saw more dust.

Beatriz hadn't followed me in. I headed back to the hallway and saw her looking into another room. There was only one window here, with a gray curtain that turned everything the color of ashes. The room seemed completely empty, but in the dim light it was hard to tell. A tumbleweed of dust rolled across the wooden floor, disturbed by our movements.

"Come on, there's nothing here," she said.

"One minute," I said. I groped for a light switch, wanting to look into the shadowy corners, but I couldn't find one. Beatriz grabbed my hand and towed me down the hall.

We came to the living room. It looked like Ms. Burden's last one, with only a few pieces of furniture and nothing on the walls.

I started inside. A long howl came from somewhere, a high note falling lower and lower, as if dragged down by sorrow.

"Fuck it," Beatriz said. "I'm out of here."

Another howl joined the first, its notes wavering in counterpoint, and then a third. I shivered despite the heat; even my bones seemed to shudder. Sweat broke out at my hairline and under my arms.

I recited the counter-spell as quickly as I could. One last howl frayed into whimpers and then stopped. Beatriz ran for the front door, and I heard the rattle of the doorknob.

I forced myself to follow her through the living room. One of the walls opened up with the change of perspective, and I saw that it was really an alcove. It held a bookshelf stuffed with books, and something round and white on the bottom shelf.

I grabbed it and hurried after Beatriz. The creatures were silent now, but I was still saying the counter-spell over and over like a prayer. I got to the door and pushed Beatriz out of the way, but I couldn't open it either. I banged on it with my palm in frustration.

"Here," Beatriz said. She grabbed a key hanging on a hook near the door and fumbled it into the lock.

For a heart-stopping moment the key didn't move. I waited, my entire body tense, for the howls to return, and the mists, and the lies, and the monsters . . .

The key turned, and Beatriz shoved the door open. We darted outside, slammed the door shut behind us, and ran down the street.

We got into the car and I lunged out into traffic. I didn't want to look away from the road, so I handed Beatriz the thing I'd stolen. "Just tell me that's an apple," I said.

"Oh, thank God," she said. "It is."

"One of Aunt Maeve's?"

"Yeah, I'm pretty sure. Though I don't have them memorized or anything."

I waited until I stopped at a light before I looked at it. Beatriz hadn't been certain, but I was; I'd spent enough time dusting them. It was the carved apple Amaranth had stolen.

"We got it," I said.

I expected to feel triumph, satisfaction. Instead I was buzzing with fear and panic. I could still hear those howls behind me, growing louder.

Beatriz was quiet as well, wrapped up in her own thoughts. I turned onto the highway and saw clouds massing in front of us; the weather was breaking, finally, though the inside of the car was still hot.

We'd driven most of the way back before Beatriz spoke again. "Do you think the apple will help?" she asked.

"I don't know," I said. "Maybe. I mean, why else would Ms. Burden want it? Why did Rantha steal it?"

I glanced at the apple again and realized that I hadn't felt anything from it, no sign that it held any power that could help us. Well, but would I recognize its power, especially when Piper wasn't here to help me?

"I just don't understand them," Beatriz said. "Kate and Rantha, and you too. Who wants to have something inside you like that? Someone who never goes away? What if you want to be alone?"

"It isn't like that."

"That's what it sounds like. It's—I don't know—it's creepy. Like a stalker."

I tried to smile. "You're the only one in the family who thinks so."

"Yeah, I know. The only normal one."

Our exit came up. I took it and drove through Woodbine, then onto the narrow road to Maeve's house. Beatriz turned and looked behind us. "Oh, shit," she said.

"What?"

"Is that her car?"

I glanced in the rearview mirror. The sun was setting but I could still make out the car behind us, a gold Camry, this or last year's model. She'd stayed well behind for most of the drive, probably, but here on this deserted road we were the only cars.

"Shit," I said. "Can you see her?"

"No, the windshield's too dark."

"It looks like hers. Like the car at her house."

"What are you going to do?"

I didn't know. She'd come back while we were inside her house, maybe, and followed us, but this time I wouldn't be able to lose her. The road we were on led only to Maeve's house, and the forest beyond that.

I turned right and dove between the trees. The car shimmied and bucked, and I heard something break underneath us—branches, I hoped, and not some essential part of the car.

"What are you doing?" Beatriz asked, startled.

"Trying to lose her."

"She's still there."

I looked back. She was following us through the trees, staying within the tracks we'd made but going slowly because her Camry didn't have four-wheel drive. I grinned, thinking about how little she knew about driving up here; our car handled so much better than hers that it would be no problem to outrun her.

Then we hit something and slammed to a stop. I pushed the gas pedal down to the floor, and the car roared but didn't move. The Camry rattled closer. "Crap," I said. "Crappity crap crap. We'll have to run for it."

I stopped the car and opened the door. "Come on," I said.

Thankfully Beatriz didn't ask any questions. We got out and hurried through the forest.

I heard a car door slam behind us, then the sound of branches cracking. "She's still following us," Beatriz said.

I knew where we were, though, and she didn't. We were near the river and the bridge, the place we'd found while looking for Amaranth. I looked for somewhere we could break away.

She came closer. I could hear her panting now, and I grinned to think that she was tiring. But I was having a tough time making my way through as well; trees were crowding around us, making it hard to see.

Then, under the sounds of our harsh breathing and stumbling footsteps, I heard the rush of water. We came out of the trees and saw the bridge in front of us.

"Stop!" Ms. Burden called behind us. "Look!"

I kept going, heading for the bridge. There was no way I'd listen to her, become enmeshed in her games again. "No, wait," Beatriz said. She pointed across the river. "Look."

The moon was starting to rise. More trees stood on the other side, white leaves picked out by moonlight and black leaves in shadow, and a path ran beneath them. Then, as I watched, the moon painted some of the trees white, so slowly that I couldn't see the moment when they changed.

The white trees formed two rows, in lines so straight they had to have been planted that way. They looked like pillars, like the ruins of an unroofed temple. The moon floated on the river like a ship at sea.

Ms. Burden came up to us, breathing hard. "The way—the way into Pommerie Town," she said.

"Really?" I said, putting as much contempt as I could fit into the two syllables. "Pommerie Town is fiction, it isn't—"

"What are those trees then?" she asked.

"And remember the part about Fo'c'sle Flynn?" Beatriz said. "He went across a river, he said, and then between some pillars that looked like ivory. There wasn't a full moon the last time we were here—that's probably why we didn't see this."

"Well, of course," Ms. Burden said. She was still panting, not from fatigue this time but from eagerness, the culmination of all her years of searching.

I looked back at the pillars. There they were, a real thing. What else could they be but the way into Pommerie Town?

Ms. Burden started toward the bridge and we hurried after her. I was sure that Beatriz and I had the same thought, that no matter what lay beyond those pillars we had to watch her closely, make sure she didn't do any damage.

Beatriz and I caught up with her, and we crossed the bridge together in silence. Partly this was because the river was running loudly now, making it hard to hear anything else. Another part, though, was that we had nothing to say to each other. How had it come to this, that I was keeping company with my worst enemy as if nothing had ever happened between us? We were like the travelers in *The Wizard of Oz*, if Dorothy had wanted to kill the Tin Woodman.

The wood of the bridge was worn through in places, so much that I had to watch my steps. I looked over at Beatriz to point them out and saw that she was being careful as well, and so, unfortunately, was Ms. Burden.

We came to the end and walked between the pillars. They were a muted white, the color of the moon or a wax candle, more ivory than marble. The path between them was silvered with light.

I wanted to touch them, to see what they were made of—they couldn't possibly be ivory, not unless the land beyond boasted giant elephants—but I was afraid of doing anything except following the directions. I was only too aware of what happened in fairy tales when someone stepped off the path.

We reached the end of the row. The forest grew sparser, and the ground sloped away in front of us. We worked our way down the incline, slipping as we went. Another path lay at the bottom, and we continued on.

Fo'c'sle Flynn had reached the town by this point, but we saw only a patchwork of land stretching out ahead of us, silent in the moonlight. We passed a farmhouse, a small wooden cottage with white walls and a red roof, then another, then four or five clustered together. Wisps of smoke rose from the chimneys, and dogs barked in the distance.

I tried to make myself believe that we were still in the real world, that these farms lay just beyond Maeve's house, even though we had never seen anything like them before. As we walked, though, a large shadow began to loom in front of us.

"Oh, my God," Beatriz said. For some reason she was whispering. "Is that the town?"

"Of course it's the town," Ms. Burden said. She looked very different: her dissatisfied expression was gone, and she seemed dazed, transfixed.

"I've done it," she said, awe filling her voice. "All those times I wrote to Adela Madden, begging her for directions. All those form letters she sent back. All those theories, those people who claimed to know the way and turned out to have no idea."

All that time you spent making us suffer, I thought. But she seemed so naked, so changed, that I couldn't bring myself to say anything.

As we came closer we saw a constellation of lights glimmering within the shadow of the town. A tower lifted high above it.

The town reached out and took us in gradually. We passed more houses, taller and wider than the ones at the farms. They seemed placed at random, as if a child had thrown them in a game of jacks, and the path wound between them, broader now and paved with cobblestones. Tall trees grew in and around the houses, and gas lamps made of iron filigree showed glimpses as we passed, a front door here, a lawn filled with flowers there.

"What do you want to do?" Beatriz asked, still whispering. "Everyone's asleep."

A dog barked, somewhere far away. Ms. Burden set off down one of the paths, moving quickly, and we hurried after her.

The path led farther into town. Scenes passed as we hurried on: white roses in front of a red-brick house, an oak butting up against a stone fence, pots of geraniums flourishing on either side of a blue door.

A flight of stone steps rose ahead of us. They were all different sizes and covered in moss, and we picked our way up them in the moonlight. At the top was a row of shops, with hanging signs that showed pictures of tobacco pipes and eyeglasses and mugs of beer.

Ms. Burden slowed and walked past them, looking into each storefront as she came to it. I could see more of the buildings now, with their gables and mullioned windows and window-boxes filled with flowers. Timber-framed balconies hung out over the road, nearly touching the balconies on the other side. The owners seemed to live on the second floors, above their work.

"What are you looking for?" I asked Ms. Burden.

"Hmmm? Nothing really, just taking it all in."

I didn't believe that for a minute. Why had she headed off so confidently, as if she'd known where she was going?

She yawned. "God, I'm tired. It's been a long day."

I was tired too, and more tired now that she'd mentioned it. She lay down on a wooden bench and closed her eyes.

Beatriz and I moved away from her. "What do we do now?" she asked in a low voice.

"Keep an eye on her. She wants something here, I'm sure of it."

"But we have to sleep too. She's right, it was a long day."

"Leave it to her to take the only bench in sight."

Beatriz just went over to a fat tree and leaned against it. She didn't complain as much as I did about Ms. Burden; I'd noticed that before. "Well, if you're going to sleep, I'll keep watch," I said. "I'll wake you up when I get tired."

She was already breathing regularly, a sound I knew from sharing a room with her. I sat down next to her.

I woke up in a world washed with green, the sun shining through leaves. A moment later I remembered where I was.

My next thought was not about Pommerie Town but Amaranth, the same worry that visited me every morning on awakening. How was she? Had she gotten worse? Had Maeve been able to cope?

We had to get back to her. Or were we supposed to find something to help her in Pommerie Town? Ms. Burden seemed to have some knowledge we didn't—but did it have anything to do with us, with Amaranth?

Ms. Burden. I sat up quickly and looked for her. There she was, still on the bench, still asleep.

A man appeared at the far end of the road, carrying a long pole. He lifted it high above him at the first lamp and doused the light, then continued on to the next. People were moving behind the ground-floor windows now, or coming outside to sweep their doorsteps.

Ms. Burden stood and stretched and looked around her. She smiled, an expression I hadn't seen in years, since she'd played all those games with us. "I'm still here," she said. "It wasn't a dream."

She seemed new-made, a different person, almost as if she had something of Piper about her. And she was right—we should be delighting in every moment, every impossible sight. But it was so strange to be agreeing with her, to find wisdom in what she said, that my mind wobbled a bit, and I nearly missed seeing her set off.

I glanced around for Beatriz, who was standing up and getting ready to leave, then hurried up next to Ms. Burden. I wanted to confront her about Amaranth, but she seemed so open that for once I couldn't bring myself to argue with her.

"What are you looking for?" I asked again, as we headed down the path.

"I told you," she said. "Nothing."

"I don't believe you. Look, just tell me the truth. If you know anything that could help Amaranth—"

"Amaranth?" She'd been looking in the windows as we passed but now she turned to me, her gaze focused to a point. "What happened to her?"

"Don't you know? You were the one who told her I could give her Piper."

"Piper, is it?" she said, looking thoughtful. "And did you? Do you still have your muse, or is he gone?"

I didn't want to answer her, of course. But I had to, I needed to know if she could help us. I told her what had happened to Amaranth, her nonsense, her moments of terror, the times when I sensed that Piper was struggling to get free.

"I honestly didn't know that could happen," she said. She used to say "honestly" whenever she lied about something, but this time I thought she might be telling the truth. "I told her she could ask you for Piper, and then she and I might convince your aunt to lend me her muse—what's his name, by the way?"

"Never mind. What do we do about Rantha?"

"I don't know. I could try to talk to her when we get back, see if I can think of something."

"You can't talk to her. That's what I've been telling you. She doesn't make sense, she's lost and confused all the time, and it's because of you. You were the one who told her to do this."

"I didn't tell her anything. All I did was explain how she might get a muse for herself."

"And why do you think you'll manage any better than she did?" I asked spitefully. "None of them wanted you so far."

So much for not arguing, I thought. I wouldn't get any answers now. She turned away from me and looked around us. The shops had given way to houses; red ivy twined up the wall of one, and a carved wooden dragon perched on the gable of another. A bird lifted off a branch and sang a quick two-note phrase into the silence, high-low, high-low.

Then she looked back at me, and I saw that she wasn't angry but unhappy, that I'd gone too deep and hit bone. I cast around for a neutral topic, something that wouldn't remind me of Amaranth, or her of her failures. "How did you know that Pommerie Town was real?" I asked.

"Of course it's real," she said. "It had to be."

"Well, but why? I never thought so, and my aunt is—" I had to hesitate here, so ingrained was my habit of secrecy. "My aunt wrote the book."

She said nothing for a long while. "My mother didn't let me leave the house a lot," she said finally, looking straight ahead. "She needed someone to talk to. Well, to talk at—she didn't actually want me to say anything. I was just supposed to nod and shake my head in the right places. Look at that!"

We'd come to a broad park. It was the first thing I recognized from *Ivory Apples*, and it cheered me to see it. The park had the trellised pavilions and meandering paths Maeve had described, the grass as green as the sea. At the far end stood the statue of the man and woman who had founded Pommerie Town.

From this angle we couldn't see their dog Oscar. According to the book, Oscar would stand up and bark if anyone threatened the town.

Ms. Burden ran toward the statue. She was going to check on Oscar, I knew, and I felt a strange kinship with her, someone who knew *Ivory Apples* as well as I did. I pushed the feeling away, and Beatriz and I hurried after her.

We reached the statue and saw Oscar between the two founders, his head on his paws. "I guess the town is safe, then," Ms. Burden said.

I wanted to get back to what she'd been telling me. "Why didn't your mother want you to talk?" I asked.

In her excitement, she'd forgotten our conversation, and she had to take a while to find her way back to it. "Well, she needed someone to echo her. I think that was how she convinced herself she was real. There's a reason, you know, that Narcissus is paired with Echo in the myth."

"What do you mean? She had to know she was real, didn't she?"

"She had no center, no core—she needed people around her to know how to act, how to be. She didn't care what I was doing, though, so I immersed myself in books, and every so often I'd look up and say something, to show her I was listening. She had no idea what happens when you read, how you go away into other worlds— she thought I was still in the room with her. We had a library, but that was only because she thought she should have one.

"And of all the books we had, the best one was *Ivory Apples*. I could hide myself inside it and never come out, never have to face her. So I knew it had to be real. I needed it to be real."

I didn't think that proved anything. We left the park and went back to the road. The town hall should be a few paces down and across the street—and there it was, just as the book had promised. It was long and low, the space of an entire block, and made out of marble instead of wood. A clocktower rose high above it.

She stood for a while, watching people go up and down the stairs to the entrance. God, she wasn't going to wait until the clock struck the hour, was she, when all the figures, large and small, came out and performed their play? The clock read 10:37, and I felt an agony of impatience; we had to move, had to get back to Amaranth.

Thankfully, she started walking again. We passed more houses, more shops, more stands of trees. "I'm getting hungry," Beatriz said. "Where's that tavern, the one Fo'c'sle Flynn went to?"

I couldn't remember. I turned to ask Ms. Burden. She wasn't there.

CHAPTER 26

"What—?" I asked.

Beatriz turned too. "Where'd she go?"

Three paths branched off from where we stood. We looked down them but couldn't see her anywhere.

I took the middle path at random, running as fast as I could, and Beatriz followed me. A while later we came to several houses standing close together, blocking our way through.

We hurried back to the crossroads and chose another path. This one turned and twisted on itself, and my hopes rose as I went around each bend, wondering if I'd see Ms. Burden on the other side. Gradually, though, the air grew colder, and weeds and grass started to encroach on the path, and we still hadn't seen her anywhere. We slowed down and finally turned and headed back.

"We should think about this," Beatriz said. "Where would she go? What does she want?"

"Well, she wants a muse," I said.

"Do they have muses here?"

I didn't know. A muse had helped create this place, Maeve's muse, but would that muse make more muses?

It was the only thing I could think of, though. "Maybe we should look for a grove, or a lake."

The path became wider, then joined the main street. We passed more places I knew from the book, and several times I wanted to stop and go inside: the bakery with its croissants that waxed and waned with the phases of the moon; the school, where Matilda Spottiswood would sometimes forget that she had died, and come back to teach her history class.

One place we did visit was the library. We wanted to see if the creek had appeared there yet, and to check if it flowed down from a lake, or into one. The creek was there, but I felt an irresistible urge to go the shelves first. They were filled with rows of seductive titles:

The Troll's Daughter, Other Wise, Practicing the Piano in the Land of the Dead.

Beatriz came over and tugged me away. We made note of where the creek came into the library and where it flowed out of it, and we went back outside.

As we left I noticed how carefully everyone stood, with their backs toward the creek and the bridge. I thought of Piper, who would at the very least shout, "Hey, look at that river!", and I felt the empty place where he should have been.

We searched all the way around the library but the ground was dry and bare, not a trickle or rivulet anywhere. The creek seemed to rise from nowhere and go nowhere, another of the town's mysteries.

We set off again. A few minutes later I saw that we were approaching the town hall, this time from the opposite direction. Bells boomed out from the clocktower, telling the hours.

I watched the figures glide out one by one, the allegory of the seasons, the procession of astrological signs, the displays of corn and carrots and other farmland produce. The clock had run backward once, along with all the other clocks in town. So much of the book was about clocks, watches, keeping time. And then, suddenly, I knew where Ms. Burden had gone.

"The Watchmaker," I said. "The book says that he has an ivory apple, and that's what she's been looking for all this time. She got Rantha to steal Maeve's, but that turned out to be ordinary, just a piece of wood."

We stopped some people and got directions. It was very close, they told us, and I thought that the Watchmaker had to be doing well for himself if he had a shop in the town center.

I wanted to run flat-out toward it, but I could only walk. Hunger was making me light-headed, and I was worn out from all our searching. Beatriz said nothing, but I knew she had to be flagging as well.

Then we saw it: a hanging sign with a picture of a beaming gold watch. I felt one last burst of energy and hurried toward it. Bells rang out as I opened the door.

Inside it was so dim that I could see nothing at first, just a silvery light glowing in the distance. Clocks and watches tocked and clicked from all over the room, and something mechanical whooshed around in circles.

The gloom lightened slowly, as my eyes got used to it. I made out shelves and glass display cases, grandfather clocks standing against the walls, a toy train sweeping through a toy town. Ms. Burden stood at the back, near the pale moth-wing light, talking to a man behind a counter.

"What are you doing here?" I asked, edging around the display cases to join her.

She sighed. "I might ask you the same thing."

"Well, we were looking for you." I saw how little she wanted us there and grinned. "And you, I guess, are looking for an ivory apple."

"I'm negotiating with Mr. Beetlestone, actually." The man behind the counter peered at us over half-moon glasses. He was old, fifty or even sixty, with a long narrow face, pinched in the middle like a waist. Thick white muttonchops had nearly colonized his cheeks. "And yes, I want to have a look at that apple."

It had been the light from the apple that we'd seen, shining from a shelf behind the counter. I looked at it and felt a sort of shocked recognition, like coming upon a friend in a place far from home. It was similar to what I'd felt when I'd seen Craig for the first time, but stronger, more insistent.

I knew from the book that the Watchmaker never let anyone hold it, or even go behind the counter to look at it, so I wasn't very worried. Still, I watched Ms. Burden closely.

"And what was it you were about to show me?" Mr. Beetlestone asked.

She found a pocket somewhere within her loose clothing and took out an apple. I recognized it, of course: it was the one Amaranth had taken from Maeve, the one we'd stolen back . . . God, it had been just a day ago. She must have gotten it from our car after we'd abandoned it in the forest.

I'd forgotten all about that apple. But she was so single-minded that it had probably never been far from her thoughts.

Mr. Beetlestone reached out for it, but she backed away. "Are we agreed, then?" she asked. "This apple in exchange for a look at yours?"

"Wait a minute," I said. "That's ours. She stole it from us."

"What's that to me?" Mr. Beetlestone said.

"Well, because she's lying about it," I said. "There's nothing special about it—it's just wood and paint, that's all."

"Honestly, she doesn't know anything," Ms. Burden said. "I'm sure she never even looked at it. She's completely ignorant."

Mr. Beetlestone took his apple down from the shelf. I tried one last time. "No, don't trust her—"

They made the exchange. The shop dimmed and grew light again. Darkness and light flickered around us, like the pages of a book flipping past. The ticking of the clocks grew louder; bells rang; jangled fragments of songs played and then stopped.

"What the hell—?" I asked.

"We're gonna rock, rock, rock, 'til broad daylight," a voice sang. In the stuttering flashes of light I could see Ms. Burden walk toward the door, her steps as jerky as someone in an old movie.

"Where are you going?" Mr. Beetlestone shouted. He'd shut himself up in the space behind the counter, and a quick flare of light showed him fumbling to get out.

She turned toward him. "Don't follow me," she said.

I hurried after her and ran hard into one of the glass displays. "We're gonna rock, gonna roooock," the voice sang, the notes stretching out and distorting.

She reached the door and opened it. The bells overhead rang out and mixed in with all the other sounds.

I headed toward the light from the door. Beatriz was closer and had already gotten there. "So you're stealing another apple?" I heard her say as I came up to them.

Ms. Burden turned to us, laughing. She reminded me of the witch in Snow White and the Seven Dwarfs, offering Snow White the poisoned apple. "You two, come with me," she said.

"Not this again," I said.

I recited the counter-spell. But somehow I found myself walking behind her, away from the shop, Beatriz next to me.

I tried again, horrified. "Oh, come, Ivy," Ms. Burden said. "Surely you know why that can't work."

Because the apple she carried, the one she had stolen from Mr. Beetlestone, was stronger than any spell or counter-spell. I strained to get away but I kept following her, placing one foot in front of the other despite anything I could do. We walked past the town hall and the park, then along some winding roads and paths. A while later we came to a row of shops I recognized; we were near the spot where we'd entered the town.

I turned to look at Beatriz. She had the same expression I'd seen in the warehouse, resigned, fatalistic. Something pricked my heart, sadness that she'd been forced back to her nightmare, guilt that I hadn't managed to save her.

A sign over one of the shops showed three mugs of beer. I hoped Ms. Burden would stop so we could eat, or at least let us lie against the trees again and sleep. But we kept going, down the stone stairs and through the town and out into the farmlands.

Finally we reached the place where we'd seen the pillars. There was only a tangle of trees in front of us, though, none of them in a straight line, and the bridge and the river were gone.

I should have worried about what she'd do with the apple, or at least about how we'd get home. Instead I felt a mean spite at this setback. "Now what?" I asked.

"Now we wait for moonrise, of course," Ms. Burden said.

I planned to keep watch on her, and to take the apple if I could. But I was so tired that even my hair felt exhausted, and I dropped to the ground and fell asleep immediately. I woke to feel someone shaking my shoulder.

"Come on, Ivy," Ms. Burden said.

I opened my eyes. The moon was up and I could see the pillars now, two rows of white candles in the moonlight. At her order we stood and walked between them, then came to the bridge and the river.

We crossed to the other shore. "Where are you going, Ivy?" Ms. Burden asked.

"To the cars," I said.

"Forget the cars. Take me to your aunt."

I tried as hard as I could to refuse her, but my steps obeyed her and I started toward Maeve's house. I looked at Beatriz. The moon had turned her as pale as a zombie, and she moved like a zombie too, slowly, reluctantly.

I must look the same way, I thought. I'd become as disconnected as Beatriz now, a fog drifting through my brain. Even the fear I felt for Aunt Maeve, and my worry about Amaranth, couldn't penetrate it. I could do nothing but continue on, hoping I'd think of something.

We came to Maeve's house, approaching it from the back. "So this is it," Ms. Burden said. Awe lit her face, making it shine like the apple she carried. "Let's go inside."

I unlocked the door and turned on the light. Ms. Burden came inside, looking around at the kitchen as if she stood on holy ground.

"Take me to your aunt," she said. I headed toward Maeve's bedroom. "No, wait. Stop. It's too late to talk to her now. Go to bed, but don't leave the house."

CHAPTER 27

I was starving when I woke up; Ms. Burden hadn't let us eat anything the night before. Amaranth's babble sounded from the living room.

"Ah, you're awake," Ms. Burden said, coming in and staring down at me. "You can take me to your aunt now."

I sat up. "Can I check on Rantha first?"

"Rantha, right."

I stood and headed for Maeve's room. "No, what are you doing?" she asked. "I said you could go to Rantha."

"No, you didn't."

"Still insolent, I see."

I was right, though—she hadn't given me a direct order. She wasn't used to speaking literally yet, and I wondered if that might help us somehow.

I kept walking. I heard her sigh behind me. "All right, let's go see Amaranth," she said.

I turned around. Now I saw that Ms. Burden had put the apple in one of her pockets; it shone with a glowworm light through her long tunic. So she didn't have to carry it, I thought. She could force someone to do her bidding just by keeping it near her.

Amaranth was sitting up on the couch. Her eyes changed when she saw Ms. Burden, grew sharper. "Kate!" she said. "You came!"

Ms. Burden looked at me, puzzled. "There's nothing wrong with her."

"There's lots wrong with me," Amaranth said. "I can't fly, for one thing. I can't talk to flowers. Well, most flowers—there's a pot of geraniums I'm friendly with."

"Can you help her?" I asked Ms. Burden. "Maybe you can, I don't know, order Piper to come out, to come back to me?"

"Well, maybe I can. I don't think I will, though."

"What? Why the hell not?"

"I think I'll just keep that in reserve. I might need you to do something for me."

"I'm already doing everything you want!"

"Well, we'll see."

She used to say that when we were younger, when she wasn't going to give us what we asked for but didn't want to say so. Just two words, and I felt the full force of my childhood anger return.

I struggled to come back to myself. I was nineteen years old now; I had negotiated with the world for my family, I'd nursed

Maeve back to health, I'd made sure that Beatriz could go to college. I could meet her as an equal, or I could have, if she didn't have that apple.

"All right," Ms. Burden said. "It's time to—no, wait. Take me to your aunt."

We went to Maeve's bedroom and I knocked on the door. "Come in," she said.

"There's someone here who wants to meet you," I said.

"What do you mean? You know I never see anyone."

Ms. Burden pushed the door open. Maeve stood there, struggling to put a robe on over her nightgown.

For once, Ms. Burden seemed to have run out of words. "Ms. Madden," she said finally. "Adela. I just—I wanted to tell you how much I enjoyed your book. It was so important to me when I was growing up. I mean—not that it isn't important now. I mean, it's my favorite book in the world."

She was just another awkward fangirl, I saw, amazed. But Maeve had backed away and put her hand in front of her eyes, as if trying to block out a bright light. She stumbled backward to the bed and sat down, looking lost.

Ms. Burden followed her into the room. "I'm Kate. Kate Burden," she said, holding out her hand to shake.

Maeve ignored her. She lowered her own hand and stared at the light from the apple as if she knew what it was. Well, of course she did—she'd been to Pommerie Town, after all, and seen the Watchmaker.

"Where were you, Ivy?" she said, sounding querulous, "You know I don't like it when you leave like that."

For the first time I remembered my promise, that I wouldn't go anywhere without telling her first. But I'd had to keep an eye on Ms. Burden, and whatever I'd done after that hadn't been of my own volition.

Still, I knew how fragile Maeve was, and I felt the weight of my responsibility. I told her what had happened, how we'd visited Pommerie Town. I thought she'd be amazed, but she didn't seem able to take it in. "It's hard watching over Amaranth, you know," she said. "I can't be expected to do it all myself."

"Don't worry," I said. "I'll do it now."

"And who is this woman? Why is she here? You know I don't enjoy having visitors."

"I'm sorry, but I had to do it this way," Ms. Burden said. "I need you to tell me about your muse."

Maeve put her hand to her heart. "My—my muse? What do you mean?"

"This is Ms. Burden, Aunt Maeve," I said. "I told you about her, remember? She killed Philip, and took over our family, and—and did other horrible things, and all because—"

"Be quiet, Ivy. You know what I'd really like?" She turned to Maeve and smiled at her. "If we could sit down and have a talk together. I've waited so long, and I want to ask you, oh, so many things. I'll tell you what. You get dressed and come out to the dining room, and Ivy here will make us breakfast. Oh, and put on some good walking shoes. We're going out into the woods later."

Maeve stood and went to her closet. "What's happening? Why am I—"

I opened my mouth to explain but found I couldn't speak, still under orders to be quiet.

To my surprise Ms. Burden turned her back while Maeve got dressed, giving her some privacy. Then Maeve and Ms. Burden went to the dining room, and I headed toward the kitchen and took out some eggs.

I heard chairs scrape along the floor as they sat down. "I can't believe this is happening," Ms. Burden said. "Here we are, just the two of us, and you're going to answer my questions. You went to Pommerie Town, didn't you? I was right about that, wasn't I?"

"Yes," Maeve said.

Ms. Burden laughed. "Oh, come now—don't be so reticent. What happened? What was it like? Did you find your muse there, or did you meet him here and then go to Pommerie Town with him? Or her? I was never able to find out if they're male or female."

"She was female, yes," Maeve said, speaking slowly. "I met her here. Pommerie Town—we created it together, the two of us. And it became real enough for us to travel there."

"That's wonderful. Do other muses work like that? Can you go to Middle Earth, or Oz?"

"I don't know."

There was silence from the dining room, and then Ms. Burden called out, "Ivy! Where's that breakfast?"

I came out of the kitchen and pointed to my throat, trying to explain that I couldn't answer. "What is it now?" she said. "Oh—I told you to be quiet, didn't I?" She laughed. "I completely forgot. I could leave you that way—it would probably be an improvement. All right, speak. Where's our breakfast?"

"I'm still making it."

"Well, hurry up. And then come and join us."

She was finding it hard going with Maeve, I realized, and she wanted me there. They weren't the cozy best friends she'd imagined they'd be. I hurried to finish the omelets I was making and took the plates in to the dining table.

Ms. Burden took a bite of her omelet. "This could really use some salt, Ivy," she said.

"I didn't have a lot of time," I said.

"I should have kept you quiet, shouldn't I? Does she talk back to you like this?" she asked Maeve.

"No," Maeve said. She'd regained some of her composure, I saw, and was looking as remote and regal as a queen. I was glad to see it.

"Well, never mind her. What else should I ask you? All right, maybe you can explain this. When we were at the Watchmaker's there were all these lights flickering, and we heard sounds, and a song . . . That wasn't in the book, was it?"

"No."

"Well, what was it?"

"It was—" Maeve struggled against the compulsion to talk but could not hold out against it. "Those were pages that were cut from the manuscript."

"What!" I said.

"Oh, my God," Ms. Burden said. "There really are parts missing from the book. People have been talking about that since the first Adela Madden Conference, even longer. Can I read them?"

"No."

She sighed, as if dealing with a child. "Show me the pages," she said.

"I can't. I threw them out, years ago."

"You threw them out?" Ms. Burden looked horrified, as if Maeve had defaced a relic. "Can you write them again?"

"No. It was too long ago."

"What were they about?"

"They were about Willa." At Ms. Burden's puzzled expression, she said, "Willa was my muse. We went to Pommerie Town, as I said, and we wandered all over, to the library and the school and the post office . . . And we came to the Watchmaker's, and somehow he understood about Willa, that I had her, that she was my muse. And he—he took her from me."

"What?" Ms. Burden said, but Maeve continued speaking. "He took her from me and put her in an apple."

Ms. Burden slowly drew the apple out of her pocket.

"That apple," Maeve said.

"Wait," I said. "You told me you lost Willa, but I thought it happened a few years ago, when you were sick. That's what you said, isn't it?"

"No, I never said that. It was a very long time ago that she left, fifty years at least."

I went over the conversation in my mind and realized that she hadn't, that I'd been the one to take that meaning from it. I wondered if she'd meant for me to misunderstand, though. If she'd told me the truth I would have pitied her, and she would have hated that. At least now I understood why I hadn't felt a muse from her, the way I had with Craig.

"How could you write the book without her?" I asked.

"I don't know. I'd already started it, and I still had the—the ability, I think. I couldn't face doing it again, though."

"So I have one of them," Ms. Burden said, looking at the apple with wonder. "I have one here, in my hand. She'd be grateful if I let her out, wouldn't she, like a genie in a bottle? Because if she granted me one wish, I know what I'd ask her."

"No, wait a minute," I said to Maeve. "The Watchmaker's just a character you made up. He can't take anything away from you—he comes from you. You can get Willa back any time you want."

Ms. Burden closed her hand around the apple, her knuckles whitening.

"It isn't that easy," Maeve said. "I don't know if even you can understand, Ivy. She was very powerful, Willa. More than Piper, I think, much more. I think Piper's very young, compared to her. And it was terrifying having her, terrifying and astonishing all at the same time. It was like living with a god, like a thunderstorm in your head forever. No one can stand that for very long. And when I saw that the Watchmaker wanted to take her, well, I let him."

"Why didn't you just go back to the grove, and tell Willa she was free?"

"I don't know, child. I was young, and I enjoyed her company sometimes—most of the time—and we were writing this wonderful book . . . I guess it was just easier to let someone else make the decision. Or to pretend that someone else made the decision, since, as you say, the Watchmaker was a part of me. I know what my sin is.

"That's why it's been so hard for me to live in this world," she went on. "Why I get so confused so much of the time. I never really got used to being without her, not even after fifty years. I know you thought that having a muse was the reason I could barely function sometimes, and I'm sorry I deceived you. But it was very hard to talk about her. About everything, really."

I had thought that. I'd thought that I would go the same way, that because I had Piper I'd end up a bewildered old woman, barely able to feed myself or leave the house. I felt a sudden bitterness that she'd lied to me, that she'd given me yet another thing to worry about.

I couldn't stay mad at her for long, though. It had been so much worse for her.

Ms. Burden was still looking at the apple, her mind continuing along its single track. "Willa, come to me," she said. "Be my muse."

We waited, not breathing, but nothing happened. "All right then," she said. She looked directly at Maeve. "Tell her to come to me."

Maeve's mouth worked as she tried to hold back the words. "Willa, go to this woman. Mrs. Berman, is that your name?"

"Burden. Kate Burden. Say it."

"Go to Kate Burden, Willa."

Ms. Burden sat back. Once again nothing changed; she remained the same as she had always been. She scowled. "Why didn't it work?"

Maeve shook her head.

"You can't disobey me," Ms. Burden said slowly. "So I know you'd give her to me if you could. Something deep inside you doesn't want to, the same way you wanted to give her to the Watchmaker. Or maybe you lost control over her when you gave her away." She thought for a while. "Tell me what you cut from the manuscript."

"I didn't cut it," Maeve said. She was looking at me instead of Ms. Burden, one writer talking to another. "It was the editor's idea. I'd written about myself, you see, and how I'd lost Willa, and what happened to me after I got home. My editor said that I'd destroyed the mood, that when I returned to reality like that it drove people out of the fantasy world. And that this ending was too sad, after most of the book ended happily, that the sudden change clashed with the rest of it. He was right, of course—I see that now."

"I thought, when the lights flickered on and off—it almost looked like pages flipping past," I said. "Like we were inside the book itself."

"Maybe you were."

"And we heard a song . . ."

Maeve laughed. "Oh, that song! It was all over, that year. 'Rock Around the Clock,' I think it was called. I couldn't get it out of my head."

I heard footsteps and conversation from the hallway, Beatriz and Semiramis. I opened my mouth to tell them to stay away, but they'd already come into the dining room.

"Careful," I said. "She can do things now—"

"I told Ramis," Beatriz said. They sat down next to me, as if to show me their support. Semiramis was wearing a necklace I had given her, with a small apple painted to look like ivory. She'd put it on as a sort of talisman, I guessed.

"Look, this isn't getting us anywhere," Ms. Burden said impatiently. "I have an idea. What if I took away something of yours, something important? You'd overcome your scruples then, I bet. If I burned your house down, for example?"

"What!" I said. Maeve groaned and hid her face in her hands. "You can't do that," I went on. "Look at everything in this house—the books, and the artwork—there might even be some notes about how she wrote *Ivory Apples*. We'll—we'll give it to you, all of it. A first edition if you want it. Maeve will even sign it for you."

"She'd sign it for me no matter what," Ms. Burden said dispassionately. Then she seemed to realize who was sitting across from her, and an unfamiliar expression passed across her face, moving as slowly as a shy speaker standing up to deliver a dinner speech. She looked contrite, almost apologetic. "I'm sorry I have to do it this way. I don't have any choice, though. If you hadn't been so selfish, if you'd just shared what you found with other people, all of this could have been avoided."

She stood and went to the kitchen. From where I sat I could see her rummaging through the drawers and slamming them closed. She made a sound of triumph and came back, holding a box of matches.

I lunged toward her. "Stop," she said.

I froze, halfway out of my chair. "None of you leave this table," she said. "Oh, sit down, Ivy. You look ridiculous like that."

I sat. She lit a match and laid it against the wall. Nothing happened at first, but the house was made out of old wood and a flame got a toehold.

She left the kitchen. I couldn't see where she went, could only imagine the damage she was doing to the rest of the house. The fire began to crawl upward, so slowly that I could have put it out, if she had let me move.

"Is she going to leave us here?" Semiramis said.

"No, of course not," I said, though I wasn't at all sure of that. "She needs Maeve for what she wants. She'll come back and get us."

We watched the fire spread along the wall, and make a start on the floor. Amaranth was still in the living room, I realized. Would Ms. Burden allow her to join us, or would she let her die?

Finally, after what seemed like hours but was probably only a few minutes, Ms. Burden came back. "All right," she said. "I can stop the fire if I want to. So. Are you ready to give me that muse?"

Maeve said nothing. I thought she was trying to do what Ms. Burden asked, to give Willa to her. Ms. Burden looked eager, but once again nothing about her seemed changed.

What if I could do it? A muse had found me congenial once; maybe this one would as well. I reached out to Willa with my mind.

A bomb went off inside my head. Fire and gales of wind hurtled toward me, threatening to annihilate me. Loud noises flew past, screams and explosions. I pulled away, terrified.

The flames were gaining strength now, gnawing hungrily on the wood. Through the doorway I saw Ms. Burden set fire to a bookshelf. Which ruin would be worse, hers or Willa's?

I pushed out toward Willa again. This time I could feel her in the whirlwind, a sense of something strong and very old. Just a touch from her could make me lose myself, make it as though I had never been.

I backed away again. Maeve was right: Willa could not be contained by anything human.

"I was sure that would work," Ms. Burden said. "All right, I suppose I'll have to try the grove now."

"What about Rantha?" I asked.

"What about her?"

"What about her? She'll die if we leave her here!"

"Very well, go get her," Ms. Burden said. "Just don't leave the house."

I ran into the living room. Smoke and heat came from everywhere, like dragons breathing all around me, and I could barely see. I opened my mouth to call Amaranth and started coughing instead. I tried again. "Rantha! Where are you?"

"Look, we have guests," she said from somewhere. "Very pretty they are, too, dressed all in bright red and yellow. They're too hot, though. Here, why don't you take off your coats?"

She kept talking. I made my way toward her voice. I coughed again, then doubled over in a coughing fit that seemed to go on forever. Finally my fingers brushed against the edge of the couch.

I fumbled onward until I reached Amaranth. "Come on, we have to go!" I said, grabbing her hand.

"But that's rude, isn't it?" she said. "To leave our guests alone like that? Shouldn't I offer them something, cold water maybe, or some ice cream . . ."

I tried to drag her toward it but she wouldn't move. I pulled on her arm, hard, and we stumbled into the dining room. We stood there a while, trying to catch our breath but only able to cough. A small flame was darting up the back of her shirt, and I grabbed the tablecloth from the dining table, spilling plates and silverware to the floor, and snuffed it out.

At first I didn't see the others; then Ms. Burden called to us from the kitchen door. "Come outside, Ivy. You too, Amaranth. And Maeve, take me to the grove."

I glanced back at the house as we walked away. I could see flames through the windows, dancing gleefully, like children capering after their parents had gone. All of it would burn, everything we own . . . the different versions of *Ivory Apples*: the first edition, the translations and illustrations, the unauthorized printing. The artwork people had sent Maeve, the papers and correspondence. Hat racks and mirrors, umbrellas and Post-it notes, pots and pans and photographs.

"Maybe it isn't really on fire," Beatriz said, coming up to me and speaking softly. "Maybe it's one of her illusions."

I hadn't thought of that. I didn't think Beatriz was right, though. It seemed to me Ms. Burden had had years of brooding, of growing anger that someone had something she wanted. She had reached the end, she had finally found the grove, and she was determined to make it count.

"Maybe," I said to Beatriz, not wanting her to lose her optimism.

We headed into the woods. We tried to talk, but all our conversations trailed off into silence. I heard leaves rustling on the trees as we passed, and branches breaking underfoot, and birds calling from a long way away. I was thinking hard, worrying about my sisters, and the grove, and what Ms. Burden might do next.

I looked back at Semiramis, remembering how frightened she'd been in the warehouse. But she was staring straight ahead, an unreadable expression on her face. Had she gone beyond fear, was she so terrified that she'd just given up?

And Amaranth had been quiet for a long time, so long that it seemed unnatural. What was happening to her, and to Piper?

And I was even more worried about Maeve. The path was treacherous for someone so fragile, steep in places and bumpy with old roots and rocks and branches. She had started out in front, guiding Ms. Burden, but she soon dropped back, and I moved close and held her arm to steady her. Finally she sank onto a rock near the path.

"Hold on," Ms. Burden said. "Everybody stop." She went back to Maeve and asked, "Are you all right?"

It was strange to see her waver between showing Maeve respect and treating her like an object, a means to an end. Maeve took several deep breaths. "I'm not used to—to this," she said.

"All right, then. All of you—we're going to rest here for a while, and when we start up again I want you to go slower. Oh, for God's sake, don't just stand there like statues. You can move around if you want." She turned back to Maeve. "How far is it to the grove?"

"Oh, I don't know," Maeve said. "Sometimes it seems closer, sometimes farther away."

"You mean—it moves?"

"No," I said. "It's about another mile, I think."

"And what happens then? Is it like Mount Helicon, where you wait to see if you're accepted?"

I'd already figured out that I couldn't lie to her while she had the apple. Now I wondered if I could keep to the truth but not give her anything useful. "I don't know—I've never been to Mount Helicon."

Her eyes narrowed "You know what I mean. Tell me—"

"They might not give you a muse, you know," Maeve said, interrupting.

Ms. Burden looked at her, startled. "Don't be ridiculous—I have Willa. Come on, let's get moving."

I gave Maeve my hand, and she pushed herself up from the rock.

We fell in behind Maeve. She went slower than before, slower than she needed to, I think. Several times Ms. Burden hurried ahead and then had to wait for her, looking impatient.

Finally I heard the familiar sounds of rushing water, of music and laughter. The woods opened out, and we came into the grove.

Ms. Burden stopped and gasped in astonishment. "Yes," she said. "Yes, after all this time."

CHAPTER 28

The sprites stopped what they were doing and came toward us, moving cautiously. One of them held blue and yellow flowers shaped like bells, and she dropped them along the path as she went. I stopped breathing, waiting to see what they would do, if they would choose Ms. Burden after all.

They ranged before her, standing on the shore, sitting cross-legged on rocks, balancing on a tree branch. They studied her, their eyes impassive. I began to breathe again.

She hadn't been chasing the muses for so many years to stop now, though. "Hello," she said, putting on her pleasant voice, the one she'd used when she first met us. "I'm asking you, petitioning you, to help me. To become my muse. I brought you an offering, to move you to think more kindly toward me."

It sounded rehearsed. Well, she'd had long enough to think of it. She took the apple out of her pocket and held it out to them.

One of them came over to look at it. He wore a conical cap stuck with a bright red feather. Thick black hair flowed from down his back, tangled like sheep's wool. "Ahhh," he said. "Beautiful."

More sprites came toward it, laughing and talking. "As beautiful as a bird, lifting from a tree," one of them said.

"As a sunset, when it changes from rose to red."

"As a snail, crawling over the grass."

"There's a muse there, Willa," Ms. Burden said. "I'll give her to you if you grant my petition."

"Willa?" the one with the red feather said. "We don't know any Willa."

Ms. Burden turned to Maeve, furious. "You told me that was her name."

"That was what I called her, yes," Maeve said. "I don't know her real name."

"Oh, what does it matter? Here, I have a muse, one who's been trapped inside this apple for fifty years. Don't you want her back?"

"Of course we do," one of them said.

"All right then."

"But we can't help you."

"Then she'll stay here, for another fifty years or longer. And it'll all be your fault."

One of them laughed. "Our fault? How can that be? It's your apple."

"By the tree—it's Talia!" someone called out. "She's in the apple!"

"Talia?" I said. The sprites echoed me, murmuring, the name passing among them.

"Who's Talia?" Maeve asked.

"Don't you remember?" I asked. "Craig told me about her. She lived on Mount Helicon, someone very old and powerful, and then she left Greece and came here. Craig thinks she might be the Greek muse Thalia."

"And this Talia—she was my muse? She was Willa?" Maeve asked. I nodded. "No wonder it was so hard to abide her. One of the Nine, the first muses."

"And she was in love with Claudio," I said. "He wanted to follow her here, but Ms. Burden captured him when she went to Mount Helicon."

"Claudio?" Ms. Burden said.

"Don't you even know their names? Well, that's typical, I guess. He's in that—that cloud you have, the ones you enslaved."

"So I have them both, Claudio and Talia," Ms. Burden said. "I have a great many of them, in fact—I should be able to do something with that. Talia, if you want to see Claudio again, come to me."

The apple glowed softly in Ms. Burden's hand. That was the only change, though; Ms. Burden still seemed her old impatient self.

"Try again," she said to Maeve. "Use her real name this time. Call Talia to me."

"Talia, go to Ms. Burden," Maeve said, her voice dull.

"Oh, for God's sake. Why don't you want to free her? She's been trapped in this apple for fifty years—what do you think that's done to her?"

Maeve said nothing.

"Tell me," Ms. Burden said.

"Maybe because—" I could see that Maeve was trying to resist, but once again she was forced to answer. "Because, well, I sometimes wonder if she was the reason the book was so popular. The reason it stayed with people. She was there in Pommerie Town, at the heart of it. She lent it her power, her glamour. And if she ever left, the town would fade away, become dull, ordinary."

"Nonsense. It's a brilliant book—that's why it sold so well. And, well, she's already left Pommerie Town, she's with me. There's nothing you can do about that. Try calling her again."

"I am trying!" Maeve said.

"Are you? I wonder how quickly this grove would burn down."

We all cried out together, me and Maeve and Beatriz and Semiramis. "No, stop! Don't do it! They won't let you!"

"Well, let's see if they will or not."

She went to the closest tree. Then, moving with the dignity of a priestess lighting a sacred fire, she lit a match and held it to the outer twigs. The fire began to eat through a branch, moving slowly.

Most of the sprites watched in fascination, but a few scooped up water from the lake with baskets and ran to the tree. Water escaped through the weave of the baskets, leaving a trail behind them.

I reached out to Talia again. The blasting wind pitched me under and spun me around, the wild noises went on and on. I wanted to turn and run, but I forced myself to call out to her instead. "Talia! Talia, we need your help."

She didn't reply. I sensed she was there, though, through all the noise and confusion. No, it was more that—she *was* the noise and confusion. That was the only way we could know her, though somewhere within all that chaos it was peaceful, the sacred stillness of a god.

"Your—Your Grace." How did you address a muse? "Would it be possible for you to leave the apple? We need you here."

I felt her answer rather than heard it. "Ah, someone with the divine spark within her. No, someone who had the divine spark but lost it."

"Yes, my muse left me—"

"No." The word seemed to negate everything, to close off all possible connection between us. But it had only felt that way because she was so forceful, because her every utterance seemed a part of creation, seemed to become real. "You lost your spirit. Your task is still to steal fire from the gods, from us. And yet you renounced that task, and instead you spend your days in drudgery. We had marked you out for something different."

But I had to do that drudgery, I thought. Who else would wash our clothes and cook us dinner and remind Beatriz to do her homework . . . But even as I was thinking how to defend myself I understood what she meant. I had grown dull, complacent. I hadn't written poetry, not one line. I'd stopped seeing all the wonderful and terrible secrets within the world.

I'd thought that this was because Piper had left me; certainly when he'd gone I'd fallen back on surfaces and stale routines. But he'd already shown me how to write, to go beyond, to look at a tree and see the heartwood within. And I'd had Maeve as an example— she'd continued working on *Ivory Apples*, even after Willa had left.

"Your Majesty, please—you have to help us," I said. "Ms. Burden is burning down one of your groves."

She looked around her, seeing everything at a glance. "It is already done," she said.

As she spoke I felt her invade me. Everything broke apart into a storm of sights and sounds that drove me to my hands and knees. Amid the turmoil I managed to hang on to one thought, that she had lost the ability to deal with us, if she had ever had it.

I struggled to stand up, to regain my balance. One tree had already burned through, and the fire was spreading to its neighbors. But the fire was turning paler as I watched, going from red and gold to the gray of a newspaper, and finally it went out.

Everyone sank to their knees in front of me. I shook my head, flustered. Then I realized that they weren't seeing me but Talia.

Together Talia and I turned to Ms. Burden. "Release my children," we said.

Children? I thought. But they *were* her children, not literally but as the descendants of the first muses, the original Nine.

Ms. Burden shrank from us, huddling into herself. The apple fell from her hand and rolled to the shore.

"Release them," we said again.

A mist formed, the horrible whiteness my sisters and I had been trapped within at the warehouse. It frayed outward, became rags and shreds of fog. Now we could see the sprites within it, moving restlessly, as if unsure what was happening.

The fog dispersed. Sprites stood and walked where it had been, looking around themselves with wide eyes.

"Claudio!" Talia said with my voice.

One of the sprites turned toward us. He was taller than the others, and with a deeper light in his eyes. More than that, though, I sensed a great age or wisdom within him, a force nearly as strong as Talia's.

"Talia," he said. "My old love, my enchanter."

I stood still and waited for Claudio to come to us, to embrace Talia, fearing that they would crush me between them. But he stayed where he was, looking at us with shining eyes.

Talia turned back to Ms. Burden. "You enslaved my children," we said. "And you tried to burn down my grove."

"I—I wanted a muse," Ms. Burden said.

"It is not for you to bind my children. They should be free to go where their fancy takes them. Tell me, what shall your punishment be?"

Ms. Burden looked up at us from her place on the ground but said nothing. Even she, I thought, could not trick her way out of this. But she surprised me once again.

"It's true—I did a terrible thing," she said. "And I'm sorry, and I'll go away and I'll never bother you or your children again. But in a way—well, in a way I did you a favor. I brought you out of Pommerie Town, and because of that you're free now, and you're together with Claudio again—"

"Quiet." The word was not loud, but it had the strength of a command, and Ms. Burden fell silent. "I want just one thing from you. Tell me what punishment I should give you."

"I—I don't know. Please—I only did what I thought was best."

I sensed Talia's anger at this. "You interfered in the work of the gods," she said. "And for that I sentence you to death."

"No!"

Much to my surprise, I found myself echoing Ms. Burden. I remembered what she had told me about her life, the wretched things her mother had done to her, the refuge she had found in Pommerie Town. Of course she would have a confused idea of what a writer did, how to go about creating a world of her own. The wonder was that she hadn't done worse.

Talia seemed to follow my thoughts. "And what fate would you give her?" she asked me.

I was silent for a while, thinking. "I would have you reveal yourself to her."

She seemed amused. "My judgment was not as cruel as that."

"I want her to see you plainly. To see what she was meddling with."

Talia left me and walked out along the shore. At first she looked the same as the others. But as I watched she seemed to kindle, to flash with grace and fire and light. She appeared to weigh nothing, and yet every step she took rang out through the grove like a gong. She shone with a dark radiance, like copper or bronze.

She moved toward Ms. Burden. Something trailed behind her like smoke, a shawl, maybe, or wings. Ms. Burden curled more tightly into herself, pressing against the ground as if trying to bury herself in it.

"Look at me," Talia said. Ms. Burden raised her head, then squinted and turned away, unable to bear her light. "I charge you to leave off your interference. To never trespass in my groves again."

Ms. Burden opened her mouth to speak but said nothing. She nodded.

"Very well." Talia turned away from her and headed for the trees.

"Wait!" I said. She glanced back at me and I burned with embarrassment. What was I thinking, to order the gods like that? "I mean, I would like your help with something. Something important. Piper, my muse—he's trapped within my sister. And she can't manage him, she has no idea what to do—"

"But that is something you can do yourself."

"No, please, wait—"

"Remember what I told you."

I had no idea what she was talking about. "That I should think about poetry more? And less about laundry?"

She laughed. "Almost. Except that laundry can be the most poetic thing."

She continued toward the trees. I expected to feel bereft after she had gone, but I was still fizzing from her visit, as if I had just finished writing a long epic poem.

My sisters gathered around me. "What was she?" Beatriz asked. "Was she a muse?"

I nodded.

"And she said that you know how to help Rantha."

"I don't, though. I don't know what she meant."

"Free," Amaranth said. "Free, fry, fro, from."

How could I free her, though? Had Talia meant that I should write a poem about her? Or had that been just a parting bit of advice, nothing to do with Piper and Amaranth?

"I don't know," I said again.

I looked around us. Ms. Burden was sitting on the ground now, her eyes glazed. Something seemed gone from her, that ambition that had overridden everything else.

The sprites had returned to their games, now that nothing remained to catch their interest. I watched them swimming in the lake, spiraling down the rocks, playing music and dancing. Something shone on the water like a rising moon.

I looked closer. It was the apple Ms. Burden had brought from Pommerie Town, now resting on the shore of the lake. I glanced at her, alarmed, but she made no move to take it. I ran toward it and picked it up.

I reached out, trying to sense what had become of it. It still held power, some residue of Talia, though less than before. I went to Amaranth.

"Piper!" I said. "Piper, come out! You're free!"

Nothing happened. I called to him again. An arm appeared from Amaranth's side, then seemed to be wrenched back inside.

"Piper!" I said again. "Come here, to me! Please. You're free, you can get away."

His leg jutted out for a moment, then it too disappeared. His hand reached out again, the long fingers groping for something, anything.

I took hold of it. He gripped me so tightly that I felt my bones grind against each other, and I had to force myself not to let go. I pulled on him as hard as I could. His shoulder appeared, and then his head. He lurched the rest of the way and fell to the ground.

He had an expression I'd never seen from him before, an almost human look, like someone forced to deal with the ravages of time and age and death. "What happened?" I asked.

"I—I don't know," he said. "I was lost. I looked for a way out but I couldn't find one. I wandered for years, centuries. Then I heard you calling me." He shivered. "Never, never ask me to do that again."

"You wanted to do it!"

"You shouldn't have listened to me."

"And it wasn't years. It was . . ." I counted. He had been gone for about six months, a long time. I decided not to tell him that.

"It seemed like years. And she had dark places, so many of them, not like you. Though even she had places of light, meadows where I could rest. If not for that, I think I would have died."

I looked at Amaranth, wondering what she would make of this. She was staring straight ahead, unseeing. Her eyes were darker than usual, like the green of the sea shadowed by clouds.

"Are you all right?" I asked her.

"No." She was shivering too, her teeth chattering. She sat down abruptly.

"Can I get you anything? A blanket?"

"No. Go away."

I drew back. Then I realized that she wasn't rejecting me, she just needed to be by herself for a while. She would come back to the world when she was ready. I hoped so, anyway.

"Look," Beatriz said suddenly. "Oh, my God, look."

I turned. Talia and Claudio were sitting together under the trees. They leaned toward each other and then, as slowly as dawn breaking, they kissed.

I'd never seen any of them kiss before. I glanced away, feeling as if I'd blundered into a hallowed place, one forbidden to humans. I had to turn back and look at them, though, unable to hold out against their enchantment

Maeve had come over and was watching them as well. "Willa?" she said.

Maeve's voice had seemed too soft to carry, but Talia had heard and turned toward her. "Yes," she said, smiling. She sounded almost human, though each word still shook and flared with her power. "That's what you called me. Willa."

"I'm sorry I made you leave," Maeve said.

Talia wanted to be with Claudio, even I could tell that. And yet she spoke to Maeve with infinite patience. "I'd used you too roughly," she said. "I'd known some who were able to withstand me, so I didn't understand how much I'd asked you to bear. You couldn't help doing what you did."

"I missed you so much. Do you—do you remember all those things we did?"

"Of course."

"Do you think we could be together again, just for a while? Or maybe I could find another muse, a gentler one?"

They regarded each other. A tear fell down Maeve's cheek, the first time I'd ever seen her cry. "I understand," she said. "I won't ask again. But can I—can I come visit you?"

Talia nodded. "You may," she said.

Claudio and Talia turned toward each other, paring their world down to the two of them. I had the crazy idea that everything that had happened, my father's death, Ms. Burden becoming our guardian, our visit to Pommerie Town, all of it had occurred just so they could meet each other again. I still wonder if that's true, sometimes.

Suddenly I remembered the fire. "Let's go, everyone," I said. "We have to see what happened to the house."

No one moved. Amaranth was still deep within herself, and so was Ms. Burden, though for different reasons. Semiramis appeared to be searching for something. Only Beatriz seemed ready to return to the world.

One of the sprites moved closer. She wore a circlet of daisies that fell crookedly over one eye. She went to Semiramis, and I saw Semiramis catch her breath, her eyes as big as teacups.

The sprite raised her hand and reached out, and Semiramis did the same. Their hands touched. The sprite leaned closer and whispered something in her ear, and Semiramis giggled with delight. Then the sprite somersaulted away and joined her fellows.

"Come on," I said. "The house is on fire, remember?"

"The house, right," Maeve said.

We started to leave the grove, all of us except Amaranth and Ms. Burden. I went back and took Amaranth's hand. Ms. Burden could fend for herself, I thought, but at that moment she stood up and followed us. She seemed docile, with no hint of the haunted woman she had once been.

We walked back slowly through the forest. For a while no one spoke, and then Semiramis said, "I thought she was the muse of comedy."

"What?" I said.

"Talia. You said she was the muse of comedy—I heard you talking to Craig about it. But she didn't seem very funny."

"Comedy used to mean something with a happy ending. Like *The Divine Comedy.*"

"Does *Ivory Apples* have a happy ending?"

"Why don't you read it and find out?"

She scowled at me. Still, I'd learned one thing as a parent; sometimes people needed to discover things for themselves.

As we approached Maeve's house I looked through the trees for smoke or the red glow of fire, but I didn't see anything. It was a good sign, or at least I hoped so.

Then I smelled smoke. I heard loud voices, and radios crackling, and the sound of cars coming and going. We stepped out into Maeve's backyard. Lights pulsed, and men and women in yellow slickers were coiling up their hoses. Others were climbing into their fire trucks or walking through the house and calling out to each other.

The living room, dining room, and kitchen were gone, everything except the stone chimney. Beyond them stood the hallway, which was flooded with water. The bedroom doors were open, but from where I stood I couldn't see inside.

Maeve made a surprised sound and put her hand to her mouth. The firefighter closest to her turned, looking startled. "Where did you come from?" he asked.

I thrust the apple behind my back. Maeve didn't answer, so I said, "Through the woods."

"Well, you'll just have to go right back," he said. "It isn't safe here—something could come down at any minute."

"It's our house," I said.

"That woman there seems to be in shock," another firefighter said, nodding at Ms. Burden. She coaxed her to the picnic table in the backyard and sat her down. "What's your name, ma'am?"

Ms. Burden said nothing. She stared, unmoving, at a spot past the woman's ear.

"Who is she?" the woman asked us.

"Her name's Kate Burden," I said. "She was visiting us and we went on a walk together. She seemed fine until we got back." I looked at the others, trying to impress upon them that this was the official story, that they could never say anything about the grove and what had happened there.

"We'll have to take her to a hospital and check her out. Is she related to you?"

"No," I said. "She's a friend."

The woman put her arm across Ms. Burden's back to help her up, and they walked to one of the trucks. The rest of us went over to the picnic table. As we sat down I noticed a book underneath one of the benches, and I bent to pick it up.

It was a first edition of *Ivory Apples*, a very rare book; it had had a small print run, and few people had held on to their copy. Ms. Burden must have stolen it from the study when she'd tried to burn the house down. If Maeve signed it, I thought, we might have enough to rebuild the house, at least the essential parts.

The house wasn't important, though. I looked around the picnic table, at Maeve and my sisters. We had all come through. It was over.

Then I realized that Piper hadn't returned with us.

CHAPTER 29

Before they left, the firefighters asked us if we wanted to go with Ms. Burden to the hospital, and seemed surprised when we said no. I was beyond caring what they thought, though. "Well, you can't stay here," one of them said. "It isn't safe, let alone dry. Go to a friend's house, or a hotel."

We kept sitting at the picnic table after they'd gone, putting off any decisions until later. "I'm hungry," Semiramis said.

I turned to her. "What did that sprite say to you?" I asked.

"She liked my necklace."

I looked at the small ivory apple hanging at her neck. Was that true? After everything that had happened, had she sought out Semiramis just to tell her something so trivial? Well, maybe she had. They had their own ideas about what was important.

"What time do you think it is?" Beatriz asked.

"Noon, I guess," I said. Already the day seemed to have lasted for a hundred years, but the sun was directly overhead.

I got up and went to the open space that was now the kitchen. I was moving slowly, as if in a dream, or an out-of-body experience. The cabinets were mostly gone, and drifts of ash spread across the floor like a frayed carpet. Inside the refrigerator, the plastic bins and shelves had melted, covering everything in what looked like cracked plastic snow.

I went back to the others. I was hungry as well, and I thought that maybe we could go to Woodbine . . . Then I remembered that we didn't have a car, or a phone, probably. "Go to one of the neighbors and call a taxi," I said to Beatriz, giving her all the money I had on me. "Take everyone to the restaurant in Woodbine. And bring back some food for me."

"What are you going to do?" she asked.

"I'm going to the grove. To see Piper."

I headed back through the forest. I worried about leaving Amaranth and Semiramis, but I thought they'd probably be fine with Beatriz. I'd make sure to check on them when I got home, though.

I saw Piper right away at the grove, as if he was waiting for me. "Um, hi," I said. I felt strangely nervous, as though we hadn't shared each other's most intimate thoughts for years. "Are you—do you want to come back to me?"

"You said one minute," he said. "That's what you said, right? And it wasn't a minute, it was a million years."

"Oh, come on. It was a few months, that's all."

"I know what it felt like. It felt like forever, like—"

"Look," I said. "I'm sorry that happened to you. I'm sorry you were so frightened. But we can talk about that later. Right now I just want to know if you're coming back."

"How will I ever trust you again?"

"What do you mean? You were the one who wanted to do this, not me. I've never broken a promise to you, never lied to you. I've lied to a lot of people, but not to you. And I never will, either."

He couldn't follow a logical train of thought like that, I knew, and I wondered why I was even bothering to argue with him. We talked some more, mostly him complaining that I had left him, but no matter what I said, I couldn't convince him to come back with me.

The house was filled with water in places ad smelled strongly of smoke, and of course all the utilities were shut off. It was obvious we couldn't stay there, but none of us could bear to leave, either. We got the car towed and fixed up and then bought some tents so we cold sleep near the house, and we drove to Woodbine when we wanted a hot meal. I found out later that a helicopter had seen the flames and called the fire department. We were very lucky in one thing: the firefighters had come so quickly that the flames had barely spread to the forest around us.

I didn't want to sell that book I'd found, the first edition of *Ivory*

Apples. But we didn't have any insurance, and so, reluctantly, I took it to an auction house. The appearance of a signed Adela Madden whipped up a flood of posts on the website, a lot of them wondering who the sellers were. The auction house had promised not to give up our names, though, and they kept their word.

We got less for the book than we wanted, and I wondered if Maeve might have been right, if interest in the book had waned now that Talia was no longer in Pommerie Town, no longer acting as its guardian spirit. Still, the money was enough to clean out the bedrooms and the study, and to make a start on rebuilding the kitchen.

Meanwhile, I kept waiting for Piper. At first I felt overcome with loss, worse than when he'd been trapped within Amaranth. Then I'd had hope that I could rescue him, but this time it was his own choice. But as the months passed I grew resigned to his absence. I felt like Maeve, like an old woman mourning the loss of her partner.

I was sorting through some debris outside when something crashed into me. Someone said, "Ooof," and all the breath left my lungs. A moment later I felt his presence, the familiar joy rising within me.

Don't think I'm here for good, he said.

After he came back I thought a lot about the advice Talia had given me. She'd wanted me to take risks, to balance my daily work with leaps into the unknown. She might not have been talking about my love life, but with Piper's help I chanced a call to Judith, holding my breath until she answered the phone.

"Hi," she said. "I was just thinking about you guys—the papers said there was a first edition of *Ivory Apples* up for auction. Was that yours?"

She always was way ahead of me. Still, she didn't sound angry, which was all I'd hoped for. "Yeah, it was," I said.

"Did something happen? Is your family okay?"

"We are, yeah. But the house burned down, and we needed the money."

"Oh, my God. What happened? No, wait, don't tell me—if you committed a felony I'd have to report you."

My first instinct was to lie, of course. Then I realized that my whole reason for lying was gone; Ms. Burden could no longer hurt us.

I could come out of hiding now, and I told her the whole story. I didn't think she believed half of it, but I didn't really care. It was a relief to tell the truth for once, and I vowed to be as honest as I could from now on.

The next minute I followed that vow to its conclusion and realized what it meant, that I had to tell her how I felt about her. What if she didn't feel the same way, what if she wasn't even interested in women? Though from some things she'd said I thought that she might be.

I took a deep breath and said, "Look. I'd really like—I'd like to get to know you better. To have coffee, or whatever you want. And I promise I won't break the law this time."

God, I was bad at this. Every other time it had been wordless, a spark, need answering need.

There was silence at her end for what felt like a year. Then she said, finally, "All right."

All right what? "So do you want to have coffee?"

"Sure. Yeah."

We were still awkward when we met, two people who, after all, knew very little about each other. But my new openness seemed to call out an equal honesty from her, and she told me what the past year had been like for her.

"I wanted to know you better too," she said. A stupid grin bloomed on my face, and I struggled to uproot it. "But you seemed so, well, so reckless. You kept doing these—these things, illegal things, some of them. You left your family and lived on the streets, and you—"

I opened my mouth to tell her that it hadn't been like that. The word "reckless" held me silent, though. I knew words, and this one fit me like a comfortable shirt.

She raised her hand to tell me she wasn't finished. "For a while I even thought you were a criminal, especially when you wouldn't give me your address. And it didn't help that you said you were going to break into Ms. Burden's house. And all of that about those—those sprites, or muses, or whatever they are—all that stuff about breaking the rules . . . Well, I'm supposed to live by rules. I'm supposed to protect people. Like a policeman, sort of."

I couldn't deny any of that. Maybe this new policy of truthfulness wasn't such a good idea after all.

"And at the same time, I was—well, I liked hearing your stories, all the things you'd done. People think being a private investigator is interesting, but really a lot of it is boring—looking up records, following people around. Your life seemed so much more exciting. I mean, your aunt is Adela Madden, for God's sake.

"And I started thinking about you and your family, and how hard you worked. The way you helped your sisters and your aunt, all that responsibility you took on. I even understood why you had to steal that apple, that you did it for your sister. Maybe you weren't the wild child I thought you were."

We kissed when we got back to my car, and then . . . but you know, I do want to keep some things private. One thing I will say, though. I'd thought being interested in women was yet another thing that would make me different, cut me off from other people, but it wasn't like that at all. It was a joining together, not a separation. An astonishment.

I wanted her to understand the muses, to see what we'd been through, so I took her to the grove. And she did say she believed me after that, but she rarely talked about it, and she would change the subject when I brought it up. Some people were just inhabitants of Pommerie Town, I thought, ignoring the magic all around them. It became a sore place between us, and we tried not to discuss it.

Now that Ms. Burden was no longer a threat I started publishing under my own name. I took Willa's advice and wrote about more mundane things, folding laundry, digging up weeds, washing windows. It had been easy to find inspiration in Piper's magic, more difficult to locate it in everyday life, and I think the poems improved because I had to work that much harder. Poetry was the combination of the two, the strange and the familiar, I thought, a bit pompously—like an ivory apple, something from nature given an unusual beauty.

I got some awards, and a small press put together a collection of my poems, and then a local college offered me a teaching post. It doesn't pay very well, but together Maeve and I covered our necessities, though very few luxuries. We did manage to fix up most of the house, and Maeve even went back to her garden.

Semiramis seemed happier, starting from the day we got back from the grove. It could have been for any number of reasons, but I wondered if the sprite had inspired her, given her a new excitement about her art—though I don't understand how saying "I like your necklace" could work that sort of transformation. Her drawings have improved, though.

I came clean with Mr. McLaren too, and he offered to help; it was the least he could do, he said, after everything Ms. Burden had taken from us. I didn't expect anything, but then one day he called to tell us he'd managed to get our old house back, though I didn't understand exactly how he did it. I thought about moving back there, but I couldn't leave Maeve, and she couldn't leave the grove.

She would go there to visit Talia, though she never told me what passed between them. She died four years later, in her sleep, at the age of eighty-three. The family discussed it and decided to bury her as Maeve Reynolds and not Adela Madden, and not to send an obituary to the newspapers. Some people on ivoryorchard think Adela Madden is still alive, at ninety years old; one of them recently claimed to have met her in a hair salon in Columbus, Ohio.

She left me the house and the copyright for *Ivory Apples*. We had to sell one of the houses, I knew, not least because Amaranth always had some project she needed money for. I called another family meeting, and after some discussion we voted to sell Maeve's place.

I'd pushed for selling Maeve's house, though I knew I'd miss it, and that we'd get less money for it than a house in Eugene. Judith had been pressing me to come live with her, and now I was able to do it. I saw the people who bought the house just once, when I came back to get some things from the garden. They were a young couple with an overactive child, and I laughed to myself, wondering if they might discover the grove, and what would happen to them. But my business with the grove had ended.

Beatriz finished college that year and became a computer programmer. Semiramis graduated in 2016 and now works as a graphic designer.

As for Amaranth, well, she continued to think that all she needed to succeed was a muse. She drifted from one thing to another, and barely worked or studied or practiced, and blamed her failure on the fact that no one helped her, while everyone else in the family had gotten all the help they needed. She's left home and come back a few times now, and each time she's harder to deal with. I still hope she'll find her life's work, though.

And Ms. Burden? I'd disavowed her when the firefighter had asked if she was family, but in a way she *was* related to us, our guardian. More than that, though, I felt an obligation to her. I'd chosen her punishment, after all.

I saw her on the street after we'd moved back to Eugene, her eyes as vacant as the house she was propped up against, and I took her home with me. She was still legally a relative, sort of, so Mr. McLaren got me appointed as her conservator, and I searched the internet for an assisted-living facility that would take her. She didn't have any money, though, so the place I found wasn't very good. They had none of those activities you see in places like that, watching movies or playing bingo, and she had to have a roommate, and the caregivers seemed to spend their time doing everything but working.

Still, it was better than the streets. I visited her a few times, partly, I have to admit, to make sure she hadn't gotten well enough to cause us trouble, but she never knew me, and finally I stopped coming.

I hid the ivory apple as soon as I came back from seeing Piper in the grove. It had far too much power to leave lying around, and I didn't like the way Amaranth looked at it. In the years that followed

I took it out every so often and held it, trying to feel my way to its heart.

As I held it I would sometimes think about the first time I saw the grove, wondering once again why the muses chose some of us and not others. The only conclusion I came to was that we might have sought that chaos, that confusion, that had so troubled Judith. You needed a mind that could shake things up, that could slip past a rule or tradition and steal a new idea from the gods. Beatriz, for all the mess she created around her, knew how to organize her life—just look at her profession. And Ms. Burden had probably been so terrified of the chaos she'd found, the lack of fixed references, that she had retreated into madness.

As the years passed I felt the apple's power more and more. Even when it was hidden it radiated an intensity so strong that I was sure other people could feel it as well, and I wondered that they didn't. It had to do with more than just controlling a muse, I realized. It was about breaking through boundaries, the rules and traditions I mentioned, but other things as well. It showed how to bring something new into the world, something no one had seen or thought of before.

A few times I almost saw where it led, but I would always stop myself from going there. I didn't know what I'd find, but whatever it was I knew that it would change things, maybe change everything.

Still, it continues to draw me. Someday, I think, I'll figure it out.

ACKNOWLEDGMENTS

Thanks to everyone who helped me with this book: Michaela Roessner, Larry Goldstein, Jayne Valenti, David Cleary, Lori Ann White, Darrend Brown, Gary Shockley, and Susan Fry. To Elisa Sconza, who answered the question "How do you burn a house down?" without turning a hair. To Bonnie the Cute Dog, who sat at my feet and inspired me. To Doug Asherman, for everything.

And thanks to the publishing folks who made this book better: my agent Russ Galen, publisher Jacob Weisman, and editor Jill Roberts, and copyeditors Rie Langdon and Anne Zanoni.

ABOUT THE AUTHOR

Lisa Goldstein is the critically acclaimed author of twelve fantasy and science fiction novels, including *Dark Cities Underground, The Alchemist's Door, Walking the Labyrinth,* and *Weighing in Shadows,* and the short fiction collections *Daily Voices* and *Travellers in Magic.* She received the inaugural National Book Award for *The Red Magician,* the Mythopoeic Award for *The Uncertain Places,* and has been a finalist for the Hugo, Nebula, and World Fantasy awards. Goldstein has published dozens of stories in magazines such as *Interzone* and *Asimov's SF,* and in anthologies including *The Norton Book of Science Fiction* and *The Year's Best Fantasy* series. She lives in Oakland, California.